LUCKY

VIA DAEMONIA MOTORCYCLE CLUB

ELISE GEDICKE

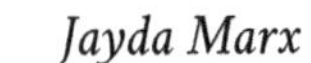

Jayda Marx
A new friend whose encouraging words got me to write book #2!

TRIGGER WARNING

This book contains references to drug addiction, violence, torture, and human trafficking.
Please be aware. Your mental health matters.

VDMC CHARACTER LIST

STEEL—PRESIDENT

Real Name: Jack Duncan
    Branch of Military: Marines (20yrs)
    Ol' lady: Jenna Duncan
    Kids: 2 sons, 1 daughter, grand baby on the way
    Job: Owns *Little Shoes* consignment store with Jenna

LUCKY—VICE PRESIDENT

Real Name: Russell McCoy
    Branch of Military: Marines (4yrs)
    Ol' lady: Harper Hannigan
    Kids: Scotty & Charlotte "Sissy"
    Job: Art Welder

BULLDOG—SERGEANT AT ARMS

Real Name: Jose Santiago
    Branch of Military: Army

Family: Mom-Louisa, Brother-Carlos
Job: Author

JUMPER–SECRETARY

Real Name: Marshall Sager
    Branch of Military: Navy SEAL (medically discharged)
    Pet: Aerial (service dog)
    Family: Brother-Gus
    Job: part-time at garage due to severe PTSD

DEMO–TREASURER

Real Name: Ron Snyder
    Branch of Military: Air Force
    Job: CPA & Club accountant/business manager

BEAR–ROAD CAPTAIN

Real Name: Terrance Collins
    Branch of Military: Marines (10yr)
    Job: Hospice Nurse

SCAR–ENFORCER

Job: Bouncer at *Demon on the Rocks*

KEYS–MEMBER

Branch of Military: Navy Intelligence
    Job: Cyber Security

ANGEL–MEMBER

Branch of Military: Army Infantry
Job: Tattoo Artist

GRUMPY–MEMBER

Branch of Military: Army
Job: Manages Garage/mechanic

CAGE–MEMBER

Branch of Military: Navy
Job: Manages construction company

PUMPKIN–MEMBER

Branch of Military: Marines
Job: Mechanic/tow truck driver

GHOST–MEMBER

Branch of Military: Navy SEAL
Job: Co-manages *Demon on the Rocks*

RANGER–MEMBER

Branch of Military: Army Ranger
Job: Co-manages *Demon on the Rocks*

BONES–MEMBER

Branch of Military: Navy (broke legs in SEAL training)
Job: Electrician for construction company

PROSPECTS

Gus "Peg Leg Gus"
    Conner
    Quinten "Q"

HONEYS

Ginger
    Cheryl
    Gracie
    Monica
    Evette
    Lacy
    Cherry (former)
    Mary Ellen (former)

COPS

Ronald Hannigan–Interim-Sheriff
    Carlos Santiago–Deputy Sheriff
    Mark Connelly–Deputy
    Bert Anderson–Deputy
    Daniel Weiss–Deputy
    Jeffery Miller–Deputy
    Scott Pan–Deputy
    Carl Kostrab–Deputy

PROLOGUE

Russell had never been so nervous in his life. His heart was racing a million miles per hour, pounding in his chest like a bass drum. He wasn't even sure he was breathing as the judge walked into the courtroom. His black robes seemed to resemble that of the grim reaper. Russell knew he needed to calm down, but he couldn't get his mind to focus. Fear that the judge would not rule in his favor a second time overshadowed logic.

The bailiff told the court to be seated. Russell was a beat slower than the rest of the room. The judge opened the file on his desk and looked up, saying Russell's name.

Russell jumped to his feet. "Yes, sir."

Judge Nolan was likely in his early seventies. His hair was stark white, with no indication of what color it used to be. He wore a pair of wide glasses on his lean face. In normal circumstances, one would consider the judge to be gruff. However, Russell felt his heart rate slow slightly when the man looked at him with sympathetic eyes.

"Mr. McCoy, I have read your file. First, off the record, let me say that I admire what you are doing here in my courtroom. It takes a rare man of honor to seek out what you are trying to accomplish here today. That being said, I am sure you can understand why I have concerns."

Out of habit, Russell clasped his hands behind his back and held his head high. "Yes, sir. Believe me, you are not the only one."

The judge's lips twitched. "I can appreciate your honesty." He closed the manila file folder in front of him. "If I was simply going off of what I read here, while tempted to grant your request, ethically I would have to deny it." Russell's heart sank. For a moment, he thought he was going to throw up. "However," the judge continued quickly, "I am not the type of man to pass judgment based on what I read in a biased report. Therefore, Mr. McCoy, I am giving you the opportunity to change my mind."

His ears started to ring. Change the judge's mind? How the fuck was he supposed to do that? He hadn't prepared anything. What was he supposed to do? Public speaking was not his strong suit. He was a grunt. He followed orders; he did not make speeches.

"Mr. McCoy?" The judge's sympathetic gaze was starting to turn impatient. "Have you anything to say in this matter?"

"Yes," Russell rushed out. "I do. I, um…" He paused. What the fuck was he supposed to say? "I just, um, wasn't prepared to have to speak."

"This is your one opportunity, Mr. McCoy. Not every man is given this chance in my courtroom. Do not waste it."

Russell nodded. "Yes. Um. Sir, I really don't have much to say other than Scotty is my brother, my family. He should be raised by people who are guaranteed to love him, not strangers."

"Mr. McCoy, do you honestly believe that, in my job and profession, I haven't seen countless situations where a child, who is *supposed* to be guaranteed love by one or more biological parent, grandparent, or guardian, is instead neglected, abused, and/or killed? Family *should* be a strong motivator to grant your request of guardianship." He looked over his glasses, directly into

Russell's eyes. "It is not. You already have guardianship of one sibling. You are twenty-four years old with a low-wage job, a rental apartment with only one bedroom, and are single. Taking in another child, blood relation or not, especially one with medical needs, is not going to be easy–"

"I don't expect it to be!" Russell interrupted and then flinched. "My apologies, sir."

The judge studied him for a long moment. Finally, he spoke again. "Son, I admire what you are trying to do, but perhaps it is not in the best interest of the child."

"Scotty," Russell hastened to add. "His name is Scotty." Russell closed his eyes for a moment, needing to catch his breath. He had survived three tours in Afghanistan but the thought of walking out of this courtroom without *both* of his siblings was scarier. He'd rather face the Taliban alone with no weapons. He *had* to succeed. Failure was not an option. Russell took a deep breath and then opened his eyes. "Sir, *I* am what is in Scotty's best interest. I may not be rolling in riches, and I will never claim that there won't be struggles, but Scotty is my brother. No one will love him, care for him, or watch over him like I will. I am a veteran, honorably discharged. As my dependent, he will get healthcare. I understand raising a child with Down Syndrome will be a challenge. I am willing to face those challenges.

"Sir, I am not our mother. I proved that when I gained custody of my little sister." Russell turned to point to his seven-year-old sister, Sissy, in the seating area. "I have been raising Sis–I mean, Charlotte for the past two years. It hasn't been easy. If any parent tells you they have it easy, they're either lying or have a staff of people raising that child in their place. We make do. Neither of us is starving. We both have clothes on our backs and a roof over our heads. She's getting straight-A's in school and reading at a third-grade level. She's even trying out for the soccer team in the fall. Does she have every latest phone or iPad or whatever device kids are asking for these days? No. But I guarantee you that kid is still just as happy and content without them."

Realizing he was rambling, Russell forced himself to take another deep breath. "Sir, I understand what that file folder states. I understand that in the eyes of a stranger, Scotty *might* be better off with a foster family and perhaps later adopted by a real one. Except he already *has* a real family: our sister and me. We are his family. We are his blood. He deserves the chance to be raised and loved by people who *already* love him."

The judge was nodding his head slowly, but Russell refused to let himself hope until he had official legal guardianship of his brother. "I am truly sympathetic to your plight, Mr. McCoy. One of my granddaughters is non-verbal autistic. I understand the challenges her parents face every day to accommodate for her needs. I am not sure you do."

"I have read every article I could find and read every book our library has on Down Syndrome. I know it is genetic and caused by an abnormal cell division. I know that means he will have intellectual delays and developmental challenges. I know he may never, quote-unquote, 'grow up'. I know he will require therapies, depending on how he develops. I also know that there will be a lot of doctor appointments and specialist appointments in our future. But I am willing to take on all that."

"Why?"

Russell blinked, not understanding the judge's inquiry. "Excuse me, sir?"

"You said that you were willing to take on all those challenges and the doctor appointments that will come with raising a child with Down Syndrome. I would like to know why."

Russell still didn't understand the question. Or, rather, he didn't understand the reason behind the question. "Because he's my brother."

"Any reasoning beyond that? Anything you can think of that is a bit more selfish?"

Again, Russell didn't understand. "No, sir." When the judge looked doubtful, Russell explained. "Sir, have you ever served?"

The judge nodded. "I did my time. I was never deployed as you were, but I put in my four years."

Russell nodded. "Whether you were deployed or not, you were still a soldier. Thank you for your service." He looked over his shoulder at his best friend, Terrance, who was also known as Bear to his friends. Silent communication passed between the two before Bear nodded and led Sissy out of the courtroom. When Russell turned back, the judge looked intrigued but didn't say anything. "If you would indulge me a little longer, sir, let me explain something that I learned while deployed. Your fellow soldiers aren't just your friends or co-workers. They're your brothers, your sisters. You live, breathe, and, in many unfortunate cases, die for them. I was nineteen years old when I saw my first fatality. It wasn't a gunshot or an explosive device. We saw it coming. A grenade was thrown into the middle of the street we were patrolling. There were six of us on patrol, but the street was packed with civilians: merchants, children playing ball in the streets, women carrying babies... There was no time to get everyone or anyone inside. My commanding officer never even hesitated. She leapt *onto* the grenade. She took the blast, so we didn't have to. I was ten feet from her when she was blown to pieces to save every single person on that street."

Russell had to take a sip of water from the glass that had been placed on the table in front of him. His hands were shaking so hard he nearly spilled it down the front of his suit.

"Over the next two years, I fought alongside my brothers and sisters in arms with a tenacity that some psychologists have referred to as hyper-awareness and overprotectiveness. I refused to lose another soldier. Of course, I did. I'm not Superman. I took two bullets and have some shrapnel in my right calf to prove what I was willing to do for my fellow soldiers."

"I read your file, Mr. McCoy. It was impressive. However, we are not here today to discuss your military record."

Russell nodded once. "I know, sir. But that's my point. You've seen my military record. You know the kind of man I am. Some might call it stubbornness, others bullheadedness. I am sure there are those who would call me an asshole. You asked me why I was willing to face these challenges to raise my medically challenged brother. This is it. If I am willing to sacrifice my life, my freedom, for brothers and sisters who are not of my blood, how far do you think I'll be willing to go for my brother and sister who *are* of my blood?"

* * *

RUSSELL SAT on the wooden bench outside the courtroom. His elbows were on his knees, his hands were clasped, and his head was down. Calm would not come. He tried the breathing techniques his therapist had recommended years ago before returning to active duty when he'd been shot, but even those techniques failed.

He heard heavy footfalls before he felt a presence beside him. Small hands and arms came around him, and suddenly that calm he'd been seeking washed over him.

Sitting up, he took Sissy into his arms. She looked adorable in her frilly pink dress with her pigtails. Many women would laugh at him if they knew how many *YouTube* videos he'd watched to learn how to do something as simple as pigtails. Braids were his next challenge. He already had some videos tagged to watch later.

Bear let out a long sigh. "I honestly had no idea how today would go. I mean, I hoped it would go your way but, damn, man, I wasn't confident."

Russell rubbed his hand up and down Sissy's back. He was sure one day she would grow out of the nickname, but he secretly loved calling her it. It reminded her, even subconsciously, that she was his sister and he loved her.

"I was terrified."

Bear snorted. "Yeah, you looked it. I thought you were going to pass out when the judge told you to change his mind on his ruling."

"Kinda surprised I didn't."

Bear nudged his shoulder. "Congrats, Daddy."

Russell let out a low chuckle. "Scotty's my brother, not my son."

"He ain't going to know that. Unlike this squirt," Bear tickled under Sissy's chin, making her giggle, "you are the only parent Scotty will ever know. You're going to be his daddy, not his brother."

Russell hadn't thought of that. He'd assumed he would be "Russ" or "Russy" like he was with Sissy. He hadn't thought of the possibility of being *Dad*. That was a heady feeling.

Russell rested his head back against the wall. Sissy started playing with his necktie. He'd loosened it after the judge had dismissed court, but he hadn't removed it. "Jesus, I need sleep. Today was so draining, I'm not sure I'll even make it home."

Bear snorted. "Dude, you have a seven-year-old and a four-month-old going home with you. You aren't going to get any sleep for at least the next eighteen years."

"Jesus," Russell repeated. Then he sat up straighter. "Where's the judge? I take it back." Even as he said the jest, he crushed Sissy closer to his chest and kissed her on her blonde head. She stretched her neck up and placed a sloppy, wet smooch on his freshly shaved cheek.

"You have got to be the luckiest SOB I know," Bear told him, indicating his chin down the hallway.

Russell turned in time to see a dumpy looking woman with clicking heels come around the corner with a baby carrier. She smiled upon seeing them.

Russell gave Sissy to Bear so he could go collect his brother. His *son*. Carefully, he lifted the underweight baby out of the carrier and brought him to his chest. The wholeness he felt in that moment was indescribable.

"The luckiest," he confirmed to Bear, his voice cracking with emotion.

Scott Mathew McCoy was finally coming home.

CHAPTER 1

*C*rash!

Russell "Lucky" McCoy bolted up in bed at the loud echo through the house. For a moment, he was back in Afghanistan under siege before his eyes corrected his mind and placed him in his bedroom in Mount Grove, Pennsylvania. He quickly rose from his bed, pulled on a pair of boxer briefs, and rushed out of the room. It didn't take him long to find the source of the crash.

Scotty stood in the kitchen surrounded by broken ceramic, milk, and mushy cereal. His chubby face was a mixture of horror, sadness, and worry. As soon as he saw Lucky enter the room, tears started streaming down his chubby cheeks.

"I'm so sorry, Daddy. I thought I could... I wanted to..." He hiccupped. "I'm so sorry."

Knowing if he didn't calm Scotty down soon it would be emotionally worse for the fifteen-year-old, Lucky immediately stepped forward. He kept his voice low and calm. "It's okay. It's just milk. And what do we say about milk?"

Scotty sniffled. "Don't cry over it."

Lucky nodded. "Exactly. Now, I need you not to move. Did you step on any of the glass?"

In a rare moment of relief, Lucky was glad Sissy was off at college and not in the house to correct him using the term 'glass'. He knew the plate set was made of ceramic, or at least thought it was. Sissy had bought the set for them when they'd moved into this house eight years ago. She'd been fourteen and so excited to *finally* have a proper kitchen. Personally, Lucky missed the simplicity of the apartment, but understood that a teenager, a kid, and an adult needed more space than the two-bedroom apartment they'd been renting since shortly after Scotty had turned two. Thankfully, a friend of a friend had known of the foreclosure on this two-story four-bedroom house. Lucky had been able to get it and the surrounding land for a steal. A bonus was that the neighbor across the street was a sweet widow in her late fifties who absolutely loved Scotty and was willing to babysit him often.

Scotty shook his head. "I didn't move. I did just as you said when something breaks. I was good, Daddy!" He glanced down guiltily. "Other than dropping the bowl…"

The rule was that Scotty could make his own breakfast as long as he didn't turn on the stove or use the glassware. There was a stack of plastic plates, bowls, and cups in the cabinet to help Scotty feel more independent when Sissy or Lucky were not around to help him. While Lucky would need to discuss why Scotty had used something breakable when it was against the rules, now was not the time.

Realizing Scotty was starting to get upset again, Lucky wanted to reassure him. "You were good. You *did* good. Do you think you could be good for just a minute longer while I grab shoes so I can get to you?"

The teenager nodded frantically. "I really need to pee."

Lucky almost laughed. His son didn't have a malicious bone in his body. He was good to his core, and Lucky would burn the world down to protect him. Both his children, though depending on her mood Sissy might argue she wasn't his child. Lucky didn't care that she was now a legal adult and in her final semester of college. He'd raised her from the time she was five years old and still paid most of her expenses so she could concentrate on getting her degree. Sissy had started calling him 'Dad' around the same time that Scotty learned to talk. Though she knew from the start that he was not her biological father, he'd never corrected her. Sissy was just as much his child as Scotty was.

In dissimilarity, Lucky was the only parent Scotty had ever known. Both children, and Lucky too, were extremely lucky (pun intended) to have thirteen pseudo-uncles and two pseudo-aunts who were both protectors and friends of the family. Scotty loved to list them alphabetically and even played a game of greeting them so.

Lucky quickly threw on a pair of boots. Without lacing them, he went back into the kitchen. While Scotty only stood at four foot-nine inches, he weighed close to a hundred and seventy pounds. Scotty liked to chuckle like Santa Claus and wiggle his belly, "ho-ho-ho" and all. Lucky had been concerned when he seemed to gain weight overnight once puberty struck, but Scotty's pediatrician assured Lucky that people with Downs tended to be obese. Hopefully, if Scotty grew anymore in height, it would even out his chunky figure. However, he'd been the same height since he'd turned thirteen. Lucky tried to watch how much processed foods they ate, but unfortunately Scotty's slew of uncles and aunts loved to spoil the kid with ice cream and sweets. With everything else Scotty had to struggle in the world with, Lucky did not want him believing there was anything wrong with his body type or weight–with the exception of if his pediatrician ever said differently.

Despite wearing shoes, Lucky was careful not to step on any of the larger shards. He didn't want to trek any glass through the house. He turned his back to Scotty, who leapt onto it with the ease of a frog. Lucky looped his hands under Scotty's butt to hold him steady since Scotty didn't have the strength to hold himself up.

"Giddy up!" Scotty yelled, making Lucky wince and his ears ring.

Much to his son's delight, Lucky skipped his way out of the kitchen and up the stairs to deposit Scotty outside his bedroom. His door was painted bright orange and decorated with the handprints of Scotty, Sissy, and Lucky in glow in the dark paint.

Scotty was a smiling, giggling riot by the time his feet hit the floor. He reached up and kissed Lucky on the nose. "You're the best daddy in the whole world."

Lucky had to remind himself that he was a manly man who didn't cry, but damn if that announcement didn't tug on his heartstrings. "You're the best son in the whole world." He pushed Scotty's glasses up his nose, since they had slipped down during the piggyback ride from the kitchen. "Get showered and dressed. I'm going to clean up the mess in the kitchen and make us pancakes instead."

Scotty's eyes widened dramatically. "Pancakes? But that's a weekend meal!"

Lucky leaned forward conspiratorially. "I know, but it's Friday and that is close to the weekend, right?"

Scotty nodded once, his face serious. "Yes. Very close."

Lucky tried to hide his smile. "You'll be a little late for school, but I think we can squeeze pancakes in this morning."

As Lucky turned to walk back towards the kitchen, Scotty grabbed his hand. "Wait!" The real panic in his voice made Lucky stop. "Does this mean no pancakes tomorrow if we get them today?"

Lucky let out a small sigh of relief that the panic was unnecessary. "Of course not. Sissy will be home tomorrow so of course there will be pancakes for breakfast. I'm sure hers will taste much better than mine too."

Sissy made her pancakes from scratch whereas Lucky's were the *just add water* kind. Lucky was beyond grateful that Sissy had chosen a college twenty minutes from their hometown. He or one of his brothers could get to her in the case of an emergency quickly and she had the excuse of coming home each weekend to do laundry. So Scotty and Lucky not only got to still see her regularly, but they also got to eat her cooking. Gourmet meals were not one of Lucky's talents. Sissy could make something out of nothing, which had come in handy during some of their leaner times before Lucky had started his own business.

Scotty nodded seriously. "Good. Then hop to it."

Lucky snorted and leaned over to kiss his son's curly hair. "Go, kid. We're going to be late as it is."

Scotty skipped off to the bathroom, and damn if Lucky didn't feel ten feet tall at how wonderful that kid had turned out. He couldn't take all the credit when it came to Scotty. It was just who he was, as well as the mentality of his affliction. Still, there wasn't a day that had gone by since Social Services had handed Lucky baby Scotty in the courthouse corridor that he hadn't feared messing up or unknowingly harming Scotty.

Realizing he was still standing in the middle of the hallway in just a pair of scuffed biker boots and black boxer briefs, Lucky stopped by his room for a pair of sweats before heading back downstairs to the kitchen to clean up the mess.

* * *

LUCKY PULLED his 2020 Ultra Limited hog over in the unloading lane at Mount Grove High School. The bright red color Scotty had picked out when Lucky had bought his sled would have stood out whether the car lane was full or empty, which it was now because of how late they were getting to school. Lucky had a hard time getting Scotty to brush his teeth after eating, claiming that he only had two hours until lunch time anyway and he never brushed his teeth after lunch.

Lucky didn't recognize the lone figure standing outside the school. When he'd called the office to let Karen, the same woman who'd been secretary when he'd attended this high school, know that Scotty would be late, she'd told him they'd have someone waiting for him when they arrived.

But Lucky knew all the aides and teachers in the special education department and this woman wasn't one of them. Despite her beautiful raven hair, which was currently pulled up in a bun, and her curvy hips encased in dress pants, and her lovely tits covered by a beige button top, and her lickable light brown skin, Lucky was not handing Scotty off to a stranger.

Scotty frantically waved from his seat behind Lucky. While Lucky admired many of the hogs and Indians his brothers had, a single-rider or a low-rider was not an option for Lucky due to Scotty and Sissy. Unlike his brothers, Lucky bought his sled knowing he'd have a backpack often. Though 'backpack' in the biker world usually referred to whomever was riding bitch, Lucky refused to use that word around his kids. Plus, Scotty got a kick out of being called a 'backpack'. He loved to ride on Lucky's hog, or with any of his uncles or aunt. Sundays were reserved for club rides followed by a barbecue. Scotty sometimes rode with one of his uncles because, according to him, Lucky drove like an old granny. This gave everyone a laugh, including Lucky. He knew he was extra cautious when Scotty or Sissy rode with him, but he was carrying precious cargo. Who could blame him?

Scotty loved that his daddy was Vice President of the *Via Daemonia* Motorcycle Club. He loved even more that he was included in that club like he was a patched member. Each member received a leather vest-like garment called a cut upon his or her prospecting. While Scotty's cut was denim due to him being a club kid and not a member, he wore it with pride and treated the cut as if it were threaded with gold. After he'd outgrown the one he'd worn as a kid and pre-teen, Scotty had demanded a set of colored Sharpies when he'd been presented with his current cut. He then went around to his adopted uncles and aunts and got them to write their names on the back. The rocker stating he was *Property of Lucky* was now surrounded by the colorful names of his aunts and uncles. Because Scotty claimed he was property of all of them.

As was the rule, Scotty waited for Lucky to turn off his sled before dismounting. He waved frantically again to the lady waiting for them on the sidewalk. A lady, Lucky noted, who did not look happy. Her scowl deepened as she eyed Lucky's leather cut.

He could understand the stereotype behind seeing such a cut. Motorcycle Clubs were notorious for being one-percenters, outlaws, and brutal towards women. Lucky was proud to say that his club was *nothing* like those clubs. It was even in their bylaws. They did not traffic or sell guns, drugs, or humans. In fact, they worked with the police department to help keep that shit out of their town. Every member of the *Via Daemonia* MC had served in the military and had clean records. All members either worked for businesses owned by the MC or legal businesses in town. They were not thugs or outlaws.

That being said, there was nothing the MC wouldn't be willing to do to protect their own or this town.

In the five years since they'd created the club, there'd only been one time when they'd had to go outside the law to protect what they claimed. Brutal, yes, but since that encounter they had not had any problems with drug dealers selling to underage kids.

Scotty knew that he could not wear his cut into school, so he carefully took it off. He then folded it inside out to protect it and placed it in the right saddlebag along with his helmet. While Pennsylvania did not require helmets, Lucky did. Some of his brothers chose to ride without, but many wore brain buckets to help encourage Scotty not to fight about wearing his. Like his cut, his helmet was decorated. He put stickers on it for each new destination Lucky took him to.

He was running out of room and would soon either need to overlap some stickers or find a new location to put them.

Not familiar with the woman waiting for Scotty, Lucky also dismounted. He took Scotty's hand as they stepped up onto the sidewalk.

"Mr. McCoy, I take it?" Damn, even her voice was sexy. Low, sultry. The kind of voice one would expect on a phone-sex hotline.

She was also young. Early to mid-twenties, if that. With Lucky's fortieth birthday in a few weeks, she was far too young for the likes of him. Even if he started to chub up at just the sight of her luscious body. He generally preferred his women a little more mature, both in mind and in body. Not that he 'had women' or got to date often, but there were club hang-arounds, patch bunnies, and club Honeys who were always willing and weren't clingy. He wasn't proud of the few times he'd taken a Honey up on what she offered, but at times he needed something more than his hand to get the job done.

Raising two kids, one with additional medical needs, was not exactly a highlight on the dating scene. His one and only girl-friend since the adoption of his siblings had been ten years ago and had only lasted two months. She'd gotten tired of his tardi-ness, absences, and/or early departures from dates, as well as refusing to allow her into his home if the kids were around. He knew Scotty would get attached and, even at the beginning, Lucky knew it was not a forever-type of relationship.

Scotty rushed forward before Lucky could confirm who she was or tell her to call him by his road name. He circled the woman in his arms and hugged her tight. "Hi, Ms. Hannigan! I spilt milk this morning and broke a glass, but I didn't get hurt. Daddy gave me a piggyback ride out of the kitchen. Then I got showered and he made me *pancakes*! That's why I'm late."

The woman's saltiness melted at Scotty's touch and words. It wasn't too surprising; Scotty had that effect on everyone. Unless someone was a total asshole, no one could stay or get mad at Scotty.

"Did he?" The woman, Ms. Hannigan, looked up at Lucky. "That was very sweet of him. What were you doing with a glass bowl?"

Scotty buried his face in her chest. It wasn't sexual and he certainly didn't mean anything by it. His height placed him exactly at her chest level. And damn if Lucky didn't feel a streak of jealousy and wishing he could swap places with his son. Scotty's voice was muffled as he answered, "All my bowls were dirty, and I thought I could use one of Sissy's bowls. She's going to be so mad that I broke it! She saved up for weeks to buy those!"

Lucky was about to step in and say something to calm Scotty down, recognizing the signs that he was starting to get emotionally worked up again, but Ms. Hannigan spoke before he could. "Sissy could never be mad at you." She put a comforting hand on top of his head. "She knows it was an accident. How about instead of worrying about if Sissy will be mad at you, you offer to help her out when she visits this weekend to help pay for a replacement?"

Scotty stepped back with a gasp. "Yes! I could work too. I'll help Sissy out and make enough to buy a new bowl!"

Damn, that was a good idea. Lucky hadn't even considered buying a replacement. It wasn't the first bowl or cup or serving dish that Scotty had broken. At least this time, it wasn't a large pan of lasagna that went *everywhere* upon crashing to the floor. To this day, most of the kitchen furniture and cabinets still had a bit of a red spotted tint to them. Tomato sauce was a bitch to get out.

He eyed the woman. Smart and sexy. She was utterly delicious.

"Good. Now you have a plan to help Sissy this weekend. Do

you mind going and waiting by the door while I talk to your dad for a moment?"

Lucky still wasn't prepared to allow her to take Scotty from him, but he approved of Scotty going towards the school. If she'd suggested any other location, he'd have stepped in. Clearly Scotty knew Ms. Hannigan, even if Lucky didn't.

Granted, Scotty considered the cashier at the grocery store his friend after he rang them up, so Scotty's stamp of approval was too worn out and overused to be considered reliable.

"It is good to finally meet you, Mr. McCoy. I'm Harper Hannigan. I'm filling in for Patricia for the remainder of the school year." She held her hand out for him to shake.

Patricia Johnson had been Scotty's Special Education teacher since he'd started high school last year. She was a wonderful woman and an amazing teacher. It took a lot of patience to work with Scotty, who had the attention span of a gnat. At times, it took bribery to get him to concentrate, but Patricia usually could get through to him before resorting to that technique.

He took her hand, noticing how smooth her palm was in comparison to his worn and callused one. "What happened to Patricia?"

"Patricia is fine, but her husband was recently diagnosed with cancer. She took the remainder of the school year off to be with him and family."

Shit. Cancer was no joke. While Lucky had no one in his bloodline with it, the MC's Sergeant at Arms, Bulldog's mother had been diagnosed with breast cancer almost nine years ago. Bulldog had been through many highs and lows with her, along with struggling to help with the medical bills, before she'd been announced in remission. Every time she coughed, had a doctor's appointment, or just felt 'off', Lucky could see the fear lurking in Bulldog's mind that the cancer had returned. The double mastectomy as well as her loss of hair hadn't killed Mrs. Santiago's spirit, and she always made an appearance at club events. Scotty was her number one fan, aside from her own children.

"I'm sorry to hear that. I think I have her cell number somewhere. I'll reach out and see if there's anything I can do. I also have a brother who's a hospice nurse. I can contact him and see if he can help or offer advice."

Ms. Hannigan, *Harper*, looked completely surprised by Lucky's words. It hadn't passed his notice that she'd been eyeing his cut and full sleeves of tattoos on his arms like they were poisonous to the touch.

"That's, uh, that's really sweet of you. I didn't know her personally before accepting the position, but I can sympathize with her situation. I'm sure a *friendly* offer of assistance will go a long way."

Lucky kept his face blank and bit his tongue. He wasn't one to hold back, but Harper Hannigan currently held Scotty's education in the palm of her hands. He didn't want to piss her off or get on her bad side. Still, he was dying to know why she'd emphasized the word *friendly* in her statement.

"Patricia has been good to Scotty. I'd like to return the favor if I can."

Harper nodded, even if a bit stiffly. "I can see you love your son very much, Mr. McCoy."

His hackles started to rise. "He's my son, Ms. Hannigan. Anything less would be unacceptable."

"Agreed." She crossed her arms over her chest, making her breasts rise slightly and increase her cleavage. That clearly was not her intent, however, because she nodded to his hog behind him. "Do you honestly believe a motorcycle is the safest form of transportation for someone like Scotty?"

This time his eyes did narrow. "The best thing for Scotty is to treat him like everyone else. If he saw his sister riding, but wasn't allowed himself, it would make him feel less. I got this bike specifically with Scotty's safety in mind. Not that it is any of your business, as it has nothing to do with Scotty's education or your position as his teacher, but Scotty loves to ride. I'm surprised he hasn't mentioned it before."

Her cheeks flushed slightly. "He mentioned riding hogs, but I mistook that to mean pigs. I assumed he lived on a farm."

Lucky snorted. "Only pigs allowed in our house are the kind served at the dinner table."

She crinkled her nose at that statement, and, despite the underlying hostility of this conversation, Lucky found the act adorable. Fuck him in the ass without lube. He was crushing on Scotty's substitute teacher like he was a high school freshman with his first erection.

"I now also understand that the club he was referring to is your motorcycle club?"

"Again, not sure what business that is of yours, but yes. Scotty loves my brothers like they're his family."

"It is my business if Scotty is being exposed to–"

"I'm going to stop you right there. It is none of your business what Scotty is exposed to outside of this school building. However, to appease your mind and to keep you from doing something you'll regret, I'll tell you that Scotty has never been nor ever will be exposed to anything illegal or inappropriate for someone of his age." Lucky tapped his chest. "That is my business as his father."

"Someone like Scotty–"

"Watch yourself," he warned, his voice deepening. Lucky hated it when someone didn't see Scotty, but instead saw someone with Downs. Or used his Downs as an excuse to talk down about or to him. To say Lucky was protective over his son was an understatement.

"I don't mean it like that. All I am saying is that people with Downs have a tendency to latch onto others or not recognize danger. He might look at a bar fight and see it as fun instead of scary."

"Since he's never seen a bar fight, I guess we'll never know how he'll react to one." When she went to open her mouth again, Lucky put his hand up. "This conversation is over. I've indulged your intrusions and blatant dislike for my lifestyle long enough. Scotty is my son. I will raise him how I see fit. *You* are Scotty's teacher. Instead of standing out here judging me for something you know nothing about, maybe you should actually go inside and do your job." Lucky put his brain bucket on but left the visor up. "His sister Sissy will be here to pick him up after school. Just in case you were concerned, she'll be driving a cage, not a sled."

Lucky straddled his hog and waved to his son, who still stood by the school. He didn't see the wave though because he was making faces back and forth with Gus, one of the school's security guards, through the glass pane on the school door.

Lucky wondered how much deeper that stick would go up Harper Hannigan's ass if she knew that Gus was prospecting for the MC and was blood-brothers with the club's secretary. Gus was a veteran and had lost his leg during his last deployment. Years of therapy and fighting with the VA had finally gotten him his current prosthetic, which gave him a normalcy in his life that he hadn't had prior. Scotty liked to call him Peg Legged Gus and had even given him a pirate patch and hat when he'd started prospecting. Being the good sport he was, Gus wore it whenever Scotty was in the clubhouse.

"Have a good day, Ms. Hannigan." Lucky flipped his visor down and sped off, knowing that he could trust Gus to keep an eye on Scotty for him. But damn, that substitute teacher of his was a piece of work. A part of him hoped he never saw or spoke with her again. Another part, a bigger part, hoped he would, and that that conversation would end with her bent over his knee and his handprints reddening her spankable ass.

CHAPTER 2

ucky pulled up to the clubhouse, his mind still on the prickly substitute teacher. Maybe he should get his club brother, Keys, to do a background check on her. Not that the school wouldn't have already done one, but because Keys would be able to provide a more thorough and inclusive one to which Lucky would also be allowed to read.

Harper Hannigan. She had some nerve questioning him like that, but he also had to give her kudos. Lucky understood that he was an intimidating man. At six-two, packed with muscle, his arms tattooed, and his cut, he wasn't a man people generally crossed or aimed to piss off. Yet Harper had stuck to her guns, questioning what she believed were valid concerns for her student.

And damn if Lucky didn't find strong women sexy.

She's at least fifteen years younger than you! He reminded himself as he got off his sled. He shouldn't be thinking about her outside of being Scotty's teacher–no fantasies, no spank-bank material.

The weekly executive meeting the club's officers held on Fridays was supposed to be at ten in the morning. However,

Lucky had texted Steel while Scotty had been in the shower that he'd been running late. Steel had sent out a group text that pushed the meeting to noon. He also said his ol' lady offered to cook them lunch. Lucky would never turn down Jenna's cooking. Because, damn, that woman could cook.

As soon as he walked into the clubhouse, he smelled something spicy and immediately started to drool.

The clubhouse building was an abandoned distillery the club had purchased upon creation five years ago. It sat on fifteen square acres of barely developed land. In addition to the clubhouse, there was a residential house, which Steel and Jenna lived in with their youngest daughter, a pavilion structure where they held cookouts and gatherings, and a building they had renovated into a garage. The club used it to work on their bikes, and to store them in the winter if needed. Lucky was grateful the house he'd purchased had a garage attached so he could store his Ultra at home.

The executive committee was made up of seven officer positions. They were the original party who created the *Via Daemonia* MC and were the only members who wore *Original* patches on their cuts. It was a small diamond on the front of their cuts above their road names.

When they had been trying to decide on a name for their club, *Devil Dogs* had been suggested. Steel, Lucky, and Bear had been Marines after all. However, they wanted veterans from any branch of the military to feel welcome to prospect. Referring to themselves as a Marine nickname would not do that. They'd taken a spinoff of the *devil* portion of *devil dogs* and thought *Demon Dogs* would be an interesting name. They'd gone round and round with it until someone had suggested *Road Demons*. Aware that there was another MC in South America with that name, Steel had suggested *Via Daemonia* instead.

When asked how he knew the Latin words for 'Road Demons' so quickly, Steel had just shrugged and said, "Catholic school."

Steel was their President. He had been Lucky's commanding officer. While he had put in twenty years, Lucky had only served four before retiring to take guardianship of Sissy when she was five years old. Steel was in his early fifties and had been married to his ol' lady Jenna for twenty-eight years. They were the love story women swooned over. They were high school sweethearts, their firsts and only, and had survived hell to get to where they were. Jenna had given him two sons and a daughter, and his oldest son was about to give them their first grandchild. Steel was over the moon about becoming a grandpa, not that one could tell from his "hard as steel" face. The only time the man showed any emotion was around his wife and children.

Lucky was the Vice President. When Steel had approached him about forming the club, Lucky had been skeptical at first. He would never do anything that would risk Scotty (and at the time Sissy) being taken away from him. Though they were officially his by way of adoption by then, he was their only parent, and he had not been willing for either of them to end up in the system if he was thrown behind bars. Steel quickly assured him the type of motorcycle club he was forming and how every dollar the club earned would be legal. Steel had come to Lucky as a favor, knowing that Lucky was in need of financial gain as well as wanting something stable to offer his small family. Lucky had saved Steel's life, taking a bullet in Steel's place when he'd spotted a sniper and selflessly tackled him. Steel never forgot the debt and offered Lucky the position as his number two.

Bulldog was their Sergeant at Arms, which placed him third in the hierarchy. It was his job to protect the club and anyone considered under their protection, like ol' ladies, kids, parents, and Honeys. He took that job very seriously. Bulldog was the type of man who would run towards danger to save a stranger. He was tough, honorable, and loyal to his core. His mother, Louisa Santiago, loved to call the club members her "boys", including their single female member.

Jumper was club secretary and Gus's big brother. Like his brother, his last tour overseas was hell and had left Jumper scarred. Unlike his brother, those scars were internal rather than external. Jumper suffered from a severe case of PTSD and often spaced out. So far, he'd never had an episode when he was driving his hog, and the club would have to reevaluate his options if that ever happened. His therapist had applied multiple times for a therapy dog for Jumper and had finally come through for him two years ago. Aerial was a German Shepard and a former police dog. She had been forced into retirement after taking a bullet in the line of duty. Jumper had adopted her and the two had been inseparable ever since. Aerial even rode in a sidecar on Jumper's Indian Chief. Sometimes Scotty mimicked Aerial's tongue hanging out during club runs.

The club's treasurer was Demo. He was missing three fingers on his left hand, which created the running joke around the club that the highest number he could count to was seven. Despite that disadvantage, the man still excelled at math. As treasurer, he also ran the books for the club businesses. While he had his accounting degree and license, he didn't practice outside of assisting the club and its members. Demo had also gotten Sissy her current scholarship after discovering that Sissy and Scotty were adopted and not Lucky's biological children. She'd had to write an essay, and Demo had gone out of his way to assist her with that too. Lucky owed Demo for that, as well as his saving Lucky a shit ton of money towards college expenses.

Lucky's best friend, Bear, was the club's Road Captain. His was the only position that didn't hold a regular vote, unless there was a tie. Then his vote was the deciding factor. While Lucky considered all the members of the club to be his brothers, Bear's and his friendship went back to their adolescence. Neither had siblings growing up and had found brotherhood in each other. Unlike the others who had only heard stories, Bear had actually been there to witness Lucky's mother's downfall. He'd stood at

Lucky's side when they'd buried his father and had been at each court hearing until Lucky had been granted guardianship of his siblings as well as their adoption hearing. Though Bear had continued to serve after Lucky had been discharged, he'd gotten out after putting in his ten. Lucky had named Bear as guardian of Sissy and Scotty if something were to happen to him. Of anyone else in the world, Lucky knew that Bear would love and protect Lucky's kids as if they were his own.

Scar was the club's Enforcer. His was the only executive position that fell under another's, which was Bulldog as SOA. Scar had a vote on the committee but the man rarely spoke. In fact, he only made his "yay" or "nay" vote with a nod or shake of his head. It was no mystery how he'd received his road name. The long scar that ran diagonally from his left temple to his right jaw made it very obvious. While the man didn't say much, his eyes said plenty. He was also the one member whose background Lucky didn't know. Obviously, he'd served, but Lucky didn't know in which branch or for how long. He didn't know how Bulldog knew him or why he'd vouched for him. If there was one word to describe Scar, it was scary. Scar always had knives on him. Always. His eyes were constantly moving, watching anything and everything going on around him. Unlike the other members, Lucky had never seen Scar partake in the use of the Honeys or patch bunnies. He'd never seen Scar associate with anyone outside the club either. While Lucky trusted Scar as a brother, he was not one that he would call upon unless the situation required deadly force. In the beginning, he'd been cautious when he'd brought the kids to the clubhouse when Scar had been around. But then one day, he'd lost track of Scotty. The entire club had been frantically searching for him, in the clubhouse and the grounds surrounding it. It had been Scar who'd located Scotty, who'd wandered up towards the road looking for (of all things) squirrels. Scar had kept Scotty safe until Lucky could get to them. He'd never asked for anything or even said how he'd tracked

Scotty down so quickly, but Lucky knew Scotty was safe with him from then on.

Angel was their only female member. When they'd created their bylaws, the gender discussion had arisen. Most MCs were male-only and would never consider accepting a woman. The *Via Daemonia* didn't share those views. They felt that if women could serve with them, they could ride with them. Angel had served with many of their members and was also a native of the area. She was the strong and deadly type, but also had a maternal way about her that Lucky appreciated since neither Sissy nor Scotty had that sort of relationship. Angel owned a tattoo shop in town and had done all of their ink since joining the club. Steel and Demo had offered to purchase her shop, so it fell under the club owned businesses, but Angel had declined. She'd worked hard to earn her shop and she wanted to keep it as solely hers.

The other members included Keys, who was a computer genius and the youngest member at twenty-three; Grumpy, who had gotten his name from Scotty when the man had shown up to prospect and *humph*'ed his way through his answers; Cage, who owned a sick 1969 Mustang and earned his road name for driving it more than he rode his sled; Pumpkin, who got his name after falling asleep as a prospect and was found cuddling a pumpkin instead of the woman he claimed he'd fallen asleep with; Ghost was a former SEAL and had kept his moniker from his time in the military; Ranger was a former Army Ranger and chose his road name to honor that service; and their newest patched member was Bones, who had suffered through a parachute accident in training to become a SEAL and had broken nearly every bone in his legs.

They currently only had three prospects with Bones recently receiving his rockers, the patches each member wore on their cuts. Gus was the only one with a nickname "Peg Leg" or "Peg Legged Gus", given to him by Scotty. Then there was Conner and Quinten or "Q".

They called what was typically known in the biker world as patch whores 'Honeys' as a nicer name to describe the position. They lived off property but came to the clubhouse to clean, do members' laundry, and cook meals. They were under club protection and were paid a small salary for their work around the clubhouse. They also had sex with the members. Steel, the only member who had an ol' lady, was very specific about the role. They were not prostitutes. They had a right to say 'no' at any time for any act, and they had a right to not sleep with any of the members ever. At no time was additional money allowed to be passed from MC member to a Honey. Sleeping with the members was their choice, not a requirement of their position. However, all of them did choose to sleep with them and even went out of their way to dress provocatively to encourage the members to seek them out.

Angel, the only female member, Scar, who was unexplainably Scar, and Steel, who was happily married, were the only members Lucky knew of who had never taken a Honey up on what they had to offer. Many of the Honeys hoped to become ol' ladies, which bumped them up in status and gave them other privileges. Lucky didn't know about his brothers, but he certainly didn't want a woman who'd been with all of his brothers regularly as a woman who would be like his wife. Becoming an ol' lady was something sacred and wasn't breakable with divorce. There were currently six Honeys.

Hang-arounds and patch bunnies were like Honeys, but they didn't work for the club, nor were they entitled to their protection. The patch bunnies just appeared hoping to bag a patched member for the night. The club hosted open parties, which involved opening their gates to allow anyone into the clubhouse to party with them. Not every party was open, nor were the Honeys invited to every party. They were just invited more than the hang-arounds. Hang-arounds were also not just female, though they referred to the female ones as patch bunnies. Many were men who were motorcycle enthusiasts or weekend riders. Some hoped to be allowed to prospect, but so far none had served in the military, which was a requirement to prospect for the *Via Daemonia*.

While Jenna wasn't present in the clubhouse, she'd set up a buffet table inside the upstairs room they referred to as "Church". This was where all executive and club meetings were held. Only patched members were allowed entrance to this room. It was kept locked at all times, unless in use. The only time anyone other than a member was allowed in was if a Honey needed to clean it (in the presence of a patched member) or when Steel let Jenna in to set up food as she did now.

Lucky was followed in by Bear. The two bumped shoulders as they picked up plates. Jenna had made a taco bar, which meant Lucky would be back for second and third servings. Jenna's guacamole was heavenly and she added diced jalapeños to her ground meat. Fucking perfect.

With his plate full, Lucky took his seat to the right of Steel's. His president gave him a chin lift in greeting and was already chowing down on his wife's cooking. That man should have been named Lucky for snagging such a great woman. Lucky's mind went back to Harper after that thought, which only made him scowl. Harper had made her opinion of his lifestyle very clear—not that her opinion should matter to him at all. Or how much he liked the idea of being around her long enough to change that opinion.

Bulldog was still getting food and would sit directly across from Lucky to Steel's left. Jumper would sit on the other side of Bulldog with Demo at Lucky's right. Bear took his seat next to Jumper and Scar, who wasn't present yet, would sit on the other side of Demo. The long conference table could hold up to twenty people. The other members didn't have assigned seats during club meetings, except to not sit in an executive member's seat.

In the center of the wooden conference table was the club's

logo: a smiling demon face with pointed horns in front of two crossing assault rifles. Curving around the top were the words *Cum Honore Ministravimus* with the words *Cum Honore Equitamus* at the bottom.

With honor, we served.

With honor, we ride.

It was words Lucky could get behind, though some of the brothers giggled like schoolgirls when they'd first read the word 'cum' on the rockers. Idiots.

As Jumper took his seat, Aerial moved under the table to lay at his feet. Despite her service vest stating that she was working and not to pet her, Jumper still had to tell many people not to touch her or try to call her to them. Stupid people thought they had a right to his service dog. It was ridiculous. Not to mention the time a restaurant had demanded to know "what was wrong with him" as to why he needed a service dog to be allowed entry to their restaurant. Not only is that shit illegal, but they tried to make Jumper sign a form stating that his dog was not aggressive and would do her business outside the restaurant. No one in the club went to that restaurant anymore. Steel said he'd be damned if that owner got a single penny out of the club again.

Lucky had seen the improvement in Jumper since getting Aerial. He'd had a long talk with Scotty, explaining that Aerial was not a pet and he needed to get Jumper's permission before he touched her. To Lucky's surprise, Scotty was fantastic with Aerial and even took her outside to "park" for Jumper when she needed to be walked. He actually had had several talks with Jumper about perhaps getting a service dog for Scotty too. Scotty was getting older and was craving more independence, but Lucky wasn't sure how much more he could give Scotty. Having a service dog, who could also be a protection dog, would give Lucky a lot of peace of mind when Scotty was out of his sight and/or on his own.

Since the meeting hadn't started yet, the guys were sitting

around shooting the shit while eating. Lucky loved being a member of this brotherhood. He'd forever be grateful to Steel for offering him this opportunity. It had not only opened up possibilities for him and his family, but the others as well. Jumper wasn't the only one with PTSD; his case was just the most severe and obvious.

Just as everyone was finishing up eating, Scar joined them. He closed the door on his way in since they were all present now. Technically he wasn't late, but the man also hadn't joined them prior to be social. He never did. He also didn't partake in the food Jenna had prepared for them. It was rare that Scar ate with them and he never drank alcohol.

For many of the members, outside of the bond of brotherhood, the biggest perks to being in the MC was the endless supply of food, alcohol, and pussy. Crude, but it was what it was. Lucky couldn't claim innocence on that last one either, since dating wasn't easy in his life as a single father. He drank too, socially. He never drank to excess, nor did he drink if Scotty or Sissy were in the clubhouse. But Lucky couldn't recall a time when he'd seen Scar partake in any of the three unlimited services the club had to offer. It made Lucky wonder, not for the first time, why the man had joined when Bulldog had offered him the position. It didn't make Lucky trust Scar less. Just as the women were not forced to sleep with the members, members didn't have to sleep with the women at the club. It was just odd that he didn't.

Steel banged his gavel down twice on the table. At first, he'd been reluctant to use "the stupid thing", but after a while realized he could threaten to hit the members' heads with it when they spoke out of turn or got too rowdy. Steel liked that idea. "Pipe down. Let's get started. We're late enough as it is."

"Sorry about that," Lucky spoke up. "Scotty had an accident this morning and it just messed up our whole routine."

"He okay?" Bear asked. Lucky hadn't had time to tell his friend what had happened.

Lucky nodded. "He's fine, but Sissy's china isn't." Some of the members were there at the housewarming party when Sissy had proudly given the new dish set to Lucky as a thank-you gift. "His new teacher suggested he work this weekend to help fund a replacement bowl. I don't even know if a replacement bowl is possible, but if Sissy brings him around for a 'job,'" Lucky did air quotes to emphasize his point, "maybe pitch in a dollar or two? In the end, it will go towards his college fund."

Ever since Patricia, Scotty's regular teacher, had shown them brochures of colleges who accepted high functioning special needs students, Scotty had been talking nonstop about going to college "like Sissy". Since Lucky had never imagined that college was a possibility for Scotty, he hadn't created a college fund like he had for Sissy. Scotty's savings had been with medical and potential assisted living needs in mind should something happen to Lucky. As soon as he'd learned that Scotty wanted to, and could, go to college, Lucky had transferred half of Scotty's savings into a college account. Unexpectedly, each member had given Lucky a check (some small and some larger) to go towards the fund too. Scotty had written each of them a thank you note and given each one a hug and a kiss too.

It was certainly a sight to see when big, burly men, and one tough-ass woman, accepted Scotty's affection so easily. He'd been worried about Jumper, due to touch being a trigger for him, and Scar, being the antisocial bastard he was, but both men had accepted Scotty's hug and kiss. Surprisingly, Scar's had been the largest donation to Scotty's fund, not that Scotty or the other brothers knew that. Lucky had kept the amounts of each donation a secret out of respect for what each member could donate. It wasn't a competition and never would be. The donations hadn't been asked for, and Lucky wouldn't tarnish what any member had been willing to give.

"I was planning on washing my sled this weekend," Demo said from Lucky's right. "Have Sissy drop him off to me Saturday afternoon and I'll take him for a few hours."

Lucky gave him a chin lift of appreciation. "I'll pass it along. Might want to wear swim trunks if Scotty's going to have control of the water hose."

A round of snickers flitted through the room. Steel brought the meeting back to order. "We'll make sure Scotty's taken care of this weekend. Might be good to make it a regular occurrence and save certain jobs until he's around. It will help give him a sense of responsibility."

That was why Lucky loved his club and his club brothers. None of them had ever seen Scotty as a hindrance and all of them went out of their way to help Scotty. Lucky would die for these men. He owed them his loyalty.

"Now, let's discuss the businesses. Demo, your report?"

"The bar is finally back in the black after the roof cave-in," Demo announced proudly. "We upped our insurance policies on all the buildings we own after that disaster. I never want to see red numbers like that again, if it can be helped."

The winter before last, the club's bar *Demon on the Rocks* had unfortunately taken some damage during a snowstorm. While Cage, who ran the club's construction business, had been assessing the damage, the roof had caved in. Thankfully no one had been hurt, but the expense of repair had been painful to stomach. The bar had had to be shut down for months, losing money and customers to other businesses in town. While under construction, the club had voted to do some upgrades. They'd put in new tables, chairs, booths, two new pool tables, dart boards, a stage for bands, and had renovated the bar itself to accommodate more inventory.

Since Ghost and Ranger managed the bar, Scar worked as the bouncer, and they usually kept two prospects on as bartenders, plus their two part-time cooks, they'd had to pull from the club coffers to keep the members and the two employees paid during construction. They'd gone from being very black to very red overnight.

Demo continued, "Bones got his electricians license a few weeks ago and is signing on with Cage. While it will up the cost of insurance for the construction company, it will save on outsourcing for those types of jobs."

Steel nodded. "Good to hear the newbie is contributing."

"He needs to watch some of the physical labor," Demo said, "but the electrician portion of the jobs should be minimal. He's still got physical therapy twice a week, but Cage says he's willing to work around Bones's needs and schedule."

Steel looked over at Bulldog. "Make sure he doesn't need anything before or after his therapy sessions. He's not alone anymore. If he finds driving too difficult or he's too sore to get himself back safely, make sure he knows to call one of us. I also don't want him to feel like he has to ride his sled if he's hurting on club run days. We can make a prospect drive him so he's still included. Hell, we can get a sidecar for him or something."

Lucky wasn't the only one who snorted at that. Bones's pride would not allow him to sit in a sidecar. He'd either force himself into a cage or not go at all. Bones could handle sitting on a sled longer than he could sitting in a cage anyway. It let him stretch out his legs instead of feeling cramped. The problem was on longer rides, Bones had trouble walking afterwards.

Bulldog ran a hand down his long beard. Scotty liked to play with his beard, but that wasn't the reason he'd kept it long. Bulldog had shorn his hair when his mom had first started chemo and had kept his head bald since. He still hadn't cut his beard, even after his mom had been declared in remission. Despite only being thirty-two, he had some gray hairs sprouting. Bulldog teased that it was from having to keep their sorry asses in line. Lucky had more of a feeling it was from the stress of his mom having cancer. Scotty sure was responsible for many of Lucky's graying hair.

Lucky wouldn't wish cancer on his worst enemy. He made a mental note to find Patricia's number and reach out. Bear had gotten his nursing license after leaving the military and now worked for the town's senior living facility's hospice department. He knew his brother wouldn't hesitate to help out Scotty's teacher if he could.

"I'll talk to Bones," Bulldog said. "I doubt he'll accept help, but I might just have a prospect show up at his appointments anyway to drive him if needed."

Steel nodded. "Appreciate it, brother."

He indicated for Demo to continue. "The garage is doing well and needs more mechanics if we're to expand as planned. Grumpy already has three who aren't members and aren't eligible to join. If we get more prospects, maybe we can throw them his way and they can learn as they go."

Jumper only worked part-time at the garage with Grumpy. He couldn't handle the noise, so he tended to work alone after closing. One of the few times he'd tried working during business hours, someone had dropped a wrench on accident and the noise had caused Jumper to have a bad flashback. Even Aerial had struggled to get through to him. Grumpy had had to call Steel and Bulldog for assistance, who had then called Jumper's therapist. Lucky hadn't been there, but from what he understood it had taken almost an hour to pull Jumper from the waking nightmare. As a result, Jumper worked different hours than the other mechanics.

Pumpkin had his CDL. He worked for the garage as a mechanic and drove as their tow driver. He was the only one licensed to work their flatbed and drive their hauler.

Steel considered Demo's words for a moment. "I don't like poaching but let's look into some of the local garages and see if there's any vets who want to prospect. Won't make it a requirement to switch to our garage but they might be inclined to out of loyalty to the club."

"We can also look into the motor pools of nearby bases," Lucky suggested. "Never know when someone is getting out and they might be interested in keeping with the profession as well as prospecting."

Steel pointed to Demo. "Have Keys look into that. I like that idea."

Demo nodded and wrote a note in his ever-present legal notepad. Two or three Christmases ago, the club had pulled a prank on their treasurer, and each gifted him a pack of a dozen notepads. At that time, they'd been around ten members, but that was still around a hundred and twenty notepads. However, Demo had turned the joke around on them and thanked them for their contributions to keeping their finances in order. He'd even gone as far as to number the notepads in thick black ink on the back cardboard.

As President, Vice President, and SOA, Steel, Lucky, and Bulldog were the only members who pulled a salary from the club. However, that salary wasn't enough for any of them to live off of.

Steel worked with Jenna at the kids' consignment store they owned. While one might think his gruff demeanor would scare away customers, Jenna openly used him and his silver-fox body to draw customers in. Steel would learn to knit if Jenna asked him to. Instead, he was used for his muscles and height assist, as well as security. There was a video somewhere of Steel wearing a Santa hat reading the Grinch book to a group of kids with their single or married mothers giggling and drooling in the background. Since Jenna had been the one to take the video, Steel couldn't exact retribution. However, he did threaten any member in possession of that video with castration if he caught them with it. They were very careful when they played it.

Bulldog worked for a nonprofit that supported cancer

survivors. With that being a volunteer position, Lucky was sure Bulldog worked elsewhere too, but he'd never asked. He didn't like to pry information that wasn't freely given. He certainly didn't want to rehash his history. While it wasn't a secret that Scotty and Sissy were biologically his siblings, no one talked about it or asked him details.

Lucky worked for himself as an art welder. He got his certification shortly after Scotty had been born. At first, he'd worked as a construction welder, but his wages had been so low that he'd also had to work part-time as a bouncer at a bar. Working one and a half jobs was not conducive to raising two kids. He'd needed something better.

He'd started making art pieces when Scotty had been about two or three. He'd been fired from the construction job after having to leave early, again, for a doctor's appointment for Scotty. Knowing he'd need to make ends meet or risk living on the streets with two kids, he'd spoken to a local entrepreneur who owned a ceramics and arts studio. Lucky asked if the owner would mind if he could work on his art pieces in the back room for a fee.

That decision had turned out better than Lucky could have ever hoped. The owner's wife had offered to watch Scotty while Lucky worked in exchange for general maintenance being done around the studio and their apartment, which was on the floor above the studio. Lucky had happily agreed, dropping the daycare and its monthly expense from his pile of bills. After a few lean years where their little family lived off of Ramen noodles and only had a few dollars to spare each month, Lucky finally found a niche in the market.

He'd created a website, dedicating a percentage of his art's profits to the NDSS, the National Down Syndrome Society. He'd marked up his art to help make up for the difference and he'd had Scotty stand, sit, or hold each piece for the picture posted on the website. In addition, he'd reached out to some local newspapers and news stations to promote Down Syndrome awareness.

It wasn't long after that that he'd been able to put a sizable down payment on their house. They certainly weren't rolling in dough, but Lucky made a decent wage from his art pieces, could continue to donate monthly to the NDSS, and put money away for the future. The best part in his opinion was, he worked for himself and at his own schedule, which meant he was always available for Scotty and Sissy without having to worry about calling off work. Once he became VP and he'd started gaining that salary too, every penny was split between the two kids' savings accounts.

Most people didn't connect the *Scotty's Creations* artist Russell McCoy with the VDMC's VP Lucky. He never wore his cut for interviews or exhibits. It wasn't that he was ashamed of either. He simply didn't want his MC life to affect the message he was stating with his art pieces.

"Where are we at with buying the motorcycle dealership?" Steel asked. "How are those numbers looking?"

Demo scrolled through some pages in his pad before answering his president. "It'll be a hit to our bottom line, but it would be awesome to own. At the moment, we have the scratch. What we don't have are employees. Can't run a dealership without salesmen."

"What about their current employees?" Bear asked.

"When we'd presented the idea for a vote, we'd stated we wanted members in cuts to be the salesmen. Bring attention to the club, possibly bring in new members, and encourage donations for the charities the club supports," Demo answered.

The two biggest charities the club supported were the Down Syndrome Society and Breast Cancer Awareness in honor of Scotty and Mrs. Santiago. They also had done poker runs and hosted fundraising events towards the local high school's marching band needing new uniforms, a local family whose house had been destroyed in a fire, and other local needs.

Demo continued, "We could purchase it, so someone else doesn't and keep the current employees until we have the members to replace them."

Lucky didn't like that idea and, from the look on Steel's face, neither did he. "What if we all take shifts?" Lucky offered.

"What do you mean?" Demo asked.

"Well, aside from you who would need to run the books, that leaves us fourteen club members plus three prospects. We come up with a schedule where we rotate shifts. None of us would work there part-time or full-time but more of an as-needed situation. I know Scotty would love to pitch in and is a natural salesman," Lucky added proudly. "I think we can all come up with four to eight hours in a week to help out. Even if it's just stopping in on our way home from our regular jobs. It would give members a break from their everyday work schedule too. Plus, I don't know about the rest of you fools, but I would love to see men suffering from mid-life crises fall head over heels for Angel as she sells them hogs and over-charges them with hidden fees for daring to check out her rack."

Laughter sprang up. Angel was certainly a force to be reckoned with. She'd gotten her moniker from having the face of an angel, but it was all a ruse to draw unsuspecting suckers into her trap.

"Personally," Bear added, "I think Scar would make a fantastic salesman. He'd scare any customer who came in into buying the most expensive sled whether he wanted it or not without even saying a word. Sales will skyrocket."

Everyone laughed again–until Scar raised his head. Then they valued their lives too much to continue laughing.

Steel scratched his chin. He had had a close-cropped beard for as long as Lucky had known him. "I want a schedule created before we offer up a penny," he told Demo. "I won't risk failing after spending that sort of money."

Demo nodded once. "I'll have it for you before the end of day. The current owner knows we're seriously interested and isn't listing the business for sale until the end of the month if we don't give him an answer first. Personally, I think he's willing to go down on the price just to get it sold outright instead of dealing with lawyers and realtors."

"I'll stop by and talk to him myself if needed," Steel said. "I'd like to get us as low as we can go, but still be fair to him. He worked his ass off building that business. I'd like to honor his hard work and see he's fairly compensated."

"I'll set up a meeting for tomorrow. It'll give me time to put together a rough schedule of members' shifts and responsibilities."

Steel nodded once and then added, "Make sure it's after two. I promised Jenna we'd take a ride tomorrow morning to visit Carter and Lucy." Carter was Steel's oldest son and Lucy was his very pregnant daughter-in-law.

Demo made a note of that request too.

"Anyone have anything else to bring to the table? We still need to discuss the cat fight between Cherry and whatever the fuck the other one's name is."

Two of the Honeys had been caught fighting–hair pulling and all–over Ranger. Since Ranger hadn't been present or aware of the fight until afterwards, he couldn't be held accountable for it. From what Lucky understood, Cherry and Mary Ellen had both called "dibs" on Ranger on the night in question. Unbeknownst to the members, most of the Honeys called out amongst themselves beforehand who they wanted to fuck that night. When both women had wanted the same member, a fight had broken out between the two. In addition to hair being pulled out and manicures being messed up, a bottle of whiskey and a bar chair had also been broken.

Demon on the Rocks was the club owned bar. It was off property and in town. However, in the main area of the clubhouse was a second bar. This one was for members and was only in use for 'business' under days when they hosted open parties. Members did not have to pay for drinks at the clubhouse or at *Demon's*. However, Honeys only got free drinks if a member got it for them at either location. Same with hang-arounds.

"Fire them," Bulldog stated.

"Hey now," Bear piped in. "Let's not be hasty. Cherry gives really good head."

Lucky snorted. Bear was an exhibitionist when it came to sex and didn't mind an audience. In fact, he loved an audience. The club rule was that sex could only be out in the open during parties where anyone under twenty-one was prohibited. Unlike other clubs where Lucky was sure women walked around naked at all times and members conducted business mid-fuck, the *Via Daemonia* didn't roll that way.

Steel's daughter, Melanie, still lived at home and was only seventeen. She had every right to the clubhouse as anyone else. Jenna personally had stated if she saw any members free balling it, they would soon be ball free. Lucky had also put his foot down about the clubhouse being kid-friendly when they'd been creating the bylaws because of Scotty and Sissy. Though Sissy was now twenty-two and could legally drink, he did not want her randomly walking to the clubhouse to find an orgy going on. Sex was to be kept behind closed doors unless it was an open party, which meant only twenty-one and older were allowed on property.

"Honeys are here to take care of us. They are not here to give you head, Bear," Steel snapped. He turned to Bulldog. "Suspend both for a month, no pay. If they choose not to return, that's on them. It'll be a lesson to both that fighting is not permitted and they are here to do housekeeping, not act like strung out strippers."

Bulldog nodded. "Agreed. They've both been with us long enough to know better."

"And you're sure Ranger did nothing to instigate it?"

Again, Bulldog nodded. "He wasn't even here. Ghost had had to leave the bar early that night and Ranger stayed late to cover him. He had no idea about any of it until I approached him."

Steel ran a hand down his face. "Shit. I know the boys love their free pussy, but damn I wish we could get rid of the Honeys."

"What about cleaning and laundry?" Bear asked.

"You're a grown-ass man. You can do your own goddamn laundry," Steel snapped. "As for cleaning, if we had more prospects, I'd give them all toothbrushes and make them scrub the floors."

"Ah, good times," Demo added with false nostalgia. "My commander at boot camp was fond of that torture. He'd even hide the toothbrushes and make us find them first."

"You aren't serious though?" Bear prompted Steel. "About getting rid of the Honeys?"

Steel let out a long sigh. "No. Since I'm the only one of you losers who seems to be able to hold onto a decent woman, I can't take away your access to free pussy unless I want a mutiny on my hands."

Bear sighed loudly and dramatically wiped non-existent sweat off his forehead. "My cock and I thank you for your generosity, prez."

Lucky fought the urge to slap his forehead at his friend's antics. Bear had always had a good sense of humor and loved to joke around.

Steel ignored Bear. "Anything else?" he asked the table.

Bulldog tapped the table in front of him. "Not sure if you all heard or not, but Sheriff Longhill had a stroke two weeks ago. I got word he's being forced into early retirement by his doctor. He still has eighteen months left on his term. Town charter states that the council can appoint a new sheriff in the interim until the next election."

"Is Carlos up for the job?" Lucky asked. He'd heard about Longhill but he hadn't thought about a replacement. Honestly, he figured the man would be back at his post after a short leave. That man lived and breathed blue.

Bulldog shook his head. "Carlos is filling in until the new interim sheriff arrives. Apparently, word got around that a former big city detective from Detroit was moving to our humble town. The council offered him the job without even considering Carlos."

Bulldog's younger brother Carlos was the town's deputy sheriff. He'd been working under Sheriff Longhill since he'd turned eighteen and joined the force. It must have been a big blow to have been passed over so easily by the town he'd served for ten years. Since Carlos had never served in the military, he wasn't eligible to prospect for the club. However, Carlos still participated in club events and openly supported the club. He also was their go-between when they came across information the police would find interesting. Since their department was so small, Longhill had also called upon the MC to back them up on a job or two. With their military experience, they had a better and faster response time than an out-of-town SWAT team.

"That sucks, man," Jumper said, speaking for the first time since their meeting started. Jumper was quiet, usually lost in his own head. He followed their conversation but generally didn't speak.

His silence was different than Scar's. The enforcer didn't fidget or make any noises. It was like he was trying his damnedest to fade into the shadows of the room to wait for an opportune moment to strike. He generally succeeded. Jumper's silence was more like he was trying to keep himself in the present by listening intently to the conversation around him.

Bulldog agreed. "Yeah. He wasn't happy. Apparently, this big shot cop is moving down with his whole family too. Wife and kids."

"When does he start?" Demo asked, taking notes.

"Two weeks, last Carlos heard. He'll continue to fill in until then."

"We had a great personal and working relationship with Longhill." Steel's eyes bounced between Lucky and Bulldog. "I want to make sure his family knows we're here in support if they need anything. Hell, his wife can bring him by *Demon's* or here just to get him out of the house and give her some free time if needed."

Lucky nodded his agreement. "Scotty's teacher's husband was recently diagnosed with cancer. I mean to reach out to her too."

"Do that," Steel said. He looked to Demo, "Have Keys get me the interim sheriff's information. I want to reach out to him too, make sure he understands we are not like other MCs and we are available to help the department as always."

"Do you know his name?" Lucky asked Bulldog.

"Hannigan. Ronald Hannigan," he added for Demo's notes.

Lucky felt his heart skip a beat at the name. Hannigan. As in *Harper* Hannigan? She couldn't be *married*, could she? Beautiful creature like her, of course she would be.

Fuck. Not only was Lucky crushing after a woman fifteen years his junior, but she was a married woman. *Fuck!*

CHAPTER 3

The weekend flew by. With Sissy's and the club's help to keep Scotty entertained, Lucky was able to throw himself into a couple of commissioned projects that had been starting to pile up. He spent the entire two days in his art studio, which was the same building he'd started in over eleven years ago. When the owners had hinted at selling and moving to Florida, Lucky had gone to Steel and asked the club to purchase the building. While the building was club owned, Lucky's art business paid rent and was able to renovate the front room to display his pieces for locals and tourists to buy. He usually kept two part-time college students working the front of the shop while he worked in the back. During high tourist seasons, Scotty and Sissy would come and help out too. Scotty loved when people stopped by just to see him.

Normally, welding and the creation of his pieces soothed Lucky. Between the occasional nightmare from his time overseas and the stress of raising two kids on his own, Lucky used this time to clear his head and gain perspective. His usual methods failed this weekend.

He was forty fucking years old–or would be in a few weeks.

Scotty wasn't as stealthy as he thought he was, so Lucky was quite aware of the annual surprise party his son was planning for the Sunday after his birthday.

Regardless of whether his birthday had come yet or not, Lucky was far too old to be mentally fucking a twenty-five (he assumed) year old married woman. But damn, every time he closed his eyes, he saw her raven hair in that tight bun and his fingers ached to pull her hair down. He wanted to pull her towards him and bury his face in her thick locks. He wanted to mark her, both with his palm print and his seed. He wanted to see her let loose and smile at him as he buried himself inside her. He wanted to–

Fuck!

Lucky mentally slapped himself. Harper Hannigan was married. Even if she was interested, and that was a big if, she was off limits. Totally and completely off limits. Lucky would never go there. He'd had married women hit on him before at *Demon's* or the clubhouse. He wasn't interested in whatever scheme they were trying to pull behind their husband's back. He was not interested in that kind of drama. No pussy was worth that.

But Harper might–

"No, you stupid fucker."

"You don't even know what I was going to ask you."

Lucky let out a snort and turned to find Bear standing in the doorway of his studio. As the building was club owned, Steel and Demo had keys. However, Lucky had also given a set to Bear just in case. The man also had keys to Lucky's house and the access code to the garage. If something happened, Lucky wanted Bear to be able to get in and get to his kids without having to fight over a locked door.

He turned off the torch. Today he wore his goggles rather than the face helmet. Taking them off, he was sure he had imprints surrounding his eyes. Scotty liked to call him a raccoon when he came home like that.

"I wasn't talking to you, asshole."

"So you were calling yourself a stupid fucker?" he inquired.

Not wanting to answer that, Lucky instead asked, "Why are you here?"

"Well, *someone*, who shall remain nameless for the sake of his dignity, forgot that his daughter needed to go back to her college dorm tonight so she could get up early for her seven-thirty in the fucking morning class and therefore needed to be home by five to take his son from her."

Lucky glanced at the clock. It was eight-thirty-three. "Fuck." Lucky put his tools down. "Why didn't anyone call me?"

"We did, asshole. You didn't answer."

"Where's Scotty now?"

"With Mrs. Henderson while I went out to search for your dead body. Sissy called me when she couldn't get ahold of you." Mrs. Henderson was their widowed neighbor who loved to watch Scotty. She refused to take payment for babysitting either. Despite her protests, Lucky still made time to help her with yard work and house maintenance.

Lucky let out a sigh of relief. "Thank you. Fuck. I was working on this piece, and I lost track of time."

Bear came closer and examined the almost completed statue. "Is that a *bear*?"

"Yeah. Some hunting company in Alaska commissioned it."

"Alaska? Damn, man. You're really getting out there."

It was freaky when he got commissions for pieces from people who lived out of state. Even freakier was the time he'd been commissioned by a family in Australia. Scotty had said 'crikey' after every other word and called everyone 'mate' for a month. There had been no more crocodile hunter episodes for him for a while.

"I can't believe I lost track of time. I thought I had an alarm set." Lucky pulled his phone out of his back pocket. It was dead. "Shit."

When he went to stand up, Bear indicated with his finger for him to sit back down. He did. Bear pulled up a chair across from him. Then he sat there and waited.

And waited.

"What the fuck, man? I gotta go get Scotty."

"Those two nutcases are probably watching some true crime episode and plotting to murder the damn squirrels who keep eating Mrs. Henderson's rosebushes. They're fine." He crossed his arms over his broad chest. "Why are you a stupid fucker?"

Lucky was not going to answer that question. They were no longer in high school. "Just a mistake I'd made while putting this piece together."

Bear didn't even look at the art piece. "You know, when Scotty lies, you tell him that you can see his nose start to grow like Pinocchio's. While that might scare the kid into fessing up, I'm aware that it won't scare you. Doesn't mean I don't see your nose growing though."

Lucky narrowed his eyes at his brother. "You are such an asshole."

"I know." He tossed his hair back dramatically. "It's one of the things the ladies love about me."

"Didn't realize you were into pegging."

"Don't knock it until you try it." Bear's smile was so wide Lucky honestly couldn't tell if the man was being serious. He'd never before mentioned anything about being interested in anal play on himself. Lucky knew all about how much the man loved to fuck women in the ass. It made Lucky suspicious but not enough to ask. He knew far too much about Bear's sex life as it was. The man didn't have a shy bone in his body. "And don't try to change the subject. We can sit here all night if needed. There might be a colony of murdered squirrels upon our return, but that catastrophe will be on you, not me."

"I don't want to talk about it."

Bear still sat there.

Lucky groaned. "You are a stupid fucker, you know that?"

"Apparently, I'm not the only one in the room. Spill."

"What are you, a ten-year-old girl?"

Again, Bear just sat there, not saying a thing.

Lucky stood, picking up his gloves and goggles. He walked over to his argon gas tanks and started the shut off procedure. He needed to send a picture of the working statue to his clients too to confirm his progress was on schedule and verify they didn't want any changes made prior to him applying a resin coat to protect it.

"I met someone," he finally admitted. He quickly stopped Bear's excitement in its tracks when he added, "She's married."

"Fuck."

"Yeah." Lucky walked over to the bear statue and started to take three-sixty-degree pictures. Bear moved out of the way, so he wasn't in the background of any. Before shipping any commissioned piece, Lucky brought Scotty to the studio to pose with it for their website. Scotty also wrote a thank you note that went in the envelope with the invoice and donation receipt in the client's name to the NDSS.

"Who is she?"

Lucky shook his head. He didn't want Bear going to the school to check her out. Since Scotty required a pick-up by an approved adult to leave the school, Lucky, Sissy, Bear, and Jenna were on his list. Lucky wished he could put every one of his brothers on that list, but the school limited it to four. Jenna's shop was close to the high school, and she could be there faster than Lucky could from his studio. Plus, if Jenna was going, Steel would follow, so it was like having a fifth person on the list.

"It doesn't matter. She's married. She's off limits."

"But you like her enough to be thinking about her, I'm assuming, days later?"

Three days. The bastard had a point.

"She was…" Lucky paused, unsure how to explain it. "It was

beyond how sexy she looked. She...challenged me. She wasn't afraid of me."

Bear, who'd gotten his nickname in the military for being as "big as a bear", was huge. He and Bulldog were the tallest in the club. Bear was six-six and Bulldog six-five. At six-two, Lucky wasn't that far below them. However, Bear had muscle that Lucky lacked. While on active duty, Lucky had been defined and muscular. After retiring and taking in the kids, he'd lost some of that structure and he started to get a classic dad bod. Once they'd moved into their new house, Lucky had converted the spare bedroom into a home gym so Scotty and he could workout. Sissy sometimes used the treadmill, but generally didn't enter that room. Scotty loved lifting weights with Lucky. He called it their manly bonding time. Slowly, Lucky had started to gain back the muscle he'd lost since leaving the military.

Bear, however, had never lost his muscle. In high school when he'd shot up to freakish heights, Bear had started lifting weights. Despite having already turned forty, being a few months older than Lucky, he still had the six-pack he'd developed in his teen years. The bastard had yet to get a gray hair too.

Lucky was aware that he was less imposing than Bear or Bulldog, but he still had an intense aura about him. More than one woman had been scared away just by him approaching their general direction. Bear had a way about him that made the ladies want to take a ride on a gentle giant. For a woman to be unaffected by Lucky from the get-go was intriguing.

"Wow," Bear said. He scratched the top of his head. "You've only met her once?"

Lucky nodded. Unfortunately, once was all it took. Harper Hannigan had burrowed her way under his skin, though she had no right to be there when she wore another man's ring.

That thought made Lucky pause. He couldn't recall seeing a ring on the woman's finger. Like Patricia, she hadn't worn any jewelry, as the students they worked with tended to have grabby hands. Maybe she didn't wear her ring to work?

"The marriage thing puts her off limits, but there's something else too." Bear raised an eyebrow and waited for Lucky to continue. "She's…young."

Bear's second eyebrow rose. "How young?"

"Old enough to be legal but young enough that I shouldn't want anything to do with her."

"So early twenties?"

Lucky nodded. "I assume so. I'd be surprised if she was older than twenty-five."

"Damn. You're taking the position of Daddy to heart."

Lucky picked up a construction pencil and threw it at his friend. Bear ducked the projectile while laughing. "That might be your kink but it ain't mine."

"Not mine either, asshole. I prefer my women gagged where they can't call me anything. Moans and groans are my language of love."

"Kinky bastard."

Bear smiled proudly. "Fuck yeah." His expression fell slightly as he asked, "What are you going to do?"

"What do you mean, what am I going to do?" Lucky started to pack up his sketchbook and laptop. He put everything in a backpack that fit in his saddlebag. Since learning the freedom of riding a sled, he truly did feel riding in a car was like the cage the bikers called them. It sucked when it was raining or the weather turned too cold to continue to ride. If it wasn't for the kids, he might have ridden anyway. "The woman is *married* and at least fifteen years younger than I am. I am not going to do anything. I can't."

"But you want to."

Lucky paused. That had been a statement, not a question. Fuck. His friend knew him too well. "Yeah, I want to. So much so it's like a burning in my gut that won't go away."

"Why don't we go to the clubhouse? Mrs. Henderson is good with Scotty for a bit. If he falls asleep, I'll help you get him home and in bed."

"What would going to the clubhouse help?" While tempted, Lucky knew that he needed to get home to Scotty.

"Maybe one of the Honeys or the patch bunnies looks enough like her that you can fuck her out of your system without actually fucking her."

Just the thought of sleeping with one of the Honeys made his stomach turn. "Eh, no."

"Really? Come on, man. Just a drink. You need to do something to get your mind off this girl and clearly making your masterpieces didn't do the trick for you."

Lucky still shook his head. "I need to get home to Scotty."

He started to walk past his friend when Bear put a hand on his shoulder to stop him. "You have proved over and over again that you are not your mom, Russ." Shit, Bear must be serious if he was calling him by his legal name. "You've proven it to the point where you're not living your life for you. You refuse to do anything even remotely selfish for fear of becoming like her. You're allowed to have a life too. You're allowed to do something *for you*. You've sacrificed everything for those kids. What about you?"

Lucky couldn't look his friend in the eyes. He knew Bear spoke the truth. He was aware that every parenting decision he made, he made with his mom's actions in mind. He knew that he was overprotective and possessive, but he wanted to give Sissy and Scotty every opportunity he could give them. Everything they would have had if Lucky's father hadn't died. Then again, if Lucky's father hadn't died, neither Sissy nor Scotty would have been born.

Lucky's childhood was normal. He had two loving parents who'd gotten knocked up way too young. Lucky's mom had been seventeen when she'd had him and his dad had been twenty-one.

With no other choice, they'd gotten married and moved in together to raise their son. There'd been resentment, sure, but towards his teenage years his parents had been more like friends who shared the same household rather than a happily married couple. He was pretty sure they had had an agreement to remain married until he turned eighteen for his sake.

Then his dad had been driving home during a snowstorm and, the police assumed, hit some ice. His car had gone over the bridge and hadn't been found until the spring when the river had thawed. His mom had been devastated. Lucky had been too, but he'd had to hold it together for her sake. In a way, his mom had lost her best friend, though legally he was her husband.

The tragedy of his dad's death had been the catalyst to his mother's downfall. She'd started small, using marijuana to calm herself down when the grief got too much. To this day, Lucky didn't know when she'd started on the harder stuff. When he'd confronted her about her drinking, he'd found her stash of needles and drugs. There'd been both meth and cocaine in the house. He'd flushed everything he'd found but, like any drug addict worth their salt, she'd gotten more.

Lucky had warned her that he wasn't going to stick around and watch her kill herself. She needed to get herself clean. Bear and Lucky had already signed up for the Marines and were due to ship out right after high school graduation. He'd gotten her into a rehab center before he'd left for Boot Camp.

He'd gotten letters from his mom throughout his service. She thanked him for getting her clean, apologized for her mistakes and pointed out that she felt lost without his father. Lucky had even stopped by to see her before being deployed. Unknown to him, his mother had been pregnant with Sissy at that time.

She'd remained clean through her pregnancy, miracle of miracles. But she had lost her job during her addiction. Lucky sent money home to her. What he hadn't known was she'd started to sell her body to make ends meet. One of her clients–

cringe—was Sissy's biological father. She had never said who and Lucky had never asked.

He knew he had a sister, but he hadn't known that his mother had started using again around her first birthday. When he'd come home between deployments, they would do quick meetups at restaurants or a park. Lucky hadn't picked up on the signs until closer to Sissy's third birthday. At that point, he had another year left before he could get out or reenlist. He'd started the process to get guardianship over Sissy almost immediately after discovering his mother was not only using in front of her daughter but also brought her clients around her. That was the longest year of Lucky's life.

As soon as he'd gotten his discharge papers, he filed his petition for custody. At first, his mom had fought him. In her drug-addled mind, she believed she was being a good mother to Sissy. But after a big fight, Lucky had convinced his mom to give up her parental rights to Sissy. That was when Lucky had discovered that his mom didn't know or didn't remember who Sissy's biological father was.

Once again, he put his mom into a rehab center. This time, thankfully, it was court-ordered, which meant she had to remain there for a minimum of six months. Even after that, though, she would have to petition to get her rights back to Sissy.

She never once asked to see Sissy or wanted her rights back after they'd been stripped.

After rehab, Lucky had tried to stay in touch with her. By this point, she'd already lost her house to the bank, and she'd had nowhere to live. Lucky was struggling with adjusting to life as a civilian, taking care of Sissy, and covering the bills, but he could have figured something out. Except his mom had refused all help.

She disappeared for almost two years. The next time Lucky had heard from her, a hospital was calling him to tell him his mom had been admitted to the maternity ward. She was so strung out she hadn't even known she'd been pregnant. Through his studying of Down Syndrome, he'd learned that his mother's drug use and alcoholism had not caused the chromosomal disorder, but it certainly hadn't helped in his development. Scotty had been born premature and severely underweight.

The police were involved, as was Social Services. Lucky had packed a bag for him and Sissy and rushed them to the hospital in Pittsburgh where apparently his mom had been living. No one ever came forward to claim fatherhood of the baby. As the closest family member, Social Services had granted Lucky temporary custody of the baby. It wasn't until Scotty was four months old that Lucky had been named the court appointed guardian.

When Scotty was five and Sissy was twelve, Lucky had officially adopted them both.

After sneaking out of the hospital fifteen years ago, no one had seen or heard from Laura McCoy since.

Lucky was sure she was dead, listed as a Jane Doe in some morgue basement. He mourned the loss of the mother he'd had growing up, but not the woman she'd become. He could only hope and pray that there wasn't another child out there in the system that shared his mother's DNA. If there was, he desperately hoped he or she had landed with a good family.

Sissy had known their mother, but claimed she didn't remember much. She recalled her singing to her and being told numerous times to hide in the pantry when Mommy's friends came over. She swore up and down that none of their mom's clients touched her.

Scotty had never known their mother. When he was twelve, Sissy and Lucky had sat Scotty down and explained that biologically he was Lucky's brother too, not just Sissy's. Lucky didn't want some stranger to break the news to Scotty and confuse him. Kids in high school could be mean and it wasn't a secret in this town how Sissy and Scotty had come to live with Lucky. Scotty had turned tear filled eyes onto Lucky and asked him if he would still be willing to be his daddy. Lucky had scooped his son up in his arms and proclaimed that he was his daddy, no matter what biology said.

That was the last time his parentage had been mentioned around Scotty.

Lucky knew Bear was right. He'd struggled to provide for his kids, wanting to give them everything and feeling like a failure the times when he couldn't afford to. There were days when Lucky had skipped a meal, not knowing if they'd have enough to stretch them until his next paycheck. As soon as Bear had discovered that fact, he'd started bringing over groceries any time he'd visit between deployments. Lucky had tried to refuse but Bear had given him the ultimatum of accepting the groceries or accepting Bear's foot up his ass.

As soon as Lucky's business had started to take off, he'd tried to pay Bear back but his friend refused. When Lucky had tried to use the same ultimatum back at him, Bear had just laughed and said he was welcome to try. The bastard.

Lucky didn't regret a single decision or sacrifice he'd made for his kids. Sissy was now thriving and in college. She was twenty-two and would soon have dual degrees in graphic design and marketing. She was such a beautiful and kind young woman. Her love for Scotty knew no bounds.

Scotty was fifteen and, despite having what society would consider to be shortcomings, was thriving. He loved his school. He loved his friends. He loved his neighbors. He loved his club. He loved life. No matter what mood Lucky was in, Scotty always brought a smile to his face. All it took was a nose-kiss and Lucky's day was automatically brighter.

He truly was the luckiest man in the world to have the honor and the privilege to raise those two amazing kids.

But maybe… Maybe Bear had a point. What had Lucky done recently that was for him? As much as he loved his MC and brothers, he'd ultimately made the decision to join for Scotty and Sissy. Steel had made it known from the beginning that both kids were welcome and included in the club. He'd wanted something stable for them, as well as uncles and aunts they could rely on beyond Lucky and Bear. He loved his MC, but even that decision had not been one he'd made for himself.

Still, it didn't matter. It couldn't matter. Harper Hannigan was *married*. To the town's interim sheriff. If there was one enemy in a town you did not want to piss off, it was the sheriff. Especially by sleeping with his young wife.

Shit. Fuck.

Lucky was going to Hell.

If there was one selfish choice he could make, it would be Harper Hannigan. Fuck. She probably thought him too old, and obviously didn't approve of his lifestyle anyway. Fuck. She was *married*. What did it matter if she approved of his lifestyle or not?

Lucky hung his head in defeat. He needed a drink, but knew if he started he wouldn't stop. And he refused to become his mother.

"I need to go home and get Scotty," he finally said.

Bear let out a long sigh and dropped his hand from his shoulder. "All right. I'll follow you and make sure you don't need help getting him down for the night."

Lucky nodded once. "Thanks."

He was grateful for Bear's offer of assistance. Scotty was no longer a small infant he could hold one-handed.

Even knowing that Harper Hannigan was off limits, he still drove home with her on his mind and still fell asleep that night with her pretty face in his dreams. He was doomed.

* * *

THE NEXT MORNING, Scotty begged Lucky to take him to school on his hog rather than take the bus. Lucky wanted to refuse, he really did, but he couldn't tell Scotty no. Unfortunately, the kid knew it too. Scotty had a cocky smile on his face as Lucky helped him strap his helmet on under his chin.

Lucky wasn't so lucky that morning as to not run into the star of his very erotic dreams the past three nights. As he waited in line for their turn in the drop-off, he spotted her almost immediately. Like last Friday, she had her raven hair up in a bun. Her business suit that day was navy blue with a green top under her jacket.

Fuck, he wanted to rip open that jacket and button-up shirt and bury his face between her tits.

He noticed she was wearing flats rather than heels. He hadn't picked up on that last Friday. It meant she was tall for a woman, probably five-eight. *Damn, tall and strong,* Lucky thought. *The full package.*

With the exception of her marriage and age.

Fuck.

Scotty started waving so frantically, he nearly whacked Lucky in the head with his elbow. Good thing he was wearing a helmet. It was proving to be more protection from Scotty than from the road.

He slowly pulled over towards the sidewalk when they were in the drop-off area. To be polite, Lucky raised his hand towards Mrs. Hannigan. He could have sworn Scotty had said Ms. on Friday, but he'd either heard wrong or Scotty had misspoken.

She responded with a polite wave and smile, like one she'd give to any other parent in the drop-off lane. Scotty dismounted as she approached. Lucky didn't raise his visor. If he didn't talk to her, perhaps she wouldn't talk with him, and he could get over this crazy obsession.

Scotty placed his helmet and denim cut in his saddlebag. He turned, gave Lucky a kiss on his visor and wished him a good day.

Then he took Mrs. Hannigan's hand and she led him into the school. Just as they reached the door, she looked over her shoulder at Lucky for exactly five seconds before she took Scotty inside.

That afternoon at pick-up, Scotty ran to Lucky as soon as he pulled his hog up to the sidewalk. Lucky waited anxiously, his eyes facing forward as Scotty donned his cut and helmet. Then Scotty mounted the bike and Lucky took off. Without looking, without talking.

They repeated this pattern the next day, and the day after that, through the end of the week. By Friday, Lucky was itching for the weekend—probably more than the high schoolers were—just to have a break from looking at her and wishing she would both talk to him and not talk to him. It was driving him insane.

The following week continued the pattern. To the point where Lucky almost begged Bear to take Scotty to school just to give Lucky a break from the battle raging inside him.

Mrs. Harper Hannigan had no right to tease him with those sexy pantsuits and that playful smile. The worst bit was, she probably didn't even know she was doing it! It was all in Lucky's mind.

The second Friday of their silent drop-off pattern, Lucky was so antsy he debated on skipping the executive meeting at the clubhouse. There was no way he could sit still or contemplate club business when Harper flooded his every waking thought. He was just as likely to say Harper's name or the color of her sexy as hell pantsuit that day as he was to answer whatever Steel said to him.

Fuck.

Still, he had an obligation to the club and so he went. Lucky wasn't sure what was mentioned prior to the topic of the new interim sheriff, whom Lucky already hated simply because the man had the woman Lucky wanted. In his bed, in his life. It was his ring on her finger. It was his claim that made her off limits to Lucky.

Over the last two weeks, Lucky had come to the conclusion

that age was just a number. Yes, she was young. Yes, there was a smaller age gap between her and Sissy than there was the two of them, whether she turned out to be twenty-three or twenty-six. Bear had made the point that Lucky didn't make selfish decisions. Making love to Harper would be a selfish decision, but it didn't change the fact that he wanted her.

She likely wouldn't want him, being the cranky old bastard he was. However, if there was a chance she did, he would jump on it.

If she wasn't married.

So somehow, despite the fact that she was still off limits to him, he'd talked himself out of their age difference being one of the reasons not to pursue her.

Except he *still* couldn't pursue her because she was still married.

Off limits.

Fuck.

He wasn't really paying attention until he heard Bulldog say, "…his wife Cindy."

Lucky's head popped up. "What?"

Bulldog's eyebrows went down as if he wasn't sure why he needed to repeat that fact. "The new interim sheriff. He and his wife finally moved to town."

Lucky waved that part off. "Her name. What did you say the wife's name was?"

"Cindy."

Lucky shook his head. "No, it's Harper. I've met her and she's been here at least three weeks."

Bulldog looked down at the paperwork in front of him. "No, it's Cindy. Cynthia, but she goes by Cindy. Oh," he pointed to something on the papers. "Looks like Harper is his daughter's name. She's a teacher and is subbing at the high school until a full-time position opens up. She moved down earlier than her parents by five weeks."

Daughter.

It was like a cool wave had washed over him, dispelling all his anxiety. She wasn't his wife. She was his *daughter*.

Holy fuck on a fuckery.

He wasn't going to go insane. He'd been ignoring her for the past two weeks for nothing. Hell, he could be fucking her right now if he hadn't jumped to conclusions.

Wait. That didn't mean she *wasn't* married. Women sometimes kept their maiden names.

"Is she married?" Lucky asked Bulldog. He would have had Keys pull background checks on the entire family.

Bulldog looks just as confused as everyone at the table, with the exception of Bear who looked amused. Fucker would have easily figured out the woman Lucky had been pining over was Harper Hannigan based on Lucky's inquiries to Bulldog and current obvious desperation.

"No record of a marriage license–"

Lucky stood up. "I gotta go."

Steel stood up too. "You what?"

Lucky couldn't explain it. He had to get to the school now. He had to talk to her. She wasn't married. He'd been going insane for nothing. She could be *his*.

The one image he hadn't allowed himself to fantasize about came to the forefront of his mind: Harper smiling, sitting on his hog waiting for him as they started their club run. Except she wasn't there as his backpack. No, the leather cut she wore proclaiming her *Property of Lucky* meant she was his ol' lady.

Bear piped up. "I'll explain." He tipped his head towards the door. "Go get your girl."

Lucky ran out of Church like the hounds of Hell were chasing after him.

CHAPTER 4

*H*arper smiled as Emily brought her wheelchair back to her assigned seating area. Emily had cerebral-palsy, or CP, and was completely paralyzed from the neck down. Her electric wheelchair was equipped with a computer that could talk for her based on certain button combinations she pushed with her chin. She was brilliant and a quick learner, but she would sadly never fit into this harsh world who judged people for their differences.

There were four students currently in Harper's classroom. She had six total, but two were able to join mainstream classes for certain electives. Tommy was in shop class with his student-aide Madison, who was a senior and received credit for assisting Tommy. Suzette was in gym class with one of the spare gym teachers assisting her.

Emily, Tonya, Carter, and Scotty were her full-time students. They followed her to their electives and did them together as a class. Harper and Emily were generally together off to the side for those electives, as Emily was incapable of performing the necessary tasks. The others could participate in home studies, shop class, gym, and the like with assistance. Actually, Scotty tended to help the other two out more, which allowed Harper to sit with Emily so she wasn't placed in a corner alone. It was unfair in so many ways that the school curriculum required her to take the electives to graduate when she was physically incapable of participating.

Tonya was deaf. She had been born so. While Harper was fluent in sign language, Tonya's parents preferred she not learn it. Per Patricia's notes, her mother had stated it was a useless language and neither her nor Tonya's father had time to learn it too. Tonya had cochlear implants in both ears. She was proficient at reading lips as well. She wasn't able to take mainstream general courses due to the fact that it was difficult for her to follow along at the same speed as the others. At times, when the world got too noisy, she'd take off her adapters and just sit in silence. To her parents' dismay, Harper encouraged her to do so at the beginning and end of the school day.

Carter was high-functioning autistic. He was super-smart and had an eidetic memory. However, his autism forced him to have his life in a certain order, and high school was far too chaotic for him to function in mainstream courses. If there was traffic in the morning and Carter arrived even a minute late, his entire day was thrown off to the point where little schoolwork was accomplished. While Harper didn't like to compare home lives and the parents of his students, Carter's mother was a saint in comparison to Tonya's parents who tried to ignore their daughter's ailment.

And then there was Scotty's too sexy father who rode up to the school like a motorcycle god. While she hadn't seen his face or spoken to him since their first introduction, the man's face had been permanently etched into her brain. He had no right to be that sexy. She had no right to be drooling over one of her student's fathers. Guess they were both in the wrong.

The man was tall, and how she loved tall men. It was the only time in her life when she felt short. Men also didn't tend to go for her because of her height. They didn't like a woman who matched or beat them in the height department like it affected their ability to 'be a man'. Not that she minded shorter men, but it always seemed to be a hit to their delicate egos and a point of resentment in the relationship.

Russell McCoy also had tattoos–and Harper *loved* tattoos. She didn't have any herself because her father would murder her and the tattoo artist in their sleep if he ever discovered she'd defaced her body in such a way. What Harper loved most about tattoos, beyond the artistry, were the stories–the meaning behind the tattoo.

Each day that Russell pulled up to drop Scotty off, she studied his right arm, which was the only arm she could see. She could only make out the T-T-Y, of what she assumed was Scotty's name, starting at his shoulder under his sleeve. His muscles bulged under his son's name. The letters were in black but the designs around them were all colored. There was a stack of books, a soccer ball, a bunch of orange handprints, and what she thought might be squirrels but figured she was seeing that wrong from her distance.

She hadn't gotten a look at the other arm and desperately wanted to. What else was tattooed on him? On his broad chest, his back, his muscular thighs…?

Did he have the logo of his motorcycle gang tattooed on his back like they did in the movies? She shouldn't find that as hot as she did.

Harper knew that his fortieth birthday was coming up. Scotty loved to talk about his dad, which included the surprise party he was throwing for him with the help of his uncles.

It sounded like Scotty had a big family. Did they approve of their son and brother being in a gang? Did they think the lifestyle was dangerous, especially for a single father with kids?

Since secrets didn't exist in Scotty's world, she probably knew far more about their home life than his father would prefer.

Harper knew that, besides Scotty, there was his sister Sissy. She'd even met the sister when she'd pick Scotty up from school on Friday afternoons. Harper loved that his sister came home from college on the weekends to spend time with her little brother.

Harper knew that Scotty's dad was an artist. She'd even gone onto his website during her lunch break out of curiosity. And damn, it warmed her heart to see the dedication the man put into his pieces and how he centered Scotty around each one in the pictures.

Scotty told her a lot about the motorcycle club. He'd corrected her a number of times when she'd mistakenly called it a gang. Scotty loved to ride on the back of his dad's motorcycle. He said he felt like a bird or Aerial, who turned out to be a service dog Scotty knew. She didn't like when she heard Scotty hung out at the bar with the bikers. Were they mean to him? Did they make fun of him? She knew bikers could be gruff and disrespectful to women. What did they say in front of Scotty? He'd never been disrespectful or said anything inappropriate that she knew of. Perhaps he didn't understand what they were saying enough to repeat it?

The biggest conflict Harper was fighting with herself about, despite the fact the man was fourteen years older than her and the father of a student, was his affiliation to that club. When her father took the sheriff position, reluctantly she might add, she doubted he'd allow for any criminal activity to last for long. Her father was a strict believer in the law. There was no gray area. There was the law and those who broke it. Black and white.

But what did it matter whether or not her father would approve of a relationship? Clearly her crush was unrequited. The man hadn't spoken to her or looked her way since their initial meeting two weeks ago. It was almost as if he went out of his way to avoid her. Maybe she'd pissed him off with her inquiries about Scotty's safety and what he was exposed to around the bikers.

She'd never been one to bite her tongue–except around her father.

Ronald Hannigan did not take kindly to being talked back to. Just like the justice system had final say in this country, Ronald Hannigan had final say over his household, whether you lived under his roof or not.

She hadn't wanted to move to Mount Grove, Pennsylvania. It certainly wasn't on her bucket list of places to live in her lifetime. But she hadn't exactly been given a choice. After her parents had decided to leave Detroit, she'd been informed she was going with them. She'd wanted to put up an argument, especially since there were no current jobs open in her field, but then her brother Richard had announced he, his wife Paige, and their two sons Michael and Nelson were moving to Mount Grove too. Harper didn't want to be the only one in the family not to move. She loved her nephews and wanted to be a part of their lives. So, she'd packed up and moved to Mount Grove alongside them.

Her parents had fought with her about her getting her own apartment. They'd wanted her to move into their new house with them. Harper had refused. She was an adult and would not be living under her parents' roof again. Her father only relented when she promised to text them when she got home safely after work and informed them if she was going out somewhere. Harper had agreed but hadn't exactly been keeping to that promise. What her parents didn't know couldn't hurt them.

Harper wanted to see this move as a good thing. This was a chance at a fresh start and a chance to meet new people. Maybe she could even meet a nice guy and settle down. She'd never do that with her parents as her wingmen.

Turns out, though, she didn't even need her parents to scare away men. She did that all on her own by opening her big mouth.

At the sound of the bell, Harper got her students together and they headed towards the lunchroom. It was eleven-thirty and she had exactly twenty-five minutes to clean up her classroom, eat her own lunch, use the bathroom, and get the material ready for the afternoon's lessons. She hadn't been sleeping well, dreams of a sexy motorcyclist keeping her awake, and she was tired enough that she debated throwing in a movie for the remainder of the day.

Inside Out came to mind. It was educational about emotions. *Possibly*, she thought wryly.

Scotty gave her a hug at the cafeteria doorway and assured her that he would watch over the others. Harper smiled down at him and thanked him. She also made sure to catch the monitor's eye and indicate towards her four before leaving. Mrs. Wallace was a strict rule follower, and she made sure the special needs group was left alone and respected. Her father would like Mrs. Wallace. She did too.

After a quick stop in the teacher's lounge to grab her packed lunch and to use the bathroom, Harper headed back to her classroom. Technically it was still Patricia's classroom. She hadn't wanted to change anything out of respect for the woman. From one perspective, Harper couldn't believe her luck that a position had opened up just as she'd moved to town. From another, she was heartbroken for Patricia.

In truth, she felt so guilty to be grateful she had this job, even if it was temporary. Maybe she should reach out to Patricia again and see how she was doing. Last Harper had heard, her husband had decided to decline chemo treatments. The cancer was too far along, and it would only delay the inevitable. Harper hated that for her colleague. It was such a helpless feeling, and she couldn't imagine the pain Patricia was going through knowing her husband was choosing to die.

Harper was so lost in her thoughts she hadn't realized her classroom wasn't empty until she was halfway to her desk. She jumped, dropping her lunchbox.

"Mr. McCoy."

The biker she'd been fantasizing about rushed forward from

where he'd been standing by the windows and picked up her lunch she'd dropped. As he handed it to her, his deep voice apologized for startling her.

"Oh. Um, it's okay. Um, how did you get in here?"

Security would not have just let him wander in, even if he was the parent of a student.

The man shrugged. "I have my ways."

Damn, that crooked smile was sexy. He had a neatly trimmed beard and mustache that surrounded his lips. It was speckled with gray hairs amongst the black, which she found utterly attractive.

"Um." Should she call for security? "Scotty is in the cafeteria eating lunch."

"I'm not here to see Scotty." He still hadn't stepped back. He was close enough to be in her personal space but still far enough away to give her the illusion of space. That illusion was failing.

She shook her head to clear it. She narrowed her eyes. She was not some lovesick teenager who didn't know how to talk to the opposite sex. "Then why are you here?"

"To see you."

Oh dear. Her heart just did a cartoon heartthrob and nearly leapt out of her chest. She wouldn't be surprised if she had little pink hearts floating around her head.

Harper forced herself to stay strong. "About Scotty?"

He shook his head, his lips twitching like he was trying to keep from laughing. Which was just great. Laugh at the poor lovesick teacher who was totally crushing on her student's super sexy dad with salt and pepper hair and a fantastic body. No dad bod for this dad.

"I came to see *you*, Harper. About you, not Scotty."

She swallowed audibly. "Why," her voice cracked. Shit. "Why would you need to see me, Mr. McCoy?"

"Lucky."

"I'm sorry?" He was feeling lucky?

"Call me Lucky." She glanced down and saw that that was the name on the patch over his left breast. The title of *Vice President* was under it.

He took a single step closer. Which left no illusion of space whatsoever. "I actually came to apologize."

"Apologize?" Damn, he smelled good. Like motor oil and man. All man. And maybe a hint of pancakes?

"I would have been here sooner but there was a misassumption on my part that prevented me from doing so."

Misassumption? She shook her head. "I don't understand."

"I'd mistakenly thought you were a married woman. I learned today that you aren't."

Married? *Her?* No. God, no. She was so single her freezer was filled with meals for one and she was contemplating starting a cat collection. "Why would it matter if I was married or not?"

He tipped his head down as if he was going to kiss her but instead stopped with his nose just above her hairline. He took in a deep breath. Was he smelling her? She supposed that was only fair, as she'd just done the same to him. Shit, had she put on deodorant this morning? Please, if there was a God, please let her have remembered to put on deodorant this morning.

He lifted his head. "I don't date married women."

Date? Did he just say date? Did bikers date? Sure, her fantasies surrounding this man involved a long-term relationship or at least a very long sex marathon weekend. But those were fantasies. Bikers liked having multiple women available. They cheated on their women. Right?

She cleared her throat and decided to clarify. "Date?"

He nodded, amusement in his brown eyes. "Date. I'll pick you up at seven tonight. Wear pants and closed toed shoes. We're taking my hog."

The man was partway to her classroom door when she finally snapped out of her daze. He hadn't actually asked her on a date. He just told her they were going on a date.

"Lucky!" Calling him 'Mr. McCoy' seemed too impersonal now, though maybe that was what she needed after their exchange.

He turned back, looking far too sexy. He had an air of satisfaction about him. Clearly, he'd accomplished what he'd come here to do.

She forced her face into a scowl when in reality her inner cheerleader was doing backflips in celebration. "I never said I wanted to go on a date with you."

He raised an eyebrow and, for a moment, she thought he was going to walk out without responding. Then he stepped forward. He slowly reached out, giving her ample time to back away if she chose to. His large, callused hand cupped her cheek. "Harper Hannigan, will you go on a date with me tonight?"

She couldn't nod fast enough. "Yes."

His smile made his eyes crinkle. She loved that.

Just as he was leaning forward to, she hoped, kiss her, the bell rang. Fuck. She'd forgotten where they were. She hadn't even had a chance to eat her lunch. It would definitely be movie time this afternoon.

Lucky didn't seem perturbed by the interruption. Instead, he leaned forward and pressed his lips to her forehead. "See you tonight, darlin'."

Then he was gone. Not five minutes later, Mrs. Wallace escorted her students, including the son of the man whom she was going on a date with that evening, back into her classroom.

As the movie started and she sat down in her desk chair, a scary thought entered her mind: what the hell was she going to wear?

* * *

BEAR DIDN'T BOTHER to knock. He just strolled through the front door like he owned the place. He was grinning like a lunatic. "Babysitter Extraordinaire is here."

"Don't you mean Asshole Extraordinaire?" Lucky asked just as Scotty came scampering down the hall.

"Uncle Bear!!"

Scotty took a flying leap into the air, but Lucky didn't worry. Bear caught him with ease. They'd done this move since Scotty had learned to run. It didn't seem to matter to either of them that he was no longer five years old.

Bear brought Scotty up to his chest, so they were face-level. Scotty's feet dangled loosely a good two feet off the ground. "What's up, Scot-Man?"

"Daddy has a date tonight, but he won't tell me who with or let me come along!"

They both turned accusing eyes on Lucky in unison. Any other situation, and he'd probably have found the choreographed move hilarious.

"Well, that's just not right, Daddy!" Bear declared. He jiggled Scotty to get his attention back on him. "How about you and I have our own date, yeah? We can do anything you want to do. Sky's the limit!"

"Really?" Scotty's eyes got comically wide. "Can we go to the clubhouse?"

Sky's the limit, and Scotty wanted to go to the clubhouse? Lucky should have known. He needed to send Bulldog and Steel a message that Bear would be bringing Scotty over, which meant anything explicit going on in the open needed to be taken behind closed doors and anyone who wanted to drink excessively needed to take it home or head to *Demon's*.

Lucky subtly nodded where only Bear could see his approval. As Bear told Scotty they'd need to go out to dinner first and then they could head to the clubhouse, Lucky quickly sent a message to Steel. Taking Scotty out for dinner would give them time to clear out the clubhouse of anything Scotty shouldn't see or be around.

It was already six-forty. Lucky needed to get going in order to pick Harper up on time.

Bear leaned over to put Scotty's feet back on the floor. The kid held on around his neck though, trapping him until he placed a nose-kiss on Bear. Lucky knew that adoring smile on Bear's face was identical to Lucky's whenever Scotty nose-kissed him. Scotty had a way of making the manliest of men feel like their hearts had grown three sizes.

Lucky grabbed his son up from behind. Lifting him off the ground, Lucky placed a bunch of kisses on his cheek. "Be good?" he said in Scotty's ear. "You listen to Uncle Bear and Uncle Steel."

Scotty nodded like a bobblehead. "I will, Daddy! I promise!"

Lucky placed one more kiss on his son's cheek before he put him down. He grabbed his cut from the hanger by the door.

Bear clasped him on the shoulder. "Good luck, man."

But Lucky didn't need luck. This felt right, like heading towards Harper was heading towards his future.

* * *

HARPER WAS PACING her living room. She had finally decided on jeans, knee-high boots with a small heel, and a black blouse with small red dots. It was loose on her and would flap in the wind as they rode his motorcycle. She also put her hair in a tight braid. She hoped Lucky had a helmet for her, because she wasn't getting on the bike until she had one.

It occurred to her around six-thirty that Lucky hadn't asked for her address. He'd simply stated he'd be here to pick her up. How did he know where she lived? Was he just now realizing he didn't know and would be a no-show? That would be just her luck, to be stood up by a guy because neither of them had exchanged numbers or addresses.

But damn, his confidence in her classroom earlier, the assertion that she would go out with him, was hot as hell. She got goosebumps just thinking about it.

As much as she was excited for this date, as long as the man gleaned her address from the cosmos, she was also concerned about it. The man was fourteen years older than her. That clearly wasn't a problem for him, since he'd been the one to ask her out. Right?

What if this date was supposed to be a hit and run type of date, as her brother called it? Ask her out, take her to dinner, fuck her, and then never see her again? That would be awkward when they ran into each other at the school. At least, it would be for her. Maybe he was used to sleeping with women and never calling them again?

He'd hinted that he'd wanted to ask her out sooner. She didn't know why he believed she was married. She didn't wear a ring. If he hadn't thought she was married, would he have tried to seduce her sooner?

Mind, there hadn't exactly been much seducing on his part. The man had opened his mouth and she'd fallen under his spell.

She heard the roar of his motorcycle, so attuned to it from his drop-offs and pick-ups at the school. Was she really about to ride on the back of it? Her parents would murder them both if they found out.

Donor-cycles was what her mother, a retired nurse, called them. Murder-cycles was what her father the cop called them.

Harper had never been on a motorcycle before. But she was dying to. Especially if she got to wrap her arms around the super sexy single dad who was pulling into a parking spot next to her car. He was sitting on it while walking it backwards with the ease of a professional.

Though he wore his helmet with the visor, there was no mistaking him or that bright red bike. She knew from Scotty that he'd chosen the color of his dad's bike. He was very proud of that fact, like he'd helped design it. The club vest he was wearing also caught her eye. She knew they were called 'cuts' from watching *Sons of Anarchy*, but planned to mess with him some. He couldn't hold all the cards here.

He got off the bike and removed his helmet. Setting it on the seat, he turned–and scowled when he saw she was already outside her apartment and walking towards him. He put his fists on his hips, looking very much like he was about to scold her.

Damn, she'd never had Daddy-kink fantasies before, but was starting to see the appeal in them. That scowl was sexy.

She smiled, ignoring his scowl, as she approached. "Hi."

"What are you doing?"

Playing innocent, she said, "Going on a date with you, hopefully."

His nostrils flared. Oh boy, her panties just got damp. "You wait for me inside your apartment to come get you. You don't walk out here on your own. Do you understand me?"

Now it was her turn to scowl. "I'm not a child. Don't treat me like one. I have a dad and don't need you to be another one."

His eyes darkened as they narrowed. "It has nothing to do with your age or mine. It has to do with safety and respect. I will always come and get you. I will always escort you to your door and make sure you lock it behind yourself. If we are in a cage, I will always open the door for you and expect you to wait for me to come around to get you before exiting. When we are walking down the street, I will always be on the outside of the sidewalk. And if my fantasies finally come true and we do end up falling asleep in the same bed, I will always be on the side of the bed closest to the door."

Holy fuck. Harper was pretty sure her ovaries just burst from the amount of testosterone coming at her.

"Um, okay."

"Good, glad we understand each other." In a quick, single

motion, he looped his arm around her waist and drew her to his front. A second later, his lips landed on hers in a hard kiss.

Harper gasped in surprise, unknowingly opening up for him. He twirled his tongue inside her mouth and against hers. He kissed her with a ferocity and a passion she'd only read about in romance novels. Like he'd die if he ever stopped.

Though startled by the initiation of the kiss, Harper gave as good as she got. She liked kissing, and she liked sex. She was not ashamed of her needs as a woman. The fact that no man had ever given her what she craved had been more bad choice and luck on her part. Some of them, she knew better going in.

But Lucky? This man was going to make her orgasm just from a kiss. He hadn't even touched her girly parts yet and she was already squeezing her thighs together, seeking release. There was a good chance that it was because it had been a while since she'd had sex, but she thought it was more likely due to the man. His confidence, his demeanor, and his alpha personality were intoxicating.

Harper wanted to cling to him and never let go.

Unfortunately, though, they had to break apart eventually. Both were breathing heavily, in dire need of oxygen.

Lucky leaned his forehead on hers. "Well damn," he gasped out between breaths. "I wasn't expecting that."

"Good or bad?"

"Good." His lips touched her forehead. Damn, she could get addicted to the man's forehead kisses as quickly as his real ones. "Very good."

Harper realized her hands were fisted into his cut. She quickly released them. "Oh, sorry."

He chuckled. "Darlin', never apologize for holding onto me."

"But I crinkled your biker vest-thing."

He pulled away from her, his eyes narrowed for a moment. "Now I know you're messing with me. Scotty was very clear he instructed you in the ways of us bikers."

Harper cursed. "Damn it. I had a really good one about calling your Harley a Moped."

Lucky flinched. "Please don't. She deserves better than that."

"She?"

"Of course. Certainly not into straddling a *him* and letting *him* purr between my legs."

Harper let out an unladylike snort. "While I am now not so sure about straddling *her* myself, I do have some questions before we go."

"If one of those questions is 'can I kiss you again?', I will inform you now, I consent to any and all kisses, no matter the time, place, or audience."

Harper rolled her eyes. "I'm not surprised in the least by that answer."

Lucky stepped back from her. He picked up his helmet so he could lean back in the bike seat. He placed the helmet on his lap— was he trying to hide his arousal or just hold the helmet? She wasn't sure. She'd certainly felt his arousal when they'd been pressed up against each other like they were trying to conform into one being. "What are your questions?"

"Well, first is more of a statement for you. I'm sure you've been wondering how old I am. The age difference between us is a bit obvious."

"Don't care."

Her spine snapped straight. "What?"

"Darlin', I don't care if you're fifteen, twenty, or twenty-five years younger than me. Actually, I misspoke on that one. If you were twenty-five years younger than me then you'd be underage, and I would care about that. All I meant is that I don't care what your age is in regard to our age difference. You are the sexiest woman I've ever met. You're strong, you're smart, you're funny, and all I want is to get to know you better. Do I want to know your age? Absolutely, but only because I want to know everything about you. Not to defend liking you or to calculate our age difference."

Damn. There went her heart again. She was going to need to keep an AED machine around if he kept making her heart flutter like that.

"It doesn't bother you?"

"Does it bother you?" he asked back.

She shook her head. "Not to sound repetitive, but you're the sexiest man I've ever met. I have some concerns about your motorcycle club. I know a lot from Scotty, but some things he's said are hard to believe. Not that I think he's lying. More of, I'd like an adult's clarification."

He nodded easily. "I'll tell you anything you want to know." He stood up off of his bike. "But maybe at the restaurant? I don't like you being out here in the open like this."

Harper agreed, but held up one finger to make him pause. "Just one quick question before I get on the bike with you. Do you have a helmet for me?"

He grinned. "Darlin', you are never getting on my sled without one."

She grinned back. "Good."

CHAPTER 5

They drove about forty-five minutes out of town to a steakhouse. It claimed to be all organic and Amish-grown. Harper was intrigued. While she was also very hungry, she wished the ride had been longer. It had been pure heaven to sit on the bike with her thighs spread around Lucky's backside and squeezing tight to him. The second seat on his bike had its own backrest and armrests, but Harper had ignored them. She'd pressed herself as close to him as she could get–just because she could.

He'd also ridden most of the way with his left hand resting on her thigh.

She hoped he took the scenic route back.

As soon as they walked in, the hostess greeted them. She gave Lucky a quick kiss on the cheek and walked them directly to a table marked 'reserved'. Harper's hackles rose at the intimate contact. Had Lucky brought her to a restaurant where he'd slept with most of the serving staff? She noticed how busy the parking lot was, as well as the number of patrons still waiting to be seated. Why had Lucky been given priority?

Why had he allowed another woman to kiss his cheek while he was holding her hand?

They followed the hostess and her swaying hips to a table towards the back. It was more secluded than the others. Lucky pulled out Harper's seat for her. She noted that he'd taken the seat that placed his back to the wall. Scotty had told her he was a veteran. Was that a military thing?

As soon as they were seated, Lucky indicated to their hostess. "Harper, this is Sally Fields. No, she is not related to the actress. Her mama was just a fan. Her family owns this place and runs an equestrian business down the road. Scotty takes horseback riding lessons from her during the summer." Well, that seemed…less intimate than she'd assumed. "Sally, this is my date, Harper Hannigan. You'll be seeing her around a lot."

That statement took Harper a moment to process. This was their first date. They'd had one kiss—mind, a very hot and intense kiss—but still only one kiss. And he was proclaiming she'd be around a lot? Did he say that because she'd just moved to the area? Did he mean around a lot *with him?*

"It's great to meet you, Harper." Sally held out her hand and Harper shook it. "Lucky here is one of our best customers. Have you met his son, Scotty, yet? He's a hoot and a half. We all love him around here."

Harper's eyes narrowed. Her woman defenses were rising again. Had Sally said that to wonder how serious they were and if Lucky had introduced her to his son yet? Was she trying to get a feel for the stability of their relationship and perhaps drive a wedge between them by pointing out that *she* had met Scotty, many times, already?

"Actually, I have met Scotty. Sissy too. I adore them both."

The older woman's eye twitched. It was slight, but Harper saw it. "Oh, well, good. Yes, I suppose you and Sissy would be friends, being the same age and all."

"Sally," Lucky cleared his throat. "Can we get a Coke and whatever Harper wants?"

"Coke is fine," Harper said.

As soon as Sally walked away, Lucky took her hand on the tabletop. "Sorry about that. I don't know what got into her. She's never been like that before."

"She's never been like that before because I'm guessing I'm the first woman she's seen you here with romantically."

Lucky gave a slow nod of his head. "You have a point. Actually, this is the first time I've been out to dinner without Scotty or Sissy in a very long time."

Did that mean he didn't date often? How could that be?

"Twenty-six."

"What?" Lucky's eyes went to hers.

"I'm twenty-six. Figured now that we're at the restaurant we should probably pick up where we left off in my parking lot."

He inclined his head. "Very well. I'm sure Scotty's already told you my age, birthday, and social security number. If my identity is stolen, I know who to turn to."

Harper grinned widely. "Actually, he could only remember the first five numbers in your social, but I'll get the remaining four eventually." She loved how his eyes crinkled when he smiled. "He did tell me your fortieth birthday is coming up in a few weeks."

"Did he tell you about my surprise party?"

She laughed. "Yes. You better act surprised, mister. That boy's so excited for you."

"I always do," he said with affection. "I've been getting a surprise party every year since he was four or five years old. His sister Sissy threw one for me when she finally saved up to buy me a cake all on her own. Since then, Scotty's taken over planning my surprise parties."

Harper felt her heartstrings tug at the obvious love this father had for his son. It took a truly good human being to love so unconditionally.

Harper turned Lucky's hand over in hers. "You truly don't mind our age difference?"

He shook his head. "I don't date often. As you can imagine, 'single father' is not conducive to an active dating life. I work and I spend time with my kids. I have no complaints," he added quickly. "But it has recently been pointed out to me that I never make a decision for myself. All my choices revolve around my kids and keeping them safe and healthy. When I saw you..." His dark eyes bore into hers. "Harper, I've never been so turned on in my life. I wanted you, even while you were scolding me for having Scotty on the back of my sled. You weren't intimidated by me and your only thoughts were for Scotty. I about kissed you right then and there."

Harper crinkled her face in chagrin. "I thought you were so pissed at me."

"I was pissed at myself, not you."

"I don't understand."

"You looked at me and saw my cut. I wanted you to look at me and see *me*."

Harper looked at his shoulders. He'd taken his cut off and stored it in one of his motorcycle saddlebags before they'd entered the restaurant. "I didn't want to be attracted to someone who breaks the law. I still don't. It's one of my biggest concerns about being here right now."

"Because your father is a cop?"

She sat back in surprise. "How did you know that?"

"Because I'm not a criminal, Harper, and neither is my club. We're all former military and we work hard to stay on the right side of the law, as well as work with the law on occasion. Our SOA's brother is the deputy sheriff, Carlos Santiago. When Longhill had his stroke, we were told of the interim sheriff taking his place."

Harper wasn't sure what question to ask first. "You're an

honest motorcycle club?" she asked skeptically. "Isn't that an oxymoron?"

"We're a bunch of vets who are brash, ride motorcycles, and love a good party, but we're not criminals."

It was like a weight had been lifted off of her shoulders. "Oh, thank God!" She lowered her head in relief.

"You thought I was a criminal and yet you came out with me tonight?" She couldn't tell from his tone if he was shocked or appalled.

"I did," she admitted sheepishly. "Honestly, I don't know why. I planned to get answers from you before we left but I got swept away by that kiss. Your very presence seems to turn my brain to mush." Harper let out a self-deprecating laugh. "It would just be my luck that I'd fall for a criminal when my dad's the new sheriff."

Lucky was quiet for a long time. "Does your dad have a thing against bikers or just lawbreakers in general?"

Finding the question odd, she still answered. "Lawbreakers, as far as I know. Why?"

"Not to mix business with pleasure, but my president's been trying to get a meeting with him, but he keeps getting blown off. We were starting to wonder if perhaps the new sheriff has the wrong interpretation of us."

Harper shook her head. "I'm sorry, I don't know. We don't discuss police business. He keeps his job close to the vest–always has. Says he didn't want that dirtiness in his house."

Lucky nodded once. "We'll keep trying." He squeezed her hand. "Tell me more about you."

Harper was about to answer when their server approached with their drinks and a breadbasket. The woman looked completely flustered. The bags under her eyes indicated how tired she was too. "I am so sorry. We are short-staffed tonight and I'm covering two sections."

Lucky waved her off. "It's okay, Piper. We're in no rush. Take care of the others first if needed."

Piper's shoulders seemed to sag in relief. "Thanks, Lucky. Oh no! I am so sorry, I forgot the menus." She looked like she was getting ready to cry.

"Hey, none of that now." He looked at Harper. "Any food allergies?" She shook her head. "Trust me to order for us?" While normally that would bother her, she was curious. He didn't seem to be ordering to take control of her but to give the waitress a break. Also, she was interested to see what he would order for her. If he dared to order her just a salad with dressing on the side or no dressing at all, she was walking out of here after stealing his steak. Because of course the man would order a steak for himself.

Harper indicated for him to proceed.

He winked at her and then turned back to Piper. "Two ribeyes cooked medium, two baked potatoes with the works, a side of broccoli, and a side of coleslaw."

Piper jotted it down on her notepad. "I'll grab you some more bread too when I get a chance and an extra set of drinks. Thanks, again, Lucky. You're the best."

"Don't mention it, sugar."

The flustered waitress hurried away. Lucky grabbed a straw and handed it to her. Then he pushed the breadbasket closer to her. "Did I pass your test?"

She feigned innocence. "I don't know what you mean."

He snorted. "You only allowed me to order for you because you were curious. So, I ask again, did I pass your test?"

She picked up a roll and started buttering it. "Two tests, actually."

"Really, teach? Tell me more."

She had the sudden image of him dressed as a naughty schoolboy. Wow, that was nearly as hot as her fantasy of him disciplining her.

"And where did your mind just go?"

Harper shook her mind clear of any naughty thoughts. Or maybe just buried them. She ignored his second question and answered his first. "You didn't order me a salad but a steak. Well done. I'm not a rabbit and don't eat like one. I'm aware I have a belly pooch. It's not something that will ever go away. Believe me, I've tried. I've accepted its presence in my life. As well as the fact that my thighs will always have a jiggle to them when I walk. It's my body and I claim it. However, this body requires sustenance." She took a bite on the roll. "I like food. I probably like food too much, especially carbs. I am not one of those girls that can eat a lettuce leaf and call it a meal. By ordering me the steak, you showed that you don't mind letting your date eat."

"First of all"–had his eyes gotten darker?–"there is absolutely nothing wrong with your body. Anyone who tells you otherwise can go fuck themselves. You are beautiful and you are all woman. Personally, I love to feel flesh, not bone, when I'm making love to a woman. Second, if you had ordered yourself just a salad or a side salad, I probably would have still ordered you a steak and threaten to withhold future kisses if you refused to eat it."

Harper loved that this alpha male had just said 'future kisses' with a straight face.

"What's the second test I passed?"

Harper indicated to the breadbasket. "You didn't withhold the bread or make a comment when I reached for a roll about if I really need to eat it." She finished off the rest of the roll and answered with her mouth full, "To which I would always say yes."

Lucky looked torn between being amused by her antics and disgusted by her words. "What utter morons have you been dating who judge you for your body and what food you do or do not eat? Hell, I'd give you that entire breadbasket if you wanted all of them."

She warmed at that sentiment. Still, she pushed the breadbasket towards him and encouraged him to eat. She did take a second roll, though.

"I'll admit my dating history and choices have been poor. At first, I dated guys whom I knew would annoy my father. Call it my single act of teenage rebellion."

"Shit, if that was all you did, your parents got off easy."

She laughed. "They don't think so, but yes. When I was in college, I tried to date guys who seemed more mature and put together. I had this image in my head that I would meet the love of my life on my first day as a freshman, we would date all through college, then get married and have two kids."

"Ah, the white picket fence fantasy. Classic. How'd that work out for you?"

"Well, since there's no white picket fence outside my apartment, I'd say poorly. The guys were all…wrong. Like they cared about the wrong things. One even told me I was wasting my life trying to teach retards the alphabet."

Lucky paused mid-chew. "The fuck?"

She nodded, ashamed she'd ever went on that date. "Yeah. I punched him in the middle of the restaurant. It was hilarious when the police showed up and it was my dad's old partner and my godfather who'd come to take the complaint."

That seemed to cheer Lucky up. "Good for you."

"Wish I'd had time to kick him in the nuts too, but I hadn't had time before management had intervened."

"Give me his name and I'll get you that opportunity."

She smiled. "Thanks, but he's not worth the jail time. Anyway, after college, my parents started setting me up with kids of their friends. None of them were worth the praise their parents or mine gave them. One of them told me I could be hot if I lost weight. Another told me he'd expect me to quit my job when we got married because I'd be too pregnant all the time to work. Another told me that he hoped I was okay with open marriages. And the last one I went on asked when my baby was due and if that was the reason my parents were trying to marry me off so quickly."

"What. The. Fuck."

Harper tried to shrug it off, but each poor experience had just lessened her faith that she'd find a great guy to settle down with. She wanted to *settle down* with a man, not settle for a man. "So, I stopped looking. I figured if I concentrated on my job and less on dating, maybe I'd be less disappointed."

"Is that why you moved here?"

Harper shook her head. "No. My parents announced their move, then my brother and his family said they were moving too. They'd all had enough of the city. I didn't want to be left behind, so I came too."

"Do you like Mount Grove?"

She shrugged. "Honestly, I haven't seen enough of it to say whether I like it or not."

"Well, I can definitely change that for you. We will take my sled out and give you a tour."

"Really?" She smiled. "I'd love that."

"Name the time and place, darlin'. We'll ride all day if that's what you want."

"What about Scotty?"

"Do you mean what about him while we're taking our tour around town or what about him when it comes to you and me?"

After some consideration, Harper said, "Both."

"Well, let's tackle the second first. Personally, I'd like to keep you to myself a little longer. I know it's inevitable that he'll find out, but I'd like to hold off on that for a bit. Not just because of how involved he'll want to be but because of how attached he gets. He'll have wedding bells playing in his head every time he sees you and I don't want to put that sort of pressure on you."

Wait, he wanted to keep their relationship a secret from Scotty because he didn't want *her* to feel pressured? In a way, that was pretty sweet. Surprising, but sweet. It also made it sound like Lucky felt like she was going to be around for a long time.

Her voice was a bit dry as she said, "I can agree to that."

"Good. As for when we take our ride through town, I can get one of my brothers to watch him or our next door neighbor. If it's a weekend, Sissy would be home and should be able to watch him too."

"When you say brothers, do you mean your club brothers?"

Lucky nodded. "Yes. They're also who Scotty means when he refers to his uncles."

She felt the lightbulb go off in her head. "Gotcha. Okay, that makes a bit more sense now."

Lucky laughed. "Picturing the Brady Bunch when Scotty was describing the family tree?"

"The Brady Bunch and the Von Trapps," Harper corrected with a half-smile. "So, you're an only child?"

The look Lucky gave her was curious. It was almost like he was studying to see if she was fishing for information. She wasn't sure she liked that look.

"I wasn't planning on bringing this up tonight, but since the subject has been raised…" He let that statement trail off. "What has Scotty told you about his mom?"

Harper shook her head. "Nothing. He only talks about you and Sissy. And his million aunts and uncles."

He rolled his eyes. "He only has thirteen uncles and one aunt who's in the club and one aunt who's married into the club."

"To be honest," Harper was hesitant but continued, "I wanted to ask but I figured it wasn't a first date conversation. I figured you were divorced."

Lucky shook his head. "I've never been married. Here's what you have to understand, *legally* Scotty and Sissy are my children. I adopted them and raised them. *Biologically*, they are my brother and sister."

Harper's mind went a little fuzzy as she tried to process that.

At first, incest had come to mind with the titles son-brother and daughter-sister. But he'd been very specific when he'd clarified legal and biological.

"How old were they when you adopted them?"

"Sissy was five. She is seven years older than Scotty. I got Scotty when he was four months old."

"And where is their… I mean, *your* mother? Where are your parents?"

"Their biological fathers are unknown. *I* am their father. We all share the same mother. While I know who she is, I don't know where she is or whether she's even still alive."

Suddenly Piper came rushing up to their table with two dinner plates in hand. She placed them down in front of each of them. "Everything look okay?"

The steaks looked and smelled delicious. Lucky looked to her first and then answered, "Looks fantastic, Piper. Thank you."

"Thanks, Lucky. I'll be back to check on you guys, I promise."

"We're fine. Take your time."

As soon as she rushed away, Lucky indicated for Harper to start eating. She cut into her steak, which melted like butter. Her mouth started to water.

"Do the kids know?"

Lucky nodded. "Sissy was old enough to remember our mom. She switches back and forth as to whether she calls me 'Russ' or 'Dad'. I think it depends on whether she's mad at me or wants money from me."

Harper grinned, took a bite of her steak, and groaned. "Oh my God. That is *delicious*."

She looked up to see Lucky had a piece of steak speared on his fork but his fork was frozen halfway to his mouth. He was staring at her with heat in his eyes.

"I promised myself I wouldn't do anything more than kiss you tonight, but, I'm warning you now, if you keep making noises like that, I'm not going to be able to keep that promise, darlin'."

Harper was tempted to groan again. But she decided to give the guy a break. "I'll try to keep the noise level down."

"Appreciated." He popped his steak into his mouth…and groaned.

"Hey," she scolded. "If I have to keep the sex noises down, so do you."

He didn't even look sheepish. "Oops."

Harper rolled her eyes. "I'm not going to ask any more about your mom or what happened. That feels like a more in-depth, private conversation. I'm just going to leave it with I'm so proud of you for taking in your siblings. Not many men in their," she did a quick calculation, "early twenties would."

"They're my family. There was no choice."

Harper loved that. It was a reminder of that unconditional love she saw in his eyes when he spoke about Scotty's quirks.

"Scotty said you served in the military but that was all he said. Will you tell me about that?"

"Marines. My best friend Terrance and I signed up fresh out of high school. If you hear Scotty talk about his Uncle Bear, he's referring to Terrance."

"Like you're Lucky."

"I'm sitting at this table with you, darlin'. Ain't no one luckier."

She felt her cheeks heat. "Don't smooth talk your way out of this. Why do you call him Bear?"

"You'll understand when you meet him."

She pondered that for a moment. "Is he a husky gay guy with lots of body hair?"

Lucky nearly choked on his steak. "No," he coughed. "He's straight. Though recently it's come to my attention that he might be a bit kinkier than I'd thought." She wasn't touching that statement with a ten-foot pole. "Let's just leave it with: you'll understand when you meet him."

She studied Lucky for a moment. "You said to Sally the Slutty Hostess that she'd be seeing me around more. You're hinting now that you want me to meet your best friend. Where are you planning on this going?"

"Darlin', if I haven't made my intentions clear, I wholly apologize." He put down his fork to take her hand. "Harper, I want to date you, go steady, be romantically involved… However, the kids are saying it these days. Calling you my girlfriend sounds a bit juvenile to me but that's the commitment level I'm going for."

"Just me?"

He shook his head, clearly confused. "Just you what?"

"You want to date just me, right?"

"Harper, I'm a single dad with a full-time career who sidelines as the vice president of a motorcycle club and barely sleeps five hours a night. I think I'd need pharmaceutical intervention if I tried to date more than one woman."

Harper couldn't help but laugh at that.

He brought the back of her hand to his lips. "Darlin', you are the first woman in years–actually no, I'm going to correct that. Darlin', you are the only woman in my entire life that I can see a future with. Any others, they don't even compare."

"Aren't bikers notorious for cheating and sleeping around?"

"Does this biker have to explain his schedule and sleep deprivation again?"

Harper shook her head. "I just want to make sure it's just us. I don't want to play games or be a sidepiece."

"Darlin', you couldn't be a sidepiece if you tried."

She leaned over the table to give him a kiss. "Thank you."

He squeezed her hand. "No reason to thank me."

"So, are you going to explain why you're called Lucky if you don't have all these women hanging all over you?"

Lucky snorted. "You're not the first one who's assumed the name has to do with my sexual prowess." She indicated for him to continue. He groaned. "Okay, fine. It started my second tour in Afghanistan. I saw a sniper my CO didn't. When I tackled him, I took a bullet in my left arm. People started to say how lucky I was."

The steak piece she'd just swallowed fell heavily into her stomach. "You were *shot?*"

"If you want to hear about my deployments, you'll never hear about my name. Choose which story you want to hear."

"Your name." Because the other story terrified her.

He pointed at her drink, telling her silently to take some. "Later when I got guardianship of Sissy, Bear called me the luckiest son of a bitch he knew. It had been a fight to get her, and there were days when I feared I'd failed, but I finally got custody of her. One of the two happiest days of my life.

"After I got custody of Scotty, Bear repeated the statement. Wanting to keep it as a reminder of how lucky I was to have my siblings under my care, I took it to heart. Started calling myself Lucky."

"That's so sweet." She took the second happiest day of his life to be the day he'd got guardianship of Scotty.

"It reminds me every day to be grateful for what I have and not spiteful for anything I may have lost along the way."

She squeezed his hand. "That is truly one of the best things I've ever heard. I love that you kept your name to remind yourself of the good in your life."

"What really makes me lucky is that the club let me keep the name when we were choosing our road names. Let me tell you about my brother named Pumpkin."

CHAPTER 6

*H*arper felt like she should have been the one nicknamed Lucky. The man was beyond sweet. In an effort to keep their budding relationship from Scotty, Lucky kept with the previous routine of dropping him off without speaking to her. The difference was, he'd now raise his visor. As soon as Scotty's back was turned, he'd wink at her and then ride away.

By the time she'd get to her classroom, there was a text message of a kissing emoji waiting for her. Sometimes it was accompanied by a text claiming how sexy she looked or how the only good thing about her walking away from him was that he got to stare at her ass.

They didn't see each other outside of the drop-off and pick-up lanes at school during the week, but they talked constantly. Mostly via text, but Lucky always called her as soon as Scotty was asleep for the night. He usually started the call off with a sensuous inquiry about what she was wearing. And while she wished they got to spend more time together, Harper realized she wouldn't trade those phone calls for anything. She got to learn about Lucky as a person, probably in more depth than they would if they were together and getting distracted by kisses and sex.

Friday nights were theirs. As soon as school let out, Harper would rush back to her apartment where she would anxiously await his arrival. Some nights they just took his bike out for a long ride with no destination. Other nights, he took her to a restaurant or a movie. By the time he dropped her off at her apartment, he was hard and she was soaked for him.

But they hadn't gone beyond kissing and heavy petting. It was...*frustrating*, but it was also sweet. Lucky kept repeating that once he got her into his bed, he'd never want her to sleep apart from him. He wanted to make sure she was ready for that. Harper also had the suspicion that he wanted to prove to her that not all bikers were sex-fiends with no control.

Saturdays Lucky kept reserved for time with his family. Sissy was only back for two days each week and he wanted to make sure to spend time with her too. Harper couldn't fault him this, though a part of her wished she could be included in those family days. She knew so much about Scotty, but not much about Sissy. With how close they were in age, she wanted, or hoped, Sissy would be willing to be friends with her. When she was introduced as Lucky's girlfriend, she wanted it to be known that she wasn't trying to be anyone's mother or stepmother.

Sundays were club days. Lucky told her that they did a club run every Sunday around ten in the morning and then came back to the clubhouse around one in the afternoon to eat lunch. The party in the afternoon was strictly club members and family. Later in the evening, the doors would open to allow the hang-arounds in.

That had been an interesting phone call when Lucky had explained the Honeys, patch bunnies, and the hang-arounds. It made her feel better when Lucky had admitted to only having been with the Honeys a few times, when he'd gotten lonely. It had never been romantic. Honestly, that admission had made her feel bad for him. The man had sacrificed so much for his kids.

Lucky always took Scotty home once the doors to the public were opened. He never let Scotty stay to see or hear the depravity going on during those events. Recently, though, he would take Scotty to Mrs. Henderson's across the street from his house and then journey to her apartment to be with her. He didn't stay late, respectful of her work schedule the next morning. Generally, they sat on the couch and watched TV while they ordered takeout for dinner.

It was hard to believe how quickly the weeks had gone by. She hadn't mentioned her current romance with the sexy biker to her family. With how busy her parents had been with the move and her dad starting his new job, they hadn't been as communicative as they normally were. It didn't stop her mother from calling to wake her in the middle of the night to verify she was safe and alive when Harper forgot to send a message that she was home. Or the time her dad had sent a deputy to the school to verify Harper was okay because she'd forgotten to hit the 'send' button on a text telling her parents good morning.

She figured it was best not to involve her parents in her relationship with Lucky until they were ready for that intrusion. Also, Lucky had mentioned that the club's president had been having a difficult time reaching out to her dad since he'd taken office. She didn't want to say anything to her dad for fear he'd ask why she was getting involved in biker affairs, which would lead to him discovering her relationship with Lucky.

She loved her parents, she really did. But sometimes it was hard to remind them she was an adult. She was twenty-six. She was not a child who needed coddling or protecting. They certainly weren't like this to her brother Richard. Probably a difference in the genders or the fact that she wasn't married. Something her mother reminded her of often.

So as much as she loved her parents, it was really disappointing when she had to cancel her Friday night with Lucky to have dinner at her parents' house. Having only arrived a month before, her parents had not yet hosted a family meal.

Harper hoped Richard and Paige would also be there with the boys. It would take the spotlight off of Harper if she wasn't alone with her parents.

Lucky wasn't upset about the cancellation. In fact, he encouraged her to go since she hadn't seen her parents in close to four weeks. That had to be some kind of record since her birth.

So, when she showed up to her parents' that Friday, she felt a sense of doom when not just one cop car was sitting in her driveway but two. "Oh no." Quickly she pulled out her phone to text Lucky.

> Harper: I'm in my parents' driveway. I think they have a blind date waiting for me.

> Lucky: The fuck? Didn't they learn their lesson about setting you up in Detroit with their friends' moronic sons?

> Harper: Apparently not. I don't want to be here.

> Lucky: Go. Darlin', it's fine as long as he keeps his hands to himself. That body is all mine.

She smiled at his possessiveness.

> Harper: I'm going in. If you don't hear from me by nine, call with some emergency to get me out of here.

> Lucky: Your father is a police officer. What emergency is he going to believe that he isn't going to want to get involved in?

Shit. That hadn't occurred to her. She thought fast.

> Harper: Pretend to be a girlfriend who has run out of tampons and needs a box of Midol.

> Lucky: Fine. I suffered through real period emergencies. I suppose I can survive fake ones too.

> Lucky: Though this will be my first period, so please bear with me if I exaggerate the amount of estrogen flowing through my system.

Harper burst out laughing. Of all the things she'd expected Lucky to reply, that had not been one of them. It was hard to imagine him in a store trying to pick out tampons for a teenage Sissy.

Feeling better about her evening, Harper knocked on her parents' door.

* * *

HARPER WAS ready to go home. She hadn't even been in the house for a half an hour and she was ready to go home. Better yet, go to Lucky's.

As she'd suspected, her parents had invited a deputy to have dinner with them. His name was Mark and he had yet to meet her eyes because he was too busy staring at her breasts. Why was that a thing? Why did men stare at women's breasts like they had x-ray vision? Were they just waiting for the bra strap to sponta-neously snap and her boobs to just tumble out while gospel music played in the background?

Pathetic.

She tried to get her dad to talk about his new job, but he kept bringing the subject back to Mark and how brave a cop the man was. Harper had a feeling, if a suspect flashed Mark, he'd be more horny than brave.

The name Carlos was exchanged between the two cops a couple of times. It sounded like her dad didn't like the officer and was looking for a way to terminate him. If she didn't know any better, she'd think her dad was implying he was a dirty cop but had no proof.

Harper's mom kept flitting about the room. She had finger-food appetizers on the living room table and was constantly refilling Harper's and Mark's lemonade glasses. The only good thing about that was Harper had a continued excuse to "use the bathroom".

She assumed they had been waiting on Richard, Paige, and the kids to arrive, but, when she'd asked, her mom had said they'd canceled. One of the boys wasn't feeling well. Harper had the sneaking suspicion they had never been invited. Great. Still didn't explain why they were waiting to eat dinner.

Mark kept scooting closer to her on the couch. Each time he got too close, Harper would get up and either feign having to pee or go to the kitchen to offer her mom help. Her mom kept pushing her back into the living room.

Geez, couldn't either of her parents or even Mark take a hint?

She really wished Lucky could have been there. It was her own damn fault for keeping the relationship a secret. If she'd told her parents that she was seeing someone they wouldn't be trying to set her up with Deputy Mark, but they also would have insisted Lucky be present at dinner.

She was stuck between a rock and a hard place.

If she hadn't accepted her parents' dinner invitation, she could be riding through the mountains on the back of Lucky's bike right now. Damn it.

"...so I've asked Mark to stop by your apartment when he's on patrol to check on you."

Harper's head snapped up. "I'm sorry. What?"

Her father's eyes narrowed slightly, the only hint of his disappointment she hadn't been paying attention to the conversation. "Mark has offered to do regular check-ins with you while he's on shift and I've agreed it's a good idea."

Before she had a chance to reply–what reply, she had no clue–her mother spoke up. "A young lady living alone in a strange new town… You should be grateful to Mark, Harpy."

Ugh. *Harpy*. She hated that nickname. Made her sound like a Greek mythological monster.

"Well, *I* did not agree to it, Dad. I don't want Mark showing up at my apartment to 'check' on me. Neither of you have the right to do so."

Her father's expression darkened. "Harper. You will answer the door when Mark knocks and you will confirm you are alone."

Alone? What the fuck? She was twenty-six years old. If she wanted to not be alone in her own apartment that she paid rent to, she had every right to do so. And Deputy *Mark*? Ew, no. Even if she was interested in him, which she wasn't, she did not want a *stranger* checking in on her. What were her parents thinking?

Heat flamed her cheeks. "No, I won't."

"You chose to live apart from your father and me when we moved here," her mother said. "We know we've been lax with checking in with you since arriving here. We've been so busy with the new house and your father learning the lay of the land. He's been in so many council meetings, *I've* hardly seen him." She smiled proudly at her husband across the living room. "I know you wish to have more freedom. Please indulge us. This is a compromise, so you don't have 'your parents'," she said it in quotes like it was some sort of joke, "checking in on you constantly. Please, Harpy. Do this for me."

Fuck… Harper closed her eyes. She knew her parents were coming from a good place. She knew that, but it didn't help the feeling of suffocation. What was she supposed to tell her mom?

No, I don't want Deputy Mark checking on me at random moments because I'm really hoping my super sexy older biker boyfriend will soon take me to his bed and never let me leave it? Or better yet, I won't be in my apartment because I'll be in his bed at his house.

Damn it. Her parents were involved in her life enough. She did not need them intruding on her sex life too.

She tried a different tactic. "I'm trying to make new friends here. Some of the ladies from work asked me to drinks. I'd like to expand my social circle. I can't guarantee I'll be home when Mark wants to stop by."

There. Let them try to argue with that! What were they going to say? That they didn't want their daughter to have friends?

To Harper's horror, her mother looked thrilled by this announcement. "Oh, that's an easy fix, honey. We already gave Deputy Mark your number so he'll be able to stop by and check on you while you're out with your new friends."

What. The. Fuck. No, no, no! She did not want Deputy Mark to have her number! What the hell?

"Mom, I am not okay with you giving my number out to strangers!"

"Mark isn't a stranger, sweetie. He works with your father."

"But he's a stranger to me!"

"How about this then?" her mom prompted. "How about the two of you take tonight to get to know each other? Your father and I will slip out of the house and go out to eat. The two of you can stay here and–"

"Absolutely not!" Harper stood up. "This is another one of your blind dates, Mom. I am not doing this again. Mark is probably just as humiliated as I am by your matchmaking."

"Actually," a voice spoke up from behind her.

"Shut it!" Harper snapped. She turned back to her mom. "I came here tonight to catch up with my parents. To have a nice meal with my *family*, whom I assumed included my brother, sister-in-law, and nephews. That list did not include, and will never include, yet another stranger you have this sick fascination of setting me up with." She threw her hands up in the air. "I'm going home."

"Sit. Down."

Harper froze at the order coming from her father. He too was standing now. To say he looked pissed would be an understatement.

Harper slowly sat back down on the couch. Thankfully there was a cushion between her and Mark.

Her father moved to stand in front of her. Over her, would be a more accurate description. It was how he spoke with Richard and Harper when they'd misbehaved as children.

"*I* stopped by your apartment numerous times since moving here. I thought perhaps I'd take my daughter to dinner or just check in with my daughter to see how she's acclimating to a new town. Except, not once, have you been home. I don't know where you're going, and I don't know who with. I do know that you haven't told your mother or me about it. You have also been lying in your text messages, claiming to be home when you have not been.

"Now, if you were seeing someone and it was serious to the point where you are not staying alone in your own bed at night, I would think it would also be serious enough where you would bring him to meet us. *Your parents.* Since you did not say you were bringing a date with you tonight, I can only conclude that either you are ashamed of this relationship *or* it's not a relationship at all and it is in fact a repeat of that teenage rebellion bullshit you pulled in high school. We are in a town much smaller than Detroit where tongues talk, Harper. I will not have you known as the town whore when I am just starting my position of sheriff here. If your mother and I like it here, in a year, I will be running for the next term. I will not have my daughter's loose morals mess up my chances of being elected.

"So you will cease whatever foolery you have been participating in since arriving here and you will be at your apartment when Mark knocks. *And,*" he added so harshly that Harper flinched, "you will be *alone*. Do you understand me, young lady?"

Harper didn't even realize she was shaking until she tried to wipe the tears falling from her eyes and felt the tremble against her cheek. She didn't even know what to say. At this point, what was there to say? Her father thought she'd come to this new town and was sleeping around? He'd called her a whore! He'd never called her that before, never even implied it.

Just wanting this conversation to be over, Harper said the only thing she could to end it. "Yes, sir."

"Good. Now let's get to the dinner table before this nice meal your mother prepared for us gets cold."

Harper followed her parents and Mark into the dining room. Still in shock, she figured the dinner couldn't get any worse.

She was wrong.

* * *

LUCKY GLANCED AT HIS PHONE. Again. It was quarter to eleven. He'd sent Harper his fake SOS message just after nine. She hadn't replied. She hadn't called. He'd called twice and immediately got her voicemail. He was starting to get worried.

Scotty was asleep. He rarely woke up in the middle of the night, but Lucky still couldn't leave him. It was far too late to ask Mrs. Henderson to come over and watch him so he could ride over to Harper's apartment. Sissy had decided to stay in her dorm room that night, so she wasn't in the house to watch Scotty either.

Frustrated and worried, he had no choice but to make a different call. He had to make sure she was all right.

* * *

HARPER IGNORED the knock on her door. It was almost midnight. If *Deputy Mark* thought she would open the door for him, he was sorely mistaken. She'd suffered through that endless dinner. She'd bitten her tongue. Worse, she'd turned off her phone. She knew the message that was coming around nine but didn't have the heart or the energy to add that to the shit pile that was her life.

Lucky.

What the hell was she supposed to do? Her father had accused her of being in a relationship that wasn't serious. Was he right? Was that the reason Lucky and she hadn't had sex yet? Harper hoped he was wrong. She wanted the relationship to be serious. Lucky was…amazing. She'd never met a guy like him.

Endless tears rolled down her cheeks. She hadn't been able to make them stop. Her father thought she was a whore? She wasn't sure there was a feeling worse than that.

She thought she was a good daughter. All she wanted was a bit of independence. She'd lived with her parents in Detroit after college. It made sense to save on rent money. Apartments were so expensive, and her teacher's salary was pretty minuscule. Why not save on rent?

When her parents had announced they were moving, Harper knew she was losing her access to a place to live rent-free. But she'd also been excited for the opportunity to live independently of her parents. That was why she'd pushed for her own apartment when she'd agreed to move to Mount Grove with them.

Maybe that was a mistake. Especially if her father believed she was sleeping around. Maybe she should move back in with her parents? It would prove to them that she wasn't sleeping around. Even if she went out for the evening, they'd see she was back and sleeping alone.

Except she didn't want to move back in with her parents.

But was that better than having Deputy Mark–who was still knocking on her fucking door!–spontaneously check in on her?

What would her dad say if she blocked Mark's number? Her phone was still off, so he might be trying to call her now. If she blocked his number, he couldn't call or text her for her whereabouts.

Fuck. Why had she come to Mount Grove? Maybe the solution was to move back to Detroit. She'd had a good job there. Friends.

Except none of those friends had reached out to her in the two months since she'd moved. Maybe they weren't friends. Maybe they were just colleagues. Friendship was a two-way street though. In their defense, she hadn't reached out to any of them either.

Harper didn't even know if she had a job after this school year. She only had a little over two more months of guaranteed employment. Then she might not have a choice about moving back in with her parents.

She needed to think. Which she couldn't do with that constant *banging on her fucking door!*

She got up off her couch and stomped over to the door. She threw it open. "What the fuck do you want, Mark?!"

Except it wasn't Mark at her door. It was a man. A very, very big man with huge muscles. He had thick brownish-red hair that curled around his ears and a full beard that fell past his chin. He wore a tight black t-shirt, dark worn jeans, and black boots. She caught sight of the knife on his belt and swallowed in fear.

Holy shit. Why hadn't she checked who was at the door before she opened it? Goddamn it. She knew better.

"Harper Hannigan?" he inquired.

She moved so the door was between her and the stranger. The very large stranger who resembled a... Her shoulders sagged in relief when she finally understood why Lucky had said she'd understand the nickname when she met him. "I take it you're Bear?"

Amusement flitted across the man's green eyes before it was

replaced with a scowl. For some reason, she didn't find his scowl even remotely sexy. She liked it when Lucky scowled at her, but Bear's scowl actually seemed menacing.

He pointed a finger at her. "Never open your door without knowing who is on the other side of it."

She sighed. "I know. I thought you were someone else."

"Who the fuck are you expecting to be knocking on your door at midnight?"

She gave him a slow once over. "Certainly not you. Why are you here?"

"Because you aren't answering your fucking phone and Lucky is going crazy not being able to reach you. He can't leave Scotty home alone, so he sent me here to check on you."

This time it was *her* turn to scowl. "Why the fuck does everyone feel the need to check on me! I'm a grown-ass woman! I have a job! I pay my own bills! I put my panties on all on my own without requiring assistance! I can even wipe my own ass! Why the fuck do I have all these men in my life wanting to *check on me?*"

She was near hyperventilating by the time she finished with her rant. Then the tears started falling all over again. She rested her head against the door. She was so fucking tired. She just wanted to sleep. Or better yet, wake up and start this day all over again.

She barely felt it when she was lifted off of her feet. Harper heard the click of the door shutting and the turning of the lock. As she was placed on her couch, it occurred to her that, even though he was Lucky's best friend, she had a giant stranger in her apartment.

A blanket was laid over her. Hell, he even fluffed her pillow. That made her cry even harder.

Harper didn't know how long she sobbed for. Every once in a while, a tissue was thrust in front of her face. She'd take it, use it, and then drop it unceremoniously on the floor.

The giant stranger just sat there in her lounge chair like it wasn't past midnight and he wasn't watching a manic lady cry her eyes out without knowing the reason. At one point she glanced at him to see he was texting someone.

"Is Lucky on his way?" Her voice sounded awful.

Rather than answer, Bear got up and went to her kitchen. He got a bottle of water from the fridge. Expecting him to drink it, she was completely taken aback when he returned to the living room and handed it to her instead.

She took it with a shaking hand. "Thanks."

As she sat up and started taking small sips, Bear sat back down in the lounge chair. "No. I told him I'd stopped by, and you were fine. Said you forgot to turn your phone back on from being at your parents' house. You promised to call him in the morning."

Harper's suspicion rose. "Why would you do that?"

"Because his girlfriend is crying her eyes out after spending the night ignoring him. I need to know why and whether whatever it is you did is going to hurt him before I tell him about it."

In a way, Harper could appreciate that. He was trying to protect his best friend. She understood.

What she didn't appreciate was his use of the phrase 'whatever it is you did'. Did he think she'd cheated on Lucky? Just when she thought she'd cried herself out, her body proved her wrong. She picked up a dirty tissue off the floor and quickly wiped her eyes before slumping back on the couch.

"Why is it that men keep accusing me of being a whore today? Is it the way I'm dressed? Some perfume I'm unknowingly wearing? What? Why would you even *think* I would do something to hurt Lucky?"

Bear watched her for a moment. He was a couple of months older than Lucky, but, based on appearance alone, she would have assumed him to be younger by a couple of years. "I'll circle back as to why I made the assumption I did after you explain who called you a whore tonight, because I know I certainly didn't."

She shook her head. She was not getting into this with a stranger. "No one."

"Who's Mark?"

Harper flinched. "How do you know that name?"

"Because you thought I was him when you threw the door open."

Damn it. She had said Mark's name when she'd opened the door. "He's one of my dad's deputies."

"Mark Connelly?" She nodded. Bear snorted. "Pompous douchebag. Longhill never should have hired him but he's the nephew of the former mayor and Longhill was basically told to hire him. Kept him on speed traps most of the time to keep the asshole out of the office all day."

For some reason, Harper felt like laughing at that.

"Still doesn't answer the question why Mark Connelly would be knocking on your door at midnight after you came home from dinner with your parents where you told Lucky you thought they had a blind date waiting for you."

"Mark was the blind date," she said, though she was sure Bear had already drawn that conclusion. "I don't want to talk about it."

"Did he hurt you?"

"What? No. I barely even talked to him." Didn't stop the creep from staring at her boobs all through dinner either. Ugh. She should have showered after coming home, but she hadn't had the energy.

"Something happened at that dinner that made you cry, turn off your phone, and ignore Lucky. Spill."

She narrowed her eyes on him. "We're not friends, Bear. I'm not going to talk to you about my personal shit. I don't know you."

Bear leaned forward, resting his elbows on his knees. "Honey, you are dating my best friend. The only reason we haven't met before is because no one in our club knows how to keep a secret. As soon as they hear Lucky is dating someone, *Scotty* will hear it. I've been helping to pitch in to watch Scotty so Lucky has more time to spend with you. Believe me, after the past seventeen years, hell even before that with all that shit with his mom, he deserves something good and solely his in his life. He thinks that is you."

Harper felt her chin start to tremble again.

"You and I will be friends. Maybe not today, but we'll be friends. Lucky is the closest thing I have to a brother. I think of Sissy and Scotty as my niece and nephew. I am in their lives. And if you join their lives like Lucky wants you to, then you and I are going to get to know each other very well.

"So, let's just skip over the getting to know you phase and you tell me what happened tonight as if we are already lifelong friends."

A tear fell down her right cheek. She didn't have the energy to bend down to grab another tissue. She wiped it away with the palm of her hand. "Is it weird how much sense that made?"

Bear gave her a wide smile. "I'm not just a pretty face."

She snorted. "Not cocky in the slightest, I see."

"See, we're getting to know each other already. Now, tell me what happened tonight and whose ass I need to kick."

"What if it's my father's?"

"Then I hope you have bail money saved up."

Harper found herself smiling at the burly guy. She had a feeling he could be terrifying in a fight, but she also had the urge to hug him like a giant teddy bear.

She wasn't really sure where to start, so she started at the beginning and, before she knew it, was dumping it all on him. How controlling her parents were, how she'd decided to live apart from them when they moved to Mount Grove, how her father had been checking on her and not finding her in her apartment, how he assumed she was sleeping around, how much it hurt when he'd accused her of being a whore, how his lack of faith in her was like a knife to the heart, how he believed she would ruin his chances of being elected as the next official sheriff, how he had assigned Mark to be her watchdog, how he'd given Mark her number without her permission, how her mom had just sat there in complete agreement with her father…

Finally ending with how she wasn't sure she wanted to stay in Mount Grove.

Bear remained silent through it all. A plethora of emotions flitted across his face as she talked, but he never interrupted. He let her get it all out, as if purging the words from her system.

After she finished talking, they were both silent for a long moment. Bear ran a big hand down his face. "Shit."

That pretty much summed it all up.

"Any alcohol in this place?"

"There's some wine in the fridge."

He grunted. "Have to be good enough." Bear stood and went to the kitchen again. As he passed her, he dropped the box of tissues on the couch next to her.

When he came back, he had the bottle but no glasses. Since she lived on a teacher's salary, it wasn't even that good kind of wine with a cork. He unscrewed the top and took a healthy gulp. Then he passed it to her.

She took it. After a moment's hesitation, Harper took her own gulp. She passed the bottle back to him.

Bear accepted the bottle. "Why didn't you call Lucky and tell him about all of this?"

She shrugged. "I needed to process it myself. I need to make my own decision, what's best for me. Plus…" Harper hesitated. "He says he doesn't care about our age difference, but I don't want to make a habit of going to him with my problems. I don't want him to view me as a child."

Bear snorted and drank. "Trust me, that man does not view you as a child. On a more serious note, though, I can also tell you that Lucky would *want* you to go to him with your problems. Some of them he'll take off your hands and handle on his own, because that's just the type of guy he is. Most of them, he'd have you solve together because he'd view it as an excuse to spend extra time with you."

Harper accepted the wine bottle from him. "You really know him."

Bear nodded. "I've known that man since he was six years old. Scrawny little thing. Had no height or muscle to him. This kid was picking on a little girl. Pulling her pigtails or some shit. Lucky walked right up to the kid, who was probably two or three grades ahead of us, and decked him. Right in the face. Knew right then that he was the kind of person I wanted to be friends with."

Harper felt herself smile, picturing Lucky as a kid and championing the victim of a bully.

"Your parents sound like real pieces of work."

"They've always been overprotective. I figured it had to do with my dad being a cop. But I had my freedom in Detroit. I went to college, I went out with friends… They've always been opinionated and some things were certainly annoying, like them setting me up on dates. But I never felt like I was being monitored." She drank some more wine. "This is different. Something is different here."

"You mean more than you living on your own?"

She nodded. "I've been in trouble with my parents before, but not since I was a teenager. Tonight, it was like I was fifteen again and got caught sneaking out."

Bear was silent for a moment. "Why did your parents move here? What prompted the move? From what I understand, they were already in the process of moving here when the council offered your dad the sheriff job."

"That's correct," she verified. "My mom's from this area. Not

Mount Grove, but a few towns over. My dad promised her after he retired from the force, they'd move back. This move's been in the works since he announced his retirement last year."

"So it wasn't spontaneous. Nothing happened to you, or your parents, in Detroit to make you want to leave?"

Harper shook her head. "No." Bear fell silent. She went to pass the wine bottle to him, only to discover it was empty. "Oops."

His lips twitched. "Got another?"

She shook her head. "I don't drink that often."

"I'm sorry for what was said to you tonight. No matter what lifestyle you live, even if you were sleeping with half the town, no one, not even your own father, has the right to call you a whore. I'm sorry."

She felt her lip start to tremble at his kindness. "Thank you. I still can't believe he said that."

"For what it is worth, I do hope you stay in Mount Grove. You make Lucky very happy. I haven't seen him like this in a long time."

Shame washed over him. "There's another reason I didn't call him tonight."

Bear raised a bushy eyebrow. "Yeah?"

"My dad… He mentioned the club." Her voice was soft, hating the admission. "And not in a good way."

"How so?" Bear sat up straighter.

"He and Mark were chatting during dinner like I hadn't just been utterly humiliated in front of my family and a complete stranger. They kept talking about the plans they had for this town, on how to clean it up. My dad said something along the lines of 'starting with those lowlife thugs who keep disturbing the peace cruising through town on their noisy bikes' and followed it up about how the good, hardworking citizens in this town were scared of you."

Bear's face was pinched in confusion. "And he was talking about the *Via Daemonia*? You're sure?"

Harper shook her head. "No, he never said the MC specifically, but what other motorcyclists around here could he be referring to?"

"Our president's been trying to get a meeting with your dad since before he came to town. Even got thrown out of the police station when he stopped by to talk to him. We couldn't figure out what was going on. We had such a good relationship with Longhill."

"I think my dad thinks you guys are criminals."

Bear let out a long breath. "Shit." Then he shrugged, "Well, in the long run, it doesn't really matter. We aren't doing anything illegal and we have nothing to hide. He can't arrest us when we haven't done anything."

Harper shook her head. "It's not that simple. My dad's relentless. Always has been. Once he takes a case, he doesn't drop it until it's solved. If he believes you're the cause of all the crime in this town, even if he can't prove it, he's going to make your lives hell."

"Like he is yours?"

She stiffened. "I can handle Deputy Mark."

"Sounds like you'll be sticking around to handle him."

Harper hadn't realized the implication of what she'd said until he said it back to her. "I need to talk to Lucky before I make any decisions."

He nodded, "And I need to talk to Steel." He stood up and then waggled a big finger at her. "Turn your phone on, little girl."

She glared at him. "That is not going to be my nickname."

He smiled. "Sometimes you don't get to choose your nickname." He opened his arms in offering.

Harper detangled herself from the blanket and stood. She threw her arms around his wide chest, pressing her cheek against his shirt. "Thank you for being my friend."

He squeezed her tight before letting her go. "What are best friend-in-laws for?" He gave her chin a little lift. "Keep your head up. If Mark starts to bother you and you can't get ahold of Lucky, you call me."

"I don't have your number."

"Get it from Lucky when he stops by in the morning."

"How do you know he's going to stop by in the morning?"

"Because, dummy, you're going to ask him to!"

CHAPTER 7

Once again, Harper found herself pacing a hole in her living room carpeting while waiting for Lucky to arrive. Except this time, it wasn't to pick her up for a date. It was so they could discuss what happened at her parents' house, the conversation she'd been privy to at the dinner table, and why she'd ignored his texts and calls once she'd gotten home. She also planned on telling him about Bear being in her apartment and comforting her, because she didn't want him to learn about that later and jump to any wrong conclusions. Open communication was key to a trusting relationship, and that was what she wanted with Lucky.

It was, what she believed, they'd had until she'd turned her phone off on him the night before.

She jumped when there was a knock on her door. Since she hadn't heard the roar of his motorcycle, she feared it was Deputy Mark. This time, she peaked through the peephole prior to opening the door. It was Lucky.

Letting out a sigh of relief, she turned her locks and opened the door for him. He stepped inside, sweeping her up into his arms as he closed the door with his boot. Harper clung to him.

Despite that he wasn't wearing his cut, he still smelled like leather. He was dressed in jeans, boots, and a blue shirt that proclaimed him the proud parent of a child with Down Syndrome.

Her chin rested on his shoulder with her nose turned towards his neck. His face was buried in her loose hair on her shoulder with his nose pressed firmly to her skin.

"I'm sorry," she said. Now that Lucky was here, and she was in his arms, she knew she'd been wrong to keep her distance the night before.

He squeezed her tighter. "I hated not being able to leave to check on you."

She shook her head. "It's my fault. Don't put this on you. If I'd just answered my phone, you wouldn't have been so worried. Even if we could only talk over the phone, at least it would have been better than silence. I'm so sorry."

Not letting go of her, Lucky walked them to her couch. He sat down. With how she was clinging to him, she had no choice but to straddle his thighs. Not that it was much of a sacrifice.

"Bear said you were fine, but I knew that was a lie. Still, he'd laid eyes on you, and I knew you were safe. Why did you turn your phone off? For real, this time."

Harper pressed her lips to his shoulder before sitting up straight. He reluctantly loosened his hold so she could. He kept his hands clasped at the small of her back.

"Dinner last night was awful, in more ways than one. I was upset and I didn't want to burden you with my troubles. I wanted time to think, but that just made me feel worse. I should have called you."

She could see the disappointment in his eyes and had to look away. "Darlin', your troubles aren't a burden. That's what being in a relationship is all about. You should be able to come to me with anything, good or bad, and I should be able to do the same. If one of us feels like a burden to the other, this will never work."

She nodded, still looking down. "I know. I couldn't... My dad said something nasty to me last night and I couldn't wrap my head around it. I wanted to talk to you. The entire dinner, you were the person I wished was there with me–or, better yet, that we weren't there at all and were riding the countryside on your bike with no cares in the world. I knew your text was coming the closer to nine it got, but I couldn't escape. I knew if I saw it, I'd beg for you to come and pick me up. It just... I couldn't deal with my parents finding out about you on top of everything else that happened last night."

She felt one of his hands leave her back. It rested under her chin, gently raising her head until she was looking at him again. He leaned forward and pressed a gentle kiss to her lips.

"Tell me," he prompted.

For the second time, Harper retold what had happened from the time she walked through her parents' door to when she'd walked through her own. Then she explained what had happened after Bear had knocked on her door.

It was probably a good thing she was sitting on his lap because there were a few times when Lucky looked like he was about to storm out of her apartment to go murder someone. Probably her dad. Or Mark. Or both. Not that Harper believed she was strong enough to actually hold him down if he really tried to get up. It was probably just the weight of her pressing down on him that was a reminder that she needed him more here than in a jail cell.

He rubbed his big hands up and down her thighs in comfort. "I'm sorry you went through that, darlin', but I don't understand why you didn't just tell me last night. I've run into Mark a few times around town, and he's got an ego the size of a football field, but he's harmless. Why not call me? I'm grateful Bear stayed to help you and talk to you, but it should have been me."

While she was grateful for Bear too, Harper did agree she should have talked to Lucky instead. "Initially, I didn't have you come and get me because of what my father said. It was like I was in shock, and it wasn't until partway through dinner that I realized I should have walked out the front door instead of following them into the dining room. Just as I was about to leave anyway, I tuned into the conversation between my dad and Deputy Mark. Lucky, they were talking about the club."

As she had done with Bear the night before, she reiterated the exchange she'd heard. While they didn't say the club's name, the implication was there.

"I don't understand why your father would believe we're criminals or that we have anything to do with criminal activity in or around the town. We've been here for five years. Most of us grew up here or around here. We have nothing against Mount Grove and would do nothing to harm it or its people."

Harper didn't have an answer for him. "Bear pointed out that it explains why your president keeps getting the brush off from the sheriff's department since Longhill went on leave."

Lucky nodded. "Unfortunately, it does."

Harper bit her lip before asking. "Are you *sure* there's nothing–"

"No," he said firmly before she could finish asking. "Harper, I was there when we created the bylaws and as VP I would know if there was anything nefarious going on. I swear to you on the lives of my children, there isn't."

She believed him. "Okay. I'm sorry. I had to ask."

He cupped a large hand around her ear. "I understand. I'm not offended."

"Do you–" Her question was cut short by his ringtone.

"AHHHH! There's squirrels in my pants!" His pocket announced. She looked down in question as he pulled the phone out.

"Scotty," he said as if saying his son's name explained the shouting coming from his phone. Which, it actually did.

He put the phone to his ear. "Yeah?" He listened for a moment before sighing. "Yeah, I'm here now." Silence again. Who was he talking to that would know Harper? "Half hour?" He paused. "See you then."

He put the phone back in his front pocket. "Steel's called a meeting. I'm going to need to go soon."

"To deal with the infestation of squirrels in your pants?" She tried to ask with a straight face but failed.

He rolled his eyes. "Scotty likes to change my ringtone. Sometimes I don't even know it's my phone ringing until someone else points it out to me."

She nodded while trying to keep her laughter in. "Sure. Go with that."

Lucky narrowed his eyes on her. "You and I are not done discussing this." He gripped her hips tightly, though not enough to hurt her. Enough to make his point. "We're a team, you and me. Or I want us to be. I slept like crap last night not knowing what was going on with you."

"Me too," she admitted sheepishly. "To be honest, I'm not actually sure I slept."

He rubbed a thumb under her eye, which she was sure was puffy. She hadn't bothered with makeup after her shower this morning. "Sissy has Scotty all day. She's taking him to a college basketball game tonight. I need to get to the clubhouse. How about you go back to bed and get some sleep? I'll stop by afterwards and we'll do whatever you want this afternoon. Just take a ride or stay in and watch a movie. Whatever you want."

Harper leaned forward and curled herself into his chest. "I would love that."

Lucky brought his arms around her and pulled her even closer. Her core pressed to his front, where she could feel his growing erection. She couldn't help but rub herself closer.

His hands immediately went to her hips, stopping her. "None of that or I won't be leaving any time soon and you won't be getting *any* sleep."

She smiled. "Tempting."

"So tempting," he agreed, his voice deepening. "But I can't."

"I know."

They stayed like that in silence for another five minutes. Finally, he moved his hands to her head. He tipped her so he could press a kiss to her forehead, then her nose, each cheek, and finally her lips.

"I need to go." His voice was rough, like a growl.

With a defeated sigh, she scooted off of his lap. She didn't move to sit on the couch though. She knew him well enough by now to know he'd demand she follow him to the door to lock it behind him after he left.

True to form, he stood, took her hand, and walked her to the door. Their parting kiss was longer, full of promise. Harper wanted to have sex with him. Several of their make out sessions had involved heavy petting, but no clothing had been removed yet. While the anticipation was frustrating, she could also appreciate it. She liked that he wanted to wait until they were both sure of each other and their relationship. Especially because it wasn't just the two of them their relationship would affect. Sissy was an adult, but she'd still be a part of it. Scotty, however, was a different story. Their romance would affect him the most, not just because she was his teacher.

And then there were her parents.

"Get some sleep," he said, his lips still brushing sensuously against hers.

She nodded.

"Lock the door behind me."

She nodded again.

"I'll text you when I'm on my way."

She nodded again.

Harper felt his smile against her lips before he pulled away. He opened the door. "I'll see you later."

She locked the door behind him. Her knees felt weak as she leaned against the wood. There was little doubt in her mind that she was falling for Russell McCoy. The way he acted around her, she could only hope that he was falling too. She didn't care what her father said or assumed: they were serious about each other. This was a serious relationship.

She'd been foolish to let her dad get into her head last night.

Harper was partway to her bedroom when there was a knock on her door. She looked over her shoulder, a smile on her lips. A quick glance in the living room showed he hadn't forgotten anything. Her love addled mind hoped he'd returned for another kiss.

She opened the door–and froze.

Deputy Mark stood there, in uniform, with his hand on his gun belt. His eyes traveled slowly down her body, leeringly. "Now, what are you going to do for me to keep me from telling your father a *Via Daemonia* just left your apartment?"

* * *

LUCKY'S MIND was reeling as he headed to the clubhouse. He had yet to meet Sheriff and Mrs. Hannigan. But he'd met and was falling in love with their daughter. He couldn't imagine someone so good and pure coming from parents who sounded like they were controlling, manipulative, and blind to who their daughter was.

He hoped Sissy never spoke about him to her friends as Harper had about her parents to him. He felt like he and Sissy had grown past the father-daughter stage and had entered into an adult friendship. Like the siblings they were, though he still thought of her as his daughter.

No matter what Sissy did in her private life, Lucky would never call her or imply she was a whore. No real father would.

Sissy was an adult. She was twenty-two and in college. She'd had boyfriends. Though it galled him to think about, he knew she was not a virgin. He'd had the safe sex talk with her. He'd taken her to the OB-Gyn to get her a birth control prescription before she left for college. It was her choice whether she took it. Sissy was a beautiful young woman. He could only hope she was safe and knew that she could call him for anything, without judgment.

He would *never* call her a whore, even if she slept with every guy on campus.

A part of him wanted to drive straight to the sheriff's office and punch Harper's father in the nose. He knew he couldn't–but, damn, he wanted to. Deputy Mark was right up there after the sheriff.

He knew of Mark. He'd graduated a few years ahead of Sissy. If Lucky recalled correctly, he'd wanted to prospect for the *Via Daemonia* when they'd first formed but had been denied due to having never served in the military. It had been a quick decline because they'd already had the discussion as to whether they would consider admitting law enforcement. Bulldog's brother Carlos had not served either. Lucky was pretty sure if Carlos had asked to join, they would have made the exception. But he hadn't and they'd decided on only military veterans being allowed to join.

Lucky wondered if Mark was egging on the sheriff against the *Via Daemonia* as some form of payback for the club rejecting him.

He parked next to Bulldog's hog. He had a sick '65 Glide. It had been his grandfather's. Bulldog had restored it himself after returning home. He'd told Lucky once that the work had helped acclimate him back into civilian life.

Though Steel hadn't specified on the phone, based on the sleds parked outside the clubhouse, Lucky knew it was only the officers meeting. While Lucky had been at Harper's apartment, Bear must have met with Steel to fill him in on what she'd over-heard at the dinner table the night before.

Lucky knew Bear. He would not divulge anything else Harper had confided in him outside of what affected the club. Since

Lucky had not claimed Harper as his ol' lady–yet–the remainder of what was said by her parents did not affect the club.

Upon entering the main area, he saw they were missing Jumper and Scar. He immediately went to where Bear was standing by the bar. One of the Honeys, Monica, was handing him a bottle of water. He accepted the water and a kiss from her.

Bulldog sat with another Honey, Gracie, on his lap. She was clothed, but their touches were definitely not platonic. Demo and Cheryl were laughing about something by his office door.

Two other Honeys, Ginger and Lacy, waved and smiled at Lucky but knew better than to approach him. He'd put his foot down with the Honeys years ago, and it was up to them to pass the word along to any new girls. Lucky had also made it very clear that if he heard one cruel word towards or about Scotty that they would be banned for life.

By his count, the only Honey missing was Evette.

Lucky clasped Bear on the shoulder as he came to stand next to him. Bear looked over and smiled when he saw Lucky.

"Talk to your girl?"

Lucky nodded. "I did. I appreciate what you did last night for her."

Bear waved it off. "I'd expect no less from you if I ever find my lady."

That was true. He also knew Bear wasn't looking for a permanent relationship. The man had had his heart shattered and broken in his mid-twenties. He'd stuck to one night stands ever since. The only repeats that Lucky knew of were the Honeys, and that certainly wasn't anything close to a relationship.

Steel walked out of his office, which was two doors down from Demo's. His sharp eyes searched the room. Lucky headed towards him.

Steel did a once over of him too. "She worth it?"

That was his president. He didn't fumble or make small talk. He went straight to the heart of the issue. That was how he'd commanded his squadron and that was how he led the *Via Daemonia*.

"She is," Lucky said without hesitation. "She's going to be my ol' lady, Steel. I don't know what this is with her father or why, but it doesn't affect who she is to me or my feelings for her. She's mine."

Steel nodded once. "About time, brother. Jenna was starting to worry about you."

"She's such a mother hen."

A rare smile appeared on Steel's lips. "That she is. You tell Scotty yet?"

Lucky shook his head. "We're waiting, but I have a feeling it's going to be soon. There's no reason to wait when I know how I feel about her, Steel."

"Whatever is going on at the sheriff's station is going to be tricky enough as it is without you adding fuel to the fire by fucking the sheriff's daughter."

Lucky's back stiffened at the crude words. "I don't care. She's mine," he repeated. "What if it was Jenna? Would you fight for her?"

"I did," Steel said smoothly. "I keep fighting for her and I'll never stop."

"Then you, out of all the clowns here, understand what I feel for Harper and how far I'll go."

Steel nodded. "And you'll have us at your back."

They clasped forearms. At the sound of a door closing, Lucky looked over his shoulder to see the last Honey enter from the kitchen. Evette had a plate of fruit, some cheese cubes, and something with toothpicks sticking out of them. She indicated to Steel, who gave her permission to go up to Church with her tray of goodies.

Both Steel and Lucky waited, silently counting in their heads. Evette emerged again less than a minute later. Any longer and they would have gone investigating as to what took the

Honey so long to exit. Church was sacred. They did not allow others in.

"Where's Jumper?" Lucky inquired after Evette was away. He didn't ask where Scar was. The man hadn't missed a meeting yet, and always seemed to show up just as they were getting ready to start. Lucky wouldn't be surprised if he was already here, hidden in the shadows. Creepy, but that was Scar.

Steel's expression tightened. "He had a bad night last night. According to Bulldog, some teens decided to light some firecrackers off. Jumper was out walking Aerial by the park and..." He shrugged. Unfortunately, Lucky could infer the rest. "A passerby called Bulldog. He was able to get Jumper to follow him home. He and Aerial are still at Bulldog's. Carlos is off today so he agreed to come over and keep him company."

Lucky rubbed the back of his neck. "He's not getting any better. Aerial helps but..."

Steel nodded solemnly. "I know. I have some inquiries in with some non-profits I know about who help vets with severe PTSD."

"I don't want him to be admitted."

"Me either, brother. But at the end of the day, we have to do what's best for Jumper."

"Demo said Jumper forgot to pay his electric bill again. Landlord thankfully called him before he defaulted, but still. If we didn't make the prospects stock his fridge, I'm not even sure he'd remember to go shopping for food."

Before Steel could respond, the echo of speeding tires barreling down the lane became audible. Everyone inside seemed to pause, all looking in unison at the closed front doors. With no roar of pipes accompanying the tires, one could only assume that the vehicles were cages.

And there was definitely more than one.

The squeal of brakes could be heard, followed by multiple car doors being slammed.

BAM! BAM! BAM!

"Mount Grove Police Department! Open up!"

Everyone looked at Steel. The man seemed unfazed. He indicated with his chin towards the door. Bulldog moved Gracie off of his lap and stood.

Before he reached the door, though, it burst open, slamming against the wall behind it and splintering it. The dual door also cracked but didn't swing open. All the Honeys screamed.

"Quiet!" Steel shouted as six men came running into the club-house with their guns drawn.

Lucky's eyes narrowed at the middle-aged man leading the charge. He was the only one he didn't recognize and knew immediately this was Harper's father.

With his gun still out, the interim sheriff stepped forward holding a folded document. "We have a warrant to search these premises!"

Shit. This was no joke. This was a show of force. The sheriff was accompanied by his entire department, except two. Carlos had the day off, Lucky knew from what Steel had just told him, and Bert Anderson was missing. Likely Bert was back at the station, keeping an eye on the rest of the town.

Ronald Hannigan was surrounded by Daniel Weiss, Jeffery Miller, Scott Pan, Carl Kostrab, and–Lucky's jaw ticked–Mark Connelly. All with guns out, though those guns were currently pointed down.

Lucky was suddenly very happy Jumper wasn't present. His brother would definitely not react well to this show of force. Especially so soon after an episode the day before.

He was also exceptionally grateful Scotty was not here and was safe with Sissy. Any other Saturday, and his son might have been here when the cops had come bursting through those doors.

Steel calmly walked forward. Lucky remained where he was, not wanting to draw attention to himself, as did the others. Though he did notice each brother who'd been with a Honey step in front of her. Lucky eyed the three Honeys who were still out in the open. Two were in a corner, which could be either good or bad. Evette was by the kitchen door and the bar. Bear was the closest to her, but not close enough to casually cover her as he was doing with Monica.

"Sheriff Hannigan, I presume?" Steel said like this was a normal introduction.

"Jack Duncan." Hannigan had a sneer in his voice when he said Steel's legal name. It was almost cocky, like he was insulting Steel by using it instead of his road name. Did the sheriff truly think Steel would get so bent out of shape by what name he was called that he would do something stupid? Like punch him?

"I've been trying to introduce myself to you since you arrived in town. We had a good relationship with Sheriff Longhill and I wanted to extend our hand to you as well."

"Are you admitting to bribing an officer of the law, Duncan?"

Steel did not let his annoyance over the purposeful misinterpretation show. But Lucky could see it in the slight stiffness of his shoulders, in the way Steel stood straighter. He matched Lucky in height at six-two. The sheriff was only five-eight or -nine at the tallest. "No, sir. I have never, nor has anyone in my club, bribed an officer of the law. You misunderstand me. My club has often helped the sheriff's office out. We wanted to offer the same assistance to you."

"Funny, I don't see a badge on your hip, Duncan. Why would I ever trust sensitive law enforcement business to a bunch of lowlife thugs?"

"Again, I believe there's been a misunderstanding. I am aware of the stereotype surrounding motorcycle clubs. We are the exception. We do not participate in any illegal activities. All my members are former military, honorably discharged, and served with honor. We do not condone or tolerate illegal activities in our club or this town. If it helps, think of us as a club of veterans who happen to ride motorcycles."

Hannigan thrust his nose up in the air. "I've never heard such utter bullshit in all my life. I could arrest you on solicitation of prostitution right now."

Lucky stiffened, as did the other brothers. Some of the Honeys made noises of protest. A single hand up from Steel silenced them.

"The women here are not prostitutes. They are our house-keeping and cooking staff."

Hannigan snorted. "I don't have time to listen to this nonsense. I have a warrant to search for illegal drugs and substances on these premises. You will stand aside and submit to this search."

"May I read your warrant?" Steel asked, though he knew he had every right to do so as well as have a lawyer present.

What was Hannigan hoping to find? There were no drugs here, or on any club properties. It was common knowledge that the *Via Daemonia* had no tolerance for drugs. They'd even confiscated and made citizen arrests when the public brought the hard stuff to a party they were throwing. After the second time Longhill had come out to arrest any dealers or users the club caught, there'd been no more incidents. All the sheriff had to do was ask around and he'd know that.

Hannigan slapped the warrant down onto Steel's hand quickly, as if he meant for Steel to drop it. Steel's reflexes were as good today as they'd been twenty years ago. He caught the paperwork easily. He pulled a pair of reading glasses out from the inside pocket of his cut. Jenna had been forcing him to wear them, even though Steel detested them. Lucky had a feeling he only pulled them out now to waste Hannigan's time.

He'd laugh if this situation was even remotely funny.

Everyone, cops and bikers, waited impatiently as Steel read over every single word on the legal document. He wasn't a lawyer, but he knew enough to be dangerous. The club had a lawyer, but Susan Black was a business lawyer, not a defense lawyer. So far, the club had never needed a defense lawyer.

Finally, Steel folded the document up again. "You have the right to search the bedrooms, storage rooms, offices, and kitchen. Please be respectful of any personal items you touch or move. You do not have the right to search our bikes or persons."

Steel pocketed the document. He'd likely be on the phone with Susan as soon as the sheriff and his posse left.

"All of you," Hannigan shouted, as if they were hard of hearing, "up against the bar. On your knees, ankles crossed, fingers laced behind your heads."

"That is not necessary, Sheriff, but we will comply." It sounded like Steel was fighting not to roll his eyes.

The five brothers moved the Honeys to the bar first, helping them down to their knees. Then they placed themselves in front of the women. As soon as the men were down with their fingers laced behind their heads, the sheriff gave the order for his men to conduct their search.

Danny, whose mom owned the town's favorite bakery, remained behind with the sheriff as the other four wandered off. He at least had the decency to look uncomfortable about being there. Lucky was not the only one to stiffen when Carl went up the stairs into the unlocked Church. They remained silent though.

Lucky wasn't sure how long they remained on the floor. It was long enough that the Honeys started to complain. All the men had their military training to keep them silent and steady. The Honeys had no training to push through the discomfort. No matter their job title or what Hannigan's personal thoughts were about their position, he should at least have the decency to not treat women so poorly. What if Harper had been here with them? Would he have made his daughter get on the floor too or have given her a break because she was family?

At one point, Mark the bastard came out to whisper something in Hannigan's ear. The sheriff told him to "search again!" and Mark hurried off.

After close to half an hour, Steel asked if the women could sit on the barstools. Hannigan declined the request.

Near an hour, Steel asked if the women could get some water. Hannigan declined that request too.

It was a very good thing Jenna was not there or Steel would not have been so compliant about how the women were being treated. The Honeys might be uncomfortable, but they were not being abused or separated from the men.

Finally, the deputies all came back to the main room with nothing to show for their efforts. Based on some of the noises they'd made, Lucky was sure they'd left some messes in their wake.

While Hannigan looked frustrated, he also didn't look surprised. If he hadn't been expecting to find drugs here, what was all this about?

With all his deputies at his back once more, Hannigan turned to the *Via Daemonia* on the floor. "Which one of you is McCoy?"

Since they all wore their cuts, the man clearly knew who was who. He'd shown that when he'd called Steel by his legal name before Steel had had a chance to introduce himself.

Lucky lifted his right hand in the air but didn't rise. With the attitude the sheriff was showing, he might take that to be an act of aggression or failure to comply. Lucky was not giving this asshole any reason to throw him in a jail cell.

The sheriff turned towards him, hands on his hips. While his gun was now holstered, it was unbuckled. "I'm warning you once, McCoy. Stay away from my daughter." His eyes landed on the women behind the brothers. "You have enough pussy around these parts, you don't need my daughter's. I won't see her turned into one of your club whores who spreads her legs for anyone you tell her to."

Lucky stiffened. He hadn't even realized he was partway to his feet until Steel rested a hand on his shoulder to push him back down. Who the fuck was this guy and why was he so inclined to believe his daughter was a whore? He didn't even know her if he thought that for even a second.

No one called Harper names! No one disrespected her so! Not even her own father.

Hannigan eyed Steel's hand on Lucky's shoulder but didn't comment on it. Instead, he spoke to the group as a whole. "Your days of terrorizing the good people of this town are over. Watch yourself. If you step one toe out of line, I will be there to slap cuffs on you and haul you down to county myself."

The sheriff walked out of the clubhouse with his head held high and his men trailing behind him like a court processional.

As soon as they were outside, Steel stood. "Church! Now!" He turned to the women. "Remain here if you wish but we will not be back for some time. You have my sincerest apologies for this."

Many of the Honeys had tears streaked down their cheeks. As a whole, they decided to stay long enough to give the cops outside time to clear out.

The five men headed upstairs into Church. The room had been tossed. The file cabinets had been forced open and paperwork was everywhere. Hell, the platter of food Evette had brought in only minutes before the raid had been tossed as if someone had smacked it carelessly off the table. Did they really think the club was hiding little baggies of cocaine inside of grapes?

Some of the chairs were knocked over, indicating they'd been searching under them to see if anything was taped to the bottom of the seats.

Bulldog's phone rang, disrupting the silence. He pulled it out and said simply, "It's Scar."

The brother usually texted. For him to call was out of character. His absence during the raid had been noticed, but also grateful. Lucky had no idea how his brother would have reacted to the sheriff's posturing.

Bulldog only put his phone to his ear for a second before pulling it away and hitting speaker. "Listen."

The five men circled around Bulldog's phone. It took a second for Lucky to figure out what they were listening to. Somehow, Scar was eavesdropping on the cops talking outside and had called Bulldog so the officers could listen in too.

"…wasn't expecting to find anything there anyway." That was their new sheriff. "The clubhouse is too public. They wouldn't keep merchandise here."

"Why did we search here then?" Lucky was pretty sure that was Jeffery Miller's voice. He'd graduated high school with Bear and Lucky.

"To shake the tree. See what acorns fall. Connelly tells me the club owns several businesses in town. That's where they'll keep the goldmine. We need to search those as well as their personal residences."

"What are you hoping to find?" That was Danny. He was one of the youngest on the force in his early twenties. "Longhill never suspected the club of doing anything illegal."

"That's because they were paying Longhill to keep quiet." The sheriff said it as if he had indisputable proof of such. Except any proof would have had to have been fabricated because they'd never paid Longhill a dime. If anything, Longhill should have been paying them for all the free assistance they'd given him over the years.

There was some grumbling amongst the deputies at the sheriff's announcement.

"Longhill was a good man. I knew him. He'd never accept a bribe." Lucky didn't recognize that voice but was grateful to the man for sticking up for his former boss.

"You never truly know anyone," Hannigan snapped back. The man certainly had a short temper. "Santiago too."

Bulldog stiffened at the mention of his brother.

"Is that why Carlos isn't here today?"

"One of the reasons." Hannigan again. "His brother is in the club and I couldn't trust he'd keep his mouth shut about the warrant. I suspended him two days ago after finding evidence that he was giving money to the club, likely for narcotics."

Lucky looked up at Bulldog, as did the others. He shook his head, indicating that he hadn't known his brother had been suspended. Based on what Steel had said earlier, it sounded like Carlos had lied to his brother. Was he embarrassed? He shouldn't be. He hadn't done anything wrong. The money he gave to the club was for the charity the club supported in honor of his mother's fight with breast cancer.

They couldn't talk further about it because Hannigan was still speaking.

"I'm holding off on the warrants for their businesses and residences for another week. I want them watched around the clock. See what we shook loose today. Most likely they'll try to switch up their hiding places after today, which means we can catch them in the act rather than having to wait on the warrants."

There was a pause and then Danny spoke up again. "Sir, we don't have that sort of manpower. It was hard enough to get the five of us together to execute this warrant."

"What did you do in the past when you needed extra hands?" Hannigan asked.

Again, there was a pause. For being the youngest, Danny seemed to have some balls. Lucky had to give it to the kid. "Honestly, we used the club. They were always willing to lend us a hand. As Steel said, they're all former military. Longhill felt safe having them at our backs."

There was a snort, which Lucky assumed to be Hannigan. "I'm sure the lazy bastard did."—Lucky did not like Longhill being called lazy or a bastard. The man had worked himself so hard and for so long the only way to get him to stop was for the universe to give him a stroke.—"They helped put other criminals away to clear the way for their illegal activities. Didn't want anyone else on their turf. I've seen it a thousand times. They help Longhill out, using the police department to do their dirty work, and then Longhill will turn a blind eye on their illegal activities."

What struck Lucky as odd was how sure of himself Hannigan was. He'd been in this town a month. How could he be so sure that the *Via Daemonia* were criminals? There had to be something behind the confidence he spoke with. But what?

"Head back to the station," Hannigan ordered. "Regroup. We'll come up with shifts to watch the bikers we suspect the most. Any overtime has already been approved."

Footsteps and voices started to fade. Wherever Scar was, they were moving away from him. There was the echo of car doors slamming over the phone and outside. Then the call was disconnected.

"How the hell did Scar get so close to them?" Demo asked.

Bulldog pocketed his phone. "Hell if I know. Man moves like a ninja."

"Everyone take your seats." Steel moved to take his. "I do not like what I am hearing. Hannigan clearly has a vendetta against us, and we have no idea why."

Just as Lucky was about to take his seat, a noise behind him caused him to turn. Scar was somehow crouched outside the second story window, using a knife to unlock the latch. He then placed the knife between his teeth and raised the glass pane. Though the window seemed too small for a grown man to squeeze through, Scar contorted his body through with ease. Ignoring his audience, he sheathed the knife, closed the window, locked it, and then walked to his seat.

Maybe they should rename him Ninja.

"What the fuck, man?" Bear asked.

Scar neither looked at him nor replied. Typical Scar. Lucky wondered why he'd come through the window though. He wasn't one for showboating. He probably needed to get away from the cops and back into the building without anyone seeing him. The window he'd come through was on the opposite side of the building from where the cop cars would have been parked. Maybe Hannigan had left one of the deputies out there to see who left first.

Steel tapped his knuckles on the table. His gavel was missing, probably on the floor underneath the paperwork strewn about. "You heard them. They're going to be going after our businesses, our homes. We all know there's nothing to find, but I will not see a brother locked up on a technicality." He turned to Demo. "Are all our licenses in order? The bar especially?"

Demo nodded. "All in order. The next to expire isn't until June. Hopefully whatever bullshit this is will be finished by then, but they can't shut us down or fine us on anything for that."

"And the books? I want everything up to date. No receipt or expenditure unaccounted for."

"All done. Most of that is automated anyway."

"Double and triple check it, D. I want no stone unturned. Cross all your T's, dot all your I's."

Demo nodded. "I'll see to it."

"Same with our donations and charities. He's hellbent to shut us down. Calling the Honeys prostitutes was a low blow, but it showed how far he's willing to go to see this vendetta through."

"Same, but I'll go over everything again."

"Pull whomever you need. A Honey, a prospect… Whomever you need to get it done, fast but accurate."

Demo nodded.

"What about the dealership sale?" Lucky asked. "Any way they can stop it or sabotage it?"

Demo shook his head. "I'm no lawyer but I don't see how. Those funds are already in escrow until the closing. They can't claim it's for anything else than what it is because of the contract between us and the dealership." Demo held up a finger as if he was thinking something through and didn't want to be interrupted. "Now they have no reason to search the dealership prior to the sale. I don't see how any judge would morally be okay with signing that warrant. However, the second it's in our name, they might."

"We'll deal with that then," Steel said. "We still have six weeks until the closing. A lot can happen in six weeks."

"What about Carlos?" Bear asked. He looked down the table at Bulldog. "He didn't tell you he got fired?"

"Suspended," Bulldog corrected. "But it sounds like Hannigan is looping him in with us so he might very well be fired. I'll need to talk to him. Without knowing the details, we can't help him."

"Might be best if we don't." The suggestion was quiet from Demo, but they all heard it. Before Bulldog could argue or defend his brother, Demo added, "Look, it's obvious the sheriff has it out for us. If we step up to defend Carlos, it might make it worse for him."

Lucky hated to admit it, but Demo had a point.

"Call Susan," Steel told Bulldog. "Or have Carlos do it so we're not directly involved. Those funds Hannigan was referring to are donations. They can be traced. He can't be fired or suspended for making a donation to a reputable charity. I don't even see how Hannigan got the backing to suspend him in the first place for it."

"Might be why it was only a suspension, not a termination," Lucky said. "They might have been able to clarify it as a 'suspension pending investigation', which would mean it could go on for however long Hannigan's bullshit investigation does."

Bulldog did not look happy to hear that. "I need to check in on Jumper anyway. I'll talk to Carlos, figure out what's going on."

"Pass the word," Steel told them all. "Watch your back, watch your brothers' backs. No speeding, no jaywalking, nothing they can come after us for. This town knows us. *That's* our advantage. Most of us grew up here. Our families are here, our kids. Hannigan is a stranger trying to knock this town down. Go out, show our faces. Do what we do. Be a neighbor, help a friend. Nothing changes. If the townspeople see that their new sheriff has a bug up his ass about us, they won't stand by and do nothing. We've done too much for them to turn their backs on us for an outsider."

"Hear! Hear!" Bear called, slapping his palm on the table.

"Lucky, yours is the only business where we own the building but not the licensing. Make sure your shit is in order. He's got his eyes on you now."

"He knows about Harper and me. I don't know how, but she's not going to be happy when she finds out, especially after last night."

"What happened last night?" Bulldog asked.

"It was the reason I'd called for this emergency meeting in the first place, but it ties into what happened today. Tell them," Steel said to Lucky.

He did. None of the brothers looked happy. Due to the raid, though, they didn't look surprised.

"You're sleeping with his daughter?" Bulldog inquired.

"I'm dating his daughter," Lucky corrected. He was not going to confirm the status of their relationship. They weren't in high school, hinting with baseball analogies as to how far his girl-friend let him go. "We've been dating for five weeks. She arrived in town about a month before her parents did. She works at the high school and is Scotty's new teacher. That's how we met."

"Lucky." He stiffened at the way Steel said his name. When he turned to look at his president, he did not like the sympathy he saw in the man's eyes. "He's going to come after you hard if you continue seeing her."

"Let him," Lucky snapped. "I've done nothing wrong. We are both consenting adults."

"He's going to–"

"I don't give a fuck." Lucky didn't care that he'd just inter-rupted his president. "He does not have the right to tell me to stay away from his daughter. Only she does. Until Harper tells me to leave, I'm not going anywhere."

CHAPTER 8

Just when Harper thought her weekend couldn't get any worse, having heard about the raid on the clubhouse, she got to school Monday morning to hear the terrifying news that Madison Mitchell, the senior student-aide who worked with one of her students, had gone missing. Her parents had called the police Sunday morning to report she was not in her room and, as far as they could tell, had not come home the night before. No one had reported seeing her or her car since she left a friend's house at ten-thirty Saturday night to drive home.

Two deputies, thankfully neither of them Mark Connelly, were at the school to interview her teachers and fellow students. Harper didn't see her father, which was also a relief. She wasn't in the mood to speak to him yet. Her mother had called and texted her over the weekend, and she'd ignored all her messages. She'd also refused to send her standard 'good morning' and 'good night' text messages.

Mark Connelly had been by her apartment twice more since Saturday morning when she'd mistakenly opened her apartment door thinking he was Lucky returning. After his clear threat of extortion, Harper had slammed the door in his face. She'd thrown the deadbolt and put the chain across.

He'd pounded continuously on her door until she heard his walkie squawk. She couldn't hear what was said, but she heard his reply that he was on his way. Based on the timing Lucky had given her of the raid on the clubhouse, she could only assume he'd gone to meet up with his fellow deputies and her father to execute the search warrant.

What a messed-up situation. Lucky swore there weren't drugs or anything illegal in the clubhouse or any of their buildings. Based on what little she knew of his mother, she couldn't see Lucky condoning the sale of drugs either.

But her father was *so sure*. He was a decorated cop. He'd hunted serial killers, murderers, rapists, kidnappers… He was a good cop. What did it mean then when he was so gung-ho against the *Via Daemonia*? Was her father wrong…or was she to believe Lucky?

She'd pondered that all weekend. Lucky had asked her if she wanted him to stay away after telling her about her father's threat. She wondered if that threat was as simply stated as Lucky's version where her father had pointblank told him to stay away from his daughter. Had other words been exchanged? Clearly Mark had told her father about Lucky having been in her apartment. At this point, she didn't have the energy to care if her parents knew she was dating Lucky.

She'd told Lucky no. He'd come over that afternoon and had been present when Mark knocked on her door in the early evening. She'd ignored the knocking and had kept Lucky from answering the door. She was not going to play her father's game. Mark, as a deputy or as a favor to her father, had no right to enter her apartment. If he did, it was trespassing. She knew the law. Hopefully he followed it.

Mark had shown up the following day too when Lucky had been out on the club run with Scotty and Sissy. Again, she hadn't answered. She'd also blocked his number when he'd tried calling her.

She'd really been looking forward to getting out of her apartment and back at school with her students. That feeling of relief she'd felt upon pulling into the school parking lot vanished as soon as she'd heard about Madison. The poor girl. Harper couldn't imagine what happened. She was a good kid. All she talked about was going to college next fall.

Harper tried to keep the news about Madison from her students, not wanting to upset them, but of course they all heard about it during lunch. The other students were not keeping quiet about Madison's disappearance. Rumors flew freely from her being knocked up and having to go into hiding to keep the baby from her parents to alien abduction.

When she heard one of the deputies question a group of students about the last time they'd seen Madison at the VDMC clubhouse, Harper got a sick feeling. She knew from Lucky that they did not allow anyone under the age of twenty-one to their parties. Madison was not only under legal drinking age but still a minor. She would not have been allowed anywhere near the clubhouse or its parties.

But once that spark of an idea had been lit, it exploded through the school like wildfire. By the time the final bell rang, Harper had heard multiple versions of students claiming they'd seen Madison partying hard with the *Via Daemonia*, including the suggestion that her "baby daddy" was one of the brothers.

As soon as she'd exited the school with Scotty, she could feel the accusatory looks being thrown Lucky's way. He sat straddling his hog as he always did, waiting for his son. Normally there were moms openly checking him out or people waving in greeting, despite the cut he wore. She'd heard both students and parents refer to him as a "total DILF". Today, one could have cut the tension with a knife.

Scotty fidgeted uncomfortably. He could hear the rumors just as easily as she could, but he didn't know how to process it.

Normally, Lucky remained on his bike. Today, he got up and walked to meet them halfway.

"What is going on?" He kept his voice low as he took Scotty into his arms. His son clung to him, burrowing his face into his father's wide chest.

"A student is missing," Harper told him, also speaking low. "Some deputies were here earlier. Their line of questioning..." She trailed off, her eyes glancing down at Scotty. "They were implying she was seen at the parties the *Via Daemonia* host."

Lucky stiffened. "A high schooler? No way."

Harper nodded. "I'm sure you can understand why this upset Scotty."

Lucky pulled his son tighter to him. His eyes flitted about, easily clocking the people staring, the pointing, and the glares. "I need to get Scotty out of here."

She nodded her understanding. "I'll, um," she put her hand to her ear indicating a phone, "later."

"Please," Lucky said as he led Scotty to his bike. "Come on, kid. Let's get out of here."

He practically lifted Scotty into his seat. He opened the saddlebag, putting Scotty's helmet on him. Harper noticed that he didn't put Scotty's cut on him, even though she saw a flash of denim in the saddlebag.

Lucky got into his seat, fixing his helmet too. He gave her a chin lift, dropped the visor, and sped out of the parking lot.

* * *

As MUCH AS he didn't like using TV as a distraction, Lucky needed to keep Scotty calm and occupied so he could make some phone calls.

Steel was his first call. He didn't have much, but his president needed to know that there were rumors the *Via Daemonia* had not only allowed a high schooler to party with them but were also somehow connected to her disappearance. Though Harper had been vague around Scotty, her implication that it had been the police's line of questioning that led to these rumors was also telling.

The question was, was Hannigan taking advantage of a terrible situation to blame it on the *Via Daemonia* or did he have something to do with the girl's disappearance to blame it on the *Via Daemonia*? The latter seemed too dark for the good cop Harper claimed her father to be, as well as his record. To think otherwise was horrible.

Neither option changed the fact that a seventeen-year-old girl was missing.

Steel picked up after the first ring. "This have to do with the missing Mitchell girl?"

"Yeah. I just picked up Scotty at school. I don't have much, Harper's supposed to call me later to fill me in on the rest, but basically the cops who were at the school today were asking specific questions that implied the girl parties with the VDMC."

"Fuck."

"Yup, and the rumor mill took it from there. Word spread fast too, and not just among the students. I had adults glaring at me as I sat there waiting for Scotty. Had no clue what was going on until I spoke with Harper."

"Well, it gets worse. Ghost and Ranger had a couple show up at the bar this afternoon demanding to know where their daughter was. Neither knew what they were talking about. Said the dad even took a swing at Ranger."

"Fuck. What the hell?"

"Exactly. Neither Ghost nor Ranger is from here. They don't know who the Mitchells are."

Lucky ran a hand down his face. "What now?"

"Wait for Harper to call. I'm going to reach out to Donna and

Stephen. I know them. Jenna and Donna are in bible study together. I've been to their house. Going to see if I can smooth things out, at least with the parents. If the parents can help us quash these rumors, it shouldn't get too out of hand."

"What about Keys?"

Steel paused. "What about him?"

"Prez, if anyone can find something on that girl, it's Keys. He probably can find out more than the police can, and faster too."

Silence filled the line. "We're under a microscope already. If Keys swears he can do it without anything coming back on him or the club, do it."

"I'll call him now."

"Call me back after you talk to Harper."

"She won't be home for a good hour. I need to spend some time with Scotty too. He's pretty upset."

"Of course. Let me know if you want me or Jenna to stop by to see him."

Lucky appreciated the offer. "Will do."

They hung up. Lucky dialed Keys.

"Madison Mitchell?" Keys asked in lieu of a greeting.

"What do you know?" Lucky asked back.

"Girl was a good student. Only one unexcused absence in the four years she's been at Mount Grove High and that was for her grandmother's funeral. Ridiculous that a family funeral counts as an unexcused absence. She volunteers a lot, including giving up her study hall to be a student aide to one of your girl's students. Anyway, kid's got a bright future ahead of her— or she did. Her phone last pinged at her girlfriend's house at ten-thirty-three on Saturday night. Next tower she hit was towards her own house, but neither her phone nor her iPad connected to the family's Wi-Fi, telling me she never made it that far."

"What's between the girlfriend's house and hers?"

"Not much. Fields, mostly."

Which didn't help narrow anything down. "Does her phone ever place her at the clubhouse?"

"Nah, man. Checked that as soon as I saw what the kids were posting about her missing and the club being involved. She's never been to the clubhouse or *Demon's*. She has been in your studio, though."

"She has? Shit, when?"

"Twice, around last Christmas. Based on credit card records, she bought a miniature swan."

Christmas was four months ago. Hopefully that was not recent enough for the cops–Hannigan specifically–to try to use that against him. He remembered the swan Keys spoke of, but he hadn't been the one to sell it. He doubted he had any direct contact with Madison himself. "Any other connections to the club?"

"Not unless she's using another device to do so."

Lucky pinched the bridge of his nose. "Nothing to indicate where her car or phone currently are?"

"I'm still working on the car. Most cars have a nav-system built in nowadays. It's satellite, which is harder for me to get access to. I'll get it, though."

"Call Steel when you do."

"Will do."

"Anything else you can tell me?"

"Yeah, Hannigan was the one who told her parents they got an anonymous tip that she's been partying with the club on the weekends."

Fuck a duck. "Where does she normally spend her weekends? Any way to give her an alibi elsewhere? Probably easier to prove where she was than where she wasn't, right?"

"Our security cameras prove she wasn't on club property, but they can always claim those were tampered with. Especially if they pull my portfolio. However, I can tell you that on the three Sundays before last, her devices were pinged at her house and in active use. We haven't had any open parties except for after club runs in weeks."

"Are you hinting we aren't partying hard enough?"

"You know, man, for being an MC, we are kind of tame."

Lucky laughed. "For you, perhaps. I could use a little boring in my life, personally."

"How's the Scot-Man?"

"He's my next target. Right now, he's rewatching his favorite episode of *Monk*. I think he's trying to figure out how the MC got framed."

"Damn. Good luck with that."

"Thanks," he said dryly.

"Maybe I'll send him a message over the TV to help cheer him up."

Lucky paused. "You can do that?"

"Dude, your TV is connected to the internet. I can do anything I want to it."

"That's...terrifying."

Keys laughed before hanging up. A moment later, he heard Scotty's laugh echo from the living room.

* * *

THE RUMORS STARTED to die down as the week went on. Mr. and Mrs. Mitchell had openly stated that they did not believe the *Via Daemonia* were involved in their daughter's disappearance. That, combined with the data Keys had anonymously sent to the police with Madison's internet data placing her at her house at the time of the last several open parties, and the police had to soon take a different turn in their investigation. Lucky saw an interview where Hannigan looked like he'd sucked on a lemon as the reporter asked yet again why the MC had been implicated in Madison's disappearance.

While it was good news that the MC had been cleared, there

was still no sign of Madison Mitchell. It had been over forty-eight hours. The statistics were not in her favor.

Harper was heartbroken for the teen. She'd moved out of the big city to get away from crime like this. It hit her hard because Madison wasn't an anonymous student that went to Mount Grove. Harper knew her, had spoken with her several times.

Lucky had asked Gus, the MC's prospect and one of the high school's security guards, to check in on her throughout the day since he couldn't. He'd rather have someone he trusted lay eyes on her to know she was okay rather than a single-word text message of her claiming she was "fine" when he asked how she was doing.

When Lucky had had his talk with Scotty on Monday after he'd gotten off the phone with Keys, he'd asked Scotty what his thoughts were if they invited Ms. Hannigan over to dinner. Scotty had been so excited he'd nearly fallen off the couch. Lucky then texted her his address and asked her to come there instead of her home when she was done at school. They'd kept their touching PG in front of Scotty, but it had been a step in the right direction towards getting Scotty used to Harper being around outside of school. Harper had also told Scotty that he could call her "Harper" at home as long as he remembered to call her "Ms. Hannigan" at school. Scotty swore he'd remember.

Though Harper had said it was silly, Scotty and Lucky followed her home on his sled and escorted her to her apartment. Just like Lucky had promised he would do on their first date. He also made it a lesson to Scotty on how to treat a lady.

Harper joined them for dinner at Lucky's house every night that week. She'd been nervous about coming over on Friday because it would be her first time meeting Sissy in a social setting. However, Sissy had said she'd come Saturday morning instead. Harper wasn't sure if that was because of her or if Sissy really did have other plans. She wasn't exactly in a position to ask for clarification without potentially insulting Sissy. With only a four-year age difference between the two women, Harper figured it was better to keep the peace and aim for a future friendship.

That was how Scotty, Lucky, and Harper ended up on the couch Friday evening watching a rerun of TV's *Monk*. According to Scotty, he was the greatest detective in the whole world. Harper made a mental note to introduce Scotty to BBC's *Sherlock* and see if he still held that opinion after watching Benedict Cumberbatch and Martin Freeman run around London.

Lucky was sitting in the center of the couch. Harper was curled against his right side with her back against him. His arm held her tightly to him, crossing over her front. Her left fingers and his right were laced together on her stomach. Scotty was on Lucky's left. He'd long since lain down with his head on his father's thigh. The light snoring told the adults he was asleep.

Lucky ran his free hand through his son's hair. He was due for a haircut soon.

"Has he been following the rule at school and calling you 'Ms. Hannigan'?" Lucky kept his voice low so not to wake the teen.

Harper smiled indulgently. "He calls it our secret game. He calls me 'Ms. Hannigan' and adds a wink afterwards."

Lucky snorted. "Any backlash from the rumors about the club? Whenever I try to talk to him about it, he says no one's said anything to him."

Harper agreed with that. "I've been keeping a close eye on him. I also told Mrs. Wallace, the lunch aide. She's made sure no one speaks out of turn around him. He seems to have put the whole thing behind him. Told me today that if more people let the small stuff go, they'd be happier."

Lucky was silent for a long moment. Harper glanced over her shoulder at him. He was looking down at his son with nothing short of paternal love in his eyes.

"I wish more people thought as he did. The world would be a much better place."

Harper agreed. "He does have a unique light about him that makes every day a bit brighter."

"I want to officially tell him we're dating. Right now, I think he thinks we're just friends, but I want to make sure he understands you're going to be around for a long time."

She couldn't help but smile at that pronouncement. "Is there a rush to tell him?"

Lucky was silent for a moment. "More of, I don't see a reason to wait–unless you do?" he asked.

She shrugged. "He's had an emotional week. I like being here with you guys, but I don't want to add additional angst if he doesn't approve of me as your girlfriend. Being a friend is far different than a girlfriend with potential maternal intentions."

She felt Lucky's lips twitch on the back of her head. "Maternal intentions?"

"Shush. He might see it that way. Not because it's me, and he knows me, but toward any woman you were dating."

"Darlin', there's been no other women I've dated. We don't know how he'll react or what intentions he's going to foresee, because you're the first girl I've ever introduced him to."

It was Harper's turn to be silent. "So," she hedged, "there's no rush then. Maybe it'd be better to wait a bit?"

"Waiting would mess up my weekend plans."

She raised an eyebrow even though he couldn't see it. "Weekend plans? What would those be?"

"Well, I was hoping you'd join me on Sunday for the club run." His arm squeezed her middle lightly. "I want to ride with you behind me."

Harper paused, and then sat up. She turned to face him, careful not to jostle him so he didn't wake Scotty. "I have some questions."

Though his face was darkened by the closed window shades, it was illuminated by the quiet playing television enough that she could make out his facial expressions. At the moment, he looked amused. She likely looked concerned.

He grabbed her hand, bringing the back up to his lips. "What questions would that be?"

Her eyes narrowed at his playfulness. She did not want to make assumptions and see more into his invitation than there was.

"If I'm riding on the back of your bike, where will Scotty ride?"

"On whoever's *bike*," he added with distaste in his voice at the word, "that he chooses. Scotty doesn't always ride with me. He says I ride like an old granny and sometimes chooses to ride with one of his uncles to 'live more dangerously.'" Harper rolled her eyes at his air quotes. "What other questions do you have?"

She hesitated on her next one. "I don't want to make assumptions. I know what an ol' lady is. I've seen *Sons of Anarchy*. Scotty told me once that you don't let anyone on your *sled*," she added for his benefit, "but him or Sissy. But you've had me on your b–*sled* multiple times. Now you're asking me to join on a club event. I feel like that's significant, but don't understand the significance."

Lucky studied her a moment before answering. "You're right. I don't let anyone but family ride on my hog with me. I knew from the moment I met you that you were special, Harper. Mind, I also thought you were married, so I never envisioned you riding on the back of my hog as you've been." He squeezed her hand. "Having you at my back means something to me. You're not random or a fling. You know this."

She nodded; she did know that. "So, does that make me your ol' lady?"

A smile touched his lips. "No. But," he added quickly, "it doesn't mean that I don't want you to be. In my world, being an ol' lady is similar to being married. Only it's not breakable. I can't claim you as my ol' lady today, break up with you, and claim someone else tomorrow. Once you're claimed, it's only broken by death. And even then, some bikers choose never to take another to honor their only."

In a way, that was sweet. The idea of an unbreakable union was very appealing. Too many marriages end in divorce. In her mind, what was the point of the marriage if those vows were so easily broken?

But to marry Lucky? That seemed like a far-off fantasy. To be Mrs. Harper McCoy. Crap, she liked the way that name sounded. No longer Ms. Hannigan, but Mrs. McCoy.

"Do you want to get married?" In her eagerness to see if her fantasy held merit, her question came out sounding like a proposal. Blushing, she quickly added, "I mean, someday? Not soon. I meant it as a general question."

Rather than smile at her babbling to put her at ease, his expression got even more intense. "I want everything with you." Her breath caught at the seriousness in his eyes. "Harper, in case I haven't made myself clear, I'm in this for the long haul. I want my cut on your back, my ring on your finger, and my baby in your belly."

That last statement broke her from her reverie. "You want more kids?" She wasn't sure why she was surprised by that, but she was.

"You don't?"

"I do," she announced. "I just didn't expect you to. You've already raised two kids, and one of them is always going to be dependent on you."

Lucky leaned forward, careful of Scotty on his lap. "I want as many kids as you're willing to give me, darlin'. If you agreed, I'd keep you pregnant always."

Geez. "Yeah, no. Maybe one or two more, but not a menagerie."

"Whatever you're willing to give me, darlin'," he repeated.

"So, just to clarify, by coming on the club run on Sunday with you, it would not make me your ol' lady. I'd just be your date."

"You're never 'just' anything to me, Harper Hannigan. And, just to clarify," he mimicked, "it does not make you my ol' lady yet. I'll get my cut on you. It won't be this week, but it'll be soon."

She swallowed hard, the name Mrs. Harper McCoy ringing in her ears. "Do I have the right to refuse it?"

His face hardened. "Of course, you do."

Harper nodded, pleased by that. "Good. Not that I want to. It's just with everything going on with my dad–"

"Has no effect on you and me, Harper. Whatever stick is currently lodged up your father's ass has nothing to do with you and me. Only we matter in this equation. If you truly want to reject my cut when I offer it to you, I hope you'll have an honest and reasonable reason that I can fix so you will say yes. Please don't let your parents influence your decision to be with me."

She shook her head. "I won't. I swear. I was thinking of the other way around. I don't want you being with me to affect you because of him. My dad's left us alone this week, but he's also been busy looking for Madison."

"I am not so old fashioned that I require your father's approval to be with you. I wish for your family's blessing, of course, but that's more for you than me. However, you and I are the only ones in this relationship that have any say in what we are or are not to each other."

"What about Scotty?" she asked. "Does he get a say?"

"If he disliked you or you disliked him, this relationship would be doomed regardless. But he loves you, so you don't have to worry about that."

Harper reached to touch Lucky's face–only to notice the time on her watch. "Oh crap. I should be getting home."

Lucky caught her hand. "Stay."

Harper's eyes widened. "Stay as in…"

"Stay as in, sleep in my bed with me tonight. We can just sleep or, if you wish, I can finally make love to you." He kissed her palm. "Whatever you decide."

"What about Scotty? He'll see me here in the morning. He'll be confused."

"Sissy will be here in the morning. If we time it right, you and I can slip out once she arrives and Scotty will never know. However, if he does discover you stayed, then I'll have that talk with him a little earlier in the day than planned." He squeezed her hand affectionately. "I don't plan on you sleeping apart from me once I've gotten you in my bed."

Her heart was racing a million miles per hour. She wanted to stay. She wanted Lucky to make love to her. She'd been fantasizing about them being together so intimately since before he'd asked her out.

"I don't… I mean, I want to, but I don't have a toothbrush or a change of clothes here."

"Harper, darlin', I have a teenager and a college student who still live in this house. I think I can find a spare toothbrush around here. As for clothes," his smile turned wicked, "I'm hoping you won't need any."

She wanted to say yes. She was ready for them to move forward in their relationship. She was pretty sure her hesitation was just about first-time nerves of being with Lucky.

"Okay."

Her voice was so low, he clarified, "Okay?"

She nodded. Then said louder, "Okay. And I'd love it if we made love tonight."

He leaned forward, taking her lips. "I have to get Scotty to bed. Go get yourself ready in my room. I'll be in after I lock up."

Feeling like she'd just won the lottery, Harper hurried off.

* * *

LUCKY LIFTED Scotty up as he stood from the couch. The kid flopped around in his arms like a rag doll. Lucky couldn't help but smile at his son. He brought Scotty up to his room. There was a small fight between Lucky and Scotty's shirt, but Lucky prevailed without resorting to getting scissors. He got Scotty's jeans off easier. Lifting him slightly to the side, he was able to get the sheets and covers over him. Scotty slept through it all. Lucky was glad he'd made Scotty brush his teeth before they sat down to watch television with Harper.

He went back downstairs to lock up and turn off all the lights. On his way past the kitchen window, he spotted the trunk of a Mount Grove police cruiser down the road from his house. He frowned. Lucky would bet all the money he had that Mark Connelly was sitting in that car watching his house.

He didn't like the idea of the police outside of his house. If Harper and Scotty weren't upstairs, he'd walk outside to have a talk with the deputy. However, he wasn't prepared to leave either of them in the house alone to do so.

Therefore, he sent a group text to Steel, Bulldog, and Bear. He knew they'd swing by, make their presence known. Hell, he half-hoped Bulldog would send Scar to scare the shit out of the deputy. It made Lucky smile to imagine Connelly losing control of his bowels when he randomly glanced in his rear-view mirror only to see Scar sitting in the back seat of his cruiser when he hadn't been a moment ago. The man certainly wasn't VDMC material, military experience or no, if he could so easily pseudo-stalk a woman against her wishes. If her father wasn't the sheriff, Lucky would have already gone to the police about his behavior.

Meaning to get his gun out of his safe when he got up to his bedroom, Lucky climbed the stairs. However, that thought left his mind as soon as he saw Harper sitting on his bed.

She was wearing one of his t-shirts and nothing else. Her legs were crossed in front of her, but the apex of her thighs was covered in shadow. He could tell she wasn't wearing a bra, and hoped she wasn't wearing panties. The vision of her in his t-shirt was one to behold. Christ, she was beautiful.

Her raven locks were down around her shoulders. He loved her hair, so soft and thick. He wasn't sure if it was weird that he wanted to brush her hair, and hoped she didn't think oddly of him if he offered to. Despite their age difference, Lucky didn't have a lot of experience with women. Sex, sure, when he got lonely. But dating? Being involved with a woman? Cohabitating with one? Never.

His cock throbbed in his pants, begging to be released.

"You look beautiful."

Harper looked up, and Lucky noticed for the first time that she had her phone resting between her legs. Her expression wasn't sensual as he'd expected. If anything, it was conflicted.

He rushed forward. "What's wrong?"

She shook her head. "Nothing."

He didn't believe her. "Harper, tell me."

She let out a long sigh and held up her phone to a text thread. Clearly the person who'd texted her texted more often than she replied. "It's my mom. She wants to meet me for lunch tomorrow."

"Have you spoken to her since the dinner at your parents' house last week?"

Harper shook her head. "No. I haven't spoken to either of them. Not from lack of trying on their parts though. My dad calls me every day and Mom texts me multiple times throughout. I haven't blocked their numbers, even though I was tempted. They're still my parents after all."

He got it. He didn't like it, but he got it. "We hadn't made any plans for tomorrow. I was hoping we'd spend the day together since Sissy will be here to watch Scotty and then the four of us could have dinner together. But if you want to have lunch with her, darlin', then go for it. I'll head to my shop or the clubhouse and entertain myself until you're done."

She bit her lip, and he reached forward to gently pry her lip out from between her teeth. She gave him an indulging smile. "I feel like I should go. I miss her. Last Friday aside, she and I have always been close. I think that's why I didn't see her siding with my dad and remaining silent about how he spoke to me coming. I think I need to meet with her. Let her say her piece and let me say mine. She obviously knows I'm upset. I want to make sure she knows why."

Lucky nodded. "Where are you meeting?"

"She didn't say." Harper picked up her phone and started texting. "But I'll take my car. I don't want you picking me up or dropping me off."

He frowned. "Why not?"

"Because you don't need to take me everywhere, Lucky. I can drive myself. Plus, it gives me a way out if I need to leave in a hurry."

He didn't like that part. "I want you to still call me if she upsets you or if Connelly shows up, invited or not."

"Promise." She put her phone on the nightstand.

Harper patted the bed next to her, but Lucky shook his head. "I'm between you and the door, remember?"

She rolled her eyes and scooted over to the left side of the bed. He caught sight of a flash of orange on her bottom as she moved. Damn, but that was hot. Had she been wearing an orange bra too? Damnit, he shouldn't have told her to get comfortable. He wanted to undress her bit by bit like a Christmas present.

Next time, he promised himself.

He waited until she looked him in the eyes before reaching behind himself and pulling his shirt over his head. He knew he wasn't as toned as he'd been in his Marine days, but he was proud of his body. The dark chest hair was sprinkled with bits of gray. He hoped she liked what she saw because, if he had his way, his was the last man's body she'd ever see like this.

Slowly, he unbuckled his belt. He left it looped to his jeans as he unbuttoned and unzipped them. Lucky could see the outline of her hardening nipples under his shirt. Fuck, he couldn't wait to get his mouth on those. He'd been dreaming about it since the day they'd met.

His jeans dropped to the floor. He stepped out of them, grateful he'd taken off his socks and shoes earlier. His black boxer briefs were all that covered him now–though his erection caused them to be so tight they left nothing to the imagination.

Lucky pulled the covers down. She lifted her butt off the bed a moment so her side went down too. He crawled into bed. His heart was racing, but not out of nerves. He wanted her, cared for her. He'd never desired any woman as he did her.

He laid down, facing her. She shifted so she mirrored him. He loved seeing her black hair laid out on his pillows. Though she'd said earlier that she wanted to make love with him, Lucky wanted to be absolutely sure this was what she wanted. He was eager to be with her, but he was also just as content to hold her all night.

Perhaps it was his age, or the fact that he hadn't had a woman in his bed overnight in almost seventeen years. Things were different with Harper. She was different. There was no comparison between her and any other woman he'd ever been with. He needed this to mean as much to her as it did to him.

Harper cast her eyes downward, looking almost shy. It was adorable. "You're just staring at me. Don't you want to make love?"

He reached forward to bring her chin back up. "Darlin', there is nothing in this world I want more than to make love to you all night long. But I also want to savor this moment. If I have my way, it's the last time you'll make love to a man for the first time."

He should have anticipated Harper's response wouldn't be romantic or timid. It was pure sass that came from her, and he loved it. "Really? All night?" She let out a low hiss with a slight grimace. "Don't you think that's a bit ambitious for a man of your advanced age?"

"Why you–" Lucky tackled her down to the mattress as Harper let out a laugh at her own joke.

Lucky ran his hands up and down her sides until she cried out, "Uncle! Uncle!"

Letting out a laugh of his own, Lucky ceased tickling her and kissed her instead. In an instant, all levity was shoved aside by lust. Her fingers dug into his sides as she pulled him closer. He settled neatly between her legs. Even through two layers of clothing, he could feel the heat of her core.

Lucky moved his lips from hers, across her chin, and then down her neck. Harper released a feminine moan. Jesus. His cock throbbed at that illicit sound, begging to be released from its confinement.

"I love seeing you in my clothes." He licked her throat. "I'm throwing away all your pajamas and making you wear my shirts to bed from now on."

He felt the shiver that ran through her body. Her nipples were hard peaks against his chest. He ground his erection against her center, imitating entering her.

Harper let out a loud gasp. "Oh God," she groaned.

"But as much as I love you in it, I'm going to love you even more out of it." Lucky reached down, gripping the hem of his shirt around her thighs. He slowly started to raise his hands.

When he got to just below her breasts, Lucky raised himself up to meet her gaze. He hovered there. He could see the plea to continue in her eyes, but he could also see pure lust. He needed to make sure that she was ready for him, not because of lust, but because of desire *for him*.

Realizing he was waiting for permission, she finally nodded.

Lucky lifted the shirt over her head. Her tan skin glistened in the light from the nightstand lamp. Christ, she was beautiful. He ducked his head and nuzzled her soft skin between her breasts. Harper locked her arms around his neck.

Lucky lowered one hand down over her tempting orange-clad ass, giving her a light squeeze, before dragging his hand even lower to the crook of her knee. He latched on, hiking her leg over his hip. At the same time that he ground his hips lower into hers, he took a luscious nipple into his mouth.

Harper gasped, her nails digging into his back. Lucky sucked harder, urging her on. He loved the idea of wearing her marks. Like she was claiming him, owning him. He would be hers as much as she was his.

Lucky's heart was thrumming so hard, it echoed in his ears. *Thump, thump, thump...* He couldn't get enough of her. Wanted more, wanted it all. Harper was everything he could have dreamed of, and he was selfish enough to want to covet her for the rest of their lives.

"*Please,*" she pleaded. "Lucky, I need you."

While he could lay for hours suckling her breasts, he would not leave her wanting. Perhaps another time he'd tie her to his bed and take his time with her. Not this night, though. This night, they both craved too much.

Lucky released her nipple with a pop. Male satisfaction filled him when he saw it was red and swollen from his suckling. He wanted to make the other one match it, but knew Harper was running out of patience. He needed to make this good for her too.

As Lucky sat up on his knees, he looked down at her. She was a sight to behold. In unison, they each reached for their underwear and dragged the last piece of clothing off themselves.

A dark patch of curls covered her pussy. They glistened with her arousal, making his breath catch. Fuck, just when he thought she couldn't look any more beautiful. He wasn't sure he was going to last. He hadn't felt anything besides his own fist in almost two years.

Taking his cock in hand, Lucky started to stroke himself. He was thick, which meant he still needed to prepare her more. Before they got too carried away, though, they needed to have a conversation that should have been had before they'd gotten to this point.

"Are you on birth control?"

Harper nodded. "I have an IUD."

For some reason, the idea of that disturbed him. Was it wrong of him that he was hoping she *wasn't* on birth control?

"I'm clean. It's been almost two years for me. I'll wear a condom if you want. I bought a new pack after we met."

She gave him a glowing smile. "Really?"

"Pretty sure all the ones I had were expired." His cheeks heated at that admission. "Harper, I've never gone bareback, but the idea of doing so with you is intoxicating. I can't get the thought out of my head. It's completely your choice though. I'll respect whatever you decide."

She reached out and he took her hand. Their fingers laced together. "I've never had sex without a condom either. I'm clean too. I had a physical before I moved from Detroit."

A dark part of his brain didn't like her statement about never having sex without a condom, because it meant she'd been with men other than him. It was a ridiculous feeling, because *of course* she'd had sex before. He had too. But Christ, he wished he could have been her first and only.

Lucky ran a finger between her wet folds. Her clit was engorged. He started rubbing circles against it with his thumb. Harper gasped, her legs spreading further.

"It's your decision," he reminded her. "Yes or no."

Harper opened her mouth to speak but let out a moan instead. Her breathing started to become short. Finally, she gasped out, "No condom."

Fuck. Yes.

Lucky laid himself flat on the bed, hooking her legs over his shoulders. He pressed his face into her center. Breathing in her purest scent. She was so sweet, like honeysuckle. He nearly shook with desire as he palmed her ass, bringing her body closer to his.

She gasped at the first lick of his tongue. Fuck, she tasted as delicious as she smelled. He drew her hardening nub into his mouth, loving the way she squirmed. He could feel her juices coating his beard.

Her orgasm came out of nowhere, surprising both of them. Harper threw her head back and yelled as he felt her body spasm under his mouth. He didn't stop, eating his way through her climax.

It was a very good thing Scotty was a sound sleeper. Lucky loved the noises she made, her whimpers and her gasps, and he never wanted to silence them due to an unwanted audience.

Her grip on his hair was starting to become painful. He slowed his licks, lessening the pressure on her sensitive clitoris.

He eased a finger inside her. She was soaked, but still incredibly tight. The orgasm helped, though he hoped to coax one more out of her before entering her.

Lucky added another finger. He licked her almost lazily as he worked his fingers in and out of her center. Her walls were still trembling with the aftershocks of her first orgasm. He worked on widening his fingers with each thrust.

She was so vocal; it was a symphony to his ears. He craved her next moan like he was a deaf man learning to hear for the first time. Knowing she needed extra stimulation to reach another orgasm, he reached up with his free hand and tweaked the nipple he'd sucked on earlier. He knew it would still be sensitive.

Harper cried out, her walls spamming around his fingers. Her back bowed off the bed, but Lucky kept a firm hold on her.

"Oh fuck, oh fuck… Fuck, fuck, fuck…"

A low, masculine chuckle loomed up from his chest. He was fairly sure that was the first time he'd heard her curse, and he loved that he'd brought it out of her.

Rising, Lucky trailed his lips from her pussy to her belly button to between her breasts to her throat and, finally, to her lips. She clung to him like her life depended on it. His sure did.

Without words, their eyes met. He shifted his hips, reaching down to guide the tip of his cock to her hot entrance. They didn't break eye contact as he pushed inside. She gasped, a slight wince on her face. He froze. He'd hoped after two orgasms she'd be ready for him.

"More," she groaned out.

Lucky was hesitant, not wanting to hurt her, but also trusted that she knew what was best for her body. Her moist heat was sweltering around his cock. He'd never felt anything so good. He slid in deeper. Christ, he could feel his balls tighten up already. He needed to hold off. He was no three-pump-chump.

Finally, he was all the way in. She felt amazing. He wasn't sure if it was because he wasn't wearing a condom or if it was because it was Harper. He was pretty sure it was a mixture of both.

She nodded almost frantically. "Move, please."

Lucky did. Slowly at first, gradually picking up his pace. She lifted her hips, meeting him thrust for thrust. He saw the fire in her eyes and knew it was mirrored in his own.

"I'm not going to last," he warned her. "You feel too good."

She nodded. "You too. I've never..." Her words trailed off into a moan.

Lucky needed her to come with him. He was not about to end this on his own. He reached down between them to find her clit.

Harper shook her head. "No, I'm too sore. I can't come again."

"You can," he vowed. "You will. Come with me, darlin'. I want to feel you come around my cock as you did my fingers."

Perhaps it was his words or his attention to her clitoris, but Harper burst around him. He swallowed her cry with his mouth, sealing his over hers. He felt the pressure in his lower back as his balls tightened up. Three thrusts later and he followed her over the edge.

CHAPTER 9

*H*arper awoke the next morning feeling deliciously sore and elated. Despite her joke about his age, Lucky really could go all night. He had taken her twice more throughout the night. She was pretty sure her pussy had been reconfigured into the outlined shape of his cock.

Holy crap. She'd never felt so good in her life.

Kisses trailed slowly up her spine. She shivered, but the truth was she wasn't sure she could take him again. Her body needed time to recover.

"What time is it?" she murmured into her pillow.

"A little after seven. Sissy will be here soon." He moved her hair out of his way so he could nibble on her ear. Goosebumps appeared on her skin. "We should get in the shower and sneak out of here while we can."

Shoot. She'd forgotten about Scotty. Geez, she hoped she hadn't been so loud last night that she'd woken him up. She was sure Lucky would have told her to be quiet if that had been a concern.

Despite her soreness, Harper could feel her arousal growing

with his touch. "Perhaps separate showers would get us out of here faster."

His low chuckle did not dampen her desire. "You may have a point. You are far too tempting, Ms. Hannigan." Harper tried to contain it, but her cheeks heated when he used her title. *His* eyes narrowed suspiciously. "Pray tell, what caused your cheeks to turn such a lovely shade of pink, malady?"

Harper buried her face into her pillow, unsuccessfully trying to hide from him. Lucky rolled her onto her back and climbed over her. She closed her eyes, not wanting to look at him or she'd spill.

Harper felt his weight shift until he was straddling her stomach. He wasn't pressing down on her though, using his legs to keep the majority of his weight off of her. "Is it dirty?"

With her eyes closed, she could feel his arms moving but didn't know what he was doing because his hands weren't on her. She squeezed her eyes and her mouth closed tighter.

"Oh, very dirty then."

Not wanting him to get the wrong idea, she shook her head.

"Not dirty?"

She nodded.

"Well, that's disappointing."

Surprised at his tone and comment, Harper's eyes sprang open. Oops. Lucky was straddled over her, lazily rubbing his morning wood. His eyes were fixated on her breasts.

She remembered how she'd felt when Mark Connelly wouldn't stop staring at her breasts during that messed-up dinner at her parents'. She'd felt gross, like she needed to take a shower just from having his eyes on her.

It was the complete opposite reaction with Lucky. He was masturbating while watching her breasts rise and fall with her breaths. She squirmed beneath him. Her nipples rose into hard points and she felt her arousal that had started to wane with her embarrassment rise again.

Some primal part of her wanted Lucky to come on her, mark her. It didn't make sense because they weren't animals. No one would know what he'd done, but the craving still existed. Because she would know what he'd done.

After each time he'd made love to her the night before, he'd gotten up and made his way to the bathroom. There he'd gather a warm wet washcloth and towel. It'd embarrassed her the first time he'd stood over her, spreading her legs to wipe her. She'd figured she do it herself. Sex without a condom was definitely messier than she'd expected. But he'd insisted.

And he'd stared.

Harper hadn't looked, but she could feel what he'd been seeing. The evidence of their lovemaking smeared between her thighs and inside her. He'd openly looked before cleaning her, like he'd enjoyed the sight. She'd even seen his flaccid cock twitch as he worked. He'd enjoyed the act.

She'd never had a lover so openly affectionate as Lucky, or so openly intimate.

Heat rose in his eyes and she saw his breath catch. "Fuck, Harper, you are the most beautiful woman I've ever seen."

She gripped his muscular thighs. "Do it. Come on me."

"Fuck," he groaned, his hand picking up speed. He reached down and tweaked her nipple. "You are so fucking gorgeous. This is how I want to wake up every morning for the rest of my life: to the sight of you, naked in my bed, with your hair messed up and your pussy sore from me making love to you. I want you to feel me throughout the day and know where I was the night before."

His dirty words increased both their arousals. His hand started moving faster, his other pinching her harder. She moved one hand to cup his balls resting on her middle. Her free hand went to her other nipple.

"Yeah, just like that," he moaned. "Harder, Harper. Pinch yourself harder. I'm so close, darlin', but not until you."

She was close too. She could feel her kegel muscles preparing to contract. But she needed something. She wasn't sure what. She was right at the edge without tipping over.

Suddenly Lucky took his hand off her nipple and reached behind him. He expertly found her clit and flicked it once.

She tipped.

With a shout, Harper felt a wave of heat rush through her as she orgasmed. Wetness hit her chest and neck as Lucky came over her, frantically still pumping his cock through the last jet.

Both were breathing heavily. They were sweaty and sticky with semen.

Lucky leaned down, seeming to not care in the least that he was crushing his ejaculate between their chests, and kissed her. When she sighed in contentment, his tongue swooped into her mouth and deepened the kiss.

When she had to pull away for much needed air, Lucky didn't get off of her. Instead, he laid himself over her, tucking his face in her neck and letting out a long sigh.

She felt light and elated…until he spoke. "I still want to know what made you blush."

Damn it. She'd been hoping he'd forgotten about that. "It's embarrassing."

"Really, Sherlock, I never would have guessed. It wasn't like you were *blushing*."

She lightly smacked him upside the head. "Not funny."

"It was a bit funny."

"Nope."

"Tell me."

She let out a sigh of frustration. "Fine, but I don't want it to ruin what we just did."

He lifted his head slightly, his eyes narrowing. "Unless your next words are 'I want to break up', nothing could ruin what we just did. It was perfect."

Harper figured she might as well just get it over with. If sex wasn't enough to distract him, then nothing would keep him from relentlessly finding out. "You called me 'Ms. Hannigan'."

He blinked, clearly not understanding. "Last time I checked, that was your name."

"But it's not a name that excites me," she hedged. When he remained silent, she groaned. "Fine. Last night when you were talking about the future and riding on the back of your *hog* and cuts and rings… I kept hearing 'Mrs. Harper McCoy' in my head." His arm across her chest squeezing slightly was his only outward reaction. She couldn't tell what he was thinking. "And I really liked how that name sounded," she said in a low voice. "It's been in my head all night too, each time you made love to me. Then you called me 'Ms. Hannigan' and it was like a bucket of cold water being thrown on me. When I realized how stupid of a reaction that was, I blushed." She met his eyes, determined not to be further embarrassed by her ridiculous thoughts. "There, you happy now?"

"Fuck, if I was fifteen years younger, I'd be fucking you again right now." He ground his hips against her, but his cock remained soft. "Darlin', you have no idea what hearing that name does to me. My blood feels like it's on fire right now and I can't do a damn thing about it."

Needing to cool herself down, Harper offered a helpful suggestion. "Maybe it's time to look into getting that little blue pill I hear men your age need to boost their performance."

A low growl emanated from him. "How was my performance last night, missy? Fairly certain I heard you begging me to stop to give *you* a break."

She grinned widely. "I have no complaints."

Lucky stretched up, kissing her gently on her lips. "Mrs. Harper McCoy. Fuck, darlin', that does sound good."

Though she agreed with him, she also felt concern. "I don't want us to rush this, Lucky. There's still so much we don't know about the other."

"I'm not proposing today, darlin'." He kissed her shoulder. "Just know that while I'm willing to wait until you're ready, I'm nearly there myself. You feel too good in my arms to risk letting you get away."

The front door closing downstairs shocked them from their intimate bubble. Crap, they'd both forgotten about Sissy, and neither of them was in any condition to greet her.

"Shower?"

She nodded, hurriedly. "Together, but no touching!"

He pulled her out of bed. "I make no promises."

* * *

AFTER PEEKING in on a still sleeping Scotty, Harper and Lucky made their way downstairs. The smell of pancakes and bacon emanated from the kitchen, where Lucky's adult daughter stood before the stovetop.

Harper had seen pictures of Sissy and they'd briefly met through the car window as she picked Scotty up from school, but they had yet to officially meet. Sissy was around five-five. She had lighter skin than Harper, like she spent a lot of time indoors. Her hair was closer to a strawberry-blonde to Scotty and Lucky's dark blonde. She could see the facial similarities between the three…siblings? No, that wasn't right. Scotty was Lucky's son.

She should have clarified before now, but she wasn't sure if Sissy referred to herself as Lucky's daughter or sister. It was definitely a unique situation. Harper believed daughter, based on how Lucky referred to her. As an adult, though, Sissy might want a more sibling-like relationship than father-daughter. She'd verify with Lucky later and just be careful of her words in front of Sissy until then.

"Good morning, Sis," Lucky said as he entered the room. He walked right over to her and gave her a kiss on the top of her head.

"Morning, Dad." She beamed up at him.

Okay, so maybe Harper didn't need to ask Lucky for clarification after all. In a way, she felt pleased that Lucky got to keep his title as father to her. He'd raised her since she had been five years old. He'd earned it, no matter what their DNA said.

Sissy looked over her shoulder at Harper. "Morning, Harper."

"Hi, Sissy. Thank you for coming over so early."

She shrugged, turning back to the stove. "Promised Scotty we'd hit the train station today. One hour there and back of nonstop train talk. Yippy!"

Harper smiled at her sarcasm, because there was no way to hide the affection in her voice when she spoke of her brother.

"I'm sure you two will have a blast today."

Sissy turned off the stovetop. She brought a large platter of pancakes and bacon strips to the table. "Better eat fast. That boy will only rouse for bacon on Saturday mornings."

Lucky filled two to-go mugs with coffee for them. "She's not wrong," he told Harper. "We're later than we wanted as it is."

Sissy threw her father an amused look. "Oh really? And what kept you from being on schedule this morning?"

He narrowed his eyes at her. "Mind your business, little girl."

Sissy's grin widened. "Oh please. After all the talks you gave me, I finally get the opportunity for a little payback."

Harper cut into her pancakes, watching the exchange between father and daughter. She didn't get the feeling of animosity from Sissy about her relationship with Lucky. If anything, it seemed like Sissy was happy. Yet, she was talking mostly with her dad. Harper didn't feel ignored, per se, but she also didn't feel included.

Hopefully she and Sissy could become friends. She didn't want there to be any awkwardness because she was closer to Sissy's age than Lucky's.

"I can still ground you, you know."

Sissy snorted. "You wouldn't ground me even when you had the legal right to."

"Fine, I'll take away your car."

"Car's in my name. You gifted me the title two Christmases ago."

"Fuck," Lucky let out.

Sissy gave a triumphant whoop.

Lucky pointed his fork at her. "Nothing that will embarrass Harper. I might have a little coming my way, but she doesn't."

"A little?" Sissy repeated skeptically. "You had Uncle Bear stalk me on my first date." She turned to Harper for the first time. "Sixteen, finally going out on my first real date with a *senior boy*, and I have a giant bodyguard following me around who would openly growl if my date touched me. Oh, and Uncle Bear glared so menacingly when it was time to pay the check, which I was perfectly fine going Dutch on, that he paid for the whole thing and therefore didn't have gas money to fill up his car for the next week."

Harper winced sympathetically. "Ouch."

"Yeah, and that's nothing compared to my senior prom."

Harper cringed, not sure she wanted to hear that story. "Sorry, Lucky, you're on your own for this one. I'm siding with Sissy."

"She wanted to go to an afterparty!"

"It was prom!" Sissy argued. "Of course, there was an afterparty!"

"With boys!"

"Well, you didn't send me to a private all-girls school. What did you expect?"

"I was not allowing my daughter to go off to places unknown–"

"Wait," Harper interrupted. "You went to her prom with her?"

A flush crossed over Lucky's cheeks. "Not exactly."

"The *entire club* came to my prom."

Oh shit. She turned wide eyes on Sissy. "If I become a casualty of the payback he has coming his way, I completely understand. I'll happily support you, even if it backfires on me."

Sissy beamed. "I knew I'd like you."

Harper met her glee with a smile of her own.

Movement upstairs reminded the adults that there was still a teenager in the house, one who shouldn't find Harper at the breakfast table. She quickly gobbled down the rest of her pancakes. Lucky ate his bacon strips three at a time. Sissy hopped up and topped off their coffee cups.

"I'll distract him. You two get out of here."

Lucky kissed Sissy on the cheek and headed for the front door to put his boots on. Since Harper was still in her clothes from the day before, their first stop was going to need to be her apartment. Her car was outside in his driveway still. She'd need that for her lunch with her mom anyway.

Crap, she thought as she got her own shoes on. She'd forgotten about that. Last night, it had seemed like a good idea to try to make amends. Now that it was only a few hours away, she wasn't sure she wanted to. Not because she never wanted to make up with her mom, but because it took away from her day with Lucky.

As Sissy hurried up the stairs, calling loudly, "Good morning, little brother!" Harper and Lucky snuck out the front door.

* * *

THOUGH HARPER HAD BEEN TEMPTED to cancel her lunch plans all morning, she decided to still go. She did miss her mom, and a lot was happening in her life that she wished she could talk to her mom about. Hell, if things continued as they were, there would be wedding bells in her near future. Harper wanted to share that with her mom.

She parked outside the diner. It was a Saturday, so they were certainly busy. She'd seen her mom's car further down the street. Hopefully she'd been able to snag them a table already.

The smell of coffee and grease hit her as she entered. Though she'd been living in Mount Grove for two and a half months, she had yet to come into this town staple. When Lucky took her out, it was usually out of town so they could get in a long ride on his motorcycle.

She spotted her mom in a booth towards the back of the restaurant and indicated to the hostess, who nodded.

Normally, she'd greet her mom with a hug and a kiss. Her mom stood as she saw Harper approach. They both looked awkward as they both hesitated, but finally hugged.

"It's good to see you, Mom," Harper said. She didn't add the *alone*, though she was thinking it. She'd half expected her dad or Deputy Mark to be sitting next to her mom, even though her mom had assured her via text that it would be just the two of them.

"You too, baby." Her mom hesitated before saying, "I don't like it when you ignore me, Harpy."

Well, I don't like it when you set me up on blind dates and remain silent when your husband implies I've been sleeping with the entire town. She bit her tongue on that sentence though. "I needed time to think, Mom. Not every day your father sticks one of his deputies on you blindly."

"It's for your own safety–"

"Against what, Mom?" Harper demanded. "This is a small town with little crime. Detroit was much busier and nastier, and Dad never made any of the beat cops up there follow me around."

Her mom remained silent though, casting her gaze downward at the table. "This is a new town. We wanted you to feel safe and Deputy Mark knows this town. He grew up here."

It sounded like her mother was reading off of an invisible script, and Harper wondered if her father had told her to say those exact words. "Deputy Mark is a creep. I blocked his number and, if I am home when he knocks, I ignore him. I *am* safe here. It's Deputy Mark who makes me feel unsafe."

Not to mention, he'd tried to blackmail her to keep her relationship with Lucky from her father. She'd shut the door in his face, which had felt damn good. Had he honestly thought she'd have sex with him just to keep her relationship a secret? *Barf.*

"You've been hanging out with that lowlife," her mother snapped. "How could you possibly feel safe around him?"

Harper took a deep breath to calm herself. "If you're referring to Lucky, Mom, he is not a lowlife. He's a sweet and caring guy, and I like him. A lot." More than a lot.

"Your father says he's a criminal–"

"Dad sees his cut and *assumes* he's a criminal. He knows nothing about the *Via Daemonia* or Lucky. He's a good guy, Mom. A really good guy."

Her mom was still looking down at the table. A waitress appeared with glasses of water and two BLTs. Apparently, her mom had ordered for them already. Harper had been looking forward to seeing what the diner offered, having never been here before. Guess she'd have to come back and have a look at the menu before someone else ordered for her.

The thought reminded her of her first date with Lucky. A reminiscent smile appeared on her face.

Her mom saw but misinterpreted it. "Oh good, you still like BLTs. I wasn't sure."

Then why order it for her? Harper shook her head. Clearly her mom had not gotten over whatever was making her act weird. Maybe it was this town? Did her mom miss the city and was trying to get Harper to want to return to Detroit too? After that disaster of a dinner, her mom had nearly succeeded.

After last night, no way.

"Mom, I wish you'd give Lucky a chance. He's an artist. He makes these beautiful sculptures and donates a percentage of his proceeds to the Down Syndrome Society. He's got two kids and–"

"Yes, your father told me he was older. Forty years old, Harpy? He's too old for you."

Harper was already shaking her head though. "Age is just a number, Mom. I don't care about his age but who he is as a man. And he's a really good man."

"Who's raising two children out of wedlock? Probably knocked up some of those sluts they keep around their club."

Harper winced. She'd never heard her mom speak so crudely before. "You're not even close, Mom, but that's his life and his choice to tell you his past. Just know you're wrong. Very, very wrong."

Her mom leaned closer over the table. "You have no reason to trust him, Harpy. Men like him cheat. It's a fact. Your father told me about the women at the clubhouse while they'd been executing a search warrant. Practically prostitutes. They were barely dressed and all over the men. *All of the men.*"

Harper was already shaking her head. Not Lucky. She trusted him. "Not all of them, Mom. Lucky isn't like that. Yes, there are women who hang around the clubhouse. They work as house-keepers and cooks for the club. Do they sleep with the guys? Sure, but they're not paid to. It's their choice."

"Which means you have no reason to trust he'll be loyal to you, Harpy. Think for a moment. Why would he stay monoga-mous to one woman when he could have any woman there? You're not thinking clearly."

Again, Harper shook her head. "Mom, you don't know what you're talking about. I trust Lucky. I know him. I want to intro-duce you to him, but not if you're already judging him for a life-style you know nothing about."

"He's a lowlife thug, Harpy. People will talk. People will think you're one of those easy women who hang around the club. Your father is trying to build a life here–"

"So am I," Harper snapped. She pushed her plate away from her on the table. She hadn't touched it and had no appetite. "Mom, if you want to have a pleasant conversation and catch up, I'm all for it. But I am not going to sit here and listen to you talk down about Lucky or my relationship with him. You and Dad don't even know him but you're spitting out facts about him like you do."

"I am trying to protect you, Harpy. You aren't thinking clearly."

"Maybe I'm not," Harper said as she grabbed her purse and stood. "Maybe he is tricking me and maybe I am falling for it. Regardless of who is right and who is wrong, it's my life, Mom. I have to make my own mistakes and choices. Please tell Dad to have Deputy Mark back off. He's circled the diner twice since we've been here."

Harper threw a twenty down on the table, not sure if that covered their meal or not, and left. Her mom called after her loudly, causing others in the diner to turn and stare, but Harper ignored her and them.

She was very grateful she'd brought her own car so she had an escape, but at that moment she also wished she'd taken Lucky up on his offer to join her or wait for her. She could really use his comforting hug right about now.

The roar of a motorcycle caught her attention just as she reached her car. It gave her a sense of comfort to hear it, even though it wasn't driving towards her.

She looked up anyway and was startled to see a red hog pull up at a clothing store down the street from where she stood. A very familiar physique sat atop it. She didn't need to see his face under the helmet to recognize those arms or torso.

But she didn't wave. She didn't let on that she saw him.

A woman was climbing off the back of his bike. A woman that was neither her nor Sissy.

I don't let anyone but family ride on my hog with me.

You have no reason to trust him, Harpy. Men like him cheat.

Her mom was wrong about Lucky, she knew that. But then why was there a woman standing there removing a helmet after having ridden on the back of Lucky's bike? A woman who wasn't family.

Though she hadn't eaten, she felt like she was about to throw up. The woman leaned down and kissed Lucky. He didn't move away and he didn't stop it. The kiss itself was quick, more of a peck, but it was still a kiss.

Lucky twisted to place the helmet in the saddlebag. Harper ducked behind her car.

Her heart was pounding like a drumline in her chest. Nausea still threatened.

Lucky had told her he hadn't been with a woman for almost two years. Had he lied? Harper put her hand over her mouth, unsure if it was to keep the sobs in or the bile down.

She'd trusted him. Who was that woman? Clearly, they hadn't had premade plans for today, because he'd been planning on spending the day with Harper before her mom had invited her to lunch. So the woman's presence was spontaneous.

But that kiss?

How could he possibly explain that? Even if he had a reasonable explanation for having a non-family member on the back of his motorcycle, even though he'd sworn he never had any woman but her ride there, what excuse could he possibly come up with for that kiss?

And, an even deeper issue, would she believe him?

You have no reason to trust him, Harpy. Men like him cheat. Her mother's words rang in her head again.

Her gut and head said *not Lucky.* But her heart? Her heart was cracking in half. Had she placed her trust in Lucky when she shouldn't have? They had sex three times last night and had shared a mutual orgasm that morning. She'd confessed to him how much she liked the name 'Mrs. Harper McCoy'. He'd seemed so open and honest with her.

And yet...?

She found herself still frozen, still crouched down beside her car, as the motorcycle's engine faded away. What if her parents were right? What if she was the fool in this equation?

* * *

THE NEXT MORNING, Lucky stared at his phone in confusion. He hadn't seen Harper since he'd dropped her off at her apartment the morning before. She was supposed to text him when she'd finished her lunch with her mom. Hoping her lack of text meant she and her mom were making amends, Lucky hadn't reached out to her until mid-afternoon. Just to make sure she was okay.

Her response back had been short and impersonal.

> Harper: Lunch was fine. I'm exhausted. Text you later.

While he wanted to spend the rest of the day with her, he understood her exhaustion. He had woken her up multiple times throughout the night to make love to her. He'd let her be.

Later on in the evening, since Sissy was in the house to babysit Scotty, he'd texted Harper asking if he could come over to spend the night. She hadn't replied. Thinking perhaps she was still asleep, he hadn't pushed the subject. He'd sent one more text to her with the clubhouse address and the time to meet the next morning for the club run. She hadn't replied until that morning.

> Harper: Not feeling well. Won't make it.

Which had caused Lucky to stand in contemplation for close to twenty minutes outside the clubhouse as his brothers, Jenna,

Angel, Sissy, and Scotty got themselves ready to leave for the club run.

Bear clasped him on the shoulder. "Where's your girl?"

Lucky put his phone away. "Do you think it's paranoid of me to think she's not okay after she's gone radio silent following a lunch date with her mom yesterday?"

Bear was shaking his head before Lucky had finished his question. "Not after the last meal she'd had with them. I don't know what is up with her parents, brother, but it's not good."

Lucky nodded his agreement. "I need to find Steel. Who are the kids riding with?" He'd already told Scotty that he couldn't ride with Lucky that day. Scotty had been thrilled.

"Sissy's with me. Not sure about Scotty."

"Can you keep an eye on him?"

Bear raised an eyebrow. "You even have to ask?"

"Thanks, man," Lucky said as he hurried away. He needed to find Steel. He was about to miss his first club run since forming the *Via Daemonia* five years ago.

* * *

THE BANGING on her apartment door was far different than Mark's usual knocking. This sounded like a fist, not knuckles.

"Harper!"

She jumped at her name. Not Mark. Lucky. Shit, she wasn't ready to confront him yet.

She'd barely slept the night before. Telling Lucky she didn't feel well wasn't a total lie. She still felt extremely nauseous. Every time she closed her eyes, her mind replayed that kiss over and over again. She was sitting on the couch, where she'd been most of yesterday and through the night. She had a blanket over her lap and a river of used tissues around her feet. Her eyes were red and puffy.

She hadn't hit the anger portion of her grief yet. She was still in the crying-her-eyes-out stage. Lucky was to blame, she knew that, but she couldn't get past how foolish she felt. She'd fallen for him so fast.

How could he spend the night sleeping with her and then kiss another woman hours later?

Harper glared at the door when he pounded again. Okay, maybe she *had* reached the anger portion. She stomped over to the door and threw it open. "What do you want, asshole?"

His eyebrows shot up. Damn, he looked good. He had on a black shirt with his cut, jeans, and his black boots. His tattoos, which she'd spent two nights ago licking, seemed emphasized by his dark attire.

That reminder angered her further.

"Well, you don't look sick." His eyes roamed her up and down. "Though you don't exactly look well either. What's going on?"

"Like you have to ask," she snapped. She hadn't had the urge to hit someone like this in a long time. "You have some nerve coming here."

He crossed his arms over his chest. He seemed to sense it wasn't a good idea to ask to come in. Good for him. She would have slammed the door in his face if he'd tried. "You know, I had a feeling something like this would happen but I didn't listen to my gut. What happened at the lunch with your mom? Did your dad show up? Did Connelly? What did they say to you?"

"Oh, lunch was great," she said sarcastically. "Didn't eat a damn thing and spent the whole twenty minutes I was there listening to my mother call you a lowlife and badmouth our rela-tionship."

His eyebrows drew down further. "Twenty minutes? Why didn't you call me? I waited for you all afternoon. I thought you were actually reconciling, and I was just being paranoid."

"Maybe I would have if you weren't so busy shoving your tongue down some lady's throat!"

Lucky looked like she'd slapped him. Good.

She went to close the door, but he put his palm against it. "What did your mom tell you? Whatever it is, I swear to you she lied. You're the only woman I've kissed."

"Liar!" Harper shouted, not caring if her neighbors heard. "My mom didn't tell me anything, *Lucky*. I saw it with my own two eyes."

His face scrunched like he was doing some quick thinking. Like she'd believe anything he had to say at that point.

Quick as a flash, he scooped her up against his chest and carried her into the apartment. He closed the door behind him.

"Hey!" she shouted, banging her fists against any part of him she could reach. "Put me down!"

He released her, taking a step back. He crossed his arms over his chest. "Tell me exactly what you saw or think you saw, Harper."

"I didn't *think* I saw anything," she snapped. How dare he come in without her approval? What would Lucky do if she called her dad? Maybe she should, to teach him a lesson, but she wasn't sure she'd survive the lecture her father would give her afterwards. He'd perfected the *I was right, you were wrong* speech over the course of her childhood. "I *saw*," she emphasized, "you ride up on your bike with a woman *who wasn't Sissy* on the back and drop her off. After she took off her helmet, she leaned down and kissed you. *And you didn't stop her!*"

Lucky nodded easily. Too easily. "That's all true."

"You lying, cheating bastard!" she shouted. Harper felt like crying again but the tears wouldn't come. Was she all dried up? How was it possible to feel her heart breaking and still be beating?

"I'm a lot of things," he said calmly, "but I'm not a liar, a cheater, or a bastard. Would you like me to explain what you *think* you saw from what I am assuming was outside the diner, which is about a hundred yards away from the consignment shop where I was?"

"I saw her on your bike! I saw you kiss her! You told me that no one but family rode on your bike! You told me I was special!"

Lucky leaned forward, his arms still crossed. "Think about what you just said and think about what you know about me, Harper. I am not a cheater. I don't bounce from woman to woman. You are special to me. So think really carefully about who could have possibly been on the back of my bike."

"Your only family is Sissy and Scotty!"

"Blood family, sure. But I have others I consider family. A Brady Bunch full of them," he added like he was giving her a clue.

She paused, recalling their referring to Scotty's aunts and uncles within the club as a Brady Bunch-like family. She eyed him carefully. He was too calm. Was it possible? Twice now he'd referred her to seeing what she *thinks* she saw.

But the kiss? She's seen the kiss.

"She kissed you," Harper argued back, though her voice had lost its fight.

Lucky nodded. "She did. On the cheek."

On the cheek? No. That wasn't what she'd seen. It had seemed more intimate than that.

Lucky sighed. "Harper, for the sake of ending this conversation so we can get to the real issue, let me explain. Yesterday after I left your apartment, I got a text from Steel, my president. His wife Jenna had been visiting their son and daughter-in-law that morning. He'd dropped her off but got held up at the children's consignment store they run because an employee called in sick. He couldn't pick her up and asked if I was available to. Not many people he trusts to pick up Jenna like that, but I'm one of them. Since you were on your way to meet your mom for lunch, and I had nothing better to do, I agreed.

"I picked her up and dropped her off outside of her store. She leaned over and kissed me on the cheek as a thank you. I drove off, completely unaware that I had had an audience. However, even if you'd been standing right outside the store, I wouldn't have done a single thing differently. Jenna's like *my* sister. I've known her for close to twenty years."

Harper felt her blood run cold. How could she have misinterpreted what she'd seen so badly?

"Now, let's talk about how you have gone silent on me for the second time after meeting with one or both of your parents?"

Harper dropped her face into her hands. She was so ashamed of her reaction and her words to him. She should have confronted Lucky. Just talked to him. How had she let herself doubt him so much? She'd done a complete one-eighty. From trusting him and defending him to her mother to hating him and believing he could betray her.

"I'm so sorry," she sobbed into her hands. Her voice was muffled. "I am so, so sorry! I don't know what happened!"

His arms came around her. "Darlin', I wish you'd trusted me. We could have avoided this whole thing if you'd just talked to me."

She nodded, her hands leaving her face to clutch his shirt. Her tears kept coming. Apparently, she wasn't as dried out as she thought. "I should have. I know I should have. I don't even know why I didn't."

"Can I tell you my theory?" She felt his lips in her hair. "Harper, you are so strong and independent, but you have a flaw when it comes to your parents. Your brain doesn't know how to fight them. They say jump, you say how high. From what you just told me, you spent twenty minutes listening to your mother berate me, putting doubt in your head. Then by some twist of fate, you witness me driving a woman you don't know around on my hog and kiss me. Your mind automatically sided with your mom's words."

She shook her head. "That's no excuse. I can think for myself. I can't put this on my parents."

"Are you sure? Because I can't help but see a pattern. I'm just grateful this time I was able to come myself instead of having to send Bear over to check on you again."

Harper gasped and stepped away from him. "Why are you here? Aren't you supposed to be riding around with your club?"

"Yes but, when you didn't show and weren't talking to me, I told Steel something had come up."

Now she felt even worse. "I'm so sorry, Lucky! I feel so stupid."

Lucky shook his head. "Do I wish you'd had more faith in me? Of course. But I can't help but notice the hold your parents have over you. It's like you're brainwashed when you're around them. You don't act like you."

"I've ignored Mark against their wishes! I don't always listen to them."

"Away from them, yes. But you told me yourself you agreed to having Connelly check in on you when you'd been at their house."

Harper flinched. She had done that. "I don't know what to say. I don't doubt you, Lucky. I do trust you. That's why this hurt so much. I couldn't fathom you betraying me."

"Never," he vowed. He reached up to wipe the tears from under her eyes. "Darlin', calling you special to me is an understatement. There aren't words to describe how I feel about you. They all seem so…cliché or overused."

She gripped his shirt tighter. "I know exactly what you mean."

"In all seriousness, though, I need your promise. I'm not going to make you choose between me and your parents. They are your parents after all. I may not like them or how they treat you, but they are still your parents. I, of all people, understand having a difficult parent. So, here's the promise I need from you: don't talk to them without me. Even if I'm just there silent in the background, promise you'll let me be there. I don't think I could handle another silent treatment."

She nodded, promising. Because she'd already been ready to

beg him to come with her the next time she had to talk to her parents. "You say I'm strong, but I don't feel very strong right now. Or independent."

Lucky placed his hands on her shoulders. "You can be strong and independent, and still lean on others in times of need. I do it with my brothers all the time."

Harper circled her arms around his chest under his cut. "I need you to promise something too."

"Anything."

"Promise to not give up on me. Clearly I have some parental-issues I wasn't fully aware of, and they're both acting strange, so there might be more Hannigan drama coming our way. Just promise me you'll be patient. I want a relationship with you and I do trust you, but I'm not sure I trust me right now. If that makes sense."

He dipped his head and took her lips. "I understand, and I promise." Then he wrinkled his nose. "So, um, when was the last time you showered?"

* * *

AFTER A LONG, luxurious shower in her too small stall, Lucky and Harper mounted his hog outside her apartment. It didn't pass her notice that there was a cruiser parked in the lot across from hers. There was no doubt who was in it, which also meant that her mom had either passed along her message and her father had ignored it, or her mom hadn't told him anything. Maybe it was time to have a chat with her dad—with Lucky at her side, of course.

She was still embarrassed for how she'd acted. It wasn't like her at all. Harper could only argue that she hadn't confronted Lucky because she'd been trying to avoid the pain that conversation would bring when she'd believed he'd cheated on her.

Some might argue that a kiss wasn't cheating. Cheating was

sex, but she didn't see it that way. Cheating was a betrayal of trust, no matter the level of intimacy crossed.

They were on their way to the club party that follows each run. The Honeys prepared it while the members were out on their ride. Lucky had once told her that it was usually a barbecue with ribs or a pig roast, or sometimes simpler with just burgers and hot dogs. Regardless, children and family members of the club were always invited. The Honeys and brothers knew to keep the party PG until later that evening when the family members went home. If a child was still around, any explicit activity was taken behind closed doors.

The club valued family very highly.

Harper loved that. She wasn't thrilled about coming face to face with the infamous Honeys. Even less thrilled because she wasn't sure which of them Lucky had slept with. She understood and sympathized with his plight that being a single dad wasn't easy and that the women had been available, and more importantly willing.

That didn't mean she liked it or planned to make friends with any of them.

She could smell the barbecue as soon as they turned onto the drive that led down to the clubhouse. She hadn't been here before, though she'd driven by it countless times since moving.

The large rectangular building was well kept. There was a house off to the side with a good distance between the two buildings. If Harper remembered correctly that house belonged to the club president and his wife.

A pavilion stood behind the clubhouse with a massive fire pit, grill, and outdoor kitchen/bar area. Adirondack chairs were strewn about with long picnic tables under the cover of the roof.

People milled around. Most of the men wore club cuts. She caught sight of Scotty in his denim one but noticed Sissy wasn't wearing hers. Harper wondered why. She saw a woman with short spiky hair and more tattoos than skin showing walking around with a cut on. Harper assumed that was Angel, the only female member. She certainly looked like she could kick some ass.

She saw other adults, but Scotty seemed to be the only child. An older Hispanic woman who wore a shawl around her head was seated in a chair by the unlit fire pit. She had one man with a cut and one man without a cut serving her a plate of food and a drink. She smiled lovingly up at them.

A very pregnant woman was sitting close to the older woman with a cushion of pillows all around her. A man who wasn't wearing a cut was placing an upside-down crate on the ground with yet another pillow and then lifted her feet onto it. She let out a sigh of contentment as she snuggled deeper into the pillows.

Two men with cuts were behind the bar, serving drinks. Since Scotty was getting what Harper assumed was a Shirley Temple from them, she figured they were in charge of both alcoholic and non-alcoholic beverages. One of them had bright red hair and she wondered if his road name was Weasley. The other, in comparison, looked almost albino. She'd call him 'Malfoy' until she learned his real or road name.

In retrospect, it wasn't at all what she expected. There was no rowdiness, no vulgarity. She couldn't even tell which women present were Honeys and which were girlfriends or friends of the club members.

Lucky walked around introducing her to people, but she had no hope of remembering who everyone was. Sensing her confusion, Lucky leaned down at one point and whispered that Scotty knew everyone and would make her a cheat-sheet. She laughed but was also grateful.

They walked up to an older couple. Both were wearing cuts and were likely in their late fifties. Though neither would understand her embarrassed reaction when Lucky introduced them as Steel and Jenna, Lucky did. He gave her an amused look. Up close, she could see Jenna's age, as well as the loving looks she kept giving her husband. The day before, at a distance, Harper had misjudged her for being much younger. She wondered if maybe there was a compliment in that.

She was thrilled when they finally bumped into Bear. Someone she knew. Harper even hugged him for being a familiar face.

He hugged her back. "Everything okay? Couldn't help but be worried, sweetheart."

She stepped back, taking Lucky's hand again. "We have some things to work out, and I have some things to work on, but we'll be fine." She squeezed Lucky's hand, and he smiled down at her. "I'm sorry for making you worry."

Bear chucked her under her chin. "Remember what I said. You can't reach this guy, you call me. Day or night, sweetheart. You're one of us now, which means you got a lot of overprotectiveness coming your way."

Harper couldn't help but feel warm at the statement. Somehow, she knew that the club's overprotectiveness would be far different and less controlling than her parents' version.

"Promise," she vowed to the big teddy bear.

"How'd the run go?" Lucky asked. Harper had a feeling he was asking to give her a chance to get her emotions under control.

"Good, though we had a cruiser tailing us."

"Me too," Lucky said blandly.

Harper winced. "I feel like my father's obsession with you guys is my fault. Maybe we should invite him here. If he could see this–"

"He'd think we'd staged a happy-go-lucky party to get him off of our backs," Lucky said sadly. "And his obsession with our club has nothing to do with you. Remember, he had that search warrant before he found out about you and me."

She nodded reluctantly. "Yeah, I know. Still feels like maybe he hasn't dropped it because of us though." Harper shrugged her shoulders, looking between the two tall men. "I wish you guys had met him in Detroit. He wasn't like this. He never blindly went after someone or put the reputation of someone or a group above evidence. This isn't him."

"People change," Lucky placated her. His eyes were sympathetic. "You also said it yourself that he keeps the cop part of his life separate from his home life. Maybe this was always him, but you're just seeing it for the first time."

Harper shook her head. "No, something's different. He's different. Mom too. When I was in high school, I was dating this really bad kid. He was into all sorts of nasty things. Drugs, smoking, stealing… I only went out with him to piss off my dad. He was furious, and rightfully so. Mom, though, sat me down and tried to talk about what was going on with me. She was the one who got through to me that I should never date someone to spite my dad. The whole don't cut off your nose to spite your face thing.

"This is different. You should have heard her yesterday. She was lecturing me on the club and how men like you cheat and how much of a fool I was being… That's not her. Both of them are acting weird."

Lucky and Bear exchanged a look. "I get what you're saying," Lucky said, "but it doesn't change anything. Not unless you can figure out why they're acting like this."

He was right, and Harper was in no mood to dive deeper into her parents' lives. If there was something going on between them, they needed to be mature enough to come and talk to her about it.

Realizing the hypocrisy of her thought, Harper stepped away from the men. "I'm going to go get a drink."

"Sit," Lucky told her. "I'll get it."

Harper wasn't really sure where to sit, but, since he hadn't been specific, she took a seat at one of the picnic tables with no one around. Lucky and Bear walked off towards the bar.

She wasn't sitting alone for long. Scotty took a seat across from her, sucking down the last of his bright red, sugary drink.

"Hi, *Harper*," he said with a wink.

She loved that wink. "Hi, Scotty. Did you enjoy the club run this morning?"

He nodded. "Yes! I rode with Uncle Demo. He's missing three fingers but he's super smart."

Harper wasn't sure what one had to do with the other, but she knew better than to ask. "If you're looking for your dad, he went to get us drinks."

"No," Scotty said. "I was looking for you. Are you dating my dad?"

Harper had not been expecting that question, but perhaps she should have. Scotty wasn't a fool. Though they'd tried to keep their relationship platonic in front of him, it was unlikely they'd been able to hide everything from him.

"I am," she said honestly. "I think he was planning on telling you this afternoon."–Actually yesterday afternoon, but she'd likely ruined those plans along with their own.–"How do you feel about that?"

Scotty pursed his lips. "I have some questions."

"Naturally. Can I answer any of them for you or do you want to wait for your dad?"

"They're questions for you."

Harper caught Lucky's eye as he started to walk over. She shook her head to indicate not to interrupt them. Scotty had a right to ask her questions and she didn't want him to feel like his dad was fielding them.

"Do you like my dad?"

Harper turned her attention back to Scotty. Lucky had gotten her message. "I do, very much."

"Are you going to marry him?"

The name 'Mrs. Harper McCoy' came to mind again. She

couldn't help but smile. "Hopefully someday, but not anytime soon and not without discussing it with you and your sister first."

"But if you marry him, you'd become my mommy?"

Shit. Maybe she shouldn't have kept Lucky away. She didn't know how Lucky felt about this topic. They'd talked about having kids of their own, but not what her relationship with Scotty would be.

In that moment, though, she realized that Lucky's opinion didn't matter as much as Scotty's did. The pleading in his eyes caught her attention. He craved a maternal figure.

She reached across the table to grab his hand. "Scotty, if that day comes, it would be my honor to become your mommy."

He grinned brighter than the sun. "Can I start calling you 'Mommy'?"

Hm, she contemplated how to approach this one. "How about I make you a deal?" Scotty liked deals and games. "How about as soon as you see a ring on this finger," she held up her left ring finger, "you can start calling me 'Mommy'? But remember, I'm still 'Ms. Hannigan' at school."

Scotty's excitement was palpable. "Yes!" He stood up suddenly, knocking over his plastic cup that now only contained ice and cherries. She noticed that none of the cherries had stems on them and thought the bartenders sweet for helping him in that way.

Harper quickly picked up his mess, since he'd already scampered off. She had no idea what he was saying to Lucky but his dad suddenly burst out laughing. Then he leaned forward and said something serious to Scotty. Scotty beamed and ran off again.

"I don't know what you said to him," a voice beside her suddenly said, "but you certainly made his day."

Harper turned to find Sissy taking a seat next to her. She felt like she owed it to Scotty's sister to be honest. "He asked me if I was going to marry your dad. I told him hopefully someday. He asked if that would make me his mommy and I told him it would be an honor to be his mom."

Sissy smiled at her. "Thank you. I think in a way it's harder on him because he never knew our mom. He doesn't remember the bad to know how good we have it now."

Harper recalled Lucky telling her that Sissy claimed not to remember much about their birth mother. She got the distinct feeling that Sissy was lying and did remember more than she let on.

She decided to take a leap of faith. "I never knew your mom and there's never been any hardness in my family other than strictness, but I'm here if you ever want to talk. I'd never tell Lucky anything you said if you wished it to remain between us."

Sissy smiled but shook her head. "Thank you, but I prefer to keep my past where it is."

She hoped that was the right decision for Sissy. "Scotty craves a mother figure. I know you don't. With how close we are in ages, that'd be a bit awkward regardless. I hope we can be friends, Sissy."

"If my dad has his way, you'll be my stepmother regardless of our ages."

"Yeah, but I'm the good kind of stepmother. I'd let you go to the ball without an escort of angry bikers following you."

Sissy let out a loud laugh. "Much appreciated, Harper." She nudged Harper with her shoulder. "Only thing I ask is that you don't hurt him. He's sacrificed enough. He deserves all the happiness in the world. He believes that's you."

Her thoughts on that morning, she spoke from the heart. "I couldn't hurt him without hurting myself in return."

Sissy gave her a nod and then stood up to walk away. Lucky took her seat. Father and daughter gave each other playful pushes as they exchanged places. Lucky put a Coke down in front of her.

"What did she say to you?"

"What did Scotty say to you?" she asked in return.

Lucky looked thrilled to answer. "He asked me to take him ring shopping."

Harper was a bit confused. "Scotty wants a ring?"

He shook his head. "No. He wants to put a ring on *your* finger."

She was even more confused. "Huh?"

"It would seem someone didn't specify *who* was going to put a ring on your finger before he got to start calling you 'Mommy'."

Harper couldn't remember her exact wording, but she had a sinking feeling she hadn't told Scotty Lucky was the one who was going to be doing the ring giving. "Oh shit."

Lucky burst out laughing. "Yeah. He now wants to know what sort of rings mommies like and how soon I can take him to go get it."

"Oh shit."

"Don't worry," Lucky chuckled. "I explained it to him that the daddy gives the mommy the ring, not the son-to-be." Harper swallowed heavily, liking the mommy and daddy titles. It was almost as good as Mrs. Harper McCoy. "I did have to promise him to take him ring shopping with me when I went to find yours."

Heat seared her veins. Suddenly Harper wished they were very much alone, and with a lot less clothes on. They'd fooled around in the shower earlier but hadn't been able to do much more due to lack of space.

Seeming to catch onto her mood, Lucky leaned forward. He crowded her. She didn't mind in the least. "I have a room here, you know. Some of the guys live in the clubhouse, but we all have rooms assigned to us. Best part, there's a lock on the door."

Harper leaned close too, brushing her teeth along his bearded jawline. "Then why aren't we there?"

Lucky picked her up and practically ran towards the clubhouse. The brothers who saw made catcalls or whoops. Some clapped. Out of the corner of her eye, Harper saw Bear covering Scotty's eyes.

CHAPTER 10

The next two weeks were fantastic. She'd joined Lucky on both club runs and had been studying Scotty's chart of who was who within the club. She started driving Scotty to and from school since she was going there anyway. Though she hadn't moved in, she'd spent nearly every night at Lucky's house. They hadn't talked about it, and she had several months left on her lease regardless. One day, she'd realized she had an extra key on her keyring.

After a stop at the hardware store, Harper had snuck a key to her apartment onto his keys as well.

They were still careful about being too affectionate in front of Scotty. There were some things he just didn't need to see. Plus, she didn't want him to say anything at school, accidentally or intentionally.

There were only two downers to her life at that point. Madison Mitchell was still missing. Keys, one of Lucky's brothers, had been able to locate her car and give the information to the police. Unfortunately, she had not been found with it. Foul play was definitely a factor, since her car had been found at the junkyard with the owner having no record of receiving it.

Mark's cruiser still followed her around. Short of calling the press on how a police officer was practically stalking her on her father the sheriff's orders, she didn't know how to make that stop. He'd ceased knocking on her door, which she took to be a good sign. Hopefully he'd take the hint.

Bear joined them for dinner some nights. Sissy was only there on the weekends. One night Steel and Jenna had joined them after receiving an invitation from Lucky. He wanted Jenna and Harper to get to know each other better.

Harper liked Jenna. She had a very easy-going, grandmotherly personality. True to form, the woman's cookies were heavenly. Jenna promised she'd teach Harper how to make them, which somehow turned into Scotty getting a promise out of Jenna to teach him too.

Scotty had recruited Harper to help him finalize Lucky's not-so surprise party. She and Bear were in constant communication to make sure everything was to Scotty's preferences. Including the piñata filled with gummy bears and Red Vines. She'd also coaxed Scotty into having more food than just the cake but found out later Jenna was already on top of that. Apparently, there was a very sugary party a few years back when no one realized Scotty had asked five different people to bring "the cake" and no other food had been prepared.

On the day of the party, the club had a run like every Sunday. Harper feigned a headache per Scotty's instructions while Jenna claimed to have a "female stomach pain". Lucky tried his hardest not to burst out laughing as the two overplayed their symptoms for Scotty's benefit. While the club left on their run, Lucky with a paper birthday hat attached to his helmet, Jenna, Harper, and the Honeys worked to get the clubhouse decorated. Since rain was forecasted for that afternoon, they were keeping the party to the clubhouse area.

To her surprise, Harper didn't mind the Honeys. A few could be catty, and she'd seen far too much of a couple who thought clothes were only a suggestion, but they seemed like good people. She hadn't found any that had a problem with her being Lucky's girl. Maybe it was because Lucky hadn't been sleeping with any prior to meeting her. No one felt displaced by Harper's presence in the clubhouse. Regardless, she appreciated their help now.

As Road Captain, Bear was taking the club on a longer route than usual to give the ladies more time to prepare. Still, there was a lot of work to be done.

Jenna was getting the last of the food on the table they'd set up along the far wall when they heard the roar of the motorcycles returning. Scotty's job was to stall Lucky from coming inside so the brothers, Sissy, and Angel could make it in to help shout "surprise".

Harper's heart swelled as she watched Lucky obediently follow Scotty to Jenna and Steel's house. She didn't know what excuse Scotty had come up with, but Lucky played along like the good dad he was.

Fuck, there went her ovaries again. Either she was getting sick or she was getting baby fever. Regardless, she couldn't seem to stop jumping Lucky any time they found themselves alone. They'd made use of her car, his car, the storage closet in her classroom, the back of his studio, his bedroom at the clubhouse, and even his motorcycle on a secluded road in the middle of the night. She knew it was too soon, but a part of her was contemplating finding an OB-Gyn in the area to remove her IUD.

The brothers, Sissy, and Angel hurried in. Scotty had said his dad would get suspicious if Sissy didn't go on the run with them. No one argued with him.

Bear started passing out more party hats and party blowers. The party's theme, which Harper had learned changed each year, was dinosaurs.

The year before was the 1950's. "To bring back memories of my daddy's childhood," Scotty had explained to her. He'd dressed the club in poodle skirts and suspenders. Jenna had laughed her way through showing Harper the pictures. Some of the brothers had worn poodle skirts and nothing else to get a rise out of Lucky. Though Scotty had been off by a couple of decades, everyone had pitched in and helped him make the party happen.

Harper was pleased to see the same happening this year.

After a little too long of a wait, Harper finally saw Scotty and Lucky headed towards the clubhouse. She also heard thunder, and knew they'd made the right decision to remain indoors.

She quieted everyone down and then waited for their cue.

"SURPRISE!" was shouted as Lucky and Scotty entered. Lucky's mouth gaped open to portray his shock of the situation but his heaving chest betrayed his internal laughter.

Harper came forward to hug him, as did Sissy.

"Well done, Mommy," he whispered in her ear. He'd taken to calling her that in private. He'd discovered the reference to their future kids got her blood pumping.

"It was all Scotty's doing," she said loudly to make sure credit was given appropriately.

Scotty beamed. "You had no idea!"

"None," Lucky assured his son. "You got me again, Scotty."

Someone turned on music—which Harper was pretty sure was the soundtrack to Jurassic Park—and the party got started. A dinosaur shaped cake was cut and served on dinosaur paper plates wishing Lucky a "Roar-ing Good Day". The brothers made it their task to scare Lucky by sneaking up behind him and blowing on their party blower in his ear. Except for the first time, Lucky had seen them all coming and only played along for Scotty's benefit, who burst into a fit of giggles each time his dad "got scared".

The rain started about an hour after the party did. It got dark out too, and the thunder could be heard even louder now. The roof of the former brewery was thankfully not metal so the party itself wasn't interrupted by the storm outside.

Lucky sat or stood with his arm around Harper. She'd try to

leave to make sure there was enough ice or they hadn't run out of food, and he'd pull her back against him. He told her to let someone else handle it, and she melted into his side.

The piñata was dropped down from one of the ceiling rafters. The brothers were good sports, but Harper could tell they purposefully missed so Scotty could get the winning hit. Even Steel had taken a turn swinging at the green cardboard T-Rex.

Lucky had a single beer before switching to water while Harper stuck with Coke. It didn't take her long to catch on that the brothers were limiting themselves to two beers each during the party.

Mrs. Santiago, whom Harper had met a couple of times now, was brought in partway through the party by her younger son Carlos. Bulldog had gone outside to meet his mother with a giant umbrella. Harper loved to see the devotion her sons had to her. She figured part of it was due to the scare they'd all suffered when she'd been diagnosed with cancer. Harper was relieved to hear Mrs. Santiago was in remission.

Harper excused herself to go to the bathroom around four. Not sure if Lucky planned on following her to have a birthday quickie in his clubhouse bedroom, she went there to use that bathroom instead of the one in the front of the clubhouse.

After close to fifteen minutes, and Lucky hadn't joined her, she exited the bedroom. She was not expecting to see party-crashers with guns when she got back to the main room.

* * *

It was only a minute or two after Harper left to use the bathroom when the clubhouse doors came bursting open. At first, Lucky thought it was the wind, but then he saw the Mount Grove police department come filing in like déjà vu.

Immediately the party ceased as once more Sheriff Hannigan raised a warrant into the air.

Lucky was standing towards the back of the main room by the stairs. While Sissy wasn't in his sights, Scotty was. He was across the room by the couch and comfy chairs. Bear was nearest to him, thank God.

Once again, Steel stepped forward to greet the sheriff. All the officers were soaked from the rain. With the doors open behind them, the storm sounded even louder. Lucky saw Scotty jump at the next clap of thunder. Bear moved closer to him. Thankfully none of the officers seemed to have noticed.

"Welcome to our VP's birthday party," Steel told the officers as if they hadn't barged in unannounced. Mind, there was a good possibility they had announced themselves, but the storm had kept those inside from hearing them. "How can we help you today?"

"We have a warrant to search these premises for Madison Mitchell!" the sheriff shouted loud enough so all of them could hear.

"Madison Mitchell has never been on this property," Steel told the sheriff. He kept his voice even. "We have surveillance tapes we'd be happy to show you to prove it."

Hannigan slapped the warrant against Steel's chest. "I have proof that states otherwise."

Oh shit, Lucky thought. Steel once again took out his glasses to read the warrant. Everyone held their breath as he read. Lucky saw each member nonchalantly slide themselves between a woman and the police. Pumpkin and Cage stood shoulder to shoulder in front of Jenna. From what Lucky could see, Harper and Ginger, one of the Honeys, were the only ones not present in the main room. He assumed Ginger was in the kitchen. Since he'd been making his way towards the back of the room to join Harper in his clubhouse bedroom, he wasn't conveniently by anyone.

Movement out of the corner of his eye made him turn his head slowly towards the back corner of the room. Sissy stood there. In front of her, like a sentinel, was Scar. Relief washed over him. If he couldn't have Bear with Sissy, he wanted Scar. His scary brother would never allow any harm to come to Sissy.

Scar caught his eye and bowed his head. A vow.

Lucky nodded his in return.

Steel's voice drew his attention back to the front of the room. "You have an eyewitness who places Madison Mitchell at our clubhouse the night of her disappearance?"

Hannigan grinned smugly. "I do. Something tells me she never made it out of here alive."

"Your eyewitness lied," Steel told him. "Yes, we had a party the night of her disappearance but she was not here. No one under twenty-one would have been allowed entry past the front gate. We are very thorough about that."

"Yeah? And what if one of your *brothers* got a taste for some younger blood? What if he allowed someone younger in for his own pleasure but didn't tell you?"

"Not possible. Our gates are monitored," Steel told him. "Two prospects guard them on party nights. One couldn't have let someone in without the other one knowing. We offered you our tapes when we were first mentioned in correlation with Madison's disappearance. You refused them. Who is your eyewitness?"

Unfortunately, Hannigan never got the chance to answer, though it was unlikely he would have answered anyway. Scotty suddenly cried out, grabbing his hair.

"No, no, no, this is all wrong! All wrong! This is my daddy's birthday party! I worked so hard on it! You're ruining it! You're ruining everything!"

Bear made to grab Scotty, but Scotty started flailing his arms around, similar to a child playing Tornado.

Lucky didn't think. He just reacted. The other officers knew Scotty. They looked towards where he had his tantrum, but they didn't turn their guns towards him.

Hannigan pointed his gun at Scotty.

Lucky rushed forward. Steel placed himself between Hannigan and Scotty. As soon as Hannigan saw Lucky charging across the room, he changed the muzzle of his gun to face Lucky instead.

Shouts came from his brothers, someone female screamed. Over all of it, Scotty could be heard crying, "No, no, no! Wrong, all wrong!"

As soon as it registered that he had a gun pointed at him, Lucky froze. He put his hands in the air. "He's my son," Lucky quickly explained. "He has Down Syndrome. Let me calm him."

"Stay where you are!" Hannigan shouted. "Don't you fucking move."

Every instinct he had told him to get to Scotty. Bear was being unsuccessful in calming him down.

"I need to go to him," Lucky tried again. "He's only going to get more agitated the longer he stays like this."

Aerial's whine could be heard somewhere behind Lucky, meaning even Jumper's dog had picked up on Scotty's agitation.

"And I told you to stay where you are!" Hannigan emphasized his words by raising his gun even higher.

Scotty let out a solid scream, covering his ears. Once again, the officers did nothing but stare on. They seemed conflicted, even Connelly, like they were aware they needed to follow orders but weren't sure those orders were right. Their boss had pointed his gun at a distraught special needs child and was refusing to allow that child's father to comfort him. But, if they disobeyed, Hannigan could have their badges as he'd taken Carlos's.

Lucky moved the moment Hannigan's gun was once more directed at Scotty. Steel was still between them, but that didn't mean Lucky was going to allow this asshole to point a gun at his terrorized son.

But as soon as Lucky reached Scotty, Hannigan ordered, "Cuff him!"

"Wait!" Lucky pleaded. "Let me talk to him."

Someone grabbed Lucky's arms. He knew it would be all the worse if he struggled. Still, he tried to talk to Scotty as his hands were being cuffed behind his back.

"Scotty, look at me. Scotty, please look at me. It's going to be okay, son." But Scotty was too far gone. He wasn't listening even to Lucky's voice. He turned to Hannigan. "Please. Take the cuffs off. Let me talk to him."

"You're under arrest for attacking an officer and resisting arrest."

"I haven't resisted anything!" Lucky shouted, and then winced realizing he wasn't helping Scotty by increasing the tension in the room.

"Sorry, man," he heard the officer behind him mutter. He was pretty sure it was Jeff, who'd graduated high school with Bear and Lucky.

"Hannigan, please–"

"I don't give a fuck about your retarded son. Whichever whore here who spat him out can take care of him."

"Ronald Hannigan, how dare you!"

The entire clubhouse, members and cops alike, froze at that stern voice. Harper came marching across the floor of the main room. Connelly went to intercept her, and she pushed him out of her way.

Meeting Lucky's eyes, she went immediately to Scotty. She nodded to Bear to tell him to release Scotty. He'd been doing a good job of nesting Scotty, but even the comforting hold hadn't been enough to calm him.

"Ruined, ruined…" Scotty was muttering. He was far in his own head now. He was pulling down hard on his hair with his fists. "All ruined. Daddy'll never forgive me…"

Lucky's heart broke. But what could he do in handcuffs with a gun between him and his son?

"Hi, Scotty," Harper said in a low, even voice. "I know everything is upsetting and confusing. I promise everything will be okay, though. You trust me. I'd never lie to you. I want you to start taking some nice deep breaths. In and out... Good. While you're doing that, I'm going to start counting down from one hundred. You can join me whenever you're ready. There's no rush. One hundred, ninety-nine, ninety-eight..."

Harper got all the way to seventy-two in a deadly silent clubhouse before Scotty started counting down with her. She kept it going until they'd reached fifty.

"Very good." She held up her hand, which he high-fived. Progress. "Can we do our ABCs now? Or would you rather a song?"

"Enough of this!" Hannigan shouted behind her. "The boy is obviously fine!"

Harper whirled around on her father. "You arrogant son of a bitch! Do you have any idea the mental damage you could have done by not allowing his father to go to him? You are selfish and power hungry." She pointed at Lucky. "Release him!"

"I don't take orders from you. The only reason you aren't in cuffs next to him is because of me."

She held out her wrists to him as if daring him to cuff her. "On what charges, Sheriff?"

"Obstruction of justice for starters."

"Go ahead," she told him evenly. "Or allow me to do my job and care for this young man who worked so hard on this birthday party that you are ruining!"

"I am looking for a missing teenager!"

"Who isn't here!" Harper shouted back. "I knew Madison. You likely didn't realize that, because your officers never interviewed me about her. She was one of the student aides in my classroom. She was a good student, a good kid. She'd never come to a party if it risked her chances of getting into college!"

"I am not discussing this with you. We have a search warrant–"

"Which is a waste of time! Let Lucky out of those cuffs."

The entire time she'd been going back and forth with her dad, Bear had taken over caring for Scotty. Now that Harper had gotten him out of his head, Bear was able to keep him calm. They were softly singing a song that Lucky couldn't hear. Bear was rubbing his hands up and down Scotty's back.

Lucky felt so helpless. Bear was taking care of his son and Harper was battling with her father while he stood there handcuffed.

Hannigan looked at her like she was a child not understanding bedtime. "He's under arrest, Harper. There's nothing I can do."

"Bullshit. You're just on some power play and Lucky's your target because I'm dating him. He was trying to get to his son. He was of no threat to you and you know it."

"I don't know it," Hannigan insisted. "I told him to freeze and he didn't. That's a Class 1 misdemeanor, as you well know."

Harper's face darkened. "I'll never forgive you for this. If you take him away, you and I are done. I'll never speak to you again."

Fuck. This had all gotten so out of hand.

Hannigan was silent at Harper's ultimatum, and Lucky actually thought he might be released for a second. But then Hannigan shrugged, like he had daughters to spare. "You do what you feel you have to. Just know this rebellious attitude you've adopted since moving here is breaking your mother's heart."

Harper winced but held her ground. "Whatever you say, Sheriff."

Hannigan turned to Connelly. "Search the grounds. Once you've done that, do it again. I want to bring closure to the family as soon as possible."

Connelly nodded, taking two officers with him.

Hannigan looked at the officer who'd arrested Lucky. "Take him to the station. I'll be along shortly."

Harper stepped forward as the hands on Lucky's cuffs tightened as if to pull him towards the door. She wrapped her arms around his neck. Since he couldn't hug her back, Lucky dropped his head to her shoulder.

"I'll be okay," he told her. "Take care of Scotty for me please."

Harper gripped him tighter. "I'm so sorry. He's doing this because of me."

"Not your fault." He kissed the side of her head. "Never your fault."

"Harper!" Hannigan shouted from behind her.

They both ignored him. Harper lowered herself down to her flat feet. She gripped his shirt under his cut. "I love you," she told him for the first time.

He smiled wickedly. "I know."

She rolled her eyes. "God, I hate that movie."

He was still smiling. "I know that too." He bent down and took her lips in front of everyone. "See you soon."

* * *

HARPER FELT like crying as two officers led Lucky out of the clubhouse, hands cuffed behind his back like a criminal. She needed her purse, but she didn't have her car. Lucky had brought her here on his motorcycle. She fiercely wiped her eyes, refusing to fall apart. "Can someone give me a ride to the station?"

"Bulldog and I will follow Lucky to the station," Steel stepped in. "Take Scotty home. He doesn't need to be here right now."

She shook her head. "No, I need to be with him–"

"Be with Scotty," Steel said more sternly. "We'll get Lucky. These are bogus charges and Hannigan knows it."

They were both talking as if Hannigan wasn't still there and in earshot. It occurred to her that her father wasn't forcing the members and party goers to kneel with their fingers laced behind their heads during this search warrant. In fact, all the officers had put their weapons away, including her father.

Had it been their goal to arrest one member, regardless of the charges, and Lucky just happened to unluckily draw the short straw?

Sissy approached then. "I need to take Scotty home."

Harper noticed one of the members, Scar, was shadowing her. To be honest, he freaked her out. Mainly because of how silent he was. She wasn't sure if she'd ever heard him speak. When Lucky had introduced her to him, he'd just nodded.

Maybe he *couldn't* speak. But Lucky would have mentioned if he had a mute brother, wouldn't he? If she tried sign language with him, would he understand and/or reply?

"Bear is taking you, Harper, and Scotty home," Steel told her with authority. He turned to Scar. "Go with them." As Sissy moved to be closer to Scotty, Harper heard Steel's voice drop lower. "And Scar? You do whatever you have to do to protect them. By any means necessary."

Scar nodded once. A chill ran through Harper. Though she was one of the ones he'd be protecting, there was a menacing air about Scar that told her to be weary of him. A part of her brain shouted *danger!* when he was near.

Scotty curled up between Sissy and Harper in the back seat of the SUV Bear pulled around. She didn't know whose car it was, since Bear had driven his motorcycle to the club run. That morning seemed so far away now. How could a surprise party go so wrong?

She was furious with her father. To arrest Lucky like that? To suspect the *Via Daemonia* had anything to do with Madison's disappearance? Why was he so fixated on them? It was like he'd decided they were guilty before ever looking at the evidence. Was it because they rode motorcycles? Harper didn't think so. There was more to this, there had to be.

Harper pulled out her phone and sent a text to her mom.

Harper: Dad arrested Lucky today on a bogus charge. Lucky was trying to protect his son and Dad had him arrested. I am no longer speaking to him and am blocking his number. If you choose to reach out to me, do so carefully. I can just as easily block yours.

Her message was harsh, but she hoped it shocked her mother out of whatever was going on. She'd never seen her father so crazed, almost fanatic in his attitude towards the club. Something was going on that went beyond her father's zealousness to bring down the VDMC. She was sure of it.

It wasn't until they pulled into the driveway of Lucky's house that Harper realized Scar wasn't in the car with them. "Where's Scar?"

Bear shrugged. "Wherever Scar feels he needs to be."

Harper went to get out, only to realize that Scotty had fallen asleep between her and Sissy. Bear opened Sissy's door. "Scooch on out of there, Sis. I'll get him. Harper, can you get the door please?"

She hurried out to aid him.

Her eyes landed on the clock in the foyer. How was it only four-forty-five? Had it really only been forty-five minutes since she'd used the excuse of having to go to the bathroom in the hopes of having a birthday quickie with Lucky in his bedroom?

She felt exhausted, like it was past midnight type of exhausted. She envied Scotty for being able to sleep like that. Suddenly she had a terrible thought: could the courts take Scotty away from Lucky if he was charged?

"What is it?" Sissy asked, closing the door. Bear was already taking Scotty up the stairs to his bedroom.

"Your dad is Scotty's adopted father, right? He's not still a guardian?"

Sissy nodded. "Dad adopted both of us officially when I was twelve. Why?"

"If the charges stick, the courts could take away guardianship. It's harder to take away a child that's adopted without some other factor like abuse."

"Even if for some fucked up reason a county DA does decide to follow through on those ridiculous charges, Scotty can't be taken away from him. And if somehow pigs started flying and Hell froze over and the courts decided to take Scotty away, Uncle Bear would become his next legal guardian. Dad sorted it out a long time ago that Uncle Bear would take us if something happened."

Harper let out a sigh of relief. "Good. Good, that's really good."

"Come sit, Harper. You look ready to pass out."

"I feel like it too."

They went into the kitchen. Harper wasn't thirsty but Sissy started making coffee.

"How come Scotty wouldn't go to you if something happened to Lucky?" Harper knew it was a personal question, but she was curious.

"When I was about to turn eighteen, Dad and Uncle Bear sat me down to discuss it. Dad said he'd prefer to leave guardianship to Uncle Bear so I could focus on my studies. Uncle Bear said he didn't mind, so we kept it as is." She poured them both a cup of coffee. "It wouldn't have mattered whether legally it was Uncle Bear or me, though. I still would have been here."

"I think you're amazing with your brother. And to give up your weekends to be with him? Between you and Lucky, I'm not sure which is more selfless." She accepted the coffee Sissy handed her with a murmured, "Thanks."

"My dad, without a doubt. Don't get me wrong, the man has definitely gotten on my nerves over the years. I think one time when I was sixteen, I actually shouted at him that he wasn't my father, and he had no say over my life." She flinched. "I wasn't exactly an easy teenager."

"I don't think any of us were."

"Did Lucky tell you about the first couple of years he had Scotty and me?" Harper shook her head. Lucky hadn't said much about then. She knew the basics, like he'd gotten Sissy when she was five and Scotty when he'd been four months old and his business hadn't been successful enough for him to buy his house until Sissy was fourteen. "We didn't have much in the beginning. Dad was working a full-time and a part-time job to make ends meet, and some months they didn't meet. He didn't think I knew, but I saw. There were days when he didn't eat to make sure there was enough for Scotty and me. I tried to lessen what I ate but Dad wouldn't have it. I claimed I wasn't hungry at some meals, even though I was. When Uncle Bear came to visit between deployments, he saw how little we had. He pitched in what he could too. That was when Aunt Jenna started coming around more too. Dad did the best he could, but raising two children on his own, and one with Downs…?" Her voice trailed off. "He may have left the service, but he never stopped being a hero. My hero."

Harper had to wipe the tears building in her eyes. "I wish I had been there for you guys."

Sissy let out a laugh. "You would have just been another kid he would have had to raise."

Harper winced. "Fair point. Still, I hate that you had such hardships."

"Our birth mom didn't give us much choice. Dad could have left us to the system. He refused. I still remember the day we stood before a family judge and Dad pleaded to get guardianship of Scotty. I was young, but I've overheard Uncle Bear and Dad over the years. I think it was a close call. I don't think the judge wanted to give Dad Scotty."

"Don't they try to keep family members within the family?"

"Normally, yes. But Scotty was a special case, and I don't think the judge thought Dad would rise to the challenge."

"Looks like he did from where I'm sitting."

"That and more," Sissy told her. "Did you know I'm not paying a dime for college? He wouldn't let me. Didn't want me to graduate with student loans hanging over my head. I applied for every scholarship I could get with Uncle Demo's help, but he's paying the rest."

Wow. Harper had been paying off her student loans since she'd graduated four years ago. "I'm not after your dad for his money. We actually haven't had that conversation yet. I don't know what he has or doesn't have…"

Sissy sent her a wry smile. "Never thought you were. Just wanted to make sure you knew how good a man you got. That man is devoted to you, Harper. Entirely. Like with Scotty and me, he'll do anything and everything he can to provide for you and protect you."

Harper felt tears start to gather in her eyes again. "I'd do the same for him. For any of you."

Sissy nodded. "Good. I'd hate to have to sic Scar on you."

Harper turned towards Sissy. She briefly recalled seeing Scar and Sissy together during the party. Not together, like holding hands, but near each other. Then, when the police came through, it was Scar who'd stood in front of Sissy, guarding her like a warrior of old.

"Can I ask you something personal?"

Sissy shrugged. "Sure. You're probably going to be my step-mother soon, so there won't be many secrets my dad won't have shared with you after that."

Harper snorted. "Don't worry, Cinderella. Good stepmother, remember?" Sissy smiled and then gestured for her to continue. "Is there something between you and Scar? I saw the way he was with you at the clubhouse."

Sissy shook her head. "Naw, Scar's just a friend."

Harper had a hard time seeing Scar having a friendly personality. "Does he talk to you?"

Sissy nearly choked on her coffee. "I've never heard him utter a word in the five years that I've known him. But Scar's a good listener, and he does this thing with his eyebrow that somehow gets his point across." She shrugged. "Sometimes I get the sense that he's lonely while other times he needs his space. It's hard to explain, but he's my friend."

Harper studied her face. A part of her believed Sissy when she claimed Scar was just a friend. But there was another part of her that thought perhaps Sissy was in denial about her feelings. Unlike Bear, she hadn't referred to Scar as "uncle". She didn't know how old Scar was but mid-thirties was likely accurate. Still, she certainly wasn't in a position to lecture Sissy on dating an older man.

Harper resolved to keep an eye on the situation. Maybe Sissy was right, and they were just friends. She had no idea how a relationship would work with a man like him though. Communication was a two-way street.

She looked around, realizing that Bear never came back downstairs. "Where's Bear?"

"Probably still up with Scotty. The last time he had a meltdown like this, Dad had to sleep in his room with him for a week. Uncle Bear will watch out for him."

Harper laid her head down on the table. "I feel like I want to sleep, but I also know that I won't be able to until Lucky is home."

"Try to get some rest. I'm sure Uncle Steel and Uncle Bulldog will have Dad out in a jiffy."

Harper could only pray Sissy was right. Still, she knew sleep wouldn't come again until she had Lucky's arms back around her.

* * *

LUCKY HAD NEVER BEEN in jail before. At first, he was grateful no one else was in the cell with him, but then boredom set in a few hours later. His phone, wallet, shoelaces, and cut had been taken from him upon entering the station. He'd been fingerprinted and placed in a cell. He got that jail wasn't supposed to be fun, but he thought the least they could do was put a TV in the corner. Just something to break the silence.

His mind whirled. He knew Harper, Sissy, and Scotty were safe with his brothers. He never doubted they'd be cared for. But damn, he wished he was the one who was there to do it.

His bed was a metal slab that was barely wide enough to fit him. Half of Lucky's legs and boots hung off the end. He wondered how many children they arrested that the metal slabs were sized so small.

Susan Brown, the club's lawyer, had stopped by earlier to tell him she'd contacted a defense attorney colleague of hers. Since it was a Sunday and the courthouse wasn't open until Monday morning regardless, Lucky wasn't going anywhere anytime soon. So there was nothing for him to do but wait.

He was trying with all his might not to stew as he did. Anger towards Hannigan would solve nothing and help no one. But damn, he wished he could get a freebie punch at the guy. The way he'd spoken to Harper, his own daughter... Fuck. It had probably been a good thing he'd been in cuffs, or he would have been anyway. The charges wouldn't have been bogus then, though.

Lucky didn't know how serious Harper was about her threat to never speak to her dad again. A part of him was grateful, having seen the aftereffects of her meals with her parents, but another part–the part of him that was a father himself–couldn't imagine the pain of never speaking to his daughter again. Did Hannigan really deserve that? Clearly, Hannigan thought Harper had been bluffing but, if so, he didn't know his daughter very well.

Despite being completely uncomfortable and dreading the back pain he knew he was going to be facing in the morning, Lucky must have dozed off to sleep. He wasn't sure at first what had woken him up. It was an echo of voices. A florescent light hummed outside his cell, but he couldn't see any people.

"…you sure?" Though the voice was distorted, Lucky felt like he knew it. He kept very still so not to make any sounds that would keep him from hearing or them from talking.

"Positive. I got the call an hour ago. The shipment will be here tomorrow night. This will be our biggest shipment yet. Boss says we need to make sure the transaction goes smoothly."

"Who's going?" Lucky was pretty sure that voice belonged to Mark Connelly.

"Just you and me. We're just there to oversee the money exchange and verify the product. That's it."

Product? Shipment? Were they talking about drugs? What the fuck?

"Pick me up here at ten tomorrow night. We've got a bit of a drive to Ohiopyle, but we should make it there with plenty of time." That was the unknown voice again.

Ohiopyle was a state park south of Mount Grove. It was a good two hour drive.

"And the boss okayed this?"

Lucky still couldn't place the first voice. He assumed it was another deputy because of the time of night and referring to Hannigan, he assumed, as the 'boss'. "Get an extra fifteen-large each if this thing goes off without a hitch."

"Shit."

Shit is right, Lucky thought. Something big was going to go down tomorrow night.

There was the creak of something. Lucky thought perhaps it was a door opening. The voices stopped. Still unsure where the two had been standing, he couldn't even tell if they were still there. Since the voices never picked back up, he figured they'd moved their conversation elsewhere.

Fuck, he thought. Hannigan was dealing drugs and Connelly was in on it.

* * *

LUCKY WAS IMPRESSED he was walking out of the sheriff's station a free man by eight-thirty the following morning. The defense attorney Susan had sent over wasn't a man as they'd all expected. Toni (with an 'i', not a 'y') Nielsen was definitely not someone Lucky would want to face on the opposite side of a courtroom.

She'd gotten the county DA to drop all charges after watching the surveillance video of Hannigan's behavior while executing his search warrant and was even filing harassment charges against Hannigan from both the club and Lucky individually. All before nine a.m. Lucky felt like a slacker in comparison.

As soon as he'd gotten his phone back, he sent messages to Harper and Sissy to let them know he was free. Bulldog and Steel were waiting for him in one of the club's SUVs since he had neither his cage nor his sled with him.

"Executive meeting," he told them in lieu of a greeting. "Now."

His phone dinged. He was almost out of battery.

Harper: I am so glad to hear it! I'm at work with Scotty. Almost called a sick day in for both of us but Scotty told me you said sick days are only for when you're really sick and we were both just tired, not sick. So thanks a lot for that. Are you headed home to get some sleep?

What he needed more than sleep was for Harper to give him a massage while naked. His back was killing him.

Lucky: On my way to the clubhouse to get my sled. Need to talk to Steel about some club business. Hopefully I'll be home soon and can pass out.

Lucky: Thank you for taking care of Scotty. Steel told me you wanted to follow me to the station.

Harper: It was Bear who took care of him, really. Sissy and I kept each other company because neither of us could sleep. Got some dirt on you now.

Lucky: I love my daughter but whatever she claims I did or didn't do or said or didn't say is a complete and utter lie.

Harper: 😊

Harper: I need to go. I'm so happy the charges were dropped. I love you.

Fuck, he loved seeing those words. Had loved hearing them from her lips even more.

Lucky: Love you too. Missed you so much last night. Never want to spend another night without you.

Harper: Ditto

Lucky put his phone away as they pulled onto the clubhouse drive. Steel, Bulldog, and Lucky got out. Since no other hogs were parked outside but theirs, he knew none of the other officers had arrived yet.

"I need a shower," he told Steel. "Can one of you plug my phone in please? It's about to die."

Bulldog reached for it. "Go. We won't start without you."

Lucky was starving but wanted a shower more than food. While he was sure the Mount Grove Police Department's top priority was to keep the jail cells sanitized, he still felt gross. The hot shower felt so amazing that Lucky nearly fell asleep against the wall under the spray.

Though Lucky had never spent the night in his bedroom at the clubhouse, he did keep a few extra clothes there for himself and Scotty. Sissy had proclaimed years ago that if there was even a hint of rain in the forecast, she wasn't getting on a motorcycle. Scotty, on the other hand, claimed only real men still ride in the rain. Beyond the need to change due to getting caught in a rainstorm while on his hog, Scotty also wasn't the neatest person around. Many a brother's shirt had fallen victim to orange juice, jelly, or soda. Scotty sometimes got animated when telling a story and would forget he had a cup in his hand. So spare clothing had come in handy at the clubhouse.

For some odd and inexplicable reason, it had never occurred to Lucky that he might need a change of clothes after spending the night in jail.

Walking down the hall, he could hear his brothers gathering upstairs. Sounded like most of them. Lucky looked longingly at the kitchen, let out a sigh, and then climbed the stairs.

A plate of bacon, eggs, and a buttered roll with jelly waited for him at his seat. His stomach growled its appreciation.

"Jenna?" he asked Steel as he sat down.

His president nodded. "She brought it over just after you went to your room."

Lucky stuffed a forkful of eggs into his mouth and groaned. The woman even made eggs phenomenally. "Thank her for me. I was starving."

"She figured."

The other officers took their seats. Scar walked into the room and closed the door.

Steel whacked the gavel on the table. "Lucky called this meeting. Let's hear what he has to say before we get into what happened yesterday."

"I'm going to eat and talk," he informed them unapologetically. "Last night I overheard a conversation between Connelly and who I believe is another officer. I couldn't see them and their voices were slightly distorted. I think they were in another room and their voices were being echoed through a vent. It's the only thing that makes sense since I was in a jail cell with no one else around.

"From what I can gather, Connelly and this other officer are meeting at the station at ten tonight to drive to Ohiopyle. There, they are to oversee the 'transfer of funds' and 'verify the product'."

"Sounds like a drug deal," Bulldog said. His face showed he was not happy at what he was hearing. "Since when does Connelly deal drugs?"

"I doubt he's dealing. I think he's just the muscle." Lucky started on his roll. "The other officer, the one I didn't recognize by his voice, he mentioned 'the boss'. Based on other events, plus Harper's insistence that her father isn't acting like himself, how far-fetched is it of me to assume that our new sheriff is the ringleader?"

They all exchanged unsettling looks.

Jumper, who generally only spoke up when he needed to, leaned forward. "After Lucky's arrest yesterday, I had Keys look into the sheriff again. This time beyond a standard background check. The Hannigans are broke. His salary as sheriff is barely covering the mortgage of that house they bought. Keys says that it's recent too. Before six months ago, they had a hefty savings account due to an inheritance that was left to them by Hannigan's in-laws."

"Wouldn't a drug kingpin be loaded?" Demo asked skeptically. "If he's the boss Connelly was referring to, wouldn't he have too much money?"

"None of us are familiar with drug dealing," Steel stated, preventing others from saying their piece. "We don't know how it works outside of the obvious. Maybe he can't access those funds for some reason. It's a cash business, so he'd have to launder it somehow. Make it legit. Maybe he hasn't found a way to do that in Mount Grove yet."

Bulldog tapped his knuckles on the table. "I think we should bring Carlos in on this conversation."

"He's not a club member," Steel argued.

"No, but he is a cop—even if he's a suspended cop. He'd know better than us how criminals work. Plus, if Hannigan is the boss, it would give Carlos an explanation as to why he was suspended."

"What do you mean?" Bear asked. "Carlos was the only deputy suspended. If, I'm assuming you're assuming, Hannigan was getting rid of all honest cops on the force so he could turn all his other officers into drug dealers, why just fire Carlos?"

"Don't you get it?" Bulldog said vehemently. "From the moment Hannigan took office, he's been coming after us. It's been a vendetta we couldn't figure out. What if it has nothing to do with us? What if it's all because, as a motorcycle club, we're an easy scapegoat?"

"You mean, he didn't count on us being ninety-nine-percenters?" Lucky clarified.

Bulldog shrugged. "Unless we get a confession, it's all speculation. But yeah, it makes the most sense. Blame all the bad he's planning on doing on the 'one-percenters' already set up in town. I think he assumed we *were* paying off Longhill and Carlos. When he couldn't find the evidence of it, he stated it was true anyway. Creating doubt."

"Who would believe the good and honest sheriff against a motorcycle club?" Steel added with venom in his voice. He slammed his fist down on the table. "That asshole is coming after what *I built* so he can sell drugs in my town!"

"It's a theory," Lucky reminded him. They weren't going to get anything done, or decided, if Steel lost his temper.

Steel let out a low growl before turning to Bulldog. His voice was only slightly calmer. "Call Carlos. Get him in here. What happens next affects him as much as us." He looked around the table. "Any objections?"

No one stated any.

Bulldog stood and left the room, pulling his phone out of his pocket as he went.

"Scar." Heads turned to the silent enforcer at the end of the table. The man didn't look at Steel, but body language said he was listening. "You're on Connelly. Do what you do. I don't care how. We need to know where this drug buy is taking place and as many details as possible before we can make too many decisions."

"Wait," Lucky stepped in. "What decisions are we making? We suspect our local law enforcement of dealing drugs or buying drugs… Regardless, who are we supposed to tell? The *cops*? Who do you go to when your cops are dirty?"

"Carlos can help us with that too," Bulldog said as he walked back into the room. He looked to Steel. "He's on his way. Says he's around the corner."

Steel nodded. "Lucky has a point though. How involved do we want to be? Until now, we've kept our hands clean."

"Except for that disposal we did for Longhill three years ago," Bear added, as if reminding them of that task.

Three years ago, a different drug dealer was trying to claim southern Pennsylvania and Amish country as his own. When the local law enforcement officers had destroyed his operation, he'd gone into hiding. Turned out his hiding place was Mount Grove. After a high schooler had been found dead with that lowlife's poison shot up his arm, Longhill had lost it. The high schooler had been his nephew. He'd hunted the dealer down and shot him.

Steel, sympathetic to the man's plight and not wanting to see a good man and cop going to jail for a drug-dealing thug, told Longhill to leave and create an alibi. Then the VDMC, much smaller at the time but growing in members, took the body. They burned the rundown shack the man had been living in to the ground. Bulldog and Scar left with the body. Only they knew what they'd done with it.

After a tense month where the *Via Daemonia* and Longhill waited anxiously to see if any other law enforcement came looking for the dealer, they eventually put it behind them. No one had come. No one knew.

It was the only time the VDMC had broken the law. The newer members didn't even know about it.

Even if Hannigan somehow figured out the drug dealer had been hiding in Mount Grove three years ago, there was nothing to trace to either the VDMC or Longhill because there'd been no investigation. Nothing was buried. It was as if that night never happened.

Everyone was silent for a time, remembering.

Eventually, Steel spoke up. "Scar, unless you have an objection, I'm transferring your vote to Bear. I need you on Connelly."

Scar stood and walked to the door. Apparently, he didn't have any objections. Surprisingly though, he left the door open.

The reason why strolled through a moment later. Carlos, in jeans and a t-shirt, closed the door behind him. He looked around the room. "Wow. So this is your Fortress of Solitude. Nice."

Steel pointed to the seat Scar had just vacated. "What is said in here, stays in here, Santiago. I don't have to tell you twice."

Carlos walked around the table and sat. "Nope. Trust me, if this has to do with whatever Hannigan is up to, I want in and damn the consequences."

"Tell us what you know," Steel prodded before they shared their new information. "You told Bulldog weeks ago that Hannigan was asking about us."

Carlos nodded. "Very first day. As soon as he walked in, he wanted to know anything and everything about you guys. Guess it was my own stupidity but as soon as I mentioned my brother was in the club, I turned into the station leper. Danny warned me that Hannigan had asked him to dig into my financials. I knew it was coming, but it was still a shock when he suspended me. Never thought he'd actually find something to warrant it. The Thursday before the Saturday he raided here looking for narcotics, he took my badge and gun."

Lucky turned to Steel. "Maybe our new hotshot attorney can look into Carlos's case too."

Steel nodded. "I've got his card in my office."

"Her," Lucky corrected. "Toni with an 'i', not a 'y'."

Steel looked intrigued. "Interesting."

Lucky looked down the table. "Susan sent a friend to get my charges dropped. She's a defense attorney. I don't have her information, but Steel does. Give her a call and see if she has any opinions on how to get your job back that Susan didn't."

"Thanks!" Carlos said excitedly. "I'm going to have to start looking for other employment soon. Never thought the suspension would hold this long."

"We think we know why Hannigan turned his sights on you." Bulldog looked to Steel, who nodded he could continue. "Lucky overheard a conversation last night that makes us suspect Hannigan is dealing drugs."

Carlos's jaw dropped. "What? No way. That guy's a straight shooter."

"We don't know for sure," Lucky added. "Connelly is definitely involved and at least one other officer that I couldn't identify. They referred to 'the boss'. I think that's Hannigan."

Again, Carlos shook his head. "Hannigan would never be involved in a drug deal. I don't know the man all that well, but he bleeds blue. He'd never betray the badge like that."

Demo spoke up. "Lucky says Harper has been saying her parents have been acting different since they moved to Mount Grove. Last night, Keys dug deeper into Hannigan's life. He and his wife are broke. What if he didn't have a choice but to turn to crime to make ends meet?"

"No. There are other ways to pay the bills," Carlos insisted.

"The man is too much of a cop to turn to drugs. That's far too extreme over some money problems."

"Regardless," Bear cut in, "of whether Hannigan is the boss or not, Connelly is clearly involved in a drug deal. We can only suspect he's escorting the product back to Mount Grove for it to be distributed. He could be taking it anywhere."

Carlos looked down the table at Lucky. "Tell me exactly what you overheard. Don't leave anything out."

Lucky did to the best of his recollection.

"Connelly's a slimeball. He's always trying for the next big score that will make him rich beyond all measure." Carlos made a disgusted face. "Longhill and I were trying to figure out how to get rid of him when Longhill had his stroke. We hated hiring him, but he was Boone's nephew. Can't exactly tell the mayor 'no because your nephew is a lazy git'. We stuck him on speed traps to get him out of the way."

"Any idea who the other officer is who would be helping him?" Bulldog asked his brother.

Carlos shook his head. "They're good guys. Bert and Jeff have been there longer than I have. Carl has an attitude that's gotten him into trouble more than once, but he's not a criminal. Scott and Danny are young, still growing into the badge. To be honest, Mark's the only one that fits the bill. If he recruited someone else from the force, I have no clue who it is."

"Also might not be a cop," Steel interjected. "Lucky said it himself, he didn't see them. It was late. Not many others around. Connelly could have called someone to the station to talk to him there."

"Can we have Keys look into it?" Bear asked. "See if he can hack into their security cameras or look to see who was on duty last night with Connelly."

"Danny was the one who brought me my dinner," Lucky said. "He was real apologetic. Whispered to me that he was sorry he had any part in upsetting Scotty."

"Shifts would have changed at twenty-two hundred. Someone would have taken Danny's place. There are two cops on night duty. All operators go home then too. One cop stays at the station, other one handles calls. If a call came in, Connelly might have stayed behind to meet with his accomplice while the other cop was out."

Steel turned to Bulldog. "Text Keys. Hell, the bastard might already be on it. I'm half-convinced he has this room bugged so he can seem like he's all-knowing when we ask him for help."

Though Steel was joking, Lucky wouldn't put it past Keys to eavesdrop if he thought he needed to. The man was former Navy Intelligence after all. That was as close to being a spy as one could get without joining the CIA.

As Bulldog pulled out his phone to text Keys, he also said, "We still need to decide how involved we want to get."

Steel turned back to Carlos. "If you had indisputable proof Hannigan was dirty, who would you give it to?"

"It'd be a bit extreme, but I have contacts at the Pittsburg Bureau office. I'd want the investigation handled properly. DOJ would rather we handle it internally. If I had my badge, technically I could arrest him like anyone else. The problem is that he can just as easily take that badge if he still technically has the authority as sheriff. So anyone on our force we ask to assist us would be risking their job. If we got the council or mayor on our side, they could suspend him and take away that power. But they'd be wanting to cover their asses as much as possible and may want to sweep the entire thing under the rug."

"What if Hannigan's crimes aren't federal? Could the FBI still arrest him?"

"It's still drugs," Carlos said to his brother. "Distribution, manufacturing, intent to sell… Those are all federal crimes."

"But we don't have any evidence," Bear pointed out. "Right now, we *suspect* that Connelly is going to oversee a drug deal tonight with at least one other guy that we *suspect* is another cop.

We *suspect* that they're doing this under Hannigan's orders. So, the question is how do we turn those suspicions into evidence we can turn over to the feds?"

"We run it like any other investigation," Carlos said. Realizing what he'd just said, he turned to Steel, "That'd be my suggestion."

"How would you do it?" Steel asked him, not seeming to mind that Carlos had spoken as if he was in charge.

"It'll take a lot of time. We need pictures, written accounts verified by at least two eyewitnesses, video and audio recordings… It's not something that will happen overnight."

"But the buy is tonight," Lucky reminded him.

"Then we go, we watch, and we take account of everything that's said and done. Taking down Connelly is small game. You guys know this, you've dealt with it overseas, I'm sure. Taking out the little guys doesn't stop what's happening. You want the big fish. Hannigan might be that fish, he might not be. Connelly might be able to lead us to him, he might not. All we can do is sit and wait for someone to mess up. Nabbing the little fish only works if he's got evidence against the big fish."

"Tell Scar to start taking pictures of anything suspicious," Steel told Bulldog. "I don't know how close he is to Connelly. If he can get anything on video, even better. But make sure he knows not to put himself in danger to get that evidence."

"I'll tell him."

Steel looked around the table. "I won't see my town flooded with drugs. Drugs lead to arms dealing and worse. I won't have that. If we do this, we follow Carlos's lead. We do it by the book. If the cops can't or won't stop this, then we will." He turned to Lucky. "Send out a message to the others. Church tonight. By then, we'll have a plan to present to them."

"What if they have objections?" Bear asked. "What we're asking of them could get dangerous."

"Volunteers only to start," Steel said, "but I doubt we'll have objections. None of our people are going to want drugs flooding our streets. We dealt with it overseas. We aren't going to deal with that bullshit here." Steel turned to Demo. "Verify everyone's firearms licenses. We do this, we are protecting ourselves. But no one carries illegally."

Demo made a quick note in his notebook. "Done."

"Carlos, can you step out for a moment while we take our vote?"

The man nodded and rose. He walked out of Church, closing the door behind his back.

"Before we vote, one more thing." Steel met each man's eyes before he continued, "We do what we have to, to protect this town, our families, and our people. Even if our hands get bloody while doing it."

Each man nodded his agreement.

CHAPTER 11

*H*arper was waiting impatiently for the school bell to ring. Lucky had messaged around noon that he was heading home to nap. She didn't know what 'club business' took him three hours to settle with Steel, but she was glad he was finally heading home.

To say Harper was pissed was an understatement. She couldn't believe her father. Were body snatchers a thing still? Maybe aliens had taken her parents' places. Harper had even contemplated that her parents were using drugs, but nixed that thought right away. Her father had been fighting against drugs and the people who used and/or sold them for the better part of his career. He'd never use them himself or allow his wife to.

Something else was going on, she was sure of it. Harper had no idea what, though. The *Via Daemonia* only had her word to go off of that her father was acting out of character. He'd always been strict, but a rule follower. She'd never known him to be blind to the facts before him. In fact, her father had received an accommodation for realizing that a convicted murderer was actually innocent and had worked tirelessly to get the conviction overturned and the real murderer behind bars.

Harper wondered if her father was being blackmailed, making him act out of character. Except, blackmailed for what? Her dad was clean cut. He'd never do anything that could come back to haunt him. How did someone blackmail someone so clean? So she threw that theory out the window.

Something had to have happened during the five weeks between when she'd moved to Mount Grove and her parents had moved to Mount Grove that had changed them. Something that was forcing her father to act this way. She needed to ask her brother Richard if he knew something or had noticed anything suspicious.

When the school bell finally rang, Harper left Scotty in her classroom to escort the other students to their assigned buses. Once she saw them off, she hurried back to finish cleaning up her classroom. Scotty helped (somewhat). Then she rushed them out to her car and drove them to Lucky's house.

She let out a sigh of relief when she saw Lucky's bike was parked in the open garage next to his rarely used car. She parked behind them.

Scotty, seeing his dad's bike too, was out of the car before she'd even turned it off. Thankfully, she'd already been in park. If she was going to keep transporting Scotty, she needed to remember to put on the child locks on the rear doors.

Surprised Lucky wasn't waiting for them in the foyer, Harper followed Scotty's voice up the stairs. She went into the master bedroom to find Lucky under the covers with Scotty laying on top of him. It looked like he'd been asleep. Despite her guilt for having woken him, Harper slipped off her shoes and joined them on the bed.

She laid down on her side of the bed on top of the covers and turned onto her side to face Lucky.

Pinned by an overexcited teenager, Lucky could only turn his face towards her on his pillow. He smiled at her. "Hey."

She smiled back. "Hey."

Scotty was babbling non-stop, telling his dad everything from the time the cops took him away until that very moment. Lucky turned his attention back to his son, but reached a hand across the bed to take hold of hers.

She squeezed it tightly.

"What happened to you when the mean cop took you away?" Scotty asked his dad. "I told Susie in the lunchroom you'd been arrested last night and she didn't believe me. I didn't have any pictures to show her. Maybe I can ask Uncle Keys for the video."

"Please don't," Lucky told his son. "Yes, I was arrested, but I was released and the charges were dropped. It's like it never happened."

Scotty's face scrunched. "So, like pretend?"

"Exactly. As for what happened to me, nothing really. I had a very boring night."

"Uncle Bear slept in my room!"

"You said. I hope you offered him a blanket. We know how much of a cover hog you can be."

Scotty laughed. "They're my covers!"

Harper found herself smiling. The bond between Lucky and Scotty was something special to witness.

"Did you listen to Harper at school today?"

"*Ms. Hannigan*, Daddy," Scotty said while rolling his eyes.

Lucky snorted. "Sorry. Did you listen to *Ms. Hannigan* at school today?"

Scotty turned towards her and winked. God, she loved that wink. "Yes, I did," he announced proudly.

"Good boy." Lucky nudged Scotty. "Hey, bud, can you give me and Harper a couple of minutes? Can you go read a book in your room?"

Scotty leaned down and kissed his dad's nose. Lucky practically beamed at the action. "Sure! Can I get a snack too?"

"There's some carrots cut up in the fridge," Harper told him. "You can have those or some blueberries."

Scotty nodded enthusiastically. "Thanks, Harper!" He wiggled and scooted off of Lucky. When he finally got his balance, he walked around the bed until he reached her side. "Come here," he waved her over to him.

Harper sat up and got herself to the side of the bed. Scotty leaned in and kissed her nose too.

Harper felt tears in her eyes as she smiled at the sweet boy. "Call me if you need help in the kitchen. Please don't try to do it yourself if you can't."

Scotty nodded. "Okay!" Then he hurried out of the room.

Harper turned on the bed to see Lucky laying on his side facing her. She found herself blushing at the adoration on his face. He pulled her close to him. "I can't wait until we have more kids. You are a wonderful mother."

His use of the present tense made her heart swell.

She reached up and touched his face. "And you're a wonderful father."

"The kid left the door open." Despite his words, Lucky still laid himself over her. Their lips met with intensity.

"Need to be quick," Harper told him.

Lucky leapt up, closed and locked the door. He stripped down as she quickly got herself out of her work clothes.

She reached for him as he neared the bed. "No foreplay. Just fuck me. I need you so badly, Lucky."

Still, as he moved on top of her, he touched his hand down between her legs. She knew he was checking to see if she was wet enough to take him. In desperation, Harper pushed Lucky onto his back. She crawled on top of him.

Though his eyes warned her to be careful, his hands helped her balance. She eased herself up. Harper gripped the base of his penis, rubbing the head along her slit to wet it. Then she sank down.

They both groaned.

Lucky kept tight hold of her hips as she lowered herself

slowly. "You are beautiful, Harper. Fuck, and all mine. How did I get so lucky?"

She grinned down at him. "I believe it started with a sniper in Afghanistan."

"Fuck," he groaned. "Less talking, more fucking."

She leaned forward. "My thoughts exactly."

Harper moved, undulating her hips. She'd only been on top once before, and that had been slow lovemaking. There was a feeling of control when she rode him that was intoxicating. As much as Harper loved the various ways he took her, she had a feeling this position would become one of her favorites.

Lucky's fingers dug into her skin. She knew he'd leave marks, and it only spurred her on faster.

Then she told him something she knew was going to tip him over the edge. "I made an appointment this morning to have my IUD removed."

The heat and excitement that rose in his eyes was beyond what she'd expected. "Fuck, you better not be kidding, Harper."

She shook her head, her hips never losing their rhythm. "I'm not. Nine days. Think you can survive it?"

Quick as a flash, Lucky rolled her onto her back. "Nine days. I better start practicing."

* * *

BECAUSE SCOTTY WAS STILL in the house, Lucky put his jeans back on when he went to unlock the door. Harper put her bra and panties on but snagged his shirt instead of hers. They laid down under the covers.

"I need to tell you something."

Harper's euphoria started to wane at his words. "Is it bad?"

They were lying on their sides facing each other. "No, but you're still not going to like it."

"Tell me." She'd always been a rip-the-Band-Aid off kind of girl anyway.

"I have to leave again tonight."

He was right. She didn't like it. "To go where?"

"I can't tell you that." When she opened her mouth to protest, Lucky put a finger to her lips. "There might be some things in the near future that I can't tell you. Call it club business and leave it at that. I need you to trust that whatever I am doing, I am doing to protect you and this family. I also need you to stay wherever it is I leave you during these times and to make sure Scotty does too."

He took his finger away from her mouth, but Harper didn't speak right away. She rolled his words around in her head. "Are you doing anything illegal?"

He shook his head. "We will try our hardest not to."

That wasn't a no. "Does it have to do with my father?"

"I can't tell you that," he hedged.

Which was definitely a yes. "Have one of your brothers come stay with Scotty. I'm coming too."

Lucky was already shaking his head before she finished. "No, you're not. You need to stay here."

She sat up slightly. "Lucky, if whatever it is you're doing has to do with my dad, then yes, I am coming. It's not because I don't trust you, it's because I have a right to be there too."

"I'm not saying you don't," he told her. There was a sympathetic look in his eyes, but also determination. He wasn't going to budge on this. She knew it. "But there are a lot of unknowns. We might be walking into a dangerous situation. I can't have you there. I need you here, where I know you're safe."

"What could be so dangerous that I can't be there, but you can be?"

Lucky drew her closer to him. "Harper, darlin', love of my life, *please* stay here. I won't be able to do my job if I'm worrying about you too. And, just to clarify, we don't know it's about your dad. We think so, but that's what we're going to go find out."

"Fine." She scowled at him. "But just know you can't use 'love of my life' to get your way all the time. This is a one-time-only situation and it will never sway me again."

He leaned forward and took her lips. "Whatever you say, love of my life."

* * *

AROUND SIX-THIRTY THAT EVENING, Jenna, Bones, and Jumper arrived with the three prospects and Aerial. With the situation unknown, Steel couldn't risk taking Bones and Jumper along. Bones was pissed about it and Jumper seemed grateful. Though Scotty was upset that Lucky was going to be gone all night again, he was thrilled to have Aerial in the house.

Jenna pulled Lucky aside and told him that all three prospects and Bones were armed. Jumper didn't have a firearms license and couldn't carry. She opened her jacket to show she had a Glock in a shoulder holster. She'd keep her jacket on until Scotty went to bed, so she didn't scare him.

Lucky leaned forward and kissed Jenna on the cheek. "Thank you."

"We'll keep them safe," she vowed. Likely, Jenna didn't know any more than Harper did. However, her relationship with Steel was powerful enough for her to know not to ask questions and to trust he knew what he was doing. Steel would tell her only what she needed to know to keep her safe.

Lucky hoped he and Harper got to that level one day. Though, Harper was stubborn enough that she might always ask questions.

He hugged Scotty and Harper one more time each. He threw a chin lift at his brothers and the prospects, then left.

By the time he got to the clubhouse, Steel had already finished explaining what was going on to the rest of the MC. Lucky saw everyone else but Scar present.

He made his way through to Bulldog, who was standing next to Carlos. "Scar still on Connelly?"

Bulldog nodded. "He's been texting me updates. He couldn't hear the conversation, but Connelly got a phone call about two hours ago that really pissed him off."

"Think the buy is still on?" If the buy was called off or something happened, Connelly wouldn't get the extra fifteen thousand he was promised. That was fifteen thousand reasons to be pissed off.

"Scar thinks so. After missing that conversation, Scar got himself closer to Connelly so he didn't miss any more intel." Bulldog pulled out his phone to show Lucky a picture of Connelly drinking a beer in his living room while watching television.

Lucky blinked and then took a closer look at the picture. "Is he *inside* Connelly's house?"

Bulldog nodded. "Probably twenty feet from the man and the guy's got no clue death is breathing down his neck."

A shiver ran through Lucky. "Fuck, that is creepy."

Carlos leaned around his brother to tell Lucky, "No matter what, I will always be on Scar's side. Even if the man hatches an evil plan to take over the world. No way am I ever going up against that guy."

Lucky agreed with him.

Steel whistled to get everyone's attention. "Last decision that needs to be made. My vote is that we leave our cuts behind. We're already taking cages, so we wouldn't be wearing them anyway. If something unexpected happens tonight, I don't want one of our cuts to be the reason it leads back to us."

"Agreed," Lucky called out. "Cuts stay here."

"Any arguments?" Steel asked the group as a whole.

"What about masks?" Angel asked. "I agree about leaving our cuts behind, but our faces are still recognizable. Connelly at least knows most of us."

"If all goes to plan, we'll never be close enough for Connelly to recognize us. Unfortunately, we don't have thirteen ski-masks to pass around. We'll just need to keep our distance and hope for the best. Those of you who've got rags can bring them."

Lucky didn't think he had any riding bandanas or doo-rags in his room. He'd have to check after Steel ended the meeting.

"Any other questions?" No one spoke up. Steel nodded. "We ride out as soon as we've gotten word from Scar that Connelly's on the move. Make sure you're ready and armed when that happens. We're estimating about two hours."

Bulldog turned to Lucky. "Did you bring your piece?"

He nodded. "Got my Ka-Bar too."

"Good. We can only hope for the best and prepare for the worst."

"A Marine is always prepared. An Army sad sack…" He let his sentence trail off with a shrug.

"At least I can wipe my own ass without having to be ordered to," Bulldog said with a laugh as he walked away.

"*Semper Fi,* bitch," Lucky called after him.

Bulldog raised his middle finger over his head and kept on walking.

Around nine-thirty, Bulldog got a message from Scar that Connelly was on the move.

They were taking three of their SUVs. Steel, Lucky, and Bulldog were separated between them so they could give orders if something unexpected came up. Keys was remaining behind at the clubhouse with Pumpkin. He'd given Steel, Lucky, and Bulldog a radio with an attachable earpiece. He didn't have enough to give to each member, something he said he'd be changing in the near future.

In Steel's cage was Demo, Angel, and Ranger. Lucky had Bear

and Carlos. Bulldog's had Grumpy, Ghost, and Cage. Keys packed surveillance supplies in each. Since no one knew how Scar was tailing Connelly, Steel had said Scar would go in Lucky's cage if he needed a ride. Just before they pulled out, Bulldog called over the radio that Scar verified he did not need a ride because Connelly was giving him one.

Lucky didn't even want to know.

They all headed south towards Ohiopyle. The state park was big, so they didn't plan to enter it until Connelly and his accomplice got closer and led them to the buy.

Bulldog called over the radio. "Scar says Connelly picked someone up from outside the sheriff's station. He does not recognize him but can confirm he is not a member of the MGPD."

Lucky heard Carlos let out a sigh of relief from the back seat. Lucky keyed his radio. "Was Scar able to get a picture of him?"

"Negative," Bulldog answered. "He's not in a position to do so."

"Too bad," Bear said to those in the SUV. "Keys might have been able to run it through FRS."

"Do I even want to know how Keys has access to a facial recognition system?" Carlos asked dryly.

"Probably not," Lucky deadpanned.

The rest of the trip was silent. They pulled off at a strip mall approximately a mile outside of the northern entrance to Ohiopyle. They parked separately so three black Suburbans in succession didn't draw attention. Then they waited.

Lucky hadn't felt adrenaline course through his system like this since his first deployment. He'd been out of the service for close to eighteen years. Bear had been out for twelve. He wondered if his best friend was also feeling the rush.

He thought of Harper and Scotty back home. It was nearing midnight. Scotty would be in bed by now. He hoped Harper was too. She needed rest to go to work the next morning. He'd heard nothing from Jumper or Bones, meaning all was quiet at his home. It should be. As far as they knew, no one knew the club was on to Connelly. Since it had been Connelly who'd been stalking his home, Lucky didn't anticipate any problems there.

Still, he worried.

He hadn't had this kind of worry when he'd been serving as Steel and many others did. He'd only had to worry about himself and his brothers with him. There'd been no one at home to worry about until he'd learned how badly their mother had been treating Sissy.

"Scar says they're taking the direct route," Bulldog's voice interrupted the silence. "Should be passing us any minute."

"Wait another ten and then we'll roll out," Steel ordered.

Bear looked to Lucky. "Shit's getting real."

"We're here to take pictures," he reminded his friend. "That's all. We're only prepared for more because that's what our training has taught us."

"I hope you're right," Bear said skeptically. "But my gut's swirling like a cotton candy machine. We need to be prepared for more."

Key's voice came across the radio. "Satellite shows a large semi-truck parked in the east parking lot. If that's who Connelly is meeting, he's taking the long way in."

"Can you get us there faster?" Steel asked.

"Not on wheels. Looks like you guys are going to be hoofing it."

Bear started up the SUV. "Showtime."

Steel's voice came across. "Switch up. Lucky, take your cage and follow Connelly. Let's make sure the semi is where he's actually going. Bulldog, you and I will take our cages to wherever Keys tells us to and we'll hike it in. Lucky, get pictures if you can. Don't get so close that he sees the tail. Remember, it's near midnight at a state park. It'll be easy to spot another vehicle's headlights."

"Affirmative," Lucky said.

"Anything new from Scar?"

"Negative," Bulldog answered. "He's gone radio silent."

"I'm sure he's got a reason for that. Keys, take us in."

As Bear pulled their cage onto the road to follow Connelly's route, Keys gave Steel and Bulldog coordinates to leave their SUVs. It was another twenty minutes before they saw Connelly's taillights. Lucky called it over the radio that they had a visual as Bear turned off their lights.

"Shit," Keys said. "Either the guy doesn't know where he's going or he's not meeting that semi."

"We're approximately two klicks out from the semi," Steel told him. "Are we turning around, Keys?"

"Keep going," Keys said, clearly frustrated. "There's no other cars or vans around. There's the campground, but he's even further from that than the semi."

Lucky turned to Carlos in the back seat. "How much drugs are we talking about if it's in a semi?"

"Most likely the drugs are being concealed by whatever is in the semi. Produce is popular because it masks the scent against detection dogs, especially when it's rotting."

Lucky called that information over the radio.

"My thoughts exactly," Keys called back. "Connelly may be taking a long route to verify he doesn't have a tail. Can you fall back anymore, Bear?"

Lucky keyed the radio and held it up next to Bear's mouth. "Not if you want me to keep a visual on him. We're already riding blind."

Lucky didn't like driving without headlights on any more than Bear did.

Fifteen minutes later, Steel called a visual on the semi-truck and four armed tangos. He told Keys they were going to spread out to take pictures and Grumpy was going to set up a video camera.

All of the surveillance equipment Keys had sent with them

would upload to his computer automatically. Lucky, who fought with his printer on a daily basis, had no idea how any of it worked. Keys had handed Bulldog a small black box and said to keep it on him.

"I'm running a trace on the truck's license plate. Interesting that it has Texas plates."

"What's Connelly's ETA?" Steel asked. "These guys look impatient."

"Based on where Lucky's cage is, I'd say about ten mikes out," using the military jargon for *minutes*.

"Affirmative," Steel replied.

"Truck comes back clean. It's registered to a produce company out of Texas, so Carlos called it. No history of suspected drug trafficking. As far as I can tell, this company isn't on any law enforcement's radar."

"Tell him that traffickers spoof legitimate trucking companies' information. The trucks are identical down to the license plate and VIN. These guys likely have no ties to that produce company at all."

"Well shit," Bear said as Lucky called Carlos's information over the radio.

"That's scary," Bulldog replied. "So they can just copy and paste the real truck's information onto this truck?"

"It's easier than you think in a computer age," Keys said dryly. "People rely too much on what a computer tells them is true. A computer could say that one plus one equals three and they'll believe it."

"He's right," Carlos said, though no one but Bear and Lucky could hear him. "And it's only getting easier as technology expands."

Keys spoke before they could reply to Carlos. "Bear, looks like Connelly is approaching the buy. There's a small turnoff just ahead of you. Park there and go the rest of the way on foot."

Lucky put the radio's earpiece in as Bear pulled off. They

dropped their phones in the center console of the SUV. They were careful to silently close their doors. Sound would carry a long way out in these parts.

"Connelly's getting out. So is his partner," Steel said over the radio. "Keys, Angel should have been in position to get a picture of him. Can you run it?"

"Checking… Yes, got it. I don't recognize him either. Probably not a local."

"Steel, we're approaching on your six," Lucky warned in a low voice.

"Oh shit!" suddenly came across the radio from Bulldog.

Lucky held up his fist to stop Bear and Carlos. Bulldog hadn't given an explanation for his outburst. Lucky didn't want to go any further until he knew the reason why.

"Bulldog, report," Steel snapped.

"Not drugs, Steel. They're not trafficking drugs! The truck is full of women."

Lucky felt his stomach jolt. For a moment, he was pretty sure he was going to throw up. *Women?* Had Bulldog just said women? As in *human trafficking?* Hannigan was involved in trafficking women?

What the ever-loving fuck?

* * *

"Repeat!" Steel's hard voice snapped Lucky out of his stupor.

"Steel, there's about thirty women in the back of that truck. Connelly's… Fuck, he's *inspecting* them. Oh God, there's a child, Steel. There's a kid in there. She's maybe nine or ten."

Cold chills ran down his entire body. *A child?* Hannigan was an even sicker fuck than they'd suspected if he was trafficking women and children rather than drugs. Drugs were one thing–the victims generally weren't completely innocent of wrongdo-ing–but *people?*

Lucky motioned for them to continue forward. He reached Steel and Grumpy just as Steel growled over the radio, "Fuck no."

"We can't let this buy happen, Steel," Lucky said to him but not over the radio. "Women and kids?"

Steel nodded. "I know. What the fuck? This was not the plan."

"I'm sure it wasn't in any of those women's plans to end up in the back of that truck either," Lucky snapped in a hurried whisper.

Bulldog called over the radio, "What's the plan, Steel? Because I don't know how much longer I can hold Angel back."

Steel turned to Carlos. "It's not drugs. It's women and there's at least one child."

All color left Carlos's face. "Oh God."

"With Connelly and his partner, plus the traffickers, that's six tangos." Steel turned to Lucky. "We go no-kill. I want answers. Did anyone bring zip ties?"

"We're going to need more than that," Lucky told him. "Those women are going to need food, water, and medical attention."

"That'll be on Bear once we've neutralized the tangos." Steel called over the radio, "No-kill. Take them down."

Though there was no way Scar could have heard the order to Bulldog over the radio, he suddenly appeared behind Connelly and his unknown partner. With quickly sweeping legs and a punch to each, the two men were down.

Angel leapt out of the tree line onto the closest tango to her. He was carrying a semiautomatic. She thrust the muzzle of the gun up in the air just as it went off. Placing the tango in a choke-hold, the man went down. She swiftly dismantled the weapon. For good measure, she also landed him a hard kick to his balls.

Bulldog must have gotten himself under the truck because he rose up behind two others, Ranger a second later. They took out those two with no shots fired.

Ghost got the last man, who'd been preparing to shoot Bulldog and Ranger. Like Angel, he expertly administered a chokehold while locking the man's legs in place with his own. The gun fell to the ground a moment before he did.

With silence no longer a necessity, Steel walked out of the tree line with Lucky, Bear, Carlos, and Grumpy. "Anyone see zip ties or rope?"

Angel hurried past, ignoring everyone in her haste to get to the back of the truck. Bear followed her. He didn't have any medical equipment with him—something he was likely kicking himself for now—but he was still a nurse and would know how to help better than any of the others. Steel indicated for Grumpy to guard the man Angel had taken out and left unconscious on the forest ground.

In an answer to Steel's original question, Scar held up a handful of flex cuffs. Lucky walked over to the man. "I'm not even going to ask why you are carrying these."

Scar raised an eyebrow as if he was questioning Lucky's sanity because he *wasn't* carrying flex cuffs of his own.

Lucky and Carlos went around putting the cuffs on the six tangos. Scar had handed Lucky eight sets of flex cuffs, so they had two spares.

Unlike in the movies, people who are placed in non-lethal chokeholds only remain unconscious for ten to twenty seconds. Angel's man was already awake and clutching his balls with Grumpy's gun pointed at his head. Ghost's too was conscious. Connelly and the mystery man were still out. The two Bulldog and Ranger had taken down were rousing as they were being cuffed.

Steel nodded to Scar. "Wake them."

Carlos walked over to Steel. "Hold on. What are you planning on doing?"

"Get some fucking answers," Steel repeated.

"And if they don't talk?"

Steel's silence was answer enough.

Carlos shook his head. "No, I won't be a part of torture, Steel.

We did the right thing in rescuing the women." His head turned towards the open back of the truck. The women's voices were growing louder. "But now is the time to call in the feds. Human trafficking is a serious crime. We do not want to get mixed up in this for the wrong reasons."

Connelly let out a shout as Scar got him conscious. Lucky would probably cry out too if he woke up to find Scar standing over him waving smelling salts under his nose.

Steel walked over to Connelly. "Trafficking women, you sick bastard? What the fuck is wrong with you?"

"You can't touch me," Connelly snapped. "You're not a cop. I know my rights."

Steel punched him in the face. Connelly, unbalanced by his hands cuffed behind his back, fell to the ground. Steel grabbed the front of his shirt and yanked him up. "And what about their rights?" Steel shouted in his face. "They're human beings! No man, no real man, would ever harm a woman. He would *die* first."

"A real man is strong enough to take what he wants." Connelly tried to look tough, but he was visibly shaking.

"And how strong are you feeling now, you piece of shit?"

Lucky had followed Steel over to where Connelly was. Scar had taken him and the mystery man down by the rear of the truck. For the first time, Lucky saw the women.

And his stomach sank even further.

They were all filthy. The smell coming from the back of the truck was nauseating. Angel was only visible among them because she was in black fatigues. The others were dressed in what had probably been white knee-length dresses but were so dirty now they looked brown. Tears could be seen streaking many of their cheeks. And there was blood.

Some of the women had blood trailing down their legs. Lucky was pretty sure the only reason some of them allowed Bear to touch them was because Angel was there to coax them.

More of Lucky's brothers came over. So did Carlos. He heard

more than one brother vomit but didn't know who. He didn't blame them in the least. He wasn't sure how he wasn't over by the woods joining them. Shock, maybe.

"Fuck," Carlos muttered. He turned his face away from the truck. "They need help, Steel. Now."

"I haven't gotten–"

"Then take it somewhere else," Carlos snapped. Lucky's jaw nearly dropped. He couldn't remember the last time someone had ordered Steel like that and lived to tell about it. Carlos continued, his voice firm. "Here's what's going to happen. I am going to step over there," he pointed to the front of the truck, "and make a phone call to get the feds and ambulances down here. While I am over there, I will be so distracted by my phone call that I won't see or hear whatever it is you feel you have to do to get answers. If some of you aren't here when I get back, then maybe you were never here in the first place."

His piece said, Carlos walked off.

It was Bulldog who spoke first. "He's right, Steel. Now is not the time or place."

Steel scowled. "Take him," he told Bulldog. "This one too." He kicked the mystery man hard in the solar plexus. "I'll deal with them later."

Bulldog motioned for Ranger and Ghost to follow him.

Lucky noticed movement out of the corner of his eye and looked to his left. Scar had lined up the four traffickers on their knees facing the side of the truck. He was going down the row tapping a knife atop their heads like he was playing a twisted game of duck-duck-goose.

Frustrated, Steel stomped over to him. "Scar, you can't kill them!"

"Please," one of the men pleaded. He had a thick Spanish accent. "It was just business. They're only women."

Steel scowled down at the man. "Okay, you can kill him."

Scar actually skipped over to the man. Fuck, that was a scary sight. Lucky couldn't imagine it being his last.

"Wait!" Steel called just as Scar's blade touched the man's throat. A wet spot had appeared at the crotch of the man's jeans. Scar had literally scared the piss out of him. Steel leaned down, his nose crinkling at the acidic smell of urine. "Where were you taking them? There's no one else here. Who else was coming to get them?"

"No one," the man shouted. Like the volume of his voice would keep him alive. "We were to take them to the auction house. Connelly and Marcos were only here to verify the transfer of payment once they'd counted all the girls were there."

Well, they now had a name for the mystery man. Marcos.

And then it registered what else the man had said. Auction house. Holy fuck. Those women had been about to be sold as slaves, most of them likely as sex slaves. And the man had the nerve to call ruining their lives *just business*.

Lucky had a mind to stand side-by-side with Scar and kill them all.

Carlos walked up then. "Feds are on their way." Lucky noticed he'd glanced over his shoulder to see Connelly and Marcos were now missing. Carlos grimaced slightly but shrugged it off.

"Tell him what you just told me," Steel told the trafficker.

The man repeated himself.

"Auction?" Carlos seemed to have trouble getting the word out. "Fuck." He ran his hand through his hair before demanding, "Where?"

Behind him, Lucky heard Angel say, "Holy fuck." Then louder, "Steel! Get over here!"

Steel and Lucky ran back over to the open truck doors. Scar had stayed behind with the cuffed traffickers.

Angel was leading a woman covered in dirt and God knew what else forward. Cage was reaching up to help her down off the high platform. Lucky was relieved to note he did not see any visible blood on her.

Once she was on the ground, she looked up at them. Lucky's jaw dropped. Holy fuck.

It was Madison Mitchell.

The FBI came whirling in in a sea of red, blue, and purple lights. They had at least a dozen red and white ambulances following them. Carlos immediately switched into cop-mode and started filling the feds in. The remaining members of the VDMC–Steel, Lucky, Angel, Cage, Grumpy, and Demo–stood off to the side with Madison. She'd recognized Steel as the husband of one of her mom's bible study friends and latched onto him. Quite literally. She clung to his arm like it was a shield between her and the world. Steel looked more than ready to take on the world for her.

Scar was somewhere unknown.

Angel offered to help get the women out of the truck, but the paramedics declined. She stared helplessly as woman after woman was carried out and led to an ambulance or stretcher.

Bear was the only one allowed to assist once he'd shown his nursing credentials for the hospice facility he worked for. The paramedics actually seemed grateful to have his assistance.

Connelly's car had been long gone by the time the feds had arrived, along with Connelly himself, Marcos, Ranger, Ghost, and Bulldog. Someone, Lucky wasn't sure who, had brought the club's SUV that Bear had been driving to the scene. It explained how the VDMC had been there. All of Key's equipment, including Steel and Lucky's radios, were now stored in the trunk. Keys had done something to wipe all the footage from the devices while still keeping the footage on his computer.

Before the feds had arrived, one of the traffickers–not the one Scar had scared the piss out of–had mentioned the name "Castillo". So far, no one had mentioned Hannigan's name. Keys was looking into the name "Castillo" in connection to Hannigan as well as in general. What he'd found so far wasn't good.

Eventually the feds told the club they can go. Carlos had told them they'd found the truck on accident and had made a citizen's arrest against the traffickers once they saw the imprisoned women.

None of the feds believed them and none of them questioned the obvious lie further.

Madison begged to be allowed to go with Steel. She'd refused medical aid, swearing up and down that she hadn't been raped. "He tried, but another man stopped him."

"Who'd tried?" the fed interviewing her had questioned.

"Deputy Connelly," she'd admitted in a low voice. "I'd gotten a flat tire and he had pulled up in his cruiser. I thought he was there to help me. Next thing I knew, I woke up in a basement. He'd..." She'd squeezed Steel's arm tighter, burying her face in his long black sleeve. "He'd started to. He'd *wanted* to. I tried to fight him, but I was naked. He..." She'd hiccupped. "He was about to when a voice called down the stairs. He stopped and cursed. Then he zipped up his pants and left. I never saw him again."

She hadn't looked up at Steel as she spoke, likely feeling ashamed. Though her feelings were unwarranted, it was a good thing she hadn't looked up or she'd have seen the murderous look on Steel's face at her story.

Carlos had taken over then, informing the fed on who Deputy

Connelly was. No one mentioned Connelly had been there that night. Not Madison or any of the traffickers.

It was a good thing the SUV sat eight. It was a bad thing that so many of the MC were large men. Steel sat in the middle section with Madison in the middle and Angel on her other side. Lucky and Bear took the front seats, because they could. Cage, Grumpy, and Demo grudgingly took the back row of seats.

The fed in charge, Agent McAlester, told Steel he'd be stopping by the clubhouse in a day or two. He seemed surprised when Steel told him he was welcome anytime. If they came on Sundays, the feds were welcome to join in on the after-run party.

Lucky knew if a federal agent ever did show up to a Sunday picnic, Scotty would never leave the agent alone and bombard him or her with endless questions.

"Can we please get to the other cages?" Grumpy snapped. "My balls are being squeezed like my thighs are nutcrackers."

Cage, though equally squished, laughed.

* * *

It was well past six in the morning by the time Lucky got home. Jumper and Bones were downstairs with the prospects. Lucky offered for them all to stay, but they insisted on going to their own homes. Most had to be awake in a couple of hours anyway to go to work. Before leaving, Bones told Lucky and Steel that Harper was in the master bedroom and Jenna was in Sissy's room. Steel did take Lucky up on his offer to stay. He didn't want to wake Jenna just to take her home to go to sleep again.

Lucky was exhausted. He hadn't slept well in the jail cell two nights ago and he'd been awake all night. Harper and Scotty would have to be up soon for school. It was hard to believe it was only Tuesday morning. So much had happened since his surprise party on Sunday.

When the club had gotten to the other SUVs parked in

Ohiopyle, Bear, Grumpy, Cage, Demo, and Angel had climbed out. Since Steel was planning on following Lucky home anyway, it hadn't made sense for those two to split up. Madison remained in the SUV in the back with Steel while Lucky drove. He would have rather Bear had stayed to drive so Lucky could have napped, but logistically that hadn't made sense.

Somehow Scar had been waiting for them at the two SUVs.

They made a stop at a by-the-hour motel so Madison could shower. Lucky had gone out and gotten clothing for her. It wasn't much but a twenty-four-hour pharmacy had had a pair of sweatpants and a "Virtue, Liberty, and Independence" shirt for her to wear. She was malnourished so Lucky had also picked up water and protein bars for her.

Then they journeyed the rest of the way to the Mitchell house. It had taken about an hour before the Mitchells were ready for Lucky and Steel to leave. The reunion had been heartbreaking. Both as fathers themselves, neither Steel nor Lucky could imagine the pain of having your child go missing. Or the relief at having them returned.

But finally, *finally*, Lucky was crawling into bed next to Harper. She roused, rolling towards him. He curled himself around her, pressing his nose into her hair.

"What happened?" she murmured, still half asleep.

"Shh…" He quieted her. He placed a kiss on her cheek. "I'll tell you in the morning."

Harper made a humming sound and then fell back to sleep.

It felt like Lucky had barely closed his eyes when there was a loud crash and *whoosh* downstairs. Lucky leapt out of bed. His gun and Ka-Bar knife were in his safe across the room.

Harper sat up in bed. "What was that?"

"Stay there," Lucky shouted as he ran out of the room. He had a bad feeling. Memories pulled at him, placing that sound. He hadn't even made it to Scotty's room before horror filled him.

Smoke was filling the hallway. He could hear the roar of a fire downstairs. "Steel!" he called out at the top of his lungs. "Fire!"

Harper came running out of the bedroom just as Lucky opened Scotty's room. His son was awake and hiding under the bedcovers.

Lucky didn't take the time to placate him. He grabbed Scotty, covers and all, and ran from the room.

Harper was in the hallway waiting for them. She was still wearing only his shirt but at least she'd put on a pair of sandals. Lucky's feet were bare. Even from the top of the stairs, Lucky could see how heavy the flames were below. Smoke was clouding their vision. Harper started coughing behind him. The heat was growing increasingly uncomfortable.

"Straight down the stairs," he told her, his voice competing with the roar below. "The front door is directly in front of you. Go!"

She went, bringing the collar of his shirt over her nose and mouth. Scotty was squirming in his arms, but Lucky kept a tight hold on him. Before heading down himself, he called one more time, *"Steel! Fire!"*

There was no movement from the guest room. He had to get his son out of the house. Harper wasn't strong enough to carry him herself.

Lucky rushed down the stairs. He could feel the heat searing the bottoms of his feet. He ignored the pain.

Harper was coughing hard now. She was struggling with the front door. Lucky pushed her out of the way with his hip and then kicked the door open with a single hit. The door splintered. There was a rush of fire as air came bursting into the house. Lucky grabbed Harper by the back of his shirt and threw the three of them outside.

He felt a raging heat at his back as he flew through the air. They landed hard on the soft grass.

Harper was hacking and throwing up. Lucky knew he was breathing heavily too. He sat up, getting his weight off of Scotty, and quickly fought the blankets off of his son.

Scotty was crying and holding his right wrist with his left hand, but he was breathing normally and otherwise unharmed. Lucky rested his forehead on Scotty's chest in relief.

He sat up, still breathing heavily, and looked over at Harper. She was crawling towards them. She put a hand on each of them, silently asking if they were okay.

Lucky nodded, then he looked back at his engulfed house.

"Steel and Jenna," Harper gasped out. Her voice was rough and scratchy.

They hadn't come out of the house. It had only been minutes since the initial crash. The entire first floor was in flames. The second would be even thicker by now with smoke. Steel was a Marine. He knew what to do in a fire, and yet neither he nor Jenna had made it out of the house.

Lucky stood back up. Harper, sensing what he was about to do, grabbed his arm and pulled on him. "Don't go."

"I have to. He would for me."

Lucky reached down and took Scotty's comforter. He wrapped it around his head and ran back inside.

* * *

HARPER CRIED out as Lucky ran back into the flaming house. *Their house.* It didn't matter that she hadn't officially moved in. It had been their house since the first night she'd stayed. They both knew it.

Tears streaked down her cheeks. She pulled Scotty into her arms. The boy was crying, unsure what was going on.

She heard sirens coming and prayed they reached them in time. Her lungs burned and she was sure she was suffering from smoke inhalation. Lucky hadn't even been wearing shoes. He'd acted so fast inside. There'd been no hesitation in his actions. She'd been too terrified to think clearly. She always thought she'd be clearheaded in a catastrophe, but she'd been wrong.

The cold metal of a gun pressing to her temple proved her nightmare wasn't over.

* * *

Even with the comforter around him, Lucky hadn't been prepared for the heat of the fire. He tried not to look at his things. The photographs on the walls of his kids growing up or Sissy's soccer trophies he'd refused to throw out even though she'd begged him to or Scotty's award on the fridge for being the classroom's best helper... His sled was still at the clubhouse, but his cage was in the garage. He had no idea if it would survive the flames.

He could barely see and stumbled his way to the stairs–or what was left of them. He looked up to see Steel and Jenna curled together at the middle of the stairs. They were trapped, caught between flames and a collapsed staircase. He remembered from his Marine days being told how quickly a structure could go up in flames. He'd seen it firsthand. Still, it was hard to believe so much destruction could be accomplished in so short a time.

Knowing they didn't have much time left, Lucky threw the comforter on the rubble that had once been the lower half of his staircase and climbed up. The blanket wouldn't resist the fire for long but at least it was something.

"Throw her!" he called to Steel.

Jenna, who was practically unconscious, didn't fight her husband as he lifted her up and tossed her like a toy down to Lucky. He caught her, tumbling down onto the now smoking comforter.

He stood up with her in his arms. Steel was waving him to take her and go. Fuck, but he couldn't leave Steel.

He moved Jenna to a small section on the floor that didn't have any flames. He prayed it wasn't so hot that it burned her.

"Jump!" he yelled to Steel.

Though he knew the man wanted to argue, he also knew the fastest way to get his unconscious wife out of the house was to comply. Steel jumped. Once again, Lucky took the weight thrust at him and tumbled to the floor. Only difference was, Steel was a lot heavier than Jenna was and he didn't have much oxygen left in him.

Steel recovered first, lifting himself off of Lucky. He got Lucky to his feet and then rushed over to his wife. Neither man was in any condition to lift her. They each grabbed her under an armpit and dragged her out of the house.

Firemen met them. Lucky could only shake his head when asked if there were any other people in the house.

There was a possibility he lost consciousness because, between blinks, he suddenly had an oxygen mask on his face. Stretchers were being brought over to where Steel, Jenna, and Lucky lay on the front lawn.

He looked around, finally finding his son. Scotty was still on the ground near where he'd left him and Harper. Mrs. Henderson, their neighbor from across the street who babysat Scotty, was kneeling on the grass next to him in a frilly pink bathrobe.

Lucky looked towards the ambulances. *Where was Harper?* It was his last conscious thought before he really did pass out.

* * *

As soon as she realized who had been holding a gun to her head, Harper became mad. But also confused.

She sat in the passenger seat of her brother's *Tahoe*, just staring at him. Richard. Her older brother. The corporate accountant who played golf on the weekends. The father of her two nephews.

The man holding a gun on her.

She hated, absolutely hated, that she'd left Scotty on the ground crying and that the last time she'd seen Lucky he'd been running back inside of their burning house. Brother or not, a gun was still a gun.

The bastard had threatened to shoot Scotty if she hadn't come with him. What the fuck?

She was very aware that she was covered in soot, wearing Lucky's shirt, a pair of panties, and sandals. She kept hacking up phlegm. Thank goodness her sister-in-law Paige had stocked the car with napkins and tissues.

Richard drove in silence. She'd tried talking to him as soon as they were in the car together, but he'd told her to shut up and then put the car in drive. She wasn't sure if she believed her brother would use the gun on her. Still, he had it for a reason and he was driving with his finger on the trigger.

Harper was furious. *Richard?* What the hell was going on? Had her *entire* family been taken over by body snatchers? What was next, the zombie apocalypse?

When she saw they were leaving town limits, she'd had enough of the silence. "What's going on, Rick?"

Like her mom calling her 'Harpy', Richard had always hated any shortened version of his name. As a teen, when she'd wanted to piss him off, she'd call him 'Ricky'.

"I told you to shut up."

"And I decided not to listen. So, care to tell me where we're going?"

"You and your stupid boyfriend messed everything up. It was supposed to be over! I was supposed to be free, but you had to stick your nose in where it didn't belong!"

The angrier he got, the tighter he gripped the gun. Harper did not like that his finger was hovering over the trigger. She didn't know much about guns. Did this one have a safety? If so, was it possible it was on?

Harper tried to use the same soothing voice she used with her students when they got agitated. "Richard, I don't know what you're talking about. I haven't done anything or stuck my nose somewhere it shouldn't be."

"How else could they have known!" Richard shouted back. "There was no way your stupid boy toy could have known about the buy unless *you told him.*"

What buy? Was that where Lucky had gone tonight? Better question: what was being bought?

"I don't know what you're talking about. Can you please put the gun down–"

"No!" he shouted. His hand jerked the steering wheel, causing them to swerve. Richard quickly righted the vehicle. "Just shut the fuck up. I have to think."

Harper fell silent again. How was it possible she was more worried about Lucky than herself? She hoped and prayed that he'd gotten back out of the house alive. Based on the fact that her brother had been at the fire and the way he spoke of blaming Lucky, she wouldn't put it past him to have started the fire.

About a half an hour later of silent driving, Richard's phone rang. He pulled it out of his pocket, somehow juggling the gun and the steering wheel while doing so. Harper had contemplated grabbing for the gun while he'd been distracted but knew, if it accidentally went off, she would undoubtedly be hit.

Richard was clearly not happy to see the name of whoever was calling. He muttered, "Fuck," under his breath and then pressed to ignore the call. Then he turned the phone off. He threw it in the cup holder between them.

Harper glanced at it. Could she reach it without him seeing? Even if she could, she couldn't turn it on without it making sounds. Maybe, if she saw the opportunity, she could pocket the phone. If she got the chance to escape, she might be able to use it later.

It was another fifteen or twenty minutes later before Richard turned off the main road. Another ten minutes after that led them down a path that Harper wasn't sure was an actual road.

Then they stopped at what looked to be an abandoned cabin. It was a single story with a wide front porch. Harper could imagine the beauty it would have once held.

"Where are we?" she asked tentatively.

"Grandpa's old hunting cabin. Mom and Dad got the land when he died. I think she forgot the cabin was even here, but he used to take me here when I was a kid before you were born."

Richard's voice held nostalgia towards the place. He spoke to her as if they were just a pair of siblings out for a ride. There was no hint of malice as he spoke or the fact that he was holding a gun on her.

They exited the car together. Harper hacked up another phlegm ball, this time spitting it into the overgrown brush. She pulled the hem of Lucky's shirt down. It covered her to her thighs, but still. She'd have preferred to have been kidnapped while wearing a pair of pants.

Then, as if her situation couldn't get any more awkward, her dad stepped out of the cabin and onto the worn porch. "What the fuck, Richard? What did you do?"

Despite her current feelings for her dad, at least he wasn't holding a gun on her. She walked towards him if only to put space between Richard and her.

"She didn't exactly leave me a lot of choice," Richard snapped. "That shipment was my last opportunity and now it's gone!"

For the first time in a long time, Harper really looked at her dad. He seemed...old. Defeated. Had his hair always been that gray and unkempt? She'd seen him tired before, but now his skin seemed to sag. His eyes were bloodshot too.

She recalled her once silly wondering about if her dad was using drugs. She'd brushed it aside as preposterous. But now...?

"Go inside, Harper," her dad ordered her. "I need to talk to your brother."

"Oh, hell no," she snapped. "I was forced out of bed this morning by my house going up in flames and then forced at gunpoint by my brother to drive an hour and a half to the middle of nowhere. What the fuck is going on? I deserve some answers."

"Language," he scolded her like she was a child.

"Fuck that and fuck you." She pointed between the two of them. "Fuck both of you. In fact, I'm out of here. I don't care if I have to walk back to Mount Grove. I'm going home."

Richard raised his gun again. "You're not going anywhere until I figure out a plan!"

"A plan for what?" she demanded. "A treasure hunt to find your brain, because you clearly lost it!"

"Harper," her father snapped. "I need you to calm down. Richard, give me that gun. Where did you even get a gun?"

Richard looked sideways like he was ashamed of the answer. "Marcos."

"Fuck," her father cursed like he hadn't just scolded her for doing the same. He stomped over to his son and wrenched the gun out of his hand. "As if you weren't a fool to get involved with these people in the first place. Now you're accepting firearms from them?"

"What was I supposed to do? He warned me that if the buy didn't go right Castillo would be done with me. *Permanently*. I needed protection."

"You idiot, it's not even loaded." Her dad put the gun in the waistband of his jeans. "Harper, I need you to go inside–"

"Fuck. That." She looked between the two of them. "One of you start talking or I walk. If you feel you need to shoot me, so be it but you're the one who'll have to explain it to Mom at my funeral."

At least her dad had the decency to wince at that.

"Tell her," their father demanded of Richard. "You're the one who brought her here. Now you have to tell her why."

Richard crossed his arms like a defiant child and turned his face away from them.

Her father scowled at her brother but allowed him to have his tantrum. He turned to her. "Your brother is in debt to the Castillo cartel for three hundred thousand."

"Dollars?" she gaped. Holy fuck nuggets. Her annual salary was just over ten percent of that. *Per year.* How the hell did someone accumulate a debt like that?

"Yes," her dad sighed defeatedly. "I didn't know he was an addict until about six months ago. I'd just turned in my papers to retire when a runner for the cartel came to me. He'd mistakenly gone to the wrong R. Hannigan."

"I was handling it on my own! You didn't need to get involved!"

"Clearly I did!" her father shot back at him. "Only I should have handled the payoff myself instead of giving it to you to do. That was my mistake."

Richard only stuck his chin further up in the air in defiance.

"Wait. Richard's a drug addict?" Had he gotten their parents addicted too?

"Gambling," her dad corrected. "He's a gambling addict. When the cartel runner came to me, he was in deep for a hundred and fifty large. It was your mother's and my savings, practically all of it, but we were willing to give it to him to save his life and then get him to rehab. We thought it was over. *I* thought it was over. He'd paid them off and that was that.

"He agreed to move to Mount Grove and start an outpatient rehab program so Paige wouldn't find out and he could still see the boys. I took the job as sheriff to help make ends meet and hopefully recoup some of our savings. But right before we left

Detroit, another runner came to our door. And this time, he knew he had the right Hannigan."

Harper turned on her brother. It didn't take a genius to figure out that three hundred thousand was double his original one hundred and fifty owed. "What did you do?"

"It was a sure thing. I couldn't lose–"

"Except you lost!" her dad shouted. "You not only lost the one hundred and fifty thousand, you doubled your debt!"

Richard looked downcast for the first time rather than defiant.

"What happened next?" Harper asked her dad. "How did you fix it? Because a cartel isn't going to let a debt like that go."

Her dad flinched, growing pale. "They… They wanted your mother. And," he stumbled, "and Paige. And…" He looked up at her. "And you. If we gave them the three of you, they would have called the debt even."

Harper's stomach dropped. "*Gave*," she repeated slowly, "as in…"

"To do with as he pleased." Her dad's voice was so slow Harper wasn't sure she'd heard him correctly. "More than likely, he would have taken the three of you and sold you into sexual slavery."

Harper stared at her dad for a single minute, then turned and vomited. What the fuck? What the *fuck!*

Her dad couldn't be serious. This was some kind of sick, twisted joke the body snatchers were playing on her. That's what this was. Her family was not involved in human trafficking. Sexual slavery? That sort of thing happened on television. She knew it was real. She knew it was a serious issue. But she'd never imagined in her wildest dreams that it would ever touch her life.

Harper spat whatever was still in her mouth out. "Obviously, you said no. What did you give them in return?" She spat one more time and then turned to face her father.

Richard looked like he was about to pass out.

"Your brother made a deal with them," he said cryptically. "The last of the payment was supposed to go to Castillo last night. Somehow the *Via Daemonia* knew about it and intercepted it."

Harper scowled at him. "Yeah, I'm going to need more information than that. What deal did he make? What was in the shipment? Drugs, money, black market art pieces...?"

Rather than answer her question, her dad stated, "I never wanted you to be a part of this. Your mother found out when I drained our savings. There was no way I could keep that from her. But I never wanted you to find out. That's why I sent Mark to keep an eye on you. I wanted you to be protected."

"Answer the fucking question, Dad! What deal did Richard make?"

Her father flinched. He looked disgusted and sad at the same time. "Castillo said if he wouldn't give him the three of you, which he claimed was a bargain on your brother's part, that he had to bring him...other women."

Harper took one look at the guilt on her brother's face, turned, and threw up again.

* * *

A RHYTHMIC *BEEP...BEEP...BEEP...* roused Lucky. It hurt to breathe, so that was unfortunate. Had someone shoved a hot poker down his throat? He felt like there was a giant boulder sitting on his chest. His eyes were grainy as he tried to blink them open. The mush that had taken the place of his brain couldn't recall what had happened. And damn, his feet hurt.

Was someone smoking?

Smoke... Fire... His house had been on fire.

Lucky tried to sit up but couldn't. His struggles must have caught the attention of whomever was in the room with him.

"Stop! Lucky, stop, brother. You're in the hospital." Bear. That was Bear's voice. He was sure of it.

Even though he was desperately blinking his eyes, he couldn't see clearly. Like there was a film over his eyeballs.

"Dad!" That was Sissy.

He turned his head in her direction. All he saw was a blurred silhouette beside him.

"Dad, stop struggling. They had to intubate you. I've called the doctor. Hopefully they can remove it now that you're awake."

Intubate him? Why had he needed to be intubated?

It explained why he couldn't move his tongue and why his throat hurt so badly. He had so many questions, but he had no way of asking them without the ability to talk. With his vision so blurry, he couldn't write either.

He felt pressure next to his hip and guessed Sissy had sat on the bed. She took his hand between her two.

"Scotty's fine. He's got a sprained wrist but no other injuries."

"Jenna and Steel too, man." Bear's voice came from the other side of the bed. "You saved their lives. Jenna's doing better than Steel, but they're both awake and aware. Steel's got some burns on his arm and his lungs are really irritated. Jenna's lungs too, but no burns. Steel protected her from most of it. Their kids are with them now."

Thank God. He tried to breathe easier with that news, but there was still one person they hadn't mentioned.

"You, um, you got hurt, Dad." Sissy's voice was full of worry and tears. "Your feet are the worst. You've got second and third degree burns on your feet and left ankle. Your right calf has first degree burns. They think your pants caught fire because they pulled fibers out of the wound. Your eyes are inflamed. They couldn't find anything in them, so they think it's just smoke irritant. Your lungs have severe damage from smoke inhalation. You're going to be here a couple of days."

He squeezed Sissy's hand to indicate for her to keep going.

Where was Harper? She'd gotten out, right? He was pretty sure he remembered that.

"Um…" Sissy hesitated.

Bear took over explaining. "We need you not to panic, Lucky. We're still trying to piece it all together. The initial fire inspector said it was one or more Molotov cocktails thrown through your living room window. Once the curtains and furniture caught, it spread fast from there. The one marshal said it only takes five minutes for a modern house to be completely engulfed."

Lucky grunted. He didn't need a lesson on how fast fires spread. Where was Harper?

"I know what you want to know, man, but I don't have an answer for you. From what we can gather from Mrs. Henderson, she saw a man approach Harper and Scotty on the lawn. He spoke to her for a minute and then they walked off together. Scotty said she knew him, asked what he was doing." Bear paused before adding, "He also said she didn't fight him."

Harper had gone off with a man while he'd run back inside to save their friends from the fire? That made no sense. She wouldn't leave Scotty alone either, especially not with a burning building only yards away from them.

Darkness took him again.

The next time he woke, his vision was better. He immediately knew that the intubation tube had been removed. His throat was still sore as fuck, but he could move his tongue. There was an oxygen mask over his mouth and nose.

While his vision was still blurry, he could at least figure out what he was seeing. Sissy was in a chair next to his bed, bent over with her head on the mattress. Bear, who looked like the chair beneath him was about to break, was slouched back with his arms across his chest. His long legs and feet were propped up at the end of Lucky's bed.

That was when Lucky noticed that his own feet weren't

covered by the sheet and blanket like the rest of him. They were covered in bandages and elevated by pillows.

He had to work up the air to speak. "Harper." It was the only thing he could say then.

Bear turned his head towards him almost lazily. Then sat up when he saw Lucky was awake. "Fuck, man. Welcome back to the land of the living."

Slipping into nurse mode, Bear reached forward and started playing with Lucky's eyelids. They tingled as he stretched them. Then he took a penlight and shined it into Lucky's eyes. It made his eyes sting.

Bear stepped back. "They're looking better, man. Less inflamed. I take it your vision is better than before?"

Lucky nodded. He wanted to move his hand up to remove the oxygen mask, but it felt too heavy. Glancing down, he saw Sissy was using it as a pillow.

Understanding Lucky's struggle, Bear lowered the oxygen mask. "Just for a minute. Your numbers are still lower than they should be. Smoke inhalation is very serious."

Lucky wasn't sure what that meant and honestly didn't care. "Where's Harper?" His voice was so scratchy that he didn't sound like himself.

"Bulldog and Keys are looking for her. We think her dad was the one who took her."

Hannigan had Harper? That should make him feel better–he was her dad after all–but then Lucky recalled they suspected Hannigan was connected to human trafficking and a slave auction. Deputy Connelly, whom the sheriff had had watching his own daughter, had abducted Madison Mitchell.

"Madison?"

"She's good," Bear answered with a smile. "Came over this afternoon to visit Steel and Jenna once word got around that they were in the hospital. Her parents finally convinced her while she was here to get a full work-up."

This afternoon? What time was it? What time had the fire been? He couldn't recall if the sun had been up when they'd gotten outside.

He remembered Sissy telling him that Scotty had sprained his wrist. Had he done that when he'd landed on Scotty? He'd been so eager to get them outside before the flashover that he hadn't checked his weight.

"I'm not sure what thought is going through your head right now, but I don't think I'll like it. You look like you want to hit yourself."

"Sc…otty…" His voice cut out before he could say more.

Bear put the mask back over his mouth. "He's fine. He's been with Jumper and Aerial all day. We figured that was best since Aerial can help keep him calm. Steel and Jenna have been discharged. They're home with the prospects as their house slaves for the next couple of days."

Scotty being fine was great to hear, but that wasn't what Lucky wanted to know. Had he sprained Scotty's wrist?

"You still don't look happy. Blink once for Scotty, blink twice for Harper."

If he blinked three times, would Bear talk about both of them? Instead, he blinked once.

"Scotty? Okay. He's been having outbursts. Keeps asking about his stuff and when he can go home. We tried to bring him over this afternoon to see you, but he freaked out before even entering the hospital. Sissy left you to go see him but then came back to be with you once Demo and Jumper had taken Scotty back to the clubhouse."

Lucky blinked once again.

"Shit, man, I'm not a mind reader. I don't know what else to tell you about him. He's upset, obviously, but he's okay. I swear."

Lucky held up his hand and bent his wrist back and forth.

"Scotty's wrist? It's sprained. It's not bad, but the doc still put a cast on him." A cast? His boy had a cast on his hand and he hadn't been there for him? "Don't worry. He's still getting it off in two weeks. The cast is simply because he has Downs and the doctor wanted to keep it as protected as possible." Bear smiled lopsidedly. "Kid's making everyone sign it. Even asked the doctor for a bigger cast so they didn't have to write so small. According to Scotty, he's loved by a lot of people."

Lucky felt warmth spread through him at those words. Scotty would be okay. Even if Lucky had been the cause of the sprained wrist, it was better to have a sprained wrist than be burnt to death.

He met Bear's eyes and blinked two times.

Bear winced. "I don't really have much to tell you. Bulldog, Ghost, and Ranger went to the Hannigan's house. The missus was there but Hannigan wasn't, nor was Harper. They checked the sheriff's station too. According to Jeff Miller, he didn't show for work today. Called in sick. Since we can't track Harper, we're trying to find Hannigan."

Fuck. Why would Hannigan take Harper? Had she been injured too? Lucky recalled her coughing but wasn't sure if she'd been hurt otherwise.

Bear's phone dinged. Lucky was sure his was a ball of melted plastic. Fuck, there was so much to worry about. Like where Harper, Scotty, and he were going to live. He didn't know if his house was salvageable but, even if it was, he doubted they'd be allowed to live in it for some time.

Bear read the message on his phone and let out a long sigh. "Fuck, man, you're not going to believe this…"

* * *

HARPER WASN'T sure how she'd gotten inside the cabin. She recalled one of them leading her in. A water bottle was thrust under her face. She rinsed out her mouth and spat into the kitchen sink. Then she chugged the rest of the bottle.

It didn't make her feel any better.

She turned on her dad and brother. "Tell me you refused again, Richard. Tell me you haven't been kidnapping innocent women in some twisted idea that you're protecting Paige, Mom, and me. Tell me you refused and have been paying him back slowly like some overpriced car loan that just won't end." When neither of them spoke, she shouted, *"Tell me!"*

Richard looked down at the floor. "I can't."

Harper turned and dry heaved over the sink. She was both grateful and not that the water she'd just drank stayed down. Cold washed over her and her body started to shake. She couldn't look at them. Either of them. "You knew?" she accused her father. "You knew he was doing this? Abducting women?"

"What was I to do?" her father asked in return. "Give up my wife, daughter, and my daughter-in-law? Live the rest of my life knowing the unspeakable horrors you three would face?"

She rounded on him. "You're a cop! You should have arrested Castillo!"

"He's too powerful!" Her dad dropped his face into his hands. "Don't you think I thought of that? Don't you think that was the first instinct I had? But even in prison, he would have still been able to come after us." He raised his head. "He knew I was a cop, about to be retired or not. He didn't care! He laughed just as you did and dared me to cuff him. Told me that while he was sitting in a jail cell, he'd send people to our house to gang-rape and kill you or your mother, whichever his men found first."

"There had to have been other options than allowing your son to kidnap women for some sick fucker who was going to sell them on the black market! Call the FBI, put us in WITSEC, *something!"*

Her father wouldn't look at her. "If Castillo goes to jail, so does your brother. His life would be ruined. Everything he's worked for, his reputation. Not to mention what it would do to

Paige and the boys, and your mother." He shook his head sorrowfully. "I couldn't do that to him."

She'd been blind. So blind. Her family had been going through a nightmare and she'd been living in a love bubble with Lucky planning a future. Scotty. Sissy. A future baby. How could she live with herself after knowing what her own brother had done, what her dad had been complicit in?

Harper glared at her dad. "You were hellbent on the *Via Daemonia*. Why? Were you hoping to place Richard's crimes at their feet?"

Her father nodded. "Yes. If I could create a trail that led between Castillo and the motorcycle gang, I thought perhaps I could turn things around on Castillo. Make such a big headache for him that he'd forget about Richard and his debt."

"You son of a bitch! They're good people! They only got involved in whatever you," she pointed at Richard, "are blaming me for because you," she pointed at her dad, "wouldn't let them be! You blamed them for Madison's–" She stopped talking. "Oh God. Madison." She looked helplessly at her brother. "You abducted a teenager? *She was seventeen!*"

Richard put his hands up as if in surrender. "That wasn't me. I never touched the Mitchell girl." He spoke as if being innocent of that heinous crime made him also innocent of his others.

"You both are sick," Harper snapped. "I'm done with this conversation. I am done with all of this. I need to get back to Mount Grove and my family. My *real* family," she added pointedly. "I hope you understand what the two of you have done. I hope you both rot in Hell. Mom and Paige deserve far better than the likes of you." She turned to Richard. "And have no doubts, I'll be telling both of them the extent of your crimes." Then she looked at her dad, "Both of your crimes."

Harper stormed towards the front door. She wasn't sure if one or both were going to attempt to stop her. She didn't know where the keys to Richard's *Tahoe* were but wasn't about to stop and ask him for them.

She wrenched the old wooden door open–and screamed.

Scar stood there. Clearly, he'd been there for a while. Perhaps for their entire conversation. He gave her a long once over and seemed to nod to himself that she was unharmed. Then he turned his menacing gaze on her father and brother.

She took a step back, allowing him entry. She wasn't sure what he was going to do, but some survival part of her brain told her not to interfere.

Scar walked right up to her brother. Without hesitation, he landed two quick consecutive open-handed strikes to the side of Richard's throat. Her brother crumpled to the floor.

Harper cried out and covered her eyes. Scar had just… Her brother? Had he just killed her brother? Her brother had done some wicked things, but he wasn't a bad person. He hadn't deserved death… Had he? What of the women he'd been abducting? They hadn't deserved to have their lives interrupted and ruined because her brother couldn't stop gambling.

She heard her father shout and then his voice cut short. She had to look, she had to know. Her father's only crime had been not stopping her brother from committing his, hadn't it? Was that worth a death sentence too?

Hesitantly, Harper peaked through her fingers to see her father standing there unharmed. A knife was imbedded in the floorboards at his feet. Scar must have thrown it as a warning for her father to stay where he was. Richard's gun was in pieces on the floor and Scar was dismantling a second gun in front of her father's face.

Scar walked behind him and kicked the back of his knees. He bound her father's hands behind his back and left him on the floor.

In a fluid motion, he hefted Richard's body up in a fireman's hold on his shoulder. Without looking back at her bound father, he walked past her and out the front door. Then he paused. With a wave of his hand, he gestured for her to walk ahead of him.

Harper stood there frozen. Should she go with him? Scar was, after all, a ride home and a way back to Lucky.

She recalled what Lucky had said to her after the first time she'd met Scar at the club's after-run party. *"He's scary as fuck. No one's arguing with you there. But there's an honor to him few get to see, Harper. He always protects. It's his first instinct. I trust him with my life—more importantly, I trust him with yours, Scotty's, and Sissy's lives."*

Those words in mind, and still wary of him, Harper walked out of the cabin.

CHAPTER 13

Once more, Harper was in her brother's *Tahoe* just staring at the driver. Only this time it was Scar and not her brother with a gun.

After leaving the cabin, Scar had thrown her brother in the back of the *Tahoe* and hogtied him. Upon closer inspection, she saw Richard was still alive. Harper had some severe mixed feelings about what she'd witnessed Scar do. On one hand, her brother had done some pretty messed up shit. Abducting women for a cartel kingpin? On the other hand, shouldn't he go to jail for his crimes? Her father might have been able to ignore his son's errors, but she couldn't.

What gave Scar the right to be judge, jury, and executioner? Or…almost executioner?

She eyed Scar as he drove. She wasn't entirely sure why she'd gotten in the car with him. He was, after all, clearly dangerous. And yet… Harper was good at reading body language. In her job, she had to be. Many of her students were non-verbal or, like Scotty, had difficulty at times expressing their emotions.

Scar's body language hadn't been aggressive or vengeful. It

had been protective. The first thing he'd done upon her opening the door was look her over to make sure she was unharmed.

Harper was also questioning his actions against her brother. She had the sense that if he wanted Richard dead, he'd be dead. And yet, from the occasional noise she heard from the open trunk, her brother was still alive. In pain, certainly, but alive.

He'd given her his jacket to cover her lower half. She thought the gesture oddly sweet for the stoic man. Beneath, he wore a strange vest with sleeves and pockets. It reminded her of Batman's infamous utility belt. There were multiple daggers crisscrossed over his broad chest. A roll of duct tape dangled by a carabiner. Zip ties were looped together and hung from the other side of a holstered gun. She could see a total of four pockets around his torso but could only guess what were in those.

In comparison to Lucky, Scar was not as muscular. He was lean, like a swimmer, but still strong. She guessed he was about Lucky's height, around six-one or -two. She was ashamed to say that she hadn't really looked past the diagonal scar on his face the first time she'd met him. That and his silent demeanor had been too prominent to take in the rest of his features.

She guessed he was in his mid-thirties. His black hair was shorn down to a buzz cut. He was clean shaven, though she doubted hair would grow over his damaged skin.

He also had more than one scar. His hands were covered in them. Without the jacket covering his arms, she saw them there too. They were different than she'd expect of battle scars. She'd seen Lucky's from his time at war. One didn't get those type of scars from getting hit with shrapnel or a bullet. They were too strategic, too evenly placed.

They were also not self-inflicted.

She wondered if they also continued over the rest of his body. Something told her they did.

"What are you going to do with Richard?"

Scar stayed silent. He kept his hands on ten and two on the wheel and stared straight ahead.

"Where's Lucky?"

At least that time he blinked at that question. That was some form of an acknowledgement. She didn't bother asking about the house or Scotty. She doubted she'd get anywhere with those questions.

"Can you at least tell me if you're taking me to him?"

To her utter surprise, Scar nodded.

"You are?" She smiled in relief. "Thank you. Where is he?"

Scar didn't acknowledge the question. Fuck.

Then she tried something. "Is Lucky okay?"

Scar nodded. It was only a single dip of his chin, but it was still an answer.

Gotcha! she thought elatedly. Scar would nod yes or no. That was the trick to getting answers from him. She just needed to phrase her questions differently. She'd had an autistic student in Detroit who was similar.

"Is Scotty okay?"

Scar nodded.

She pondered her next question. She couldn't ask about Jenna and Steel without getting the details she wanted to know. If Lucky was okay, she hoped they were too.

"Were you trying to kill Richard, my brother?"

Scar's chin shook side to side. Minuscule though the movement was.

So she'd been right. His actions, while violent, had not had the intention of being lethal. Why do it then? She had to also wonder at the precision not killing someone took. The human body was so fragile. Scar's actions had been so quick and accurate. He'd known exactly what he was doing.

That was a scary thought, because a skill like that took practice.

"I want to ask how you found me, but I know you won't

answer that. I don't have my phone on me so you couldn't have traced me. Were you even looking for me or were you there for another reason? Had you followed my brother? No," she answered that question herself before he could. "You had no reason to follow my brother. I hadn't suspected him of being involved. I never told Lucky anything about him. You wouldn't have known to follow him unless you're psychic. Are you psychic, Scar?"

Again, he shook his head. This time, though, she caught a flicker of amusement on his face. It was quick, but it had been there.

She'd made Scar smile. Even if it was only internally. Harper felt like patting herself on the back.

"Too bad," she said, keeping the conversation going. "If you hadn't been following my brother, then you were following my father." She thought about what Richard had said about the buy that the MC had interfered with last night. "You were following my dad to see what his reaction to you guys interrupting the buy last night was. Oh shit!" Her brain had just put it together. "The buy. It had been women, hadn't it? Oh, God. The women my brother had been abducting to give to Castillo! You guys went after the women?"

She felt like throwing up again.

"How did you know though? It's too big of a jump to automatically assume human trafficking. My dad was acting weird, sure, but I'd figured he was using drugs or been body snatched by aliens. I never even suspected human trafficking, so how could you guys?"

She thought over the conversation she'd had with Lucky the afternoon before. He'd said *might* be dangerous. Not would be. If they were knowingly going after human traffickers, he wouldn't have used the word *might*. He'd also clarified that they weren't sure her father was involved.

Then who?

"It was an accident, wasn't it?" she asked Scar in a quiet voice. "You guys left last night thinking you were going to find something else or maybe even were just looking for something to lead you to my dad. Instead, you walked in on the buy my brother had set up. You hadn't known you'd find those women, did you?"

Scar dipped his chin. She was right.

"What happened to them? Where are they? Fuck, that's not a yes or no question. Um, are they safe?"

He nodded.

Harper supposed that was as good as she was going to get. At least the women were out of harm's way. She still couldn't believe her brother would do something so heinous as abduct women. Gambling was one thing, but abducting *women?* Knowing their horrific fates, even if he didn't have a direct hand in where they ended up?

He'd claimed not to have been involved in Madison Mitchell's abduction, but she wasn't sure she believed him.

Harper shook her head, trying to get her questions back on track. "Something happened last night to make you follow my dad, though. That's how you knew where I was."

He nodded.

She needed details, but there was no way she could guess those with yes or no questions.

She hadn't realized they were nearing the outskirts of town until he pulled into a fast-food drive-thru. Shit, so much had happened that she hadn't even realized she hadn't had anything to eat that day. Granted, if she had, it likely would have been thrown up a while ago.

They waited patiently in line, as there was only one car in front of them, and then Scar pulled up to the speaker box. He rolled down his window before looking at her expectantly.

She raised an eyebrow at him.

The voice over the speaker asked, "Can I help you?"

He raised an eyebrow back at her.

She *was* hungry. She leaned over the center console. Scar pushed himself as far back in his seat as he could. Harper pretended not to notice. She placed her order and then glanced at Scar. "You look like a meat-kind-of guy." She added a triple cheeseburger meal to the order for him.

As they pulled up to the pay counter, Scar pulled a wallet out of one of the pockets on his holster vest. She saw her brother's license when he opened it. Scar pulled two twenties out of the billfold. Harper noticed that he turned his face away from the cashier as he did. Was he avoiding the cameras or the person?

How much of his silence was self-administered and how much of it was protection? Was he silent to freak people out or to keep an invisible shield around himself?

They got their food and drinks. Harper noticed the worker kept glancing at Scar's face. She knew her first reaction to Scar hadn't been pleasant. She'd felt scared of him. That shamed her. Especially in her profession, she should know better than to judge before knowing the cause of a person's differences. But the way the cashier kept looking at Scar. It was in a morbid fascination kind of way.

Like she wanted to get a better look at the freak in the car.

Harper scowled at her as Scar pulled away. She put straws in each of their drinks. "The front one is yours," she told him. Then she started working on getting their sandwiches unwrapped. She dumped the fries into the bottom of the paper bag and placed it in the cubby under the media station. "Figured that was easier for you."

She handed Scar his half-wrapped massive burger. To her surprise, though, he shook his head.

"Is it because you're driving?"

Again, he shook his head.

She looked down at the burger. "Do you not eat meat?"

He shook his head.

"Then what's wrong? I figured you'd like this. We can go back. You can point at what you want and I'll order it for you."

Again, he shook his head. Scar pulled back onto the main road.

Shit. She felt terrible. She'd gotten her food but guessed wrong on his order. She wrapped the giant burger back up. "Will you eat the fries?"

He shook his head.

Harper paused. Maybe it wasn't the food but the type of food. "Do you not eat processed foods?"

He nodded.

"Oh! Well, we can stop somewhere else. I'm not exactly wearing pants, but there's got to be somewhere around here where you can eat."

Scar shook his head.

"Well, now I feel bad." This time when he nodded his chin, it was more of a point than an acknowledgement. "Are you telling me to go ahead and eat?"

He dipped his head down once.

She hesitated, but she really was hungry. Now that she was smelling the food, her stomach was realizing it was empty.

She tentatively took a bite of her much smaller burger. "I owe you an apology."

Though he didn't take his eyes off of the road, his eyebrows scrunched downward.

"No, I do," she corrected him. "When Lucky first introduced us, I took your silence as off-putting and even scary. I'm sorry about that. I should have taken the time to get to know you better."

This time he did look at her—and it looked like he was questioning her sanity.

Harper let out a short laugh. "I get that you're standoff-ish, but that's no excuse. Sissy says you're a good friend. I didn't understand before, but I do now, and I'm sorry for how I treated you."

Harper almost dropped her sandwich as Scar abruptly pulled off to the side of the road. He threw the gear into Park. To her surprise, he turned to face her fully. She couldn't remember meeting his eyes before now. They were a deep shade of blue, like sapphires.

They sat there staring at each other for a moment. She wasn't sure what Scar's intention was, but she let him process what he needed to. There was clearly a lot going on behind those intense eyes.

Scar tipped his head slightly, still studying her. Slowly, watching her for any sign of discomfort, Scar reached a hand across to her. He laid his palm on her shoulder and squeezed gently.

Harper smiled at him. "Thank you for forgiving me."

He squeezed again. Then wrenched his hand away like she'd burned him. Harper got the feeling he didn't touch people often—at least in a non-violent way. And even less often that people touched *him*.

Carefully, she reached across just as slowly. His entire body tensed as she drew nearer. He froze, but he didn't stop her. She gently laid her hand on his shoulder too.

Scar seemed to sag under her touch. She wondered what sort of life he'd led that he feared a friendly touch, not knowing if it would hurt him. She knew in that moment, no matter what else came at her, she would make sure Scar was included in her life.

Sensing he'd reached his limit, she took her hand away. "Can we go see Lucky, please? I'm sure he's really worried."

Scar nodded once and put the car back in drive.

* * *

LUCKY FELT a pressure on his right side when he next woke up. He didn't remember wanting to sleep, but the pain meds they had him on kept knocking him out. He remembered Bear telling him that was normal.

Expecting to find Sissy as the cause of the pressure, his heart leapt with relief when he instead saw raven hair spread across his chest. Harper had squeezed herself against him on the narrow hospital bed. She had herself pressed tightly to his side without putting any weight on top of him. Someone, he suspected Bear, had put the railing up to keep her from falling off.

The room was darker than before. He wondered if the sun had set. The overhead lights were off with only a lamp above the bed dimmed for minimal light. He glanced around but didn't see Sissy or Bear. He hoped Sissy at least had gone home to get some rest.

Then he remembered their home had been burned down. Fuck. Lucky did not want to think about everything he had to handle between insurance and finding them somewhere else to live right then.

Movement out of the corner of his eye drew his attention to the corner of the room by the door. Scar stood there. Lucky wondered for how long.

"Were you the one who found her?"

He nodded.

"Thank you. I don't know how to repay you."

Scar tipped his chin towards Harper.

"I'll take care of her. I can promise you that."

He nodded again.

"Was it Hannigan? Did he take her?"

Scar shook his head.

Fuck. Who had it been if not her father? "Do you have who it was?"

Scar nodded.

"Save him for me. He's mine."

Again, Scar nodded.

Harper started to stir. Lucky hugged her tighter to him. He looked over one more time, but Scar had left the room. He didn't know the details, but he knew he owed his brother for his woman's life. It was a debt he knew he could never repay.

* * *

THE NEXT MORNING, his fellow officers were crowded around Lucky's hospital bed. He was sitting up finally and only needed the oxygen mask occasionally. He'd taken the oxygen hose off, to Harper's annoyance, for this meeting.

Harper was sitting on the bed next to him. She was wearing a pair of teal scrubs and had her dark hair in some messy bun that looked sexy as fuck. He was tempted to see how much force a hospital bed could take once this meeting was over. Unfortunately, Harper would have to do most of the work, but, then again, Lucky was okay with that.

Carlos was also present. Though he'd been working with the FBI on the human trafficking ring, last Lucky had heard, he had not yet been reinstated with the MGPD.

Steel, to his utter horror, was in a wheelchair. Jenna had rolled him into the hospital room and threatened them all to withhold her food from them if they allowed her husband to stand up from the "stupid fucking thing"–Steel's words, not Jenna's. No one was willing to risk being on Jenna's shit list, so they all were watching him to ensure he stayed in the chair.

Before leaving, Jenna had given Lucky a kiss on his cheek and thanked him for both their lives. Lucky had blushed and tried to shrug her gratitude off, but she wouldn't allow it. She'd also left him a crustless peach pie so he could eat it without irritating his throat. He asked her if she was willing to divorce Steel and marry him instead.

To everyone's complete shock and surprise, Scar had entered

the room and gone straight over to Harper's side of the bed. She'd smiled widely at him. Though there was caution in the action, Harper reached over and placed her hand on Scar's shoulder. The man flinched slightly before seeming to sag, like a weight had been taken off him. When she lowered her hand, Scar reached over and touched her shoulder.

Lucky didn't know what to say or do. Neither touch was intimate, but something profound had passed between the two of them. He'd never seen Scar touch anyone–unless he was threatening them.

No one else seemed to know how to take the exchange either. Eventually, Steel cleared his throat. "Harper, we're so glad you're okay. I'm sorry you were taken in the first place."

"It's no one's fault but my brother's," she told Steel. Upon waking that morning, Harper had filled Lucky in on what had happened to her after he'd gone back inside the burning house. Lucky still couldn't believe they had suspected the wrong Hannigan the whole time. Not that the elder Hannigan was entirely innocent of wrongdoing.

Bear leaned forward in his chair. "Demo and I have been in touch with the fire marshals and your insurance company. I'm sorry, but the house is a total loss."

Lucky had expected as much. The damage to the stairs had hinted so. "Thanks for taking care of it for me, man," Lucky said. His voice was still scratchy. He looked to Demo and Jumper. "Scotty too."

"Kid's definitely upset. He's at Angel's shop with her and Aerial today," Demo said. "He slept at Jenna's and Steel's last night."

At the mention of the dog, Lucky noticed for the first time her absence at Jumper's side. He looked at his brother in concern. "You're okay without her?"

Jumper shrugged. "He needs her more."

On top of everything else he had to deal with due to the fire, Lucky knew he'd just resolved to get Scotty a service dog.

"Harper," Steel said, bringing the meeting back to task, "if you don't mind, can you fill the others in on what happened to you yesterday? *Everything*," he added like he knew she'd been planning on leaving something out of her story.

Lucky laced their fingers together between them as she started. He hadn't been there for her when she'd needed him most. She'd never know how much he regretted that. It was a conflicted sort of regret though. He knew it had just been bad timing. There was no way he could leave Jenna and Steel to die inside the burning house. And yet…if he hadn't gone back in, her brother wouldn't have been able to take her.

Harper repeated what she'd told Lucky that morning. The others' reactions ranged from shock to outrage to dismay to disgust.

Towards the end of her tale, she looked at Steel. "Where's my brother?"

"He's where he needs to be," Steel said vaguely. "He'll be dealt with accordingly for his crimes."

"You're turning him over to the police?" Harper looked at Carlos.

Carlos looked like he was trying desperately to pretend he had earplugs in his ears.

"We'll make sure he faces justice," Steel told her.

Harper looked at him then Lucky then Scar and then back at Steel. "I want to talk to him."

Steel shook his head. "Not a good idea, Harper."

"He's my brother," she argued back. "I don't care that he abducted me yesterday. I care that he's been abducting other women. I need to know what he's done. What if there are others out there that weren't in the shipment you found?"

Lucky squeezed her hand, making her look at him. "Darlin', we'll make sure the right questions are asked and we'll make sure he pays for his crimes. The more you know, though, the more danger it could put you in. You know too much for my comfort already. Can you please just leave this to us to handle?" She looked like she wanted to argue. Lucky leaned in and kissed her gently. "Please, love of my life?"

She scowled at him. "Not going to work…"

He kissed her again.

She sighed, the fight draining out of her. "Fine." He smiled. "Arrogant bastard."

He smiled wider.

Harper turned back towards Steel, ignoring the fact that their intimate moment had had an audience. "What about my dad? He isn't guilty of committing my brother's crimes, but he certainly isn't innocent either."

Carlos stepped forward. "As far as the law is concerned, it doesn't matter. He knew about it. That's aiding and abetting."

"I'll have a talk with Hannigan," Steel said darkly. "We need to see what he specifically knows too."

Carlos did not look happy with Steel's response. "You said you were going to do this the *legal* way, Steel. So far, I'm not seeing a whole lot of legality. I don't know how much more I can be complicit in."

Steel met Bulldog's eyes from across the room and then turned towards Carlos. "We understand. Our hands will get dirty, even bloody. We all know this isn't the end. A cartel is trying to move into our territory. Richard and Ronald Hannigan led them to our town. It's going to be our job to defend it, guard it. We can do what the police can't, Carlos. If you don't feel comfortable being in the know, then we understand. You're still family. You're still one of us, but we'll do our best to shield you."

Carlos looked conflicted. "There's a right way and a wrong way of doing things," he finally said. "I also know that the justice system is flawed." He looked at his brother. "You do what you have to do. I won't stop you, but I also can't support you."

Bulldog nodded. "We understand."

Carlos looked around the room one more time and then left.

In the silence that followed, Harper raised a shaky hand like one of her students in her classroom. Steel's hard face turned amused. "Yes, Harper?"

She lowered her hand. "I know you want to protect Jenna and me. The less we know, the less we can say, right? You could also claim we're innocent of wrongdoing if the law comes after you. But don't leave us so much in the dark that we're blind to what's coming. Please? I know Jenna feels the same way."

Steel looked to Lucky. Of all the brothers, he and Lucky were the only ones with ol' ladies. They were the only ones who had to worry about what to tell their significant other.

"We'll tell you what we can, Harper, but perhaps it would also be best not to ask questions you know we won't answer."

She frowned at that. "Fine. Just remember, though," she looked back down at Lucky, "that we control your sex lives when you're trying to figure out what you should or should not tell us."

CHAPTER 14

Something roused Ronald Hannigan from his sleep in the middle of Wednesday night. As soon as his senses told him Cindy and he were no longer alone in their bedroom, he bolted upright in bed. His hand went for the gun on his bedside table, but found it absent. Cindy screamed.

Three men wearing leather cuts stood at the foot of their bed, illuminated by the moonlight coming through the window. Hannigan recognized all of them. He'd anticipated a confrontation like this, which was why he slept with his gun so close.

"Get dressed," Steel told them. "It's time we talked."

Then the men exited the room together. Hannigan reached for his phone with the intention of calling Connelly, but also found his phone missing. Looking across the bed, he saw Cindy's was missing too. There was no way for him to get help now.

He took off the covers. Steel had said he wanted to talk. If he wanted Hannigan and Cindy dead, they could have easily done so without their knowledge. Waking them this way was a scare tactic. Taking his gun and their phones was to make them feel alone and defenseless.

"Stay here," he ordered his wife.

Downstairs, Steel, Bulldog, and Scar waited for the sheriff. Lucky had wanted to come, but was in no condition to. His feet still had several weeks of healing ahead of them and any form of exertion caused him to have coughing fits. Steel knew he owed Lucky his life, as well as Jenna's. Especially Jenna's. If Steel had survived and Jenna hadn't… He flinched. A world without Jenna was unfathomable to him.

Jenna hadn't wanted him to leave. She'd been hovering over him since waking up in a hospital bed beside him. Steel knew his body well enough to know he wasn't a hundred percent. He also knew that he owed Lucky. He needed to do this, to repay the man for his selfless sacrifice.

The sheriff certainly kept them waiting. It took him close to twenty minutes before he came down the stairs. He had his badge attached to his belt, like the piece of metal would protect him.

"Your wife too, Hannigan," Steel instructed. When Hannigan made to protest, Steel swore, "She won't be harmed. You have my word. Of the two of you, she's the only one innocent and we don't hurt the innocent."

The threat was clear.

Hannigan scowled. He grudgingly went back up the stairs. It was another twenty minutes before the couple returned. Cindy Hannigan cowered behind her husband.

Steel tried to catch her eye, to reassure her, but she kept her face down. He understood the woman was frightened, and he felt regret for that.

He took a seat in the lounge chair and gestured for the sheriff and his wife to sit on the couch facing him. They sat, though Hannigan placed an arm across Cindy's front. Bulldog and Scar placed themselves behind the chair where Steel sat. Steel caught Scar's eye, and the enforcer put the knife he'd been playing with away.

He looked between the two. Like any interrogator, he let the silence draw out a while before speaking. "Harper told us an interesting story this morning. You've been very naughty, Sheriff."

Cindy let out a low whimper. Hannigan silenced her with a look. "Where's our son?"

Steel ignored the question. "My brother Keys is digging through your life, your son's life. He's looking for evidence you were more involved than just the knowledge of your son's despicable crimes. In the meantime, I suggest you reinstate Carlos Santiago and resign your position. It'll be better for you in the long run. Less embarrassing."

"If I'm going to prison anyway, I might as well take you with me. I can have *him*," he pointed but didn't look at Scar, "arrested for murder right now."

Again, Steel ignored him. "Your son's still alive, Sheriff, but his life is over. We'll see to that. Based on what we've found so far, we can circumstantially link him to five missing persons' cases in Detroit. Multiple business trips place him in other areas around the timings of even more missing women. We're estimating around a dozen. Are you aware of the statistics, Sheriff? Whether they would have been forced into forced labor or sexual slavery, less than one percent of victims are rescued. *His* victims were lucky. They were of that one percent. Far too many are not. Despite that his victims were rescued, I still believe jail would be too good for the likes of your son. Do you agree, Mrs. Hannigan?"

Tears had been streaming down her face, but the submission had seemed to leave her once she heard and understood the extent of her son's crimes. She clearly knew, or suspected, that Richard's involvement in the Castillo cartel hadn't been over.

"While we cannot link you to any missing women, we are aware you knew of it and turned a blind eye, Sheriff." Steel continued to use Hannigan's title, not out of respect, but as a reminder of the job and law Hannigan had failed to uphold. "You knew Madison Mitchell went missing. You suspected your son but decided to put the blame on my club instead. Here's the real kicker though: your son was innocent. This time. Your own deputy, whom you put in charge of your daughter's safety, was the guilty party. *Was* being the opportune word there, Sheriff. If you do not want to join the late deputy, I expect to hear the announcement of your retirement by the end of tomorrow's workday."

Steel stood. "The Castillo cartel isn't going to leave you alone, Sheriff. You're in too deep. You know too much. They'll link you with your son's debt and seek you out for compensation." He looked to Cindy. She met his eyes for the first time. "If you need anything, you come and find me. Our clubhouse is always open to you."

She stood up, despite her husband's protests. "What about my daughter?"

"She's MC property now, Mrs. Hannigan. She's under our protection." He looked at Hannigan when he added, "And no longer a concern of yours."

* * *

Lucky was finally discharged from the hospital Thursday morning. With no idea where else to go, they decided to head to Harper's apartment. Scotty was still staying at Steel's. Since Harper's apartment was only a one-bedroom, they'd need to figure something else out soon.

The burns on Lucky's feet kept him from being able to walk. He was wheelchair bound for the next several weeks, and not happy about it. The wheelchair legs were raised high, so his feet stood out straight like lances. Thankfully Harper's apartment was on the first floor.

Bear was a huge help, Lucky grudgingly had to admit. Though it annoyed Lucky that his best friend and not his woman was helping him bathe, the truth of the matter was Harper wasn't strong enough to help hold Lucky up to get him in and out of her stall shower. Bear insisted he be called 'Nurse Bear', which Lucky refused to do and Scotty did too much.

Lucky had to put all his art projects on hold. Though his computer and drawing pads had been destroyed, his computer files had been backed up to the cloud. Keys brought him a new computer with all his information already loaded onto it. He'd messaged the clients who had active commissions, explaining his situation and injuries. Most were sympathetic and agreed to wait the additional time. A couple were less than pleasant and took their business elsewhere. Harper and Jenna made a plan to check in on his store to make sure the college students were handling things appropriately. At least he could still sell the pieces he'd already made.

The dirty business of what to do with Connelly, Marco, and Richard came three days after he'd been discharged. Bear came to collect Lucky, claiming that he wanted Lucky's help with something at his house. Harper didn't look like she believed them for a minute but also didn't argue or demand the truth.

It wasn't commonly known that the clubhouse had a cellar. It wasn't on any floor plans, and the club hadn't known about it when they'd bought the buildings and land. They suspected the former distillery owners kept certain collectibles or expensive bottles there and off their records.

The last time Lucky had been down in the cellar, it had been nothing more than a musty old room. It was probably half the size of the main room above it. It was concealed by a hatch in the floor and had old wooden stairs that looked very breakable.

Though Lucky wasn't happy about it, Bear had to carry him down those creepy old steps while Bulldog brought down his wheelchair. It had only been three days and Lucky was ready to torch the thing while singing *Kum Ba Yah* around it. He didn't think he was going to last several more weeks.

Long chains now hung from the ceiling with manacles

attached. There were eight of them in total, four pairs. Only three of them were currently in use.

Richard was Lucky's. They all knew it. Harper's brother was slumped over, his chained arms the only reason he was still vertical. His legs had completely given out on him.

Mark Connelly hung in the middle. He was standing on his own two feet but looked ready to drop at any moment. His lips were cracked and dry, and his mouth kept moving like he was trying to say something. Likely he'd screamed himself hoarse and was now unable to speak.

Marcos was on the end. He was still a mystery to the club. Keys had not been able to find anything on him. Most likely he was an illegal, smuggled in from Mexico by the cartel. The tattoos on his body indicated he'd spent time in prison, likely more than one stint, but Keys couldn't find his records.

All three men were naked. Twice a day, the prospects came down and threw buckets of ice-cold water on the men to "shower" them and to keep them additionally uncomfortable. The cellar wasn't connected to the HVAC system upstairs and had a draft. Once a day, they were given water and bread. The drain in the middle of the floor and a power washer was their bathroom.

They certainly weren't staying in the Ritz Carlton.

Quinten, one of the prospects, threw a bucket of water on Connelly. They were starting with him, since he was more likely to talk than Marcos.

Connelly's yell was rough. His eyes were half-lifted as he looked around as if just noticing his audience. His mouth gaped up and down like a fish.

"Hello, Mark. Here's the deal," Steel said. "I'm going to ask you a question. You're going to answer that question honestly. If you don't answer honestly or I don't like your answer or I think you're holding something back, my brother Scar here will throw a throwing star at you. He might miss, he might not. Do you understand?"

Connelly started sobbing, all the arrogance and confidence he'd once portrayed gone. "Please. Please let me go. I'll give you anything. I won't tell anyone what you did. Please. Just let me go."

Steel nodded to Scar. Quick as a flash, Scar threw a star at Connelly. It whizzed right by his face, nicking his cheek before it imbedded itself in the concrete wall behind him.

Connelly cried out.

"Perhaps I should have specified that I don't want to hear any whining, pleading, or bargaining. I just want answers."

Connelly nodded quickly. "Fine, fine. I'll tell you anything."

"Let's start off with some easy questions and go from there," Steel said, feigning amusement. "Why were you in Ohiopyle Monday night?"

"I was told to go there to oversee a shipment–"

Scar threw a star. This time, it cut deep into the underside of Connelly's raised bicep. He yelled out in pain.

"A bit more detail," Steel scolded. "Told by whom, what type of shipment… You get the idea."

Connelly swallowed. "I don't know who he is. I've only ever called him 'boss'. I've never even met him. Marcos and I were ordered to go to Ohiopyle to oversee a shipment of women who were being bought for auction."

"Who was the buyer and who was the seller?"

"I don't know who runs the auctions. I know the Castillo cartel were the ones who organized the sale of the product." He said the word *product* so easily, like they were talking about diamonds, not women.

"Was this the first time you've overseen a sale like this?"

Connelly hesitated. Scar threw a star. It took a lock of hair off of his head. "No!" Connelly shouted. "No. There was another one, but it wasn't women. That time it was heroin."

"To be sold here?"

Connelly weakly shook his head. "No, stored. I can tell you where if you let me go."

Scar threw a star. The blade embedded itself in the meat of Connelly's left thigh, missing the artery. Connelly screamed in pain and blurted out the drug's location without further prompting from Steel.

Steel looked over his shoulder at Bulldog. "Tell Carlos. Anonymous tip." Bulldog nodded and pulled out his phone. Steel turned back to Connelly. "How did you get involved in the cartel?"

Connelly glanced to his right before answering, "Hannigan. He didn't mean for me to get involved. I don't even think he knows. I figured out what was going on, why he was having me watch his daughter. I spotted Marcos in his office one day, overheard him threaten Hannigan. I followed Marcos, but he told me I had to prove myself."

"And how did you do that?" Steel asked, though they already knew that answer.

"I kidnapped Madison Mitchell." Scar threw another star. This time, it landed in Connelly's upper right pectoral. Connelly cried out. Blood started seeping from the wound. "I was telling the truth! That was the truth!"

"Yeah," Steel said with venom in his voice, "but I didn't like it."

Connelly's head hung low. "There's nothing else to say. That's all of it."

"Not quite. *Why* did you get involved with the cartel?"

"I thought it was some easy money. Sell some product, get some cash. Maybe I'd be able to get out of this goddamn town."

"Oh, you'll be leaving it all right. Just in a body bag," Steel informed him. "But don't go dying yet. I want to talk to your friend Marcos first."

"Please, I told you everything. Just let me go. I was barely involved."

"Barely involved?" Steel shouted. *"Barely involved!* You

abducted Madison Mitchell. You tried to rape her! I'd be killing you myself for that, but sadly that was only the tip of your crimes. Whatever peace you feel you need to make between you and your god, I'd start doing so. Your time is up as soon as Marcos here is finished talking. Tick-tock…"

Connelly was too dehydrated to cry, but his body still shook with sobs. Steel ignored him and turned his attention on Marcos.

"You're awake and have been listening. You know the rules. Are you going to talk or is my brother going to get some more practice in?"

"No habla inglés," Marcos said, somehow getting the strength to smirk as he did.

Scar threw a star before Steel could reply. Marcos cried out, throwing his head back in agony, as the outer shell of his ear landed on the floor. Blood coated the side of his face, his neck, and his shoulder.

"I think you understand English just fine," Steel said. "Who is the boss Connelly was referring to?"

"Mateo Castillo," Marcos gasped out. His head lulled forward. "He's Juan's little brother. Wants to expand his business, separate from Juan. Doesn't want to have to report to him anymore."

"Who knew blood loss allowed someone to speak perfect English?" Steel asked sarcastically. "Which Castillo does Richard Hannigan owe money to?"

"Mateo. He's in Detroit but wants to move. Wanted to break ground here before coming down himself."

"Where is Juan Castillo?"

"Los Angeles."

"Is Juan Castillo involved in Mateo's drug running or human trafficking?"

"Juan doesn't deal in labor. Says too hard to control. Mateo wanted to prove him wrong. He started small but then started to grow. He doesn't ship internationally, though. Just here in the

States." Marcos said that like it helped his boss's cause. A star landed in his chest, just below his heart.

Marcos screamed, losing his footing.

"Where was the auction Monday's shipment was meant to go to?"

"Won't matter." Marcos's words were starting to slur. "They change. Never the same place twice."

"Who runs the auctions? If Castillo was selling the women to the auction house, that means he doesn't run it. Who does?"

"Only know him as Cameron. Don't know if that's his first name or last name. Only met him twice. He's some rich guy with too much time and money on his hands."

"Describe Cameron."

Marcos stopped talking, like he was fading off to sleep. Steel snapped his fingers and Quinten threw a bucket of ice-water at him. Marcos jumped awake and then winced in pain. "What…!"

"Describe Cameron," Steel repeated through his teeth.

"Uh, maybe mid-forties. Eccentric. Likes his girls young. Too young, if I'm being honest. Got a pet panther or tiger, I think."

"Where did you meet him? At his house?"

"Nah, man." Marcos was starting to slip into unconsciousness again. "Auction houses. One in Chicago, other in Miami. He wasn't at the one in Baltimore."

Shit. There'd been thirty-four women, plus Madison and the nine-year-old girl in the trucking container Monday night. If the other three auctions that had been successful had had the same number of women auctioned off, that was over a hundred. A hundred women and children who were likely suffering through unspeakable tortures at the hands of people who weren't even fit to be called human. Monsters was a better title.

Lucky had an overwhelming need to know where Sissy was right now, right that second. He needed to make sure she was safe. Sissy was twenty-two. A college student. Beautiful. She was such an easy target.

Bear's hand went to his shoulder. Lucky still wasn't calm, though. There were so many monsters in the world. How could he have let his baby girl out of his sight for even a second? He was a terrible father.

Lucky reached into his pocket and grabbed his phone. Not knowing what she might hear in the background if he called, he texted, even though he would have preferred to call. Sissy hadn't been happy about going back to college, but he'd insisted. He'd been fine with Harper and his brothers to take care of him. She needed to go back to school. He'd been such a fool.

Lucky: Where are you? Text me back ASAP.

Her reply was immediate.

Sissy: I'm in my dorm. What's up?

Lucky: Stay there. One of your uncles will come and get you.

Sissy: You okay?

No, he wasn't. Not when monsters like Mateo Castillo lived.

Lucky: Just need you safe.

Sissy: Okay. I'll be waiting.

Lucky: Wait inside. Do not wait outside. They'll come to your dorm.

Sissy: You're scaring me, Dad. What's going on?

Fuck. He hadn't wanted her scared. Bear was reading over his shoulder. He grabbed the phone out of Lucky's hand.

Lucky: It's Bear. Your dad's fine. Everyone is fine. He's having a bit of a panic attack thinking you're not safe at college. After the fire, he's in overprotective mode. Are you okay with coming home or do you need to stay?

Sissy: I'll come home. I can do my classes remotely tomorrow.

Lucky: Still Bear. Thanks, Sis.

Bear handed his phone back to him. Though he didn't appreciate Bear making it sound like Lucky was mid-freak out, he was grateful Sissy wasn't fighting coming home.

Steel walked over to where Bulldog and Bear were standing and Lucky was sitting. Scar was... Well, he was terrorizing the already terrorized. Was he *drawing* on Marcos? With what?

That was when Lucky realized he wasn't using a red marker. He was using a tip of a throwing star to slice designs into Marcos's skin. Was that a smiley face? Lucky shuttered.

"Any other questions you can think to ask?" Steel asked them. Quinten was the only prospect in the cellar. Demo and Jumper had remained upstairs. Jumper because he didn't want what was said or done in the cellar to trigger him and Demo because he said the cellar creeped him out before Bulldog and Cage had added chains. Angel had begged Steel to allow her below. She hated when she saw her gender abused and put down. Steel, however, had told her no, since she couldn't guarantee not to kill the bastards before they got their required answers. Most of the others were at their places of work.

Lucky hadn't been paying attention to the last couple of minutes in his need to talk to Sissy. He thought over everything that had been said.

"The entire thing is fucked up," Bear commented. "Connelly only got involved because of greed. Marcos seems like a psycho with no empathy whatsoever. And Hannigan is a selfish bastard who hurt countless people to save his own skin."

"I say we leave them down here with Scar," Lucky added. "Let him do what he wants to them and then, if they're alive in the morning, we ship them off to the older Castillo in Los Angeles to show him what his baby brother has been up to."

"Not a bad plan," Steel murmured. He rubbed a hand over his close-cropped beard. "What about Hannigan?"

"As much as it pisses me off to admit it, I'm in no condition to do to him what I want to." Lucky growled in frustration. "I can't even take a shit without Nurse Bear over here having to hold my hand."

Bear smiled widely. "Happy to be of service."

"Give him to Scar?" Bulldog asked. "Guy's already halfway done in anyway just from being down here five days."

"We still need to talk to him," Steel reminded them. "We need to make sure the thirteen women Keys has linked him to were the only ones he was involved in. He's still crosschecking to make sure all those women were recovered in Ohiopyle too."

"Got it." Bear snapped his fingers. "Be right back. Look after my patient for me," he added to Bulldog. Then he rushed up the stairs and opened the latch.

Bulldog looked down at Lucky. "Does he really hold your hand while you take a shit?"

"He tried to once, but I punched him in the nuts and he hasn't tried to again."

Bulldog snorted.

Connelly let out a whimpered cry behind them. Scar had moved onto his next victim.

A few minutes later, Bear returned. He had a self-lighting hand torch in his hands. He'd most likely gotten it from the garage on club property. He handed it to Lucky. Then he unlocked Lucky's wheelchair and pushed him towards Hannigan.

"The guy burnt your feet. I figured it was only fair you returned the favor."

Lucky smiled over his shoulder at Bear. "I'm actually impressed." He nodded his head towards Hannigan. "Can we lift him up anymore?"

* * *

Hannigan hadn't remained conscious for long. The flames had awoken him from his stupor. Steel had been able to get some answers out of him before he'd passed out again.

It would be a long time before Lucky would be able to eat barbecue again. Especially because Bear kept commenting on how the cellar smelt like burnt chicken.

Before they left Scar alone with the three doomed men, Steel asked one more question to each of them. "Did you rape any of the women?"

Marcos had shaken his head.

Connelly hadn't wanted to answer but, after some prodding from Scar, had admitted that he'd raped two women in his lifetime. Steel had gotten their names and the dates of the attacks too. Bulldog was texting as Connelly talked, and Lucky knew he was sending the information for Keys to verify. Connelly confirmed it had been Marcos who'd stopped him from raping Madison Mitchell the night he'd abducted her.

Richard sobbed as he admitted Mateo had made him to prove his loyalty to their deal. In his defense, he'd only done it once.

"Some cultures believe that proper punishment for a thief is to take his hand. What do you think the proper punishment for a rapist is, gentleman?" Steel turned to Scar. "Do what you want with them. These two," he pointed to Connelly and Richard, "take their cock and balls while they're still breathing. We'll bag them and ship them with their bodies to their destined Castillo brother."

* * *

HARPER WAS WAITING up for Lucky when he got back to her apartment. Scotty was still at Jenna and Steel's since they didn't have a bed for him here. Lucky had said he'd had an idea about a house for them but had wanted to run it by Steel first. She didn't know what the idea was and hoped he'd remembered to talk to Steel after whatever it was Bear took him to do tonight.

A part of her knew it had to do with her brother. The other part was trying to ignore that first part.

She waited for Bear to help Lucky out of the wheelchair and into her bed. Bear was teaching her how to clean and re-bandage Lucky's wounds. Even after he healed, both the burn doctor and Bear had said that Lucky's feet would be sensitive. There were cushioned socks and shoes Bear was going to help Lucky shop for once he was allowed to walk again.

The top of her dresser had been taken over by medical supplies and pain pills. The silver lining of having not moved fully into Lucky's house was she still had some clothes and most of her things at her apartment. She'd lost minimal in comparison. Since Steel was the closest to Lucky's size, Lucky had been wearing some of his old sweats and shirts. They'd gone online and ordered an entire wardrobe replacement for Scotty and Lucky, but some things took time. Jenna had taken Scotty shopping a couple of days after the fire too.

Her phone and school bag had been destroyed in the fire. Thankfully, she'd been given the week off of work to get herself situated. Her principal was very sympathetic to her plight. Lucky was also keeping Scotty home.

Lucky had lost everything. All his memorabilia, the kids' things, pictures, clothing, furniture... Even his car had been damaged beyond repair. Thankfully his motorcycle had been parked at the clubhouse at the time of the fire, so that was safe.

Not that he could ride it though. Her car was their only mode of transportation.

After Bear was done, Harper walked him out so she could lock up. He gave her a hug and a kiss on the cheek before reminding her to call him if she needed anything. Harper promised.

She crawled into bed next to Lucky. It wasn't that late, but she could see the exhaustion pulling on his face. He had an arm thrown over his eyes.

"Sissy's on her way. Cage went to go pick her up. She's going to stay in my room at the clubhouse."

"Why? Is she okay?"

Lucky let out a long sigh but didn't lower his arm. "I had a bit of a panic attack tonight. Had it in my head that she wasn't safe at school and sent one of my brothers to go get her."

Harper paused. "Is she safe at school?"

Lucky made a face under his arm. "As safe as anyone in this world could be, I suppose. I wasn't thinking straight and panicked. A little."

It sounded like he'd panicked *a lot*, though she didn't correct him. If her suspicions of what the club had been up to that night were correct, she could understand why he'd reacted so. After the fright of the house fire and seeing the horror her brother had had a hand in, it was understandable why he'd want to verify his daughter was safe.

"You know, you're going to have to ease up on the overprotectiveness when we start having kids. I'm not going to be one of those delicate pregnant women who can't function in her 'condition'."

That got Lucky to lower his arm. "I make no promises."

She smiled. "Did you talk to Steel? Because I hate to break it to you, big guy, but this apartment is just too small for you, me, Scotty, Sissy on the weekends, *and* a future baby."

"I did and he agreed. I hope you don't have plans tomorrow because Bear is picking us up at nine to go shopping."

"Shopping? House shopping?" Why had he needed to talk to Steel about house shopping? That had nothing to do with Steel.

"Not exactly. With everything going on, I want to make sure that my family is as safe as I can make it. I asked Steel if I could buy a plot of land on the club's property. Actually, when we went out to look tonight, the best one is right by his and Jenna's house."

"We're going to build a house by Jenna and Steel?"

He shook his head. "Modular home. Fast, easy, and most importantly *fast*."

She laughed at his redundancy. "Fast is good. This apartment seems to be getting smaller by the day."

"Tell me about it," he rolled his eyes. "You know, the apartment I had when I got guardianship of Scotty was smaller than this one. Still no clue how I raised two kids in it before that two-bedroom opened up. Fairly certain that couch I used to sleep on is the cause of all my back pain today."

"Because it has nothing to do with just having turned forty?"

He snorted. "Of course not."

"So Bear's taking us modular house shopping tomorrow?"

Lucky nodded. "You, me, Bear, and Scotty. Not sure how easily it will be getting me in and out of some of the models, so you'll need to take pictures for me to see."

Harper bit the inside of her lip. "Will this be *our* house?"

He tipped his head down at her. "Of course, it will be our house. I'm not sleeping apart from you–"

"No, I mean *ours*. Financially. I don't have that much saved up, Lucky, but I need to contribute if my name is going on the title. My credit score is good but I don't have a full-time job for the mortgage application."

"Based on the pricing I looked up for a modular home, we won't need a mortgage."

"What are you talking about? Are you saying you've got hundreds of thousands of dollars just lying around?"

"I owned my house, Harper. As in I owned it. I paid off my mortgage years ago. Insurance will be paying me back that value."

"That's still months, if not a full year, away."

"True. I'll have to do some finagling with my accounts to pool the money together, and I'll reimburse the proper accounts once insurance pays out."

"But that sounds like it'll be *your* house then, Lucky. If you're really able to pay for it, more power to you and financially I'm jealous, but that still doesn't give me a part in it."

"Well, the way I see it, once we're married, it's *our* money. Not mine."

Her heart leapt in her chest. "But we're not married."

Lucky looked over at the suitcase propped up against the wall. "Top zipper." He nudged her with a gentle elbow. "Go on."

Slowly, like she was moving through molasses, Harper got up off the bed. She went over to the suitcase and squatted down. A trembling hand unzipped the top pouch before reaching inside and pulling out a small black box.

Harper stood back up and faced Lucky. He was still sitting on the bed, exactly as she'd left him.

"This isn't exactly how I'd pictured doing this." He gestured to his feet. "I'll owe you getting down on one knee sometime in the future." He lifted his chin towards the box. "Open it."

Her hands were shaking so bad, she had no idea how she got the hinge open, but she did. Inside was a sapphire cut diamond ring set on a silver band.

"Remember that day about two weeks ago when I told you Scotty and I had to go up to Sissy's college because he forgot his favorite shoes in her car?"

Harper nodded almost robotically. Her eyes fixated on the ring in her hands.

"Well, I lied. We did go up to Sissy's college, but only to pick her up. Then the three of us went ring shopping. I had to bribe Scotty with that new train set he'd had in his room before the fire to keep him quiet."

Sissy and Scotty had helped their dad pick out the ring? That meant they supported them getting married, right? Sissy hadn't even hinted, and they'd been texting a lot recently.

"What do you say, darlin'? Ready to be Mrs. Harper McCoy?"

She let out a sobbing laugh. "You know what that name does to me."

He looked wickedly sexy as he said, "Does the same to me, darlin'."

Harper pulled the ring out of the box. It fit her finger perfectly. More importantly, it felt *right* on her finger. She crawled back into the bed and straddled him. "Yes, Lucky, I'll marry you."

She bent down to kiss him and, to her complete shock, he stopped her. "One more thing." He pointed back at the suitcase. "Way bottom."

Her eyes narrowed, but she climbed back off of him and went to the suitcase. Down at the way bottom of the borrowed clothes Jenna had dropped off to him was a leather cut. On the back was the club's logo. The top rocker said *Property of.* The bottom rocker said *Lucky.*

Harper walked back to the bed. Never losing eye contact, she stripped down naked. Then she put the cut on. The leather was cool against her skin, making her nipples pebble.

She crawled back onto the bed and straddled Lucky once more. His eyes were ablaze with desire. The borrowed sweat-pants did nothing to hide his arousal.

"Can I kiss you now, ol' man, or is there anything else you'd like me to get from your suitcase?"

"Not unless you have a positive pregnancy test hidden in there." His voice was deep, sensual.

"Not today," she leaned down close. "Maybe tomorrow." Then she kissed him.

It wasn't over. The cartel was still out there. Keys was still trying to track down the missing women Richard had abducted that weren't on the produce truck in Ohiopyle. There was their house to be built and a wedding to plan. Harper didn't know if she had a job next school year. Mrs. Hannigan would soon reach out to Harper, wanting to make amends. Together, the women would have to figure out what to tell Paige, Richard's widow, and her two sons. Lucky still had to find a service dog for Scotty. Sheriff Hannigan had reinstated Carlos Santiago but had yet to turn in his own resignation notice.

But in that moment, none of it mattered. In that moment, with his ring on her finger and his cut on her back, Russell McCoy truly did feel like the luckiest man in the world.

AFTERWORD

Human trafficking involves the use of force, fraud, or coercion to obtain some type of labor or commercial sex act. Every year, millions of men, women, and children are trafficked worldwide – including right here in the United States. It can happen in any community and victims can be any age, race, gender, or nationality.

To report suspected human trafficking to Federal law enforcement: 1-866-347-2423
For more information, please visit: https://www.dhs.gov/blue-campaign/what-human-trafficking

BOOKS IN THE SERIES

1. Lucky
2. Bear—available May 10, 2024
3. Bulldog (coming summer 2024)
4. Jumper (coming summer 2024)

FOLLOW ME ON SOCIAL MEDIA

Follow me on Social Media for Updates, Promos, and Announcements!
@elisegedickeauthor

Contact Me!
elisegedickeauthor@gmail.com